PRAISE FOR JOY

"Talented author Joy Avery regales her readers with a well-written story and a plot twist that validate her place among the great storytellers of romance."

—Brenda Larnell, RomanceinColor.com

"There are few things more exciting than a Joy Avery book; it is sensuous, exciting, and a veritable utopia of beautiful prose."

—Stephanie Perkins, Book Junkie Reviews

"When I read a book by Joy Avery, whether it's a novella or a longer story, I'm always captivated by the way she writes her characters. Their personalities jump off the pages, and I feel as if I'm right there in the story with them. You can always count on her to take your imagination to another level and [write] a romance that makes you want to believe in true love."

—Shannan Harper, *Harper's Court Literary Blog*

something so sweet

OTHER TITLES BY JOY AVERY

Additional Titles

In the Market for Love

Smoke in the Citi

Cupid's Error

One Delicate Night

A Gentleman's Agreement

The Night Before Christian

Another Man's Treasure

Hollidae Fling

Collaborations

A Bid on Forever (Distinguished Gentlemen)

Sugar Coated Love (Carnivale Chronicles)

something so sweet

JOY AVERY

Published by Montlake, Seattle

www.apub.com

Amazon, the Amazon logo, and Montlake are trademarks of Amazon.com, Inc., or its affiliates.

ISBN-13: 9781542034135
ISBN-10: 1542034132

Cover design by Hang Le

Printed in the United States of America

Dedicated to the dream

CHAPTER 1

Lunden Pierce liked Dick.

However, she liked him more when he wasn't dropping colossal problems at her feet. Then again, whose feet would he drop them at other than those of the esteemed mayor of Honey Hill, North Carolina?

The small town nestled two hours outside Raleigh just so happened to be the topic of today's discussion. According to Richie Dickerson—the town's penny-pinching, budget-cutting finance director—their slice of heaven was losing more money than it was bringing in. An unfortunate result of the untimely death of the woman most would call the town matriarch, Shugga Hawthorn, and the closing of her pride and joy, the Inn on Main. Until its closing several months ago, the inn had been a staple in the farming community and a viable source of revenue for the other local businesses due to its popularity as the perfect escape destination.

Lunden closed her eyes and kneaded her temple. "How bad is it?" she asked.

"Well, we won't go belly up anytime soon, if that's what you're asking."

Her eyes popped open, and she eyed Dick curiously. If they weren't in serious straits, why in the hell was he here stressing her out? She shook her empty coffee tumbler and sighed.

At ten in the morning, it already felt as if she'd been awake the entire month of April. That morning, she'd overslept when her alarm hadn't sounded. She'd burned breakfast, attempting to multitask. Then, through no fault of his own, her six-year-old son had spilled an entire cup of apple juice in her back seat when she'd been forced to slam on the brakes to avoid mowing down her neighbor's peacock.

The whirly bird had obviously deemed it a good idea to cross the road bright and early on a Monday morning. A second later and it would have literally gotten to the other side—not of the road but of the peacock pearly gates high in the sky. Or wherever peacocks went after they died.

Thank God she hadn't hit it. She would have never lived it down. Especially if Lady Sunshine had gotten wind of the news. Lady Sunshine was many things to Honey Hill, including their walking, talking gazette. If she didn't know it, it wasn't news. The actual town paper—the *Honey Hill Herald*—had actually blamed Lady Sunshine for its decline in subscribers.

Yep, she was definitely glad she wouldn't become known as the peafowl killer of Honey Hill. That title made for a great crime novel but was no good for her reputation.

Dick continued, "But unless we find a way to supplement, we'll be forced to cut several line items from the budget. The square renovation. Updated playground equipment for the park. New provisions for the sheriff's department."

Heck, it wasn't like they were crime central. The HHSD's "provisions" should still work like new, as they were rarely put to use. About the only criminal activity they saw in Honey Hill was Old Man Patterson and Sam Whitman—rival farmers—trying to kill each other every time Sam Whitman's pet raccoon moseyed onto Old Man Patterson's farm and terrorized his bevy of peafowl.

"We'd also have to scrap plans for the community pool," Dick said.

This drew Lunden's immediate attention. Dick eyed her as if expecting a reaction. Understandable. She'd been the one who'd painstakingly convinced the city council to approve the costly addition to the state-of-the-art community center—another one of her crusades. Though that one hadn't been so difficult to pass, because she'd had the full support of Ms. Shugga.

Dick smoothed a hand over his close-cut jet-black hair. "In the document I've given you, a five-year operating budget projection is included on page eight."

Lunden flipped through to the corresponding page. Her brows furrowed as she read. She didn't see the problem. Glancing up, she said, "Our reserves are close to three million."

"I prefer it closer to five. What if . . . ," he said.

Oh, how Dick loved his what-ifs. "What would you suggest we do?" Lunden asked, despite already knowing what his answer would be.

"Sell the inn," he said plainly.

Yep, she knew the man well. Or at least well enough to know he didn't view the inn with her same sentimental regard. Then again, why would he? He hadn't grown up here. Hadn't experienced the true wonder and magic of the inn as she had. As many here had. "The inn is not the town's to sell." But if it were, she would fight tooth and nail against it.

The Inn on Main had been the catalyst that had made Honey Hill what it was today. Because of the inn, this wasn't simply a community of eccentric residents. Ms. Shugga had single-handedly brought their small town together with her festivities at the inn, making Honey Hill not just a place to live but a place to call home, with friends that were more like family.

The inn also held some of Lunden's best memories. She'd attended Easter egg hunts there as far back as she could remember. Had celebrated her first father-daughter dance there. Had learned to swim there, which had ultimately led to her being offered a swimming scholarship to UNC. But probably her most notable memory was losing her innocence there.

Lunden couldn't think about that stormy night in July without thinking about *him*. Quade Cannon. The boy who'd deflowered her at the tender age of fifteen, Ms. Shugga's nephew, and the man who was now the new proprietor of the inn.

Lunden grumbled under her breath, remembering *all* that had occurred that summer so many years ago.

"Did you say something?" Dick asked, looking up from his notepad, pushing his gold-rimmed glasses farther up his narrow nose.

Lunden shook her head.

Quade Cannon had captured her heart and her virginity. But after all this time—twenty-three years, to be exact—she still harbored ill will toward him. She'd offered him two of her most precious gifts. Her heart and her virginity. How had he reciprocated? By taking them, then vanishing from Honey Hill and never returning.

Lunden groaned to herself. Even as a teenager, she'd attracted losers. She hoped Quade had gained two hundred pounds, suffered from male-pattern baldness, and had a lazy eye, warts, and an unmanageable case of bromhidrosis. That would be retribution enough for her. She laughed aloud, then dismissed her silliness with a wave of the hand when Dick eyed her with a raised brow.

Back on track, Lunden said, "I'm willing to entertain *postponing* the pool installation."

"That investment group out of Charleston has shown renewed interest in the property," Dick said. "Maybe the inn's new owner will sell. That's if he ever makes an appearance. It's been several months since he was notified of the inheritance. Heck, if he doesn't show, we'll just claim the property as eminent domain."

Lunden noticed the twinkle in tricky Dick's gray eyes. And she knew why. Said company had been willing to shell out several million for the property, which sat on more than thirty acres of prime real estate.

"Maybe Ms. Shugga's nephew would be open to selling. With what they're offering, he'd be a fool not to."

Lunden ground her teeth. She'd be damned if she stood by and watched as some conglomerate that cared little about the inn's history—and even less about Honey Hill and its residents—swooped in and gobbled it up. They would probably turn it into some kind of exclusive golf resort that no one in town could afford—or be welcomed—to visit.

First the inn, then they'd surely attempt to entice other businesses to sell. Before you knew it, Honey Hill would be like a mini New York City, overflowing with crime, pollution, and rude people. Nope. Not on her watch. Honey Hill, Ms. Shugga, and the inn meant too much to her to witness their legacies get swallowed up by greed.

The Inn on Main would return to its original glory. She would make sure of it. All she had to do was play nice with Quade Cannon, especially since the big-city hotshot held the fate of the inn—and ultimately the future of Honey Hill—in his (probably) baby-bottom-soft, manicured hands.

Quade Cannon missed Charlotte already, but it was too late to turn back now. He'd already terminated the lease on his condo, placed all his belongings in storage, and sold his stake of the commercial real estate brokerage firm he'd co-owned with his best friend, Pryor.

Was he really doing this? Voluntarily giving up city life to live in small-town USA for the next six months? He eyed the HONEY HILL 30 MILES sign. Yep, he was. A knot tightened in his stomach, which was odd, because he never buckled under pressure. If anything, that's when he excelled.

He couldn't explain it, but something in his gut told him Honey Hill would present him with a whole new set of challenges. Maybe this was why he'd put off coming the past several months. That and the fact he didn't want to field all the questions he was sure people were just waiting to ask him. *Where have you been all these years? Why didn't you ever visit Shugga? Why would she leave you her inn?*

The last he couldn't answer, because he didn't get it himself. Though he was grateful, he didn't understand why an aunt he hadn't seen or spoken to in years would will him all her earthly possessions. Surely there had to have been a more suitable option. The mailman. Grocery store clerk. Newspaper-delivery guy. Heck, even her beautician. Folks she'd probably interacted with on the regular. Not a nephew she hadn't seen since he was fifteen. *Twenty-three years.*

Until he'd received the call from the attorney representing Aunt Shugga's estate, Quade hadn't so much as thought about the place he'd spent most of his summers as a child in years. How was that even possible? Some of his fondest memories had been made there.

Maybe he'd blocked it out because his mother had told him Aunt Shugga had died years ago. He remembered how he'd bawled for two days straight. How could his mom have betrayed him this way? He would never get the opportunity to ask.

An image of Aunt Shugga filtered into his head, causing him to smile. Wispy, unruly, fire-engine-red hair whipping in the wind. Fluorescent-pink lipstick that painted her teeth more than her lips. Baby-blue eyeshadow, rosy-red cheeks, and an eccentric vibe that matched it all. The flamboyant woman was steeped in confidence and courage. Maybe that was partly where he'd gotten his *I can conquer the world* attitude from.

A feeling of sadness washed over him at the idea that the woman who'd once been like a second mother to him had died alone. *I should have been there.* But how could he when he'd had no idea she was still alive? *Why didn't she contact me before now?*

Quade harbored his share of regrets in life, but at the top of his list was the fact he would never get the opportunity to tell Aunt Shugga just how much she'd meant to him. He swallowed hard to free the lump of emotion lodged in the back of his throat.

To this day, he still had no idea why his mother had forbidden him to return to Honey Hill after that last summer. The one time he'd sneaked and called Aunt Shugga, he'd been caught and put on punishment for a month. It had been worth it just to hear her voice.

The sound of the telephone ringing gave Quade a brief reprieve from his troubling thoughts. Pryor's name flashed across the in-dash screen. Hitting the phone icon on his steering wheel, he said, "Hello?"

"I really can't believe you are moving to way-out-yonder USA," Pryor said.

Quade laughed. "Trust me, I won't be there any longer than absolutely necessary."

"You say that now," Pryor said. "But you might meet yourself a country girl, decide to settle down and have a few rug rats."

"Oh, I won't be in Honey Hill long enough to forge that kind of bond."

"Six months can be an eternity. People have fallen in love in far less time."

Yeah, but those people had probably been looking for love. Quade wasn't. He'd made that mistake once, and he wasn't the type of man to make the same mistake twice. Marriage wasn't for him. And kids? Definitely not. They ruined relationships. At least, according to his stepfather—an unlikable man he'd loathed until the day he'd died.

"Didn't you say the girl you lost your virginity to is from Honey Hill? What was her name, again?"

"Lunden," he said absently. "Lunden Pierce."

Quade thought about the woman who'd ushered him into manhood. The best damn two and a half minutes of his young life. Lunden had been one of the most ambitious girls he'd ever known, so he doubted she was still cooling her heels in Honey Hill. And even if she was, it would change nothing. He had one goal. Get in, do his time, and get out. Simple as that.

"Don't take it personally if I don't come for a visit," Pryor said. "I hate small towns."

"Didn't you grow up in a small town?" Quade asked.

"Exactly. You be careful. There is no such thing as personal business. Everyone knows everything. If you decide to bed someone, just know the entire town will be privy. Townsfolk love to gossip."

Quade laughed.

"You're laughing, but I'm dead-ass serious."

Quade sobered, Pryor's words rattling him. He cherished his privacy, so this was just another strike against small-town living. Though he didn't recall the folks in Honey Hill being overly nosy. But a lot of time had passed. Who knew what the place was like now?

Pryor continued, "I have several parties interested in the property. Just say when, and I'll arrange a site visit."

"Thank you for handling this for me, man. I appreciate you," Quade said.

"You know I've got your back. I just wish you'd reconsider leaving the firm. The place won't be the same without you."

"My heart's just not in it anymore," Quade said.

The unwavering hustle and bustle of corporate America paired with the constant fight to be—and stay—on top had burned him out. He needed this temporary reprieve. And in six months, he'd sell the inn, collect his windfall, and use it to fund a new hustle.

He hadn't decided just yet what said hustle would look like, but whatever it was, he would make sure it made him happy, not just rich. Aunt Shugga's passing had triggered something inside him, reminding him just how short life could be. He didn't want to continue to just exist. He wanted to live for once.

"Well, I'm not giving up on you just yet," Pryor said. "Look, I have to jump on a conference call. Check in when you get settled. And don't get yourself mauled by a bear or attacked by coyotes."

Bears? Coyotes? Pryor made it sound as if he were moving into a cabin in the forest. In all his summers of visiting Honey Hill, he'd never seen either creature there, so he felt confident he wouldn't meet his demise via wildlife. Boredom, maybe. Saying goodbye to his friend just in time to see the white-and-green WELCOME TO HONEY HILL sign, Quade chuckled at the *Population: Still Growing* wordage.

Wow was Quade's immediate reaction upon his arrival in Honey Hill. The town was definitely not how he remembered it. Gone were the dull, time-hardened structures. Modern-looking brick buildings now lined both sides of Main Street, housing the usual places one would imagine in a small town—grocery, hardware store, bakery, hair salon—and some that one might not have expected to see here: microbrewery, specialty food shop, coffee café, massage parlor.

This was not exactly what he'd expected. In his head he'd pictured unoccupied, dilapidated buildings and shops hanging on by a thread. In actuality, the town appeared to be thriving. Apparently, it had great leadership.

Seeing the condition of the town, Quade was even more confident he'd get a decent price for the inn. With any luck, it wouldn't be too time consuming to get the property ready for sale. With the proceeds, he'd be able to purchase a kick-ass condo in Miami. *No, New Orleans.* Heck, he might just buy a place in both. He wasn't sure where he'd wind up. All he knew was he didn't belong in small-town USA.

Where did he belong? *Nowhere* seemed like the logical answer. He had no home. No family. No roots. He dismissed the prickle of sadness. The world was huge. He'd find somewhere to call home. But until then, he would—

"Shit!"

Quade slammed on the brakes. The tires of his Range Rover clawed the asphalt and kicked up a thick cloud of white smoke. The rancid smell of burnt rubber filled the cabin of the SUV. The woman who hadn't bothered to look left or right before crossing the street now glanced up. She closed her eyes and tossed up her hands. The papers her face had been buried in moments earlier flew through the air like windblown leaves.

Quade blew a sigh of relief when the vehicle came to a screeching halt, thankful he hadn't plowed down one of Honey Hill's residents his first day in town. That would have certainly given the town something to gossip about.

After several seconds had ticked past, the brown-skinned beauty cracked open one lid, glanced down at her body as if to make sure she was still in one piece, lifted her gaze to him, and scowled.

"Are you insane?" she yelled loudly enough for him to hear through the closed windows. "The speed limit through town is fifteen miles per hour, not fifty."

Honestly, Quade wasn't sure how fast he'd been going, as he'd been a little distracted by his thoughts. Yeah, perhaps more than fifteen, but he was darn sure he hadn't been traveling fifty miles per hour. And why was she pinning all the blame on him? She'd been the one who'd strolled out in front of him as if she were made of rubber.

Yep, his gut never lied. Quade exited his vehicle. Several cars crept past, gawking at the scene. After nodding at the curious onlookers, he approached his first "challenge" of the day. "Are you okay?" he asked, rather than reminding her that she, too, was at fault.

"Do I look okay? You nearly killed me," she said.

Actually, she looked beyond okay. Ms. Made of Rubber was several inches shorter than him, which put her around five feet eight, if he had to guess. Those brown eyes bored into him as if she were willing him to disappear. Her smooth, medium-brown skin glistened as if it had been spritzed with a light coating of water. It was more likely sweat from nearly becoming roadkill.

"Do you typically walk into traffic without looking both ways?" Quade instantly regretted his question when those brown eyes turned a shade darker and her features hardened. While he wasn't looking to make friends while he was here, he didn't want to make any enemies either. Deciding to be the bigger person, he flashed his hands in mock surrender. "I apologize for nearly hitting you. I take full responsibility."

"I don't want your apology," she said. "I want you to slow down. We have kids here."

"Are you okay, Mayor?" came from someone inside one of the passing vehicles.

Mayor? This woman was the mayor? Weren't public officials supposed to be warm and welcoming? Well, Quade guessed you got a pass from being cordial when you were nearly flattened in the street.

"I'm fine. Thank you," she said, her tone warm and welcoming toward the concerned citizen.

Returning her attention to him, she rolled her eyes, moved away, and knelt to collect her scattered papers. Quade's first instinct was to get into his vehicle and get as far away from this bitter woman as he could, but when he saw the unicorn-shaped birthmark on her right shoulder, it stilled him.

"Lunden?"

CHAPTER 2

As it turned out, Lunden not only liked Dick, but she needed him too. The man was good at running interference, and with the town's newest arrival, she was going to need all the help she could get.

How could she not have seen it before? The eyes should have been a dead giveaway. Probably because she was blinded by rage. Surely her behavior could be excused this one time. She'd almost become a fixture atop that shiny SUV. Now she knew how that poor peacock must have felt, seeing her barreling toward it.

Okay, she could recover from this sour first impression. Taking a deep breath, she turned to face Mr. Lead Foot, a.k.a. Quade Cannon.

This was definitely no longer the gangly boy who'd sweet-talked her panties right off. The specimen in front of her was *all* hot-bodied man. Every lofty, muscular inch of him. In steel-gray suit pants, a light-gray button-down shirt, and dark-gray suspenders, he looked ready to conquer the world.

Sadly, there was no extra two hundred pounds. The man had a body that looked as if he dedicated hours to working out. No baldness. Instead, he had a full head of jet-black hair cut close and neat. Neither one of his dark-brown eyes—hooded by long, curly lashes and thick brows—was lazy. She could still hold out hope that he had warts or stinky feet, though she seriously doubted it. *Dammit.*

A five-o'clock shadow dusted Quade's strong, square jaw. The sight of him staring at her all grinny and sure of himself made her grind her teeth. *Play nice,* she reminded herself. Relaxing her jaw muscles, she smiled, hoping it looked genuine enough. "Quade Cannon." Her tone was plain yet friendly. At least, friendlier than earlier.

"You remember me, huh?" he said.

His question caused a tiny fraction of her disdain to return. How could she *not* remember him? He'd been the first boy who'd ever made her cry. "The ears," she said. "They're still a bit on the big side." Okay, so she really needed to work on that *play nice* thing.

Quade gave a smooth laugh while simultaneously running a hand over one of his ears. Was he still self-conscious about them? When they were younger, his ears had been far too big for his head, but he'd grown into them nicely. No one could call him Chocolate Dumbo now.

"Still got that sense of humor, I see," he said.

She shrugged.

Like everything else, Quade's voice had changed. It was far deeper than she remembered. Definitely not the soft and innocent timbre of the fifteen-year-old who'd whispered *I love you* in her ear right before he'd inched inside her.

"It's been a long time, Lunden," he said, taking a step toward her.

"Yes, it—" *Wait. What is he—*

Before her brain could process Quade's actions, his arms wrapped around her in a warm, firm, familiar manner. *Too* familiar. She didn't do hugs, especially from him. Despite this, she found herself melting into his chest. The impact of their connection was instant, sending powerful currents zapping in every direction through her entire body. A minute ago, she'd almost forgotten how it felt to be held; now, she was forgetting she harbored a grudge toward him.

Inhaling satisfied her sense of smell. Oh, how she loved a good-smelling man. And this one smelled damn good. Like soap and expensive cologne. A car horn sounded, forcing Lunden to remember her current situation—downtown, in the street, clinging to Quade like a wet T-shirt. The perfect ingredients for crafting one tasty rumor pie that would likely feed the entire town. While this had been nothing more than a friendly hello—one that Quade had initiated, for the record—not everyone would view it that way.

Like most small towns, Honey Hill had its share of rabble-rousers. She'd learned that her first week back in town after her divorce. All kinds of ridiculous rumors had swirled. Foolishness like that she'd been caught in their marital bed with her ex-husband's brother. That her ex had kicked her out of the house because she wouldn't work. And the most ludicrous one: her ex-husband had learned her son was not his. Just because her ex acted as if Zachary wasn't his child didn't make it true. The actual truth—had anyone bothered to ask—was that *he'd* been the unfaithful one and, in the process, had fathered a child outside their marriage.

Lunden pulled away and took a step back. Quade eyed her as if attempting to read her mind. Oh, he definitely didn't want to know her thoughts. Especially the one where she wanted to kick him in the balls for being so damn distracting.

Kneeling again, Lunden began to collect the papers that hadn't gone with the wind. Quade joined her. "You don't have to do that. You're obviously in a hurry," she said.

"I have a few minutes to spare." He flashed a dazzling smile. "Besides, one kind gesture deserves another, right?"

Lunden's brows knit. "Kind gesture?" she asked.

"You didn't push me out into oncoming traffic. Though at one point you looked like you wanted to."

Lunden fought back her laughter. "And I would have been justified. You nearly took out the mayor."

"Mayor," Quade said. "How do you like being a politician?"

"It's not as glamorous as it might sound," she said. "But as mayor, I'd like to officially welcome you to Honey Hill. Actually, I guess *welcome back to Honey Hill* would be more appropriate."

"Thank you," he said.

His lips parted as if he wanted to say more, but a second later, they clamped shut, and he returned his attention to the scattered papers. After several seconds ticked by, he said, "It's been too long."

Lunden wasn't sure if he was talking to her or himself. "You have my deepest sympathies for your loss. Ms. Shugga meant a lot to Honey Hill. A lot to me. She'll be missed tremendously. But thankfully, her memory will live on through the inn."

There was so much more Lunden wanted to say, but she knew it wasn't the time, the place, or any of her business. The last didn't always deter her, but in this instance, it did. Especially after she witnessed the cloak of sadness that covered Quade's face. She recognized the expression. Genuine pain.

"Thank you." Quade glanced at his watch. "I, um . . . should get going. I have a meeting."

When he returned to a full stand, Lunden did as well. Quade passed her the pages he'd collected, smiled, then moved away.

Stopping, he said, "It was good seeing you, Lunden, and I'll try my best not to mow you or any of your citizens down while I'm here."

"Make sure you do. Next time, I might not be so forgiving."

"I'll see you around, Mayor."

Lunden gave him a single nod. "Not if I see you first," she mumbled to herself.

Quade parked in front of a deep-blue Victorian-style home with white trim and a beautiful wraparound porch, then double-checked the address he'd been emailed. According to the GPS, he was at the right place for Marshall Joyner Law; however, the location looked more like a private residence than a law office.

Quade made his way inside. High-end modern furnishings in cream, chocolate, and gold, as well as fancy drapes, hardwood flooring, and a crystal-and-gold chandelier, outfitted the swanky space. A woman with rainbow hair sat behind a hand-carved, expensive-looking solid wood desk. GREE POINTER, the nameplate read. In a lemon-yellow pantsuit, the colorful woman seemed out of place among the severe furnishings.

After providing his name, he was directed to an equally stylish seating area with high-backed brown-leather-and-gold chairs. While he waited, Quade recalled his encounter on Main Street. He couldn't believe Lunden was still in Honey Hill, let alone its mayor.

An image of her flickered through his mind. Time had been good to her. The asymmetrical pixie hairstyle suited her, framing her heart-shaped face perfectly. The golden highlights in her auburn hair brought out her brown eyes. The dress she'd worn did little to highlight her curves, but they were definitely there and noticeable under the lavendar-colored fabric.

She still had a nice shape, just more pronounced now. Her thin waist flowed down into perfectly proportioned hips, a nice ass, and long, shapely legs. He'd checked her out, without checking her out.

Mayor? He chuckled to himself. The position suited her. She'd always been kind of bossy. He'd known Lunden would go far in life; however, he'd assumed it would be farther than Honey Hill.

"Mr. Cannon, I'm Marshall Joyner."

Quade stood and accepted the man's outstretched hand. For some reason, he'd expected someone older, midsixties or so. Marshall Joyner looked to be around his own age. A few pounds heavier, several inches shorter, a shade or two lighter, with a headful of reddish curls and a thin mustache that looked as if a hairy centipede had crawled across his top lip and fallen asleep there.

"Call me Quade, please."

"Then call me Marshall."

Quade gave a nod, then followed the man into his office. Unlike the lobby area, this space felt informal. There were photos scattered throughout the room. Definitely family, because the resemblance between Marshall and the folks in the shots was uncanny.

Marshall directed Quade to a small round conference table. The man retrieved a packet from his pristinely organized desk and joined him.

Marshall rested his hand atop the table and intertwined his long, skinny fingers. "First, let me say how sorry I am for your loss. Ms. Shugga was a wonderful woman and a pillar of this community. She will sorely be missed by all."

Quade knew he would have to get used to folks offering their condolences. He just wished he had prepared himself better for it. Every time it happened, his heart broke a little more. He'd been forced to live through Aunt Shugga's death once; now he was forced to relive it all over again. "Thank you," he said. "Marshall . . ." Quade paused a moment. "I'm still a bit confused as to why my aunt would will her estate to *me*."

"From what I understood, you are her only living relative, correct?"

"Yes, but I hadn't seen or spoken to her in a number of years." A fact that embarrassed him to admit aloud, despite the lie that had resulted in his absence. "I'm not sure I can even be considered family. I didn't—" He stopped shy of admitting he'd had no idea Aunt Shugga had been alive all these years, but something told him Marshall already knew this.

Marshall relaxed against the back of his chair. "Your aunt was an interesting woman." He chuckled. "Some of the things she asked of me seemed . . . peculiar, for lack of a better word. However, I didn't question her, because one thing I'd learned about Ms. Shugga was that absolutely nothing she did was without thorough planning, consideration, and purpose."

Quade considered the man's words but was no closer to understanding the why than he had been ten minutes before.

"She sure was proud of you," Marshall said.

Marshall's words sliced through Quade's thoughts. "What?"

"She was proud of you. Your accomplishments. Especially when you received your MBA and started your own company. I don't think there was a more delighted aunt this side of the equator."

Quade pinched his eyes shut, more confused than ever. "Wait. How . . . ?" His words dried up.

"Though she may have done it from the sidelines, she kept tabs on you," Marshall said, correctly interpreting his question.

"Why didn't she reach out? Why didn't she . . . ?" Words escaped him again.

"Like I said, your aunt was an interesting woman. But I'm sure she had her reasons."

The latter comment made Quade suspect Marshall knew far more than the man was divulging. What reason could have been more important than a connection with her only nephew?

Marshall opened the folder he'd brought with him to the table. "We should get down to business. I know you're eager to get settled in."

Quade shifted in his chair before broaching an uncomfortable subject. "How did she die?" he asked.

Marshall's eyes lowered to the folder he held. "Metastatic breast cancer that spread to her lungs and liver. She refused treatment this time."

"*This* time?" Quade asked.

Marshall nodded. "Sadly, she'd battled breast cancer several years back but, thankfully, went into remission. When it returned, she chose to live life on her own terms for however long she had left. I don't know how she did it, but she operated the inn up until the day she died."

Just like Aunt Shugga. Determined to the very end. "I'd like to visit her grave site. Can you tell me where it is?"

"There's not one," Marshall said. "Your aunt didn't want folks fussing over her in life or in death. By her request, there was no official service. She was cremated and her ashes sprinkled in several locations that were dear to her. The creek behind the inn—so she could move through Honey Hill one last time, she said. Among her beehives. And a small patch of earth, under—"

"A centuries-old sycamore tree," Quade finished.

"Yes. How did you know?" Marshall asked, a quizzical expression on his face.

Because it had been *their* tree. The place they'd had deep, heartfelt conversations. The area they'd buried a time capsule. The spot where she'd told him she would always have his back. Quade ran a hand over his lips, gripped by emotion. "Lucky guess," he said. He could tell Marshall didn't believe him, but that was okay. He didn't need to convince the man of anything. "You mentioned beehives," he said.

Marshall chuckled. "Yes. Ms. Shugga was extremely passionate about saving the bees. Several honeybee hives occupy her property—pardon me, *your* property. A handful of the locals have been caring for them since Ms. Shugga's passing. But now that you're here . . ."

Now that he was here? What in the hell did that mean? Quade lifted a hand, pausing Marshall. "Marshall, I don't know anything about beekeeping." And he didn't plan on learning.

"No problem. I'm sure someone will be willing to show you the ins and outs." Marshall pressed his finger into his chin as if recalling something important. "Let's see. There's Sam Whitman. Randy Pitman down at the hardware store. Though he should be your last resort. He's . . . unique. Even our may—"

Quade lifted his hand again. "Sorry. Maybe I wasn't exactly clear. I don't want to learn anything about beekeeping."

"Well, I sure hope you're open to compromise, because unfortunately, you don't get the inn without it."

CHAPTER 3

After her near-death experience, Lunden had needed retail therapy, but now she needed coffee. Like, a whole lot of it. Black and piping hot. An image of Quade materialized in her head. The man was both black and hot, but she couldn't sip him from a cup. Nor would she want to. She liked quality coffee. He probably tasted bitter, weak, and lukewarm. She laughed at herself and continued her stroll along Main Street.

God, she loved Honey Hill. No blaring horns. No plethora of people. No polluted air. In fact . . . she inhaled a deep breath. All she smelled was cinnamon and fresh dough, which made her need to get to Pastries on Main even greater. In addition to coffee, she needed something sweet and decadent. This time she envisioned a cinnamon roll rather than mucking her thoughts with Quade Cannon and how sweet he might or might not be. But . . . if she had to, she'd wager on his being stale and salty.

Every shop she passed along the way, folks inside flashed wide smiles and tossed up their hands in greeting, not because she was mayor but because here, that was what people did. She matched their enthusiasm, smiling wide enough to eclipse the sun. You couldn't get this kind of small-town hospitality in some big city. Another reason she loved their intimate community. The idea of their harmonious landscape changing troubled her. She liked things just the way they were.

Pastries on Main was the most colorful building along the strip. A wooden structure painted a royal blue with a yellow-and-white striped awning. Sunflower wreaths hung on either side of the entrance. A huge window provided an unobstructed view of the interior. As always, most of the small round tables inside were occupied. Probably because no one baked like Rylee Harris—owner of Pastries on Main and Lunden's best friend. What she didn't see, however, were any of the ladies she was here to meet to finalize plans for the town's June Jubilee event.

Lunden loved the cozy feel she got every time she moved through the french-style doors. And not just because the shop housed all the answers to a stress eater's wildest dreams. Though that certainly didn't hurt. Large glass vases were scattered throughout the space and held yellow, blue, and white gumballs. Hand-painted images of delectable desserts adorned the pale-yellow walls. But the focal points of the room were the dual glass display cases overflowing with an assortment of mouthwatering sweet treats.

Several good-morning greetings were directed at Lunden, and she stopped at a few tables to chat with some of the townsfolk. When she finally made it to the area that had been fashioned to accommodate their group, Rylee joined her after setting down an assortment of freshly baked pastries arranged on a silver platter. *So fancy.* But that didn't surprise Lunden. Rylee did everything with an attention to detail.

Rylee was close to six feet tall with a figure most women would pay to possess, despite having the appetite of a woman pregnant with twins. Her blonde hair was cut in a short, curly style Lunden wished she had the nerve to attempt, and her almond-brown skin was flawless.

"Coffee's brewing," Rylee said on approach.

The woman knew her too well.

Taking a seat, she continued, "So I hear you were in the middle of the street all hugged up with a stranger." Her brown eyes twinkled with mischief.

If scientists wanted to learn more about warp speed, all they had to do was visit Honey Hill, because that was how news traveled around here. "Did this chatter bird also tell you I was nearly plowed down in the middle of the street? I'm fine, by the way. Thank you for asking." Lunden rolled her eyes playfully.

"*Awww.*" Rylee stood, wrapped her arms around Lunden, and shook her back and forth. "That poor baby. Are you okay?"

Lunden sounded like a wounded toddler recovering from a boo-boo when she spoke. "Yes."

"Did your life flash before your eyes?"

Actually, it had, but the only thing she'd seen was Zachary. Probably because that little boy *was* her life. Her entire life. Which was kind of sad when she thought about the fact that her only excitement these days derived from the daily antics of her six-year-old son.

Before Lunden could respond, the bakery doors swung open. The Chamber sisters entered, displaying their usual level of energy and style. Lunden smiled just seeing the snazzily dressed ladies. If anyone could redeem her shitty day, they undoubtedly would with their colorful personalities.

Ms. Bonita and Ms. Harriet were the three Ss. Sassy, sixty-something, and shameless. While they weren't twins, they looked so much alike it was uncanny. Same natural afros—which looked freshly groomed. Same smooth chestnut skin that gave them both a more youthful appearance. Same happy hazel eyes. Oh, and they both loved meddling in other people's business, as did many of Honey Hill's more mature residents.

"Where's Ms. Jewel?" Lunden asked once the women had settled at the table.

"Probably somewhere getting someone straight," Ms. Harriet said.

They all laughed, because they knew the woman was right.

"I'm sure she'll be here any minute. But in the meantime, why don't you tell us about this handsome hunk you were spotted clinging to earlier," Ms. Bonita said. "Quade's his name, isn't it?"

As if the woman didn't already know she was right. This was Honey Hill. *Everyone* knew his name by now. "I wasn't clinging to anyone." Lunden's cheeks burned under the women's unwavering scrutiny, suggesting neither one of them had believed her weak explanation. "It was a friendly hug between old fr—" She stopped abruptly, nearly making the mistake of calling Quade a friend. He hadn't been that in a long time. "Between old acquaintances," she corrected, but even that felt like a stretch.

"I heard that man's strong arms were wrapped around you so tight that you could probably feel his heartbeat," Ms. Bonita said.

Who comes up with this stuff? "Not true," Lunden said. "Not true at all." Lunden hated how defensive she sounded. In an attempt to divert the conversation, she said, "Maybe we should go ahead and start the—"

"Well, I heard the man is some kind of good looking. Tall, chocolaty, and built like a freight train. *Choo choo,*" Ms. Harriet said.

When Rylee failed miserably at stifling a laugh, Lunden scowled at her.

"Sorry," Rylee mouthed.

"We're not getting any younger, child. Is he good looking or not?" Ms. Harriet asked. "Like Billy Dee." The woman's hazel eyes twinkled. "*Mmm-mmm.* I used to love me some Billy Dee Williams. If he's that good looking, the man is in trouble. All these lonely, thirsty women in this here town."

"Sister, it sounds like you might be looking to quench *your* thirst," Ms. Bonita said. "Now let the child answer."

In the hot seat again, Lunden scratched at the side of her neck. "I . . . um . . . didn't really pay that much attention to him like that." Which was a lie. She had checked him out. Every strong, solid inch. And while she would never admit it aloud, she'd liked what she'd seen.

Picking up one of the pages she'd salvaged from her run-in earlier, she attempted to wrangle this wayward conversation again. "For the jubilee, I was thinking that, instead of a DJ, we could—"

Ms. Bonita cut her off midthought. "Well, Happi at the beauty parlor said he looks like a chiseled mythical god straight from the heavens."

"*Mmm-mmm,*" Ms. Harriet hummed. "I sure do like mystical creatures."

A wide smile curled Ms. Harriet's lips as she stared off as if lost in a satisfying fantasy. Lunden didn't even want to imagine what was running through the woman's head. Whatever it was, Lunden was sure it would turn her stomach.

"About the jubilee . . . ," Lunden said.

"Is he involved?" Ms. Harriet asked. "I'm not asking for myself," she said when quizzical eyes landed on her. "I'm old enough to be his . . . auntie."

"Hon, I believe you mispronounced *grandmother*," Ms. Bonita said.

Lunden and Rylee both snickered at an appalled-looking Ms. Harriet.

"I'm curious too. Is he involved?" Ms. Bonita said, directing the question at Lunden.

Why would they think she knew the answer? "I have absolutely no idea," Lunden said in a defeated tone, stuffing her mouth with a cinnamon bun and really wishing she had that cup of coffee.

"Well, if he's single, he won't be for long. I hear a few of the town desperates are already lining up to shoot their shot," Ms. Bonita said. "I guess the good sheriff and Sebastian are no longer the only eligible bachelors in Honey Hill."

"Oh, I think the sheriff's relaxing his stance on love. Word on the street is he's entertaining that Sweeney gal over at the diner," Ms. Harriet said.

Heads whipped toward Rylee when she knocked over her glass, sending water webbing across the table.

"*Shoot*. I-I'm sorry," Rylee said, bolting to her feet.

They all grabbed napkins to help clean up the mess.

Lunden eyed a frazzled-looking Rylee.

"Excuse me while I grab some towels from the back," Rylee said before hurrying away.

Ms. Bonita and Ms. Harriet watched until Rylee had disappeared. Turning, they smiled at one another.

"Well, I guess that confirms what we suspected, sister," Ms. Harriet said.

"I think it does, sister," Ms. Bonita said.

Confused, Lunden said, "What did you suspect?"

"That our baker extraordinaire is sweet on the sheriff," Ms. Bonita said.

Lunden eyed the direction in which her friend had escaped. "What?" That was ridiculous. Rylee would have told her if she had a crush on Canten. Every time they were together, the two bickered like brother and sister. *Wait . . .*

"She hides it well, but nothing gets past these eyes," Ms. Bonita said. "She ought not to worry. It won't last with that Sweeney gal. She's too loose for the sheriff."

"I'm just glad she's starting to open up again. I was starting to worry about her," Ms. Harriet said.

Oh my God. Rylee *was* sweet on the sheriff. It brought a smile to Lunden's face. Things made sense now. Why Rylee consistently shot down any man in town who showed interest. Initially, Lunden had thought it was because of Lucas, Rylee's husband, who'd been killed by a roadside bomb in Afghanistan. Now she knew better. Rylee hadn't wanted any of them; she wanted Canten.

The sisters continued their assessments of the situation. While Lunden didn't like the fact they'd manipulated her best friend to prove a point, she was kinda glad the focus was off herself. Did this make her a horrible friend? Probably. "Excuse me," Lunden said, rising and then making her way to the back of the restaurant to check on Rylee.

If Lunden had harbored any doubt before about the sisters' claims, she didn't any longer, watching her friend pace back and forth inside her office, gnawing at her nails. Something she did when she had a lot on her mind. "Ry?" Lunden said.

Rylee stopped. "Oh, hey. I was just . . ." Her words dried up, as she probably knew Lunden would see right through any lie she would tell.

"Why wouldn't you tell me you're in love with Canten?" Lunden asked.

Rylee's eyes widened. *"Shhh."* Her voice lowered. "I'm not in love with anyone. But I . . . I feel something for him. Something I haven't felt in a long time. Something I don't want to feel. Not to mention he's Sebastian's best friend."

"Speaking of brothers, does Sebastian know?"

"I think he suspects, but he won't say anything until I do." Rylee hugged her arms around herself. "I swore I would never fall for another man whose profession puts him in harm's way. Not after Lucas." Rylee tilted her head back and batted her eyes rapidly. "God, I still miss him so much. And these feelings I have toward Canten burn like betrayal. And as much as I want to banish them . . . I can't."

While it had been four years since Lucas's death, Lunden imagined the pain was still as fresh now as it had been the day the news had been delivered. Lunden wanted to remind Rylee of two things: One, Honey Hill wasn't a hotbed for crime. And two, it was okay to move forward with her life.

Canten and Rylee made the perfect pair. They'd both lost someone they loved to violence. What could build a tighter bond than that? But who was she to give anyone advice about moving forward? Since her divorce, she'd been in a holding pattern. Not quite trusting love, but not quite distrusting it either. *A broken heart has two choices,* her mother used to say—*heal or halt.* She was in between the two.

"Guess it's a nonissue now," Rylee said. "Canten is seeing someone. It's probably for the best. I'm not sure I'm ready for a relationship anyway. I'm happy for him." She smiled, but it didn't quite reach her eyes.

"Do you want me to beat her up and tell her to leave your man alone? I will," Lunden said.

They shared a much-needed laugh.

"You know I don't condone violence," Rylee said. "Plus, how would that look? Our esteemed mayor yanking someone's wig off their head." Rylee threaded her arm through Lunden's. "But thank you for having my back. Come on. I'm sure the ladies have some more Quade-related questions for you." Rylee snickered.

Lunden didn't have the heart to tell Rylee that *she* was now the topic of discussion. "If I never hear his name again, that would be okay with me."

When they emerged from the back, Ms. Jewel had finally arrived; however, she wasn't the only one who'd joined their table. Quade stood there, chatting with the short, stout woman. Ms. Jewel said something, and he glanced in Lunden and Rylee's direction and smiled.

"Happi was right," Rylee said. "That is one good-looking man. And I do mean good looking. I don't think I've ever seen a man wear business attire so impressively. Yep, he's certainly about to cause a ruckus in Honey Hill."

Dear Lord. Not Rylee too. Happi, her hair stylist, thought most men were good looking. However, Lunden had to admit the man could definitely pose a threat for a desperate woman—which probably made Lunden one of the few safe women in town, because one thing she was not was desperate. Her bumblebee vibrator kept her plenty satisfied. Multiple speeds. Always at the ready. Never complained. And damn good at touching her in just the right spot. She shrugged one shoulder. "He's all right, I guess. I mean, if you like that type."

"Tall, dark, and devastatingly handsome. Is that the type you mean?"

Lunden groaned.

"Oh, sweetie. I'll get that coffee. You look like you could use it," Rylee said, snickered, and walked off.

Ignoring Rylee, Lunden plastered on her mayoral face and approached the table.

Wrapping an arm around Lunden's waist, Ms. Jewel said, "Hey, dear." She eyed Quade. "I understand you've already met our esteemed mayor," she said.

"Yes. We ran into each other earlier," Quade said with a grin.

Ha! Ha! Offering what she hoped was a convincing smile, Lunden said, "Speeding make you hungry?"

"Actually, I bumped into Ms. Jewel, and she said this place had the best pastries in the state. Sadly, I have a ferocious sweet tooth. I couldn't resist."

"Well, you've definitely come to the right place," Lunden said.

"He sure did," Ms. Jewel said, a wide grin on her face. "Mayor, once Quade's all settled, maybe you'd like to give him a tour of our beautiful town. I'm sure a lot has changed in twenty years."

No, she would not like to give him a tour. And yes, a lot had changed in twenty years, including her tolerance for Quade Cannon. But since she had on her official face—despite the scowling-Lunden face clawing to break free—she said, "That sounds like a *wonderful* idea. Whenever you're ready, just contact my office."

"Lawd, child, he'll spend all day inside that automated phone maze y'all got down there at the town hall. I don't know whose bright idea that was," Ms. Jewel said. "'Press one now. Dial three for English. Say zero for the operator.' A hot mess."

It had been Lunden's hot mess idea, but she remained silent.

"Why don't you give him your cellular telephone number. That'll make it much easier for him to reach you," Ms. Jewel said.

That was the thing. She didn't *want* him reaching her. Before Lunden could object, Quade had his cell phone out, ready to input

28

her number. Well, what could be the harm? It wasn't like she intended to answer if he called anyway. She'd just say she'd thought it had been a telemarketer because she hadn't recognized the number. With that in mind, she happily rattled off the digits.

"You should probably take mine too," Quade said. "I wouldn't want you to mistake my call for one of those annoying telemarketers."

Lunden's brows furrowed. *Did he read my mind?* "G-good thinking," she said, the confidence she'd felt moments earlier waning. After inputting his number into her phone, she forced something she hoped could be construed as a smile. "Got it. All safe and sound in my device. I sure hope I don't drop it in the toilet or anything." She laughed for effect.

"That would be awful," Quade said. "Guess I'd just have to track you down at town hall."

"Or you could just walk to her house, seeing how you two are practically neighbors," Ms. Jewel said. "Just a hop, skip, and a jump away. How convenient is that?"

Quade's brow arched. "Neighbors? Really? Huh."

"Yep," Ms. Bonita and Ms. Harriet said in unison. "Neighbors."

"Good to know," Quade said.

"Why?" Lunden asked.

"You know, in case of an emergency," Quade said.

"In case of an emergency, you'd probably want to dial 9-1-1," Lunden said.

Quade chuckled, a sound so smooth and sexy it made Lunden's skin prickle. And when he silently stared at her with those penetrating dark eyes, it sent a jolt of awareness she hadn't experienced . . . ever.

"I should let you ladies get back to your meeting," Quade finally said, breaking eye contact with Lunden.

"We're finalizing the details of our annual June Jubilee celebration," Ms. Harriet said. "Will you be attending, Billy Dee? I mean, Quade."

Quade's lips parted, but Ms. Jewel spoke before he had a chance.

"Yes, he will," Ms. Jewel said.

Lunden bit back her laughter at the perplexed look on Quade's face. Something told her that wasn't the answer he'd intended to give. Regardless, he didn't correct Ms. Jewel. Smart man.

"So what do you plan on doing with the inn?" Ms. Bonita said. "We sure do miss visiting. Ladies' Day brunch, high tea."

"Taste-Testing Tuesday," Ms. Harriet added, referring to the once-a-month event when Ms. Shugga would invite folks over to taste and critique potential new additions to the food or beverage menu.

Lunden eyed Quade with anxious anticipation. She, too, wanted to know the timeline for the inn's reopening. Maybe they could plan a celebration around the date.

"I plan—"

"Good Lawd, Bonita. The man hasn't been in town long enough to even form an opinion about the weather, let alone plans for the inn. Let the man breathe. He'll let us all know his intentions next week at the town hall meeting."

"Town hall meeting?" Quade asked.

"Yes. Next Wednesday at seven p.m. You *will* be attending, right?" Ms. Jewel asked.

Though she'd framed it as a question, it didn't quite sound as if Quade was being given much of an option.

"Next Wednesday at seven p.m. Wouldn't miss it," he said.

Was it wrong for Lunden to find so much pleasure in Quade's discomfort? Yeah, but it didn't stop her. She'd pray for forgiveness later.

Ms. Jewel gave Quade a warm smile as she patted his arm. "Good. Now run along and get your pastries. Us ladies gotta get to work. A handsome fella like you is just too distracting."

Quade beamed. "Yes, ma'am."

Lunden could see his head swell with the compliment, so she had to deflate it a bit. She wouldn't want him getting stuck in the doorway on his way out. "It's okay if he stays. He's not really all that distracting."

Of course, she regretted the words the second they'd escaped because, aloud, they kinda sounded as if—

"Are you trying to say you want me to stay, Mayor?" Quade said with a faint smirk.

—she wanted him to stay. Lunden ground her teeth at his arrogance. Rebounding, she said, "It's a public meeting."

They eyed each other for a long, heated moment.

"Unfortunately, I have some things I need to take care of," Quade said.

"Aww, shucks," Lunden said, hoping he was hit by every cold drop of sarcasm. "Welp, maybe next time."

"Definitely, next time," Quade said.

The way he'd released the words, exact and firm; the confidence of his expression, like he'd just made a master move on the chessboard; the certainty in his eyes, as if he knew they would definitely have a next time—it all rattled Lunden for some unknown reason.

"It was nice meeting you, ladies," Quade said to Ms. Bonita and Ms. Harriet. Facing Lunden again, he said, "Mayor, until we meet again."

Smug bastard. She gave a simple nod, then watched as Quade approached the counter. Taking her seat, Lunden ignored Ms. Bonita's and Ms. Harriet's accusatory stares. "So shall we begin?"

"What did I miss?" Rylee asked, returning with an Airpot and cups.

"Sparks," Ms. Bonita said.

"No, sister," Ms. Harriet said, "that was a full-fledged blaze. I'm still sizzling from it."

"Lawd, will you two quit your meddling," Ms. Jewel said.

Lunden appreciated Ms. Jewel's intervention. The last thing she needed was rumors about some nonexistent, fairy-tale attraction between herself and Quade Cannon. She slid her attention across the restaurant toward him, as he stood waiting in line to order. As if he'd sensed her eyes on him, he tossed a glance in her direction and smiled.

Nope, there definitely hadn't been any sparks, because had there been any from her, she would have used them to turn Quade into a pile of ash. Imagining him as a heap of smoldering embers made her smile back.

Quade wasn't sure what in the hell had just happened. In the span of five minutes, he'd committed to both a June Jubilee and a town hall meeting. He didn't even like crowds. Especially ones where he knew he'd be asked a thousand and one questions by a hundred and one people wanting to know a little too much about him. *Damn. I should have declined.* But it wasn't like he'd been given the option.

He thought about Ms. Jewel and chuckled. *Oh, she is a slick one.* And, something told him, not one to be messed with. Why was he stressing? He could handle these small-town country folks. He'd give them what they wanted by feeding them a little info, just enough to nibble on, and then he'd simply shut 'em down. Just like a business deal. Let them walk away feeling as if they'd won when, in actuality, he'd been the true victor.

Yeah, this town hall meeting will be a breeze. The jubilee, on the other hand . . . that was a whole other story. The last time he'd attended a function solo—a charity gala—he'd spent most of the night listening to mothers and grandmothers tell him all about the eligible women in their family. He just hoped no one attempted to push him off onto their daughters or granddaughters this time. The thought made him antsy.

Pushing his bitter concern aside, he replaced it with something a little more palatable. He hadn't been the only one who'd been strong-armed by Ms. Jewel. If he had to guess, Lunden hadn't wanted to give him her cell phone number. And she damn sure hadn't wanted him to know they were neighbors. Why had it been such a big deal? It wasn't like he'd show up at her doorstep, asking for sugar or begging for a home-cooked meal. He pinched his brows together. Could she cook? Didn't matter. Something told him hell would freeze over, thaw, and freeze over again before she invited him to her dinner table.

Something else told him he definitely wouldn't be getting that tour if she had to give it. He laughed. That woman was nothing if not interesting. If he didn't know any better, he'd swear he wasn't one of her favorite people. But why? All he'd done was nearly turn her into a hood ornament. But he'd offered her a heartfelt apology. He shook his head. *Some people.* They just couldn't let things go.

The more he thought about it, maybe it wasn't him at all. Maybe she simply hated all men? Nah, it was him. But she would warm up to him. The notion filled him with far more delight than it should have. Especially when he'd vowed not to become intimate with anyone in Honey Hill. And that included the woman who'd been his first love. *Especially her.* He couldn't risk anyone catching feelings, namely Lunden, because, thanks to his ex, he was immune to love.

The big question was, Could he actually survive another six months without sex? *Yes, you can. You've done it before.* Quade did something he didn't like doing—thought about his ex, Rachel. After their split, he'd gone an entire year without sex. Surely he could do it again if he had to. And what better way to curb his sexual appetite than aligning himself with a woman who he was sure would prefer to toss him to the wolves rather than sleep with him?

He and Lunden didn't have to become best friends, but no doubt they would run into each other around town. It sure would be nice if she didn't act as if she wanted to boot him off the island every time they crossed paths. A tiny glimmer of hope swirled inside him when he thought about the fact she'd returned his smile at the bakery. That had to be progress, right? He chuckled. The woman was too damn beautiful to be so damn ornery.

The second the inn came into view, a calm washed over Quade. This place held so many great memories for him. The oversize house was just as beautiful as he remembered. The historic home sat on several dozen acres. Hundreds of flowers bloomed with colors so vibrant they looked hand painted. Grass—lush and green. Flowering bushes—big and small. Trees—massive and sturdy. It all gave the landscape a true countryside, southern-home appearance and feel.

After pulling into the circular drive, he placed the SUV in park, relaxed against the seat, and stared at the white structure. "Aunt Shugga, I'm so sorry I wasn't here for you." Emotion lodged in his throat, and he swallowed hard to free it.

Quade's eyes swept across the extended porch as he remembered how he and Aunt Shugga used to rock there and sip lemonade—like two old-timers, she used to say. And when a car had passed, Aunt Shugga had always had a story to tell about its occupant. She'd once told him that had she put half of what she knew about the residents of Honey Hill into a book, it would have been a bestseller.

She'd never shared any scandalous tales with him, though he imagined there had been plenty. But bad-mouthing hadn't been her thing. In fact, she'd talked so positively about everyone that as a boy he'd believed Honey Hill was only filled with saints, not a single sinner. As an adult, he realized now how unlikely that was. There were bad people everywhere. *Sometimes in your own household.* An image of his stepfather filtered into his head.

Pushing the disdainful man from his thoughts, Quade eyed the detached garage and recalled the moments he and his dad had spent in there. Leaving memory lane, he finally exited his vehicle. Deciding to leave his luggage inside until he'd scoped out the place, he ventured in.

Though the place had sat vacant for several months, he felt the lingering love the second he entered. He'd never known an unhappy day within these colorful walls. The foyer was still painted a bold red, undoubtedly refreshed several times over the years. The color of love, Aunt Shugga would say. *And that's exactly what I want people to feel when they walk through those doors. Love.* Recalling her sweet voice in his head filled him with joy.

He explored the first floor. Instead of the pea-green appliances that had once occupied the kitchen, it was now filled with state-of-the-art stainless steel. The formal dining area housed the longest dinner table he'd ever seen outside of a movie screen. It, along with the chairs and what he assumed was a china cabinet, was covered in white cloth.

When he entered the spacious sitting room, he could almost see Aunt Shugga in one of the chairs, crocheting or teaching one of her guests how to. She made the place feel like home, even to complete strangers. Moving to the bank of windows, he stared into the backyard, the sycamore tree jumping out at him like a cardinal in the snow. He would visit it, but he just couldn't right now.

His gaze slid to the owner's cottage Aunt Shugga had used for storage. It, too, looked as he remembered, minus the several broken windows. At a greater distance, he saw dozens of stacked white boxes. *Those damn bees.* Had Aunt Shugga really believed he could harvest honey? Or whatever the correct term for it was. Well, she'd always told him he could do anything he put his mind to. In a thousand years, he never would have imagined putting his mind to beekeeping. He wasn't exactly *buzzing* with excitement about it.

He backed away from the window and snatched up the white cloth from the sofa. The released dust particles caused a sneezing fit. Settling, he eased down onto the welcoming blue-and-gray floral-printed piece and stretched out. He draped an arm across his forehead and closed his eyes for just a second. *This entire day has been exhausting. Overwhelming and exhausting . . .*

Quade bolted forward, jarred by the sound of breaking glass. *What . . . ?* His eyes frantically swept the room. It took several seconds to gather his bearings, then realize he'd fallen asleep. He thought he'd dreamed the shattering until he heard it again. He came to his feet, rushed to the window, and peered out. Kids were tossing rocks at the windows of the cottage.

"Hey! Hey! Stop that!" he yelled, then realized they probably couldn't hear him. Rushing outside, he ran toward them. "Stop that!"

"Let's get out of here," the chubby one said, running toward one of the three waiting bikes.

Two got away, but the third—the kid who'd only been observing the other two misfits—was having trouble getting his bike going. A second later he fell to the ground, the bicycle crashing down on him.

"I'm sorry. I'm sorry. I tried to make them stop," the kid said. "I even threatened to tell my mom."

Apparently, his mother wasn't intimidating enough. Quade pulled the bike off him, then helped him to his feet. The kid looked to be around six, maybe seven, with medium-brown skin and black hair freshly groomed. Wide, uncertain light-brown eyes stared up at Quade. "Are you hurt?"

"N-no, sir."

Good manners. Quade eyed him a long second. A scare tactic. "Shouldn't you be in school instead of running with those hoodlums?"

"We get out at three o'clock," the boy said.

Quade checked his watch. *Four thirty?* Damn, he'd slept longer than he thought he had. "What's your name, kid?"

He appeared to relax a bit. "Zachary. Zachary Chandler Griggs," he said, his tiny chest heaving up and down as if he'd been running a marathon. "I'm sorry. I'll help you clean up."

"Are you also going to help me pay for replacing the glass?"

Zachary's expression was perplexed. "I have a piggy bank. And five dollars." He slid his tiny hand into his jeans pocket, pulled out a folded bill, and pushed it toward him.

Quade chuckled. "Keep your money, little man."

Zachary smiled, revealing a missing bottom tooth. "Thank you."

Obviously, he had plans for the bill. "Did they knock your tooth out too?" Quade asked.

Zachary laughed. "No. My mom did."

Quade's head jerked back. "Your mom?"

"We were playing catch with a football. She doesn't really know how to throw, but I don't tell her. I like when she plays football with me. Do you have kids?" Zachary asked.

"Me? No," Quade said, thrown off guard by the question.

"Oh. Well, I bet you'd play football with them if you did," he said.

"I sure would." But that was an opportunity he'd never get, because kids weren't in the cards for him. Quade knelt. "What's going on with your bike?"

Zachary brushed a hand through the air. "My chain slipped. It happens sometimes."

Quade could see why. This rusty once-blue contraption appeared to be on its last legs. Clearly, it was well used. The kid definitely needed a new bike. Quade tinkered with the chain for about five minutes with no luck. "Sorry, man, I don't think I can fix it."

Zachary shrugged. "That's okay. My mom knows how to fix it."

Quade returned to a full stand, rubbing the black, oily gunk from his fingers. "Your mom knows a lot, huh?"

Zachary nodded. "Yeah, she does. She's *awesome*. Is your mom awesome too?"

A pang settled in Quade's chest. "Yeah, she was."

"Is she here with you?"

Zachary looked past him and toward the house as if expecting her to walk out. Oh, how Quade wished she would.

Ignoring the question, Quade said, "Let's load your bike into my vehicle, and I'll drive you home."

Zachary flashed a troubled expression. "I'm really not supposed to get into a car with strangers."

Smart kid. But Quade wondered if that was the only reason Zachary didn't want him to take him home. Afraid he'd tell his mother about his vandalism activity? While he was technically innocent, he was guilty by association. Quade stuck out his hand. When Zachary placed his small hand against it, he continued, "I'm Quade Augustus Cannon." Zachary gave him a surprisingly firm shake.

"It's nice to meet you. Why are you in Ms. Shugga's house? Did you know her?"

Quade nodded. "I did. She was my aunt. But I hadn't seen her in a long time." He cringed. Why in the hell had he said that?

"Oh," was all Zachary said. "I knew her too. I miss her a lot. She always baked me fresh cookies. Can you bake cookies?"

Quade laughed. "You wouldn't want my cookies."

"That's okay. I can't bake cookies either. Do you live here now?"

"For a little while," Quade said.

"Cool. Are you going to swim in the pool?"

Quade crossed his arms over his chest. "Probably." He noted the hopeful look on Zachary's face. "Can you swim?"

Zachary's eyes widened with excitement. "Yes!"

Quade glanced at the pool with its cover still intact, then back to Zachary. "Well, once I get the pool ready for use, and as long as I'm here and your mom"—because he got the impression his dad wasn't in the picture, or at least in Honey Hill—"says it's okay, you can swim anytime you like."

Zachary pumped a tiny fist into the air. *"Yes."*

"So are we still strangers?" he asked.

"Nah. I think we can be friends," Zachary said.

"Cool," Quade said.

Moments later, they loaded up and headed out.

"Your truck is awesome," Zachary said.

"Thanks. Her name is Josie."

"You named your car?"

Quade nodded. "It's good luck."

"Cool." A second later, Zachary said, "You should have dinner with us tonight. My mom's an awesome cook."

Quade wondered what Zachary's mother would think about his inviting a stranger to dinner. "We'll see," he said, though he had no plans to accept the kid's invitation. For one, he didn't eat everyone's cooking. To a growing boy, everything tasted good. His mom was probably a horrible cook. For two, all he wanted to do was get back to the inn, take a hot shower, and decompress from this crazy day.

"Are you going to tell my mom I busted your windows?"

Quade eyed Zachary a second, his face long and sad. "That depends. Do you know anything about beekeeping?"

Zachary laughed as if it were the funniest thing he'd ever heard. Settling, he said, "No."

It wouldn't have surprised him had the kid said his mom did. The woman sounded like some kind of small-town superhero. *The Honey Hill Crusader to the rescue.* He laughed to himself.

"You're going to like my mom. She's awesome," Zachary said.

"Is your mom a superhero or something?" he asked for kicks.

"Yes. She's the mayor."

Quade whipped his head toward Zachary. *No way. There is no possible way . . .* With hesitation, he asked, "Is your mother named Lunden?"

Zachary looked astonished. "You know my mom?"

"Yeah. We're kinda old friends," Quade said, feeling uncertain about the tag.

"Cool."

Quade was beginning to think *cool* was the kid's favorite word. When Zachary pointed out the brick ranch-style house, Quade pulled into the driveway. Ms. Jewel had been right. They were practically neighbors. The quaint home had a cozy-looking porch with ferns hanging several inches apart, a two-car garage, and impeccable landscaping.

"I bet my mom's going to be *really* happy to see you," Zachary said.

Somehow, Quade doubted it. But he had to admit he was looking forward to seeing the look of astonishment on her face.

CHAPTER 4

Lunden paused the electric pasta maker when she thought she heard a car door close. Chalking it up to her imagination, she continued. She was probably the only person in Honey Hill who chose to make their pasta by hand instead of simply purchasing it from the market. For her, making pasta was therapeutic. After the day she'd had, Lord knew she needed it.

As if Quade nearly plowing her down hadn't been enough, he'd had to crash her meeting too? Did he not have anything better to do than to keep invading her space? Lunden laughed at herself for being so dramatic. He had just as much right as she had to go anywhere in town he liked. Thankfully, and with any luck, she wouldn't have to see him again until the town hall meeting, when he would announce a reopen date for the inn.

When Lunden heard, again, what sounded like a car door, she washed her hands and headed to the front. Jherico Whitman—with his fine ass—was supposed to drop off some produce from his family farm, but not until after six. Maybe he'd found an opening in his schedule. Looking out the window, she instantly recognized the shiny black SUV parked in her driveway. *What is he doing here?*

A second later, Quade stepped from behind the vehicle, carrying Zachary's bike. Lunden gasped, her heart leaping into her throat. She rushed outside and sprinted across the yard. "Quade Cannon, did you run my child off the road with your erratic driving?" She dropped to her knees in front of Zachary and inspected him from head to toe, front to back, side to side. "Are you okay? Are you hurt?" She didn't see any obvious scrapes, bruises, or blood. But that didn't mean he didn't have internal injuries.

Zachary laughed. "Yes, Mom. My chain popped off my bike again. Quade helped me."

Lunden froze, blinked several times, then said, "Oh." After several long seconds, she rose to a full stand, brushing debris from her knees. "I see."

"No need to thank me. I'm just glad I could help," Quade said.

Lunden eyed Quade. By the smug look on his face, he'd enjoyed watching her make a fool of herself. *Don't do it, Lunden. Just say thank you, and let him get on his way. Don't be petty. Just say thank you.* Still eyeing Quade, she said, "Son, what have I told you about getting into a car with strangers? There are some real lunatics out here."

If the jab had offended him, he didn't show it. Simply flashed a low-wattage smile and crossed his arms over his chest. Lunden was knocked a little off balance by the way the shirt pulled taut against his body, revealing the hard lines underneath the fabric.

"Quade's not a stranger. We're friends," Zachary said.

Quade grinned wide now, then stuck his hand out, palm up, for Zachary to smack. Zachary did, with a little too much enthusiasm for Lunden's liking. Feeling overly possessive, she pulled her son closer to her.

"Thank you, Mr. Cannon, for giving my son a ride home. We won't inconvenience you any longer. I'm sure you have—"

"Mom, I invited Quade to dinner. Can he stay? Pretty please? He did help me, and you *always* say deed one is always good to deserve another."

Lunden fought back her laughter. While he might not have gotten the quote just right—*one good deed deserves another*—at least she knew he was listening. At this moment, she regretted instilling such niceties in him.

"Please, Mom, please." He looked at Quade. "My mom makes the best lasagna in the whole world."

Zachary's praise made Lunden glow.

"Really?" Quade said.

Zachary nodded wildly.

Lunden looked down into Zachary's adorable face. She always liked to lead by example, and she'd never been able to say no to him when he flashed that innocent puppy dog face . . . until now. "I'm sure Mr. Cannon has a ton of other things to do. We don't want—"

"Actually, I don't," Quade said, cutting her off midsentence. "And lasagna just happens to be one of my favorites."

Play nice, Lunden. You can tolerate him for an hour. It's not like you're welcoming the Antichrist into your home as he plans to steal your soul. He's just a man. A good-looking, great-smelling, hard-bodied—stop it. "Well, I guess I'm outnumbered," she said. "If Mr. Cannon would like to stay for dinner, it's fine with me."

🐝

There were two reasons Quade had accepted Lunden's less-than-enthusiastic dinner invitation. One, she seemed so dead set against it, and two, he was starving. But if he was being truly honest, it was mostly because Lunden seemed so dead set against it. He wasn't sure why, but he was starting to enjoy getting under her skin.

Please let her be able to cook.

The delicious aromas that slapped him in the face the second he entered the house gave him hope. The smell of spices and fresh bread stirred his hunger even more. He also picked up hints of lavender and vanilla, then spotted a lit candle flickering on the fireplace mantle, alongside several framed pictures of Lunden and Zachary, smiling, happy. It brought him delight. What he didn't see was a man in any of the images, including her brother, Lexington. Lex, as Quade used to call him. The three of them had been so close when they were younger, so to not see at least one picture of him around the room struck Quade as odd.

The house was cozy and felt like a home. Teal, gray, and yellow decorated the space. From where he stood, the open floor plan provided an unobstructed view of the living and dining rooms and the kitchen. Large windows allowed a lot of natural light to stream in.

Focusing on the happenings in the kitchen, he saw dough dangling from a pasta machine. *Who makes their own pasta? Lunden, apparently.* Why did that not surprise him? The sight put him at ease. A woman who made her own pasta had to be a great cook, right?

"Make yourself comfortable. Dinner will be ready soon. Can I get you something to drink?"

Wow. She's actually being cordial. Was that a good or a bad thing? He laughed at himself. "I'm okay, thanks." She started away. "Lunden?"

"Yes?"

"Please stop calling me Mr. Cannon."

For a moment, it looked as if she would protest, but she finally said, "Okay."

Progress.

"Come with me, Quade. I'll show you my room," Zachary said, taking his hand and pulling him down a hallway.

Zachary's room was decorated in dark blue and red and was surprisingly neat for a six-year-old boy's room. A tall bookshelf packed with books sat next to a small desk holding more books. Obviously, the kid liked to read. They had this in common.

"Check this out," Zachary said.

Quade accepted the postcard-size paper with the words *Tooth Receipt* printed in large letters across the top in black ink. Zachary's name populated the appropriate space, along with his age, a date, a payment line—twenty-five dollars was indicated—and a quality-of-tooth scale: good, great, excellent. *Excellent* was circled. There was also a diagram that indicated which tooth had been received.

"It's from the tooth fairy," Zachary said. His tone lowered to a whisper. "It's really from my mom, but don't tell her I know she's the tooth fairy, okay?"

"Okay," Quade said.

Zachary challenged Quade to a game of Operation, which he eagerly accepted. It had been one of his favorites as a child. And not to pop his own collar, but he had been pretty good at it. And so was Zachary, he soon found out, when the kid won three of the four rounds they played.

"You're better at this than my mom," Zachary whispered. "But don't tell her I said that, okay?"

"My lips are sealed."

"She's really good at Connect Four. If you play her, you'll probably lose. So don't bet any candy, because she'll take it all. But she'll share. Do you have a girlfriend?"

Stunned by the question, Quade opened his mouth, closed it, then opened it again. "Oh. Um, no, I don't."

"Me either. My mom says I'm not old enough yet. That's okay, because all the girls in my class are *mean*." He rolled his eyes heavenward. "But they're pretty. Not as pretty as my mom, though. Do you think my mom is pretty?"

Damn, kid. You're killing me. Was he trying to play matchmaker? "Your mom is very pretty," he said honestly.

Zachary flashed a wide smile.

An hour or so later, Quade, Lunden, and Zachary sat at the dinner table. Quade couldn't recall the last time he'd had such a filling meal.

The lasagna was among the best he'd ever tasted. While he didn't want to be greedy, when Lunden asked him if he'd like a second helping, he'd said yes before she'd fully gotten the question out.

Zachary burst out laughing. "You must really like my mom's lasagna," he said.

"It's amazing," Quade said. Actually, everything was delicious. The salad tasted so fresh he wondered if Lunden had a garden in her backyard. The garlic bread was soft and buttery. Even the sweet tea was perfect. If he ate like this every day, he'd have to add another mile to his daily run.

Even though Lunden tilted her head like she didn't want him to see, Quade noted the soft smile that touched her lips.

"Wait until you taste her honey pie," Zachary said.

The words made Quade swallow wrong, and he coughed several times. "I'm okay," he said, not that Lunden looked the least bit concerned. *Taste her honey pie?* Only a man who hadn't had sex in several months would find sexual innuendo in the innocent statement.

"I doubt Mr.—" She stopped abruptly. "I doubt *Quade* will have room for pie," she said.

Recovering, he said, "I always have room for dessert. Especially honey pie." *Whatever that is.*

"Of course you do," Lunden said half-heartedly. "I'll grab it."

When Lunden stood and moved toward the kitchen, Quade couldn't help noticing the way the shorts she wore hugged her ass. She'd definitely filled out nicely. As if sensing his eyes on her, Lunden glanced over her shoulder. Their gazes only held a second before she turned away.

"The honey is from Ms. Shugga's bees," Zachary said, drawing Quade's attention. "I think some of the bees are living in our walls," he continued around a mouthful of lasagna.

"Don't talk with your mouth full," Lunden said.

Curious, Quade said, "Why do you think bees are living in your walls?"

Zachary swallowed. "Because I hear them buzzing at night," he said. *"A lot."* He made an animated expression while rolling his eyes to the ceiling.

Quade glanced at Lunden, who didn't seem the least bit concerned with Zachary's claim as she loaded the dishwasher. Obviously, she was used to the kid's vivid imagination.

Zachary continued, "They sound strange. Like they're on a roller coaster or something. They buzz fast, then slow, fast, then slow. *Buzz-buzz-buzz. Buzz . . . buzz . . . buzz.*"

Quade's brows bunched. Maybe the kid really was hearing bees. Once, online, he'd watched a beekeeper remove a large hive that had formed inside someone's attic. He shivered at the thought of discovering such a thing inside his home.

"They drive my mom crazy, because every time they start buzzing, I hear her moaning and groaning. I guess she can't fall asleep or some-thing," Zachary said with a shrug.

Quade forked another helping of lasagna into his mouth. Buzzing, moaning, and groaning. He laughed to himself. It almost sounded like Zachary was describing—

Quade bit his tongue when Lunden shrieked, scaring the hell out of him.

"Zachary!" she said, eyes wide, mouth agape.

Both Quade and Zachary flinched from the urgency in Lunden's voice.

Her stunned expression relaxed, and she flashed a wobbly smile. "I'm, um . . . I'm sure you're just hearing praying mantises." Her hands swept through the air. "They're everywhere. All over. Um, sweetie, could you help me with the pie, please?"

Zachary bolted out of his chair. "Yes, ma'am."

If Lunden's intent had been to distract Zachary from the current conversation, it had worked, because he dropped the bee talk. However, Quade couldn't get the buzzing out of his head. He'd learned something new about Lunden. Apparently, she liked to masturbate. A lot, according to Zachary.

Although he tried, Quade couldn't stop the image of Lunden flat on her back, hands between her legs, pleasing herself, from filling his thoughts. He squirmed in his seat, the visual becoming too much to handle. He stared across the room at a fully clothed Lunden. Did she not have a man to satisfy her needs, or did she have a man who *wasn't* satisfying her needs?

No pictures of a man on her mantel nor a live one sitting at the dinner table with them, so he settled on it being the former. Her being single didn't surprise him. After sex, she probably bit her lover's head off like a praying mantis. Quade laughed aloud, drawing Lunden's and Zachary's attention. Since he had no explanation for his amusement— at least, not one he could share—he simply looked away.

Zachary had been right. Quade did love his mother's honey pie. Rich and flavorful. But he shouldn't have had it, because now he was so full that all he wanted to do was take a nap. Something told him Lunden would not cosign him stretching out on her sofa for one.

"Okay, young man, I know you have homework, so hop to it," Lunden said to Zachary.

"Ah, man," Zachary said, but he didn't plead or protest beyond the *ah, man.* He slid from his chair and stood in front of Quade. "I'm going to do my homework really fast. Don't leave, okay?"

"Peanut, we can't hold Quade captive all night," Lunden said.

"*Mom,*" Zachary whined. "Don't call me Peanut in front of company," he said.

"But you are my little peanut," she said.

Lunden might have been a closed book, but one thing was wide open for the world to see: the love she had for her son.

"I love you," Lunden said.

Haunted briefly by the past, Quade felt the numbers 1-4-3 float through his head. Three numbers that had once meant something so powerful to him. Lunden, too, if he had to guess. He shook the decades-old memory away.

Zachary ambled over to his mother and lazily draped his arms around her. "I love you too."

Lunden popped him on the behind. "You better. Now go and do your homework."

"I'll be back in a little bit, Quade," he said, then sprinted away.

"He likes you," Lunden said, standing and beginning to clear the table.

Quade stood, too, gathered his dishes, and followed Lunden into the kitchen. "I'm a likable guy." Lunden didn't appear convinced. "Where's Zachary's father?"

Lunden paused and stared at him. "That's an awfully personal question, especially coming from a man I've only known a few hours," she said, moving again to place their plates into the dishwasher.

"Sorry. I didn't mean to pry. And for the record, we've known each other a lot longer than a few hours."

Lunden faced him. "I knew the boy. I don't know the man." She turned away. "But if you must know, we're divorced. He lives in Greensboro with his new family."

"Are he and Zachary close?"

Lunden laughed. "More questions? Are you writing a book about my life?"

Quade rested his backside against the counter and anchored his hands on either side of his body. "Just curious, I guess."

"I think you mispronounced *nosy*."

He chuckled and flashed his hands in mock surrender. One thing that hadn't changed over the years: she still didn't bite her tongue.

"To answer your question, no, they're not close."

"That's unfortunate. He's a great kid. Must be hard raising him alone."

Lunden eyed him as if trying to decipher why he was so interested. "Why do you assume I'm raising him alone?"

Quade's lips parted, but before he could respond, the doorbell rang.

"Excuse me," Lunden said, wiping her hands and walking off.

Moments later, Lunden returned, trailed by a tall, brown-skinned brother carrying a wooden crate overflowing with fresh vegetables. When the man's eyes landed on Quade, a brief look of surprise spread across his face. He nodded, and Quade mimicked the greeting.

"Jherico, Quade; Quade, Jherico."

Jherico placed the crate on the counter, then extended his hand toward Quade. "Nice to meet you, man."

Quade matched the firmness of the man's shake. "Same here."

Quade thought for a moment that maybe he'd been wrong about Lunden not having a significant other. Not that it mattered either way. He wasn't interested in her like that. Just . . . curious. Quade's brow arched when Lunden rested a hand on Jherico's back, almost reminiscent of an affectionate lover. *Almost.*

"Are you hungry?" she asked in a gentle tone.

Much gentler than any she'd used with him, Quade noted. Lunden cut her eyes to him as if to make sure he was watching the scene unfolding in front of him. Oh, he was watching and observing. Their chemistry. Their body language.

To the untrained eye, it would have been a winning performance, but he was versed in reading people. It was how he'd been so good at his job. Observing these two, he knew one thing for sure. They weren't romantically involved. They lacked lovers' energy. That spark that seared everyone around them.

Quade got the sneaking suspicion Lunden wanted him to think they were involved. What he didn't know was why.

CHAPTER 5

When Lunden moved through the auditorium doors inside the city hall building, her eyes widened and her head jerked. What in the world was going on? Why were all these people here? Not only had their usual seven attendees been joined by others, the female count had quadrupled. Half of these women she hadn't seen at a meeting in years, the other half, ever.

Judging by the dolled-up, runway-ready women, they weren't here to listen to the council discuss streetlights, flowers in the square, or the summer parade. They were here for one reason and one reason only. To shoot their shot at Quade.

Her gaze slid across the room, landing on Quade, who was gracing the town with one of its rare sightings of the man. Well, he certainly knew how to draw attention. While most wore jeans and T-shirts, Quade wore a black, long-sleeved, button-down shirt—with several buttons left unfastened at the top—a black belt with a gold buckle, black slacks that fit almost too perfectly, and expensive-looking shiny black shoes. The man stood out like a stealth panther in a field of sheep, but Lunden couldn't ignore how damn good he looked, despite desperately wanting to.

She hadn't seen Quade since he'd had dinner at her place over a week ago. Not that she'd been looking. Had she seen him out in public, she'd probably have gone the opposite direction. Especially when she thought about Zachary's bee story—and the look on Quade's face had pretty much revealed he'd known exactly what Zachary had been describing. Not the sound of bees but the sound of his mother masturbating . . . a lot, according to him. Though she truly doubted she did it more than the average sexually deprived female.

That debacle had spawned a second one: her foolish attempt at making it appear she and Jherico were a thing. She groaned at the level of her own stupidity. What had she been thinking? Why did it even matter whether Quade thought she was single? The answer came quickly.

To a big-city type like Quade, it probably looked as if she had nothing going for herself. A divorced single mother still living in the small town she'd grown up in. She couldn't have him thinking she was lonely too. Even if that was in fact the case. In hindsight, she wished she could erase the entire evening. Well, maybe not all of it, because Quade's presence had seemed to bring Zachary so much joy. That alone had been worth the hours she'd been forced to spend with Quade Cannon.

As if he could sense her eyes on him, Quade glanced in her direction. Like the good mayor she was, she greeted him with a smile. He returned her greeting with a dazzling smile of his own, then turned away. Damn, that man seemed to get finer each time she saw him.

And speaking of seeing him . . . Had he intentionally been keeping a low profile? Was he a private person or just antisocial? While folks had commented that he clearly wasn't looking to make friends in Honey Hill, that didn't seem the case now as he chatted it up with the sheriff and Sebastian.

"See something you like?"

Lunden turned to face Rylee. The woman's accusatory look caused Lunden's cheeks to heat. "No." Then she flipped the script. "Do you?"

Now Lunden wore the smirk and Rylee the incriminating expression. But Rylee's look of defeat only lasted momentarily, replacing itself with one of certainty.

"I had a very interesting chat with my nephew. Seems his mother— my very best friend in the whole wide world—somehow forgot to mention she'd had dinner with a certain town newcomer."

Dammit, Zachary. Lunden loved her son, but the kid couldn't hold water. "It wasn't dinner. At least, not the type you're making it out to be. Zachary invited him."

"Uh-huh."

"Whatever," Lunden said.

"Zachary seems to really like him," Rylee said.

Lunden gave an exasperated sigh. "Zachary's six. Quade's like a shiny new toy to him. He'll lose interest soon, trust me. I have a garage full of discarded gadgets to prove it."

"I'm sure you're right," Rylee said.

Too bad Lunden hadn't believed a word she'd said. This was exactly why she hadn't told Rylee about Quade having dinner at her house. In true Rylee fashion, she'd blown the entire situation out of proportion, making it out to be far more than what it had been.

Promptly at seven, Lunden called the meeting to order. Instead of taking a seat, Quade watched from the back of the room, one arm folded across his chest, the other massaging his stubble. Things started with the usual format: a greeting; the charge to respect each attendee and their comments, statements, and opinions; and an ask for the attendees to conduct themselves in a respectful and courteous manner.

They breezed through roll call and approval of the agenda. With so many people in attendance, announcements took far longer than usual, as half the room wanted to chime in. Lunden found herself inconspicuously checking her watch. Though the room teemed with people, she constantly found her gaze trailing to the back of the room. Every time her eyes landed on Quade, his were already settled on her. His scrutiny was a bit unsettling, and she couldn't explain why. Maybe because his dark, probing gaze made her skin hot to the touch.

Announcements were followed by the call for petitions, the recap of old business, and finally the call for new business. Once all pending business had been addressed, Ms. Jewel introduced Quade. The soft hum of chatter reverberated in the room as he made his way to the front. If he was in any way nervous about addressing the town, it didn't show. He carried himself with his usual grace and confidence.

When Lunden locked stares with Rylee, a mischievous gleam was present on her face. Lunden rolled her eyes away from her soon-to-be *ex*–best friend. Unfortunately, they landed back on Quade. Something long dormant awakened inside her that made her entire body warm and tingly. Red-hot desire. Disgusted with herself, she feigned disinterest by pretending to read the pages in front of her. With all the men in Honey Hill for her to lust over, why did it have to be this particular one?

Quade settled at the front of the room and reintroduced himself, stating he was the new owner of the Inn on Main, as if the *entire* town didn't already know this. Heck, most had probably known it before he had.

Mentioning he was the nephew of Ms. Shugga seemed to rattle him. Was it grief or guilt? For the first time that night, Quade looked . . . vulnerable. His shoulders slumped, and his posture relaxed. The room filled with sounds of sympathy, words of encouragement, and kind-hearted sentiments, which made him appear even more uncomfortable.

Witnessing his unease prompted her to intervene. "Mr. Cannon, I'm sure the town is eager to hear about your timeline for reopening the inn," Lunden said.

She certainly was. The town had rallied together and maintained the upkeep of the inn when Ms. Shugga had become too weak to do it all by herself and after her death, so Lunden knew it wouldn't take much to get it up and running again. Three, four months, tops. And since Quade might not actually be as bad as she'd made him out to be in her head, she'd be open to assisting him where needed. It was the mayoral thing to do.

Quade recovered quickly, his bold self-assurance returning instantly. Squaring his shoulders and firming his stance, he said, "Well, Mayor, I don't intend to reopen the inn. I plan to sell it."

By the way Lunden's once-vibrant smile dimmed, Quade suspected he hadn't given the answer she'd wanted to hear. Surely she hadn't thought he would stick around small-town USA to operate an inn. Six months would be torture enough. Permanently? That would *never* happen.

"You can't do that," Lunden said.

Her expression looked as if she was teetering between frustration and forced cordialness. Quade's brows knit. "I believe I can, Mayor. I own it." While sounding arrogant hadn't been his intent, he needed to remind her and anyone else who had an issue with his decision that he could—and indeed intended to—sell the property.

"Selling the inn would be a mistake. For many of us here, it's far more than a commodity to leverage toward the highest bidder simply as a means of lining one's pockets."

By *one's pockets*, he was sure she meant his, but he ignored the jab. The hum of chatter swirled around him, most in attendance seeming to side with their esteemed leader. Though he suspected there had to be one or two who saw his vision. Not everyone in town could be as closed minded as Lunden. Or could they?

Quade would have thought Lunden would be on the front line campaigning for the sale of the inn. "As mayor, surely you considered how the sale of the inn would benefit Honey Hill," he said. "The right growth and development could boost the local economy and generate local government revenue by the millions."

There were oohs and aahs from the room, but Lunden didn't seem the least bit impressed by his information.

"You forgot to mention that in the midst of your 'growth and development,' Honey Hill will be stripped of its small-town charm. Our quiet, intimate community will become a bustling, overpopulated, and commercialized mini city."

This time there were groans and moans. They brought a smug smile to Lunden's face. Probably because she knew the masses had crossed back over to her side of the line.

"That—"

Lunden cut him off. "And when this growth and development pushes most of the locals out because they won't be able to afford to live in the place they've called home all or most of their lives, what then?"

This generated grumbles and growls, seemingly directed at him.

"That's—"

"You might not understand this, *Mr. Cannon*, being from the big city and all, but we like our slice of heaven just the way it is. We're okay with depending on local assets to seed our growth. We're not all servants to the almighty dollar."

When Quade barked a laugh, Lunden's expression turned to stone. If she had been able to shoot daggers from her narrowed eyes, he would have been a dead man.

"Am I amusing you, Mr. Cannon?"

"Yes, you are. Mostly by the way you keep insinuating money is my driving factor."

"Isn't it?"

"I can assure you I don't need the money," he said. While he usually didn't go around touting his financial well-being, he'd felt compelled to do so this time.

"Then why sell?"

"Because I—" He paused, deciding against revealing his plans for the proceeds, to start a nonprofit for at-risk young men. It was none of her business. Or anyone else's in this room, for that matter. Starting again, he said, "Because I have no desire to operate an inn."

Lunden went silent, but it didn't last long.

"Have you once considered Ms. Shugga? She wouldn't have wanted this. The inn was her heart."

At the mention of his aunt's name, Quade stiffened. Lunden had definitely hit below the belt with interjecting Aunt Shugga into the conversation. Recovering from the blow, he said, "With all due respect, Mayor, isn't it a bit arrogant for you to assume to know what my aunt would have wanted?"

"No," Lunden said plainly. "I spent time with her every single day. Talked to her every single day. Listened to her talk about y—" Lunden clammed up, inhaled a deep breath, then released it slowly before starting again. "You hadn't seen her in, what, twenty years? I think I might know better than you what she would have wanted."

"Yet she left me the inn, and I do intend to sell it."

Before Lunden could get out another word and dig even deeper under his skin, he thanked the council for their time, turned, and left the room. Outside, he drew in a deep breath of fresh air and released it slowly. A second later, a door banged open. By the way the energy shifted, he didn't need to turn to know who it was.

"Do you think I'm going to stand by and watch you sell the inn?" Lunden said behind him.

Quade whipped around. "Do you think you have a choice?" When Lunden flinched, he felt horrible for making her do so. He inhaled deeply to center himself, then exhaled slowly. "Lunden, I'm not the enemy here."

Lunden barked an emotionless laugh. "That's funny. Funny that you actually believe you're not."

Watching her stalk away, Quade shook his head. One thing was certain. This damn town was not big enough for the both of them. *Six months. Six months and I'm out of here.* The time couldn't elapse fast enough.

CHAPTER 6

One of the first things Lunden did when she took a seat behind her desk the morning following that disastrous town hall meeting was prep an email to the town attorney, letting the woman know exactly what she needed her to research. *The nerve of him.* Thinking about the meeting swelled her with anger, causing her fingers to move even faster over the keyboard.

Who does he think he is? She stabbed at the keys. *Bastard.* Did he actually believe he could just barrel into town like a maniac and knock her—the town, she corrected—off balance like this? *Who does he think he is?* Her fingers stopped abruptly. "He's the new owner of the inn," she mumbled to herself, the fact making her stomach curl. "Why, Ms. Shugga?" she said.

At this point, the why no longer mattered. Ms. Shugga had chosen to leave the inn to Quade, instead of—she stopped shy of completing the sentence. Lunden was sure the woman had never dreamed he'd sell it. Clearly, she'd wanted him to carry on her legacy, not off-load the treasured landmark to the highest bidder. She groaned at the possibility of what could happen if the inn fell into the wrong hands. *Another set of wrong hands.*

After hitting send on the email, Lunden crafted a second to the Land and Use Department head, then reconsidered before sending it.

Couldn't risk too many people being privy to her plans. Her mother's voice played in her head. *If you have to hide what you're doing, you probably shouldn't be doing it.* "This is different, Mom," she mumbled.

At ten forty-five, she gathered her things and headed to the library for her weekly storytelling hour with the preschoolers at the local daycare. Twenty minutes later, she sat in front of a group of eager-to-listen four-year-olds.

Lunden always loved how interactive they all were. When she mooed, they mooed. When she barked, they barked. When she clucked like a chicken, so did they. All the laughter worked wonders on her previously shitty mood.

Glancing up, Lunden said, "Okay, who's ready for another story?"

"Me, me, me," rang out in unison.

"Perfect. Let's . . ." Her words trailed off when she looked past the group to see Quade across the room, staring at her. Her cheery disposition took an instant nosedive. It was all she could do not to bare her teeth as she sneered in his direction.

"Ms. Lunden, what's wrong?"

The tiny, delicate voice helped Lunden regain her composure. Eyeing the children, she smiled and said, "Nothing. Where were we?"

"Another book. Another book," they all cheered.

Unable to resist the urge, she glanced up again to where Quade had been standing. He was gone. Refocusing on the kids, she cracked the cover of another book and lost herself in the playful story.

After story time wrapped up, Lunden chatted with Helena Gentry, Honey Hill Public Library's only librarian. As always, the woman thanked her profusely for sparing her time to read to the kids, wrapping it up with her favorite line, "It's fundamental." When she turned to walk away, Lunden stopped her.

"Helena?"

Helena faced her again. "Yes?"

"Was that the new owner of the inn I saw earlier?" As if she didn't already know the answer.

The woman's brown eyes lit up, and she turned a lock of her brown hair around her finger. "Why, yes, it was."

"What was he doing here?" As if the answer weren't already obvious. It was a library. He'd probably been getting books.

"He applied for a library card and checked out several books. Pieces by James Baldwin, Richard Wright, Toni Morrison, and Octavia Butler, if I'm remembering correctly. Oh, he also checked out several beekeeping books. Women do love a well-read man, don't we?"

While Helena giggled like a schoolgirl, Lunden mentally rolled her eyes at the woman.

"I informed him about our extensive e-book offerings, thanks to our mayor. But he said he preferred the feel of holding a book in his hands. By our conversation, he loves to read and—"

"Well, that's good for him," Lunden said, done talking about the overzealous man. Clearly, he'd hypnotized Helena—a married mother of five—with his charms, but Lunden wouldn't be so susceptible.

On Lunden's walk back to her office, she refused to give one single second of thought to Quade. The jerk deserved not another minute of her time. He definitely didn't deserve the inn. And if she had anything to do with it, he wouldn't get it. She just prayed Zeta found something, anything, she could use as ammunition. For most people, she would have attempted to appeal to their more compassionate side. Lunden highly doubted that imp had one. Oh, he could best believe she wouldn't take this lying down.

For a brief moment, she had an irrational thought. Maybe selling the inn wouldn't be so bad. Maybe it would be the boost to their reserves Dick wanted to see. What was she saying? Apparently, the beaming rays of the sun were getting to her. Selling was bad. Real bad. In Dallas, she'd seen firsthand how gentrification destroyed communities like theirs. She wouldn't allow that to happen.

"Why, don't you look real pretty today, Mayor."

The familiar voice placed an instant smile on Lunden's face. She turned to see one of her favorite people. Ms. Jewel. "Thank you. So do you." Ms. Jewel wore a clover-green dress with yellow flowers peppered all over.

"Mind if I walk with you?" Ms. Jewel said, threading her arm through Lunden's.

"It would be my pleasure."

"I've been meaning to stop by your office. I wanted to chat with you about the other night at the meeting."

How had Lunden known that would come up? "I apologize. I . . . could have handled the situation better," she admitted. "I allowed my emotions to get involved."

"You're passionate," Ms. Jewel said, patting her hand. "That's why you're so good at being mayor. You authentically care about the town and its residents. Never apologize for your convictions."

"Not everyone at the meeting seemed as committed to the inn after *he* made that comment about millions of dollars potentially flowing into the town." *But at what cost?* Lunden had always valued Ms. Jewel's opinion, so she said, "Do you think I'm wrong for wanting to save the inn, potentially the town?"

"I think you've deemed it a battle worth fighting. As such, might I offer some input on your strategy going forward?"

The fact Ms. Jewel hadn't given a direct yes or no to her question hadn't been lost on Lunden. But if she was offering advice, she had to support Lunden's efforts, right? "Absolutely," Lunden said.

Lunden listened as Ms. Jewel offered some good advice and, in her opinion, some not-so-good advice. Especially the part that loosely translated to *you get more bees with honey than vinegar*. Well, getting bees wasn't the problem. Keeping them safe was. And she'd rather be pelted with acorns by the mischievous albino squirrels that roamed around town than make friends with Quade Cannon. Still, Lunden didn't object, just listened.

"Well, this is me," Ms. Jewel said, stopping in front of her fabric shop. "Just think about what I said."

Lunden gave a nod. "I will." Anyone else, she would have dismissed the advice as soon as it had been given, but because it was Ms. Jewel, she would consider it.

Thankfully, the remainder of the week whizzed by. Lunden had looked forward to this moment—a peaceful Friday night on her deck, glass of wine in hand, enjoying the warm night breeze and the sounds of nature—but Rylee was ruining it. The very last thing Lunden wanted to do was talk about Quade Cannon and the debacle at the meeting earlier in the week; however, from the moment they'd settled into the chairs an hour ago, it was all they'd discussed.

Regardless of the numerous times she'd attempted to change the subject, they somehow found their way right back to Quade. Thankfully, the two glasses of peach moscato she'd consumed helped to make the conversation less daunting. Plus, despite how Rylee made it sound, she wasn't at fault here.

"Okay, so I'm . . . passionate." Because that was how Ms. Jewel had labeled it. "Is that such a bad thing?" Lunden said.

"Sweetie, you mispronounced *stubborn as hell*," Rylee said, finding amusement in her own words.

Too bad Lunden didn't. After Rylee's laughter dried up, Lunden said, "So what if I'm *stubborn* about a town and landmark I love? Is that a crime?"

"Of course not."

Lunden could sense a *but* coming. *Three, two, one . . .*

"*But . . .*"

Yep, she knew the woman well. "But what, Ry?" Lunden asked, eyeing her sympathetic-looking friend.

"Don't get me wrong—you made some really good points at the meeting, but so did Quade. Would selling the inn truly be such a bad thing?"

Yes! Lunden wanted to scream. Instead, she gave a heavy sigh, then feigned disgust. "Don't tell me you're Team Quade too." Since the meeting, she'd had several similar conversations. Was she the only one who saw the ramifications of such expansion in Honey Hill? It was how gentrification started. Big corporations taking little nibbles until the town was all gobbled up, leaving the residents with nothing but crumbs to snatch after like beggars. The thought angered her even more. How could Quade so easily kick aside Ms. Shugga's legacy? *His* legacy. He had no idea of the value—and not the monetary one—of the gift he'd been given.

"I'm Team Lunden all the way, but who's putting up this fight? Mayor Pierce or Lunden?"

Confused, Lunden said, "They're one and the same." And they both wanted what was best for the town.

"No, they're not. Lunden is allowed to be emotional, hasty, and stubborn as hell. The mayor can't be those things. She has to look at the big picture, focus on making and keeping the town viable, and do what's right for the town as a whole, regardless of how much *Lunden* may or may not like it."

Feeling attacked, Lunden said, "Haven't I done this?" And wasn't that exactly what she was doing now?

"Yes, and you've done a hell of a job, thus far."

Lunden gave a lazy smile. "Thank you," she said, despite knowing . . .

"But . . ."

. . . a but was coming.

". . . sometimes you have to be open to things that may not please Lunden but must, at least, be considered by Mayor Pierce."

"I hear you." Lunden took a sip from her glass, considering Rylee's words. As mayor, she was duty bound to do what was best for the town. Not in a million years did she—Lunden or the mayor—believe selling the inn was what was best.

"What does Ms. Jewel think?" Rylee asked.

Just like Ms. Shugga, Ms. Jewel was highly respected by the townsfolk. Just as many people went to her for advice as they had to Ms. Shugga. So it had been a no-brainer Lunden would seek her counsel and wisdom. "She hasn't supported or opposed the idea. All she said was if I stood a chance, I couldn't tell a man like Quade why the inn was so important to Honey Hill; I had to show him." The only thing she wanted to show him was the way out of Honey Hill.

"I see how showing him some goodies could be persuasive," Rylee said.

Lunden swatted at her friend. "Get your mind out of the gutter."

"What?" Rylee said, attempting to sound innocent. "I was simply agreeing with Ms. Jewel." She smirked. "But honestly, you can't tell me you haven't fantasized about sleeping with Quade. I saw how you looked at him at the meeting before the shit hit the fan."

Briefly, Lunden recalled how sexy Quade had looked, then scolded herself for appreciating his assets. "Did you see how calm he acted? Like he knew he had the upper hand." *Asshole.* Lunden took another sip from her glass. "He gets under my skin," she said more to herself than to Rylee.

"You know why he gets under your skin, right?"

Knowing she would regret asking, Lunden said, "Why?" And if Rylee said something foolish, like that she still felt something for Quade, Lunden would disown her. The only thing she felt toward Quade Cannon was the desire to run him over, like he'd nearly done to her. That would solve all her problems. *Ugh.* The man affected her so negatively he was turning her violent.

"Because you want him," Rylee said.

Rylee laughed as if she were listening to her favorite comedian perform onstage. Made sense she would find the humor in the words, because what Rylee had just suggested was a joke. "I want him all right. I want him to plunge face first into a shoal of piranhas."

"All this anger you're exhibiting toward him is just pent-up sexual frustration. You need some. And that man looks like he can definitely knock down walls."

Only to herself, Lunden agreed with Rylee. She most definitely needed some, and Quade most definitely looked like he could deliver all of it with one stroke; however, one thing was for absolute certain . . . "Quade Cannon will *never* get anywhere near my walls," she said. "He probably sucks at knocking down walls anyway." If only she actually believed that, then maybe the space between her legs would stop throbbing. She chastised her body for its betrayal.

"Men are such complications," Rylee said.

Lunden couldn't have agreed more. Still . . . "I do miss being in someone's arms. I just want a good guy for once. Is that too much to ask for? Someone who looks at a dandelion and sees a wish, not a weed." Lunden wasn't even sure where the words had come from, because dating was the last thing on her mind.

"Maybe—"

Both Lunden and Rylee yelped when a bang sounded in the kitchen.

"Zachary?" Lunden called out.

"Sorry, Mom," he said.

"What are you doing?"

"Getting water. I was thirsty. I'm okay now. Good night. Love you. Love you too, Aunt Rylee."

"Love you, Petunia," Rylee said.

Lunden snickered when Zachary whined, *"Aunt Rylee."* Between Peanut and Petunia, the kid had it rough.

Lowering her voice, Rylee said, "That kid is like a cat burglar. The other day, he nearly gave me a heart attack. I didn't even hear him enter the kitchen at the bakery. When I turned, there he was, smiling up at me with all that cuteness. I nearly dropped an entire tray of cupcakes."

"Yep, that sounds like him. He moves like a ballerina. Maybe I should get him a bell necklace."

They laughed.

"My godson nearly broke his neck on that rickety old bike when his chain popped off. *Again*. I'm going to get him a new one for his birthday," Rylee said.

"Don't bother. I've tried. His dad gave him that bike." One of the few things the bum had ever given their son. "He cherishes that heap of rusted metal. I guess it's the only reminder that he actually has a father." Feeling renewed strife toward her ex-husband, she downed the remaining contents of her glass, then refilled it. "I really hate men."

"Well, you should hate *that* trifling dog, for sure, but not *all* men. There are some good ones out there. Zachary seems to really like Quade. He was all he talked about. How cool he is."

Lunden had made the same observation about how much Zachary seemed to like Quade. She made a mental note to tell Zachary to stay away from the man. "He's six. He likes everybody."

"You owe him an apology," Rylee said.

Confused, Lunden said, "Zachary?"

"No, not Zachary. Quade."

Lunden whipped her head toward her. "Excuse me? An apology? For what, standing up for something I believe in?"

"No, for the jabs at him about Ms. Shugga. That hurt him. You could see it all over his face."

There was not a damn thing Lunden could say to counter Rylee's claim, because she'd witnessed the same thing. Instead, she turned away and studied her glass, replaying the events in her head. An image of a dispirited Quade filtered into her thoughts, causing her chest to tighten. Maybe she had cut a little too deep. But like a wounded animal, she'd reacted, in hindsight, perhaps a little too hastily. Why did she always strike first and assess the target later? Swallowing the painful lump of guilt lodged in the back of her throat, in a tiny voice she said, "You're right." Maybe she regretted her words. But what was done was done.

This was what Quade called a perfect Saturday afternoon. Lounging on the patio, sipping bourbon, and reading. He wasn't used to too many moments like these, when he wasn't being pulled in fifty directions at once. In the past, his entire day would have been spent either working in the office, meeting with clients, or doing commercial site visits. Sometimes all three in one day. He shook his head at his old practices. But while his previous life had been hectic, he'd loved it . . . until he hadn't.

Glancing up from the book, he surveyed the tranquil backyard. *A man could get used to this.* Actually, he couldn't. This was a little too quiet for his taste. No car horns. No sounding alarms. No sirens. None of the luxuries of city living. Yet being here would help him satisfy his goal of finding peace and the time to enjoy life more.

Finding time wouldn't be a problem. It was the peace thing that would probably be a challenge for the next six months. His jaw tightened as he thought about Lunden and how she'd thrown the bit about Aunt Shugga in his face. He got she'd been upset about his decision, but to drag his dead aunt into the conversation had been a low blow. If she'd meant so much to his aunt, why hadn't she inherited the inn instead of him?

"Hey, Quade? You busy?"

The sound of Zachary's voice drew Quade from his thoughts. The kid moved toward him, pushing that hunk of metal he called a bike. The front wheel wobbled, but Zachary didn't seem to mind. He could definitely use a new bike. Quade closed his book. "Never too busy for you, dude. What's up?"

Zachary allowed the bicycle to drop to the ground, then slid into the lounger next to Quade. "Nothing much. Are you and my mom mad at each other?"

Odd question. But it made Quade curious. "Why do you ask?"

"Because my mom told me I couldn't come here anymore."

This made Quade even more salty toward Lunden. What was her plan? To turn the town against him, starting with Zachary? The fact that Zachary was here told him he had an ally in the kid. Even if the rest of the town came after him with pitchforks, it wouldn't force him to change his decision. And after Lunden's stunt at the meeting, he was even more eager to off-load this place. "Then you should probably get home. I don't want to get you into trouble for being here. Friends don't do that," he said, a hidden message in his words.

"You're worth it," Zachary said.

Quade smiled lightly. "You're okay with me, kid."

"So are you. And I bet you're really good at knocking down walls."

Quade's brow furrowed. What in the heck was Zachary talking about? "Knocking down walls?"

"My aunt Rylee said you look like you can knock down walls, but my mom said you will never come near her walls and that you probably suck at knocking them down anyway. I didn't even know she wanted the walls knocked down. Wouldn't the house fall?"

So Lunden and Rylee had been discussing him sexually. Did Lunden really think he would suck in the bedroom, or had she simply been trying to convince herself? He was tempted to relay a message to her by Zachary. That he could knock down her walls with one stroke. That would piss her off, for sure.

"Don't tell her I told you, okay?" Zachary said.

Well, damn. There went his message idea. "I won't. This is man talk."

Zachary smiled wide. "Will you come to my birthday party? It's in July."

Lunden would probably have a fit if he walked into the party. She'd probably spend all her time uncomfortable and scowling at him instead of enjoying herself. His presence would probably make her day miserable. Something wicked lifted one side of his mouth. "I wouldn't miss it for the world."

Zachary pumped his little arm into the air. "*Yes*. It's going to be so much fun. It was supposed to be a pool party, but the community pool isn't built yet. Maybe it'll be ready next year."

Quade almost offered up his pool, but since he was sure Lunden would never go for it, he remained silent.

"Are you a good guy, Quade?"

Quade considered the randomness of the question before saying, "I try to be."

Zachary's smile grew wider. A second later, he slid out of his chair. "I have to go. Before my mom gets home. I'll come back tomorrow, okay?"

"Okay," Quade said.

Zachary grabbed up his bike and started away. Stopping, he lowered the kickstand, ran back to Quade, and hugged him. "Bye, Quade."

Zachary was gone before Quade recovered from the surprise of the kid's actions, not allowing him to return the show of affection. "Hey, Z," he called out.

"Yes, sir?"

"You be safe, all right?"

"Okay, I will."

While Quade held no desire to have kids, if—and that was a huge if—he did, he'd like to imagine they would be as mannerly as Zachary. While Quade questioned Lunden as mayor, he couldn't question her parenting skills. She'd done a great job with him.

Quade couldn't help thinking how Zachary's father was missing out on getting to know him. He thought about his own father. A pain-filled smile curled his lips as he remembered the man who'd been bigger than life to Quade. In his eyes, Horace Cannon had been a superhero. Then he was gone. His hell had begun shortly afterward.

The sentimental feelings toward his father's memory were swallowed whole by the scornfulness he experienced anytime he thought about the Beast, the nickname he'd given his stepfather. Tossing his book aside, he decided to go for a swim. After removing his shirt, he jumped in. He swam laps until his thoughts were completely clear of the man his mother had married a few months after his father's death from a massive heart attack. His father's supposed best friend.

When his cell phone rang, Quade's initial thought was to ignore it, but he decided to take the call. After making his way out of the pool, he lifted the device from the table. Pryor's face filled the screen. Making the call active, Quade said, "What's up, P?"

"I'll tell you what's up. Multiple millions. That's what's up. These folks are champing at the bit for your inn. Shit, is there gold buried somewhere on the property?"

The only thing Quade knew for certain was buried there was his and Aunt Shugga's time capsule. For him, that was gold. But in the form of memories.

"I have seven companies already interested and feelers out to several more. When is the earliest I can bring them for a site visit?"

Quade knew Pryor wouldn't have any trouble selling this place. It had so much charm and appeal. With a few minor upgrades and added amenities, this place could definitely become a five-star getaway destination. Couple that with such a charming town, and the place practically sold itself. "Better hold off awhile. I don't think Honey Hill would be too welcoming to any more newcomers right now."

"Damn, you just got into town. You've made enemies already? That's a record. Even for you," Pryor said.

"Just one. Who just happens to be the mayor," Quade said, drying off and easing down into the lounger.

"That could be a problem," Pryor said. "Typically, in small towns the mayor is like a cult leader with a dedicated following. No faster way to run off a potential buyer than a bunch of disgruntled citizens. Any chance of winning him and his flock over?"

"Her," Quade corrected, his jaw tightening at the thought of Lunden. And he doubted it.

"Her? I take my earlier assessment back. There's no problem. Just dial up that Cannon charm. You'll have her eating out the palm of your hand in no time."

If Quade offered Lunden his hand, he was fairly certain she'd lop it off. "I wouldn't be so sure about that. That woman is a viper wrapped in barbed wire and booby-trapped with explosives that are liable to explode with the slightest touch."

Pryor laughed. "Sounds like you're overexaggerating. She couldn't be that bad. And on the off chance that she is, what's the problem? You've charmed far more menacing serpents than a small-town mayor."

Quade appreciated all the confidence Pryor had in his powers of persuasion, but he didn't *want* to charm Lunden. He wanted to stay as far away from the woman as humanly possible. Besides, he didn't need to waste his energy trying to persuade Lunden of anything. Legally, he had every right to sell his own property, and she couldn't do a damn thing about it but complain, because the law was on his side. He just hoped it wouldn't get that far.

CHAPTER 7

Lunden usually found solace at Sunday service, but that changed the second Quade strolled through the doors of Honey Hill United, the town's nondenominational church, where all were welcome. Apparently even the wicked. He'd done a good job of hiding during the past month. What had prompted him out now?

Rylee bumped her. "Do you see who just walked in?"

Oh, she'd felt the presence of evil as soon as it'd entered the sanctuary. Since she stood in the house of the Lord, Lunden refrained from thinking any negative thoughts, like about bopping Quade on top of the head with her Bible.

"Fine as h—" Rylee paused. "*Heck*, and a man of God."

Lunden seriously doubted he was here of his own volition. This had Ms. Jewel written all over it. Lunden laughed to herself. She would have loved to have been there for that conversation. There was a chance she could be wrong, that Quade was indeed here of his own accord. Highly doubtful, but possible.

"Look at those vultures, swarming him already," Rylee said, her face scrunched in displeasure.

Lunden couldn't help but wonder if Rylee's discontent had anything to do with the fact Katrina Sweeney, Canten's . . . whatever, was among the women vying for Quade's time. Lunden looked on as Quade said something and the women tossed their heads back in animated laughter. Whatever it was couldn't have been that funny.

Lunden took in Quade's attire. A shirt checkered with green, white, and black paired with navy-blue slacks. Okay, so she had to admit he looked . . . nice. Lunden patted herself on the back. See? She was capable of giving him a compliment. Quade glanced in her direction. When his eyes landed on her, the toothy grin he wore melted from his face, and he turned his back to her. *Asshole.*

"I'm guessing there's still a bit of animosity between you two," Rylee said.

"Animosity? Absolutely not. I harbor no ill will toward him," she said with a straight face.

"Is that so?" Rylee asked, her tone revealing she hadn't believed a single syllable of what Lunden had just said. "Okay, if you have no ill will toward him, say something nice about him."

What were they, five? Lunden sighed but played along. "Okay." She eyed Quade again, fighting the urge to bare her teeth. "Those are nice colors he has on. They go together well."

"See, that wasn't so hard, was it?" Rylee said.

"I told you. No animosity. He must not have known we're a come-as-you-are church."

"What makes you say that?" Rylee asked.

"Because he's not wearing red, horns, and a tail."

Rylee barked a laugh that drew the attention of several of the other parishioners. "Oh my God, did you just call that man the devil?"

Lunden simply shrugged. "I call 'em as I see 'em."

After service, everyone gathered on the back lawn for the church picnic. The breezy eighty degrees made it a perfect day for an outdoor function. Lunden made a point of avoiding Quade, and he seemed to be doing the same, which was a-okay with her.

"There's Lendell with that camera," Rylee said. "And you know he's heading this way to snap his favorite mayor. That man sure does like taking pics of you. You think he jacks off to them at night?" She made a pumping motion with her hand.

Lunden playfully swatted her friend. "*Eww.* No." Lunden eyed the older gentleman. "He's harmless."

Lendell Pruette was Honey Hill's unofficial town historian. There hadn't been an event or celebration over the past sixty years he hadn't captured on tape or video. Many considered him a nuisance, always wielding a camera or recorder—sometimes both—but not Lunden. She appreciated his ability and passion for capturing moments.

Truthfully, she felt bad for him. He lived in that big old house all alone. As far as she knew, he'd never been married, and she couldn't recall ever seeing him with a woman. Didn't have any kids. At least, if he did, they never came to visit. Just had himself, an adorable pygmy goat named Spud, and his camera and video equipment. Yet he seemed happier than most folks in town. Strange how that happened sometimes. The people with the least were happier than the ones with the most.

"And here he comes," Rylee said under her breath.

Lendell reminded Lunden of her former postal carrier back in Texas. Though Lendell had about forty years on him, they had similar builds and the same deep-brown complexion, both always happy and smiling, both able to talk your ear completely off.

"Look at two of the most beautiful women in Honey Hill. I just gotta capture this. Smile for the camera," Lendell said.

Lunden and Rylee moved closer to each other, then cheesed as if their images would appear on the cover of *O* magazine.

"Perfect," Lendell said, looking at the shots he'd just taken on the tiny camera screen and walking away before either of them could ask to see.

Lunden and Rylee looked on as he approached the Chamber sisters, both knowing this would be entertaining. Lunden didn't know any two women who loved posing for the camera more than these two. As customary, they required Lendell to snap several shots from several different angles. When he attempted to move away, they held him hostage and urged him to take just a few more. When they made the mistake of turning away, Lendell fled like a convict experiencing freedom for the first time in years who feared being led back to captivity.

"Those two are—" Rylee stopped abruptly. "Oh God. Here she comes."

Confused, Lunden said, "Here who comes?"

"Lady Sunshine. I'll be back." Rylee scrambled to her feet. "Can I get you anything while I'm up?"

"No, I'm good. Why do you always run from Lady Sunshine?"

"Because she's too good at extracting information. Or maybe I'm just too bad at holding on to it. Either way . . . I'll be back when she's gone," Rylee said, then hurried off.

Loud laughter drew Lunden's attention. She glanced in the direction it had come from. *Of course,* she thought as she zeroed in on Quade and his harem. Rolling her eyes away, she popped a meatball into her mouth. Was she the only one in town who had an issue with him for selling the inn? She scowled. If she had to fight the good fight alone, so be it. The inn was here to stay, regardless of any plans Quade had for it. *Why couldn't he have simply stayed gone?*

"He's quite the attraction, isn't he?"

That was one way of putting it. Lunden glanced up to acknowledge Mrs. Cora Jane Ridley. Better known as Lady Sunshine, because she always left a little warmth everywhere she went. But mostly because she was always hot with gossip.

"Mind if I join you?" Lady Sunshine asked.

"Not at all," Lunden said.

Lady Sunshine was a hair over four feet with big, brown, expressive eyes, dark-brown skin, and auburn-red dreadlocks that usually hung to her waist. Today they were wrapped in a messy bun atop her head. A kente-printed scarf was wrapped around her head and matched the dress she'd undoubtedly made herself. In addition to being their walking gazette, she was also the best seamstress and dressmaker in the state, possibly the South.

Lady Sunshine stared across at Quade. "Shugga loved that boy like he was her very own. It broke her heart when his mother snatched him away all those years ago." Lady Sunshine shook her head. "A shame."

Snatched him away? What had that meant? Despite not wanting to appear overly interested, Lunden needed elaboration. "Snatched him away. What does that mean?" she asked nonchalantly.

"Well, you know I ain't the one to go round spreading folks' business," Lady Sunshine said.

Was this woman serious? Was she really going to sit on sacred land and tell such a humdinger of a tale? Lady Sunshine was more informative than CNN. However, this was one time Lunden wanted to know what she knew, so she said, "Of course not."

"And I would hate for word to get around that *I* told you anything about anybody," Lady Sunshine said.

"My lips are sealed."

Lady Sunshine stared at her a moment. "Well . . ." She surveyed her surroundings before continuing. Apparently satisfied that no one was eavesdropping, she continued, "Shugga and Rose—Rose was her sister, Quade's mother," she clarified. "They'd had a huge argument about the man Rose started dating shortly after Horace died, the boy's real father."

Lunden was saddened to hear Mr. Cannon had passed. She'd really liked the hilarious man.

"The way I heard it, he was mean and controlling," Lady Sunshine said.

Mean and controlling. The words reverberated in Lunden's head, because they were ones she'd used to describe her ex.

"Shugga didn't like the way he treated the boy." Lady Sunshine pointed toward Quade with her chin.

The way Lady Sunshine made it sound, Mr. Cannon had died when Quade was younger. But when? Quade hadn't mentioned anything to her back then about losing his father. But now that she thought about it, that last summer he'd visited Honey Hill, his mother had been alone when she'd brought him. Mr. Cannon usually accompanied them. Why hadn't Quade shared the loss with her?

"How did he treat him?" Lunden asked.

Lady Sunshine's expression turned somber. "Like he hated him, from what I was told. Always yelling at him. Belittling him. Making him feel like he didn't belong. You know, that can have dire consequences on a child in their formative years."

Lunden knew this. It was one of a list of reasons she'd left her marriage. There was no way she could continue to expose Zachary to such a toxic environment. While her ex hadn't been physically abusive, his words had sometimes cut like a knife and felt that way. Lunden's gaze slid to Quade. Instead of the contempt she usually felt toward him, she experienced something different now. Empathy. Was this why he wanted to rid himself of the inn? Did it remind him too much of a past riddled with pain?

"Now, I can't swear to this, but I believe the man she took up with was her dead husband's best friend." Lady Sunshine shivered as if the notion had given her the chills. "But whoever he was, I don't think Rose loved him, according to the information given to me."

That was one thing Lunden could say about Lady Sunshine. She never revealed her sources.

"Rose just couldn't stand to be alone, I reckon. Probably didn't *know* how to be alone. She went right from her parents' house to Horace's. Lord, that man loved him some Rose."

Lady Sunshine stared off as if remembering the two as a couple. Lunden herself recalled how happy Mr. and Mrs. Cannon had always seemed together. She smiled, recalling the time Mr. Cannon had slid a wildflower behind Mrs. Cannon's ear, whispered something that had made her giggle like a schoolgirl, then kissed the tip of her nose. What they'd shared had been real. Maybe Mrs. Cannon had just wanted to experience that bliss again. Didn't sound as if she'd gotten it, though.

"Some men prey on vulnerable women," Lady Sunshine said. "And what's more vulnerable than a woman who's just become a widow?"

While Lunden had learned a lot in the last few minutes, she still needed to know one thing. "What did you mean about Quade being snatched away?"

"That last summer they visited, Shugga suggested the boy come to live with her, permanently. Rose flew into a rage. Accused Shugga of trying to steal her child away. Even mocked Shugga for not being able to have kids of her own. Rose and the boy left Honey Hill that summer, and Shugga never saw either of them again, just as Rose had promised."

Baffled by what she'd learned, Lunden's heart pounded against her rib cage. Quade hadn't used her for sex. He hadn't returned to Honey Hill because he couldn't return. It'd had nothing to do with wanting to avoid her. A part of her experienced relief. But while the revelation stripped away one source of contention, another one still remained.

Lady Sunshine continued, telling Lunden how Ms. Shugga had attempted to reach out to Rose, to no avail. The way the letters she'd written to Quade had been marked *return to sender*. Lunden's heart broke, because she knew how much Quade had loved Ms. Shugga. *She's like a second mother,* he used to say.

"When Shugga learned Rose was sick, the cancer, she visited her in the hospital, hoping that after all those years they could patch things up, I guess," Lady Sunshine said.

"Did they?" Lunden asked. However, she guessed they hadn't.

Lady Sunshine shook her head. "Some folks cling to the past like an anchor and allow it to plunge them into the depths of bitterness. That's exactly what had happened to Rose. Even on her deathbed, the stubborn woman refused peace."

"Wow," was all Lunden could muster.

"That wasn't the saddest part of it all. Not only did she snatch the boy away, Rose had gone and told that child Shugga had died, then told Shugga she didn't want her contacting him. And she never did. A piece of Shugga really did die that day."

Overwhelmed with emotion, Lunden felt an unexpected tear slide down her cheek. Truthfully, she didn't know whom she was crying for, Ms. Shugga or Quade. *Both,* she settled on, because they'd both been denied something precious. Each other.

Using the back of her hand, she wiped the tear away before anyone witnessed the scene. God, she could only imagine the pain Quade had felt when he'd learned Ms. Shugga had died . . . again. This time for real. It had to be an immeasurable blow. Coupled with the fact it had been his own mother who'd orchestrated the deception. An overwhelming feeling to glance up prompted her to do so. When she did, Quade was watching her, a perplexed expression on his face. Thankfully, something drew Quade's attention, and Lunden released the breath she hadn't realized she'd been holding.

Quade had intentionally avoided both physical and eye contact with Lunden, but when one of the women in the group that had become his shadow said something about her crying, he had to see for himself. When she dragged a hand across her cheek, his brows bunched. What had brought her to tears? And why did he care?

Lunden glanced up, and their gazes locked. For the first time, he didn't get the impression she wanted to strangle him. Despite the distance between them, he could see . . . tenderness in her eyes? No, that couldn't be right. She would never grace him with such kindness.

"She's probably crying over the stupid inn," the blonde woman whose name he couldn't remember said.

"Sorry," she said, when he eyed her with a sharp look.

Blondie continued, "What is it with her and that place? If Shugga wanted her to have any say-so over it, she would have left it to her instead of *you*, right?" She pressed her manicured finger into his chest and gave him a roguish grin. It gave Quade the willies.

"I just want you to know I support your decision to sell," she continued. "And if our mayor can't get on board and embrace progress"—she flashed an innocent look and shrugged—"well, then maybe it's time for new leadership."

Like drones, the other four women agreed. Why did he get the impression Blondie wanted Honey Hill's top spot? Apparently, small-town women could be just as vicious as big-city ones. While Lunden wasn't his favorite person, he wouldn't be party to any plans to overthrow the current regime. "Will you ladies please excuse me?" he said, then walked off.

Quade didn't believe for one minute Lunden was crying over the inn, but something had caused her tears. What? Again, why did he care? *I don't.* He checked his watch. At a little after two; now was the perfect time for him to make his escape. He hadn't wanted to come, but just like before, he'd allowed Ms. Jewel to somehow finagle a yes out of him. *That woman is good.* She could probably sell stripes to a zebra.

Honestly, he'd actually enjoyed meeting some of Honey Hill's finest, among them Mr. Ammons, who ran the thrift store; Mr. Conroy, who ran the sign shop; Mr. Elmo, the town mechanic; and several more of the town elders. With the exception of the woman who ran the bakery—Rylee, if he remembered correctly—most of the shop owners in town were older. Obviously, the younger demographic had discovered that the world and their potential were far bigger than Honey Hill. He couldn't blame them for getting out. Why would anyone want to stay here permanently?

To his surprise, he hadn't been peppered with questions as had been expected. He had, however, been inundated with condolences, which had been equally taxing. While he'd done his best to appear gracious, all the attention had been draining. Maybe because he hadn't felt deserving of the genuine sympathy they had all shown him.

Saying his goodbyes to the pastor and several deacons, Quade headed to his vehicle. An apparent glutton for punishment, he couldn't resist tossing one last glance in Lunden's direction. All visible signs of sadness were gone, and she was smiling and laughing again. *Back to her old self.* That was a scary thought.

"Walk an old lady home."

Quade glanced over his opposite shoulder to see Ms. Jewel approaching. "Absolutely. Is she on her way?"

Ms. Jewel swatted him playfully. "Go on, you charmer, you."

It was good to know his charisma worked on someone. "I have my SUV; I can drive you," he said.

"No. I like to walk. Get to see the sights and hear the sounds of nature. Plus, I need to work off that big meal I just ate," Ms. Jewel said. "You didn't eat anything. Aren't you hungry?"

"Um . . . no, ma'am. I had a big breakfast."

Ms. Jewel threaded her arm through his. "I don't eat everybody's cooking either," she said, then led them on.

Quade chuckled.

"I notice some tension between you and a certain mayor," she said.

Not so subtle, was she? "I have no ill will toward Lunden, but it's clear we're never going to agree on the matter of the inn, so it's best to remain in our respective corners. After the scene at the meeting, I want to keep things as tranquil as possible."

Ms. Jewel laughed. "You do know the mayor's going to eventually find her way over to your corner? She's nothing if not determined. I sure hope you're ready."

Ms. Jewel made Lunden sound like a female version of the Equalizer. Righting wrongs one bad guy at a time. Only thing, he wasn't a bad guy. *And Lunden would know this if she talked less and listened more.* "I get that she and Shugga were close, but why is she so invested in the inn?"

"Now that would be a good question to ask her," Ms. Jewel said.

"I'm the last person she'd entertain any questions from." The way she'd shunned him at the picnic made it fairly obvious she wanted nothing to do with him. And he was a-okay with that.

"Oh, she's not as hard as she comes off. In fact, she's one of the most gentle souls I know."

Quade's head jerked in surprise. *Gentle?* That was definitely not the word he'd have used to describe the Lunden he'd encountered. *Abrasive. Pigheaded. Rude.* But not *gentle*.

"Mayor's like a little worker bee. Always buzzing around, doing this, doing that. Planning the June Jubilee. Organizing the summer market. The Thanksgiving food drive. The town Christmas celebration. Spearheading any worthy cause."

All those projects, it didn't sound like she had much of a social life to him.

"Lawd, I don't think I've ever known any one person who loves Christmas as much as that child. Every year when she's done, the entire town looks like a Christmas village right out of one of those holiday movies. You'll see."

Actually, he wouldn't. He planned to be long gone well before Christmas.

"Mayor gets the entire town involved. Even Sylvester Crump and his old cranky ass." Ms. Jewel patted his arm. "Pardon my language. But the man's personality is rougher than sandpaper. Anyhow. That mayor of ours is one of a kind."

Why did it feel as if Ms. Jewel were trying to sell him a mule? Well, in this case, a Lunden. A purchase he'd never be interested in making. "Sounds like she stays pretty busy."

"I think it's her way of keeping her mind occupied. I did the same after my divorce. Avoided processing all those emotions. We sometimes believe if you don't think or talk about them, they just go away. Truth is they simply eat you up inside. But I understand her hesitation not to relive that hell." Ms. Jewel clammed up, then laughed. "Lawd, listen to me, sounding like Lady Sunshine. All up in everybody's business. Have you met her yet?"

Quade marveled at how effectively Ms. Jewel had changed the subject. Especially when he'd wanted to hear more. "No, ma'am, I haven't."

"Well, when you do, take my advice. Don't tell her anything you don't want broadcast to at least fifty people."

"Yes, ma'am," he said. Luckily, he was good at keeping his private life private.

Silence fell between them. Ms. Jewel stared up at the trees lining their walk and smiled as if she saw angels hovering above them.

"You know, the June Jubilee is coming up soon. I bet you're going to look mighty fine in that suit."

Was this her way of determining whether he was going? He hated to disappoint her, but crowds just weren't his thing. "Oh. Um . . . I, um, hadn't planned to attend." The townsfolk weren't interested in getting to know him. And at this point, the feeling was mutual.

"Well, that's too bad. I think you'd have a lot of fun."

Quade pushed his brows together. Wait. That was way too easy. No sooner had he thought that, Ms. Jewel glanced up at him.

"Maybe you should go," she said. "No need to stay cooped up in that big house alone. Shugga would want you to get out and mingle. And so do I."

"I just don't think—"

She patted his arm. "It's settled. You're going to have an amazing time. Make sure you save me a dance."

Tell her you're not attending. Tell her you have better things to do than be meat for fodder. "Yes, ma'am." *Dammit.* In his career, he'd swayed astute businessmen over to his way of thinking. Now, here he was, unable to say no to one little old lady wearing an oversize church-mother hat.

"Something tells me you're going to garner a lot of attention that night."

That was exactly what he was afraid of. He didn't want attention. Despite his dynamic personality and ability to address a room filled with a hundred people, he most preferred to melt into the background, being seen and not heard. A side effect of living with a stepfather who craved dominance. Correction—the man who'd married his mother. He didn't deserve to be called a father, in any form.

Ms. Jewel stopped walking and glanced up at him. The overly excited expression on her face scared him a little. Actually, scared him a lot. What was she up to now?

Excitement danced in her brown eyes. "I have an excellent idea. Why don't you escort the mayor to the June Jubilee? She doesn't know this, but we're honoring her with an award of excellence for all she's done and continues to do for the town."

Quade barked a laugh. Not at the honor—he was sure Lunden deserved it—but at what Ms. Jewel had suggested. Him? Escort Lunden? With all due respect, had Ms. Jewel lost her damn mind? Had she forgotten that he and Lunden were like a match and a jug of gasoline? Sure, things had the potential to get hot, but not in a good way.

Did Ms. Jewel realize that what she'd just proposed would take a pure act of God? Well, as it turned out, he *was* capable of telling her no, after all.

CHAPTER 8

What the hell am I doing here?

Lunden had asked herself the same question a hundred times over a five-minute span. Instead of meeting Rylee at Doggone Delicious—their favorite hot dog spot—for lunch, she'd come here, to the inn, to chat with Quade. Though she hadn't fully committed to getting out of her car, trekking across the yard, climbing the stairs onto the porch, and ringing the bell, she'd at least made it into the driveway.

Truthfully, she didn't want to be here and definitely didn't want to face Quade. But if she stood any chance of convincing him not to sell the inn, she had to be the bigger person, apologize, and play nice. She'd gotten the feeling that Pastor White's *love thy neighbor and enemy* sermon the other week had been directed at her.

Well, her neighbor and enemy were one and the same, and she wasn't sure she had that much love to go around. When a pain shot through her lower belly, she heard her mother's voice in her head. *See? God don't like ugly.*

"It's nerves, not God," she said aloud as if her voice would travel to her mother in heaven. But when a second, more powerful pang traveled through her gut, she reconsidered. Once the discomfort passed, Lunden exited her vehicle.

"Hey, Mayor."

Lunden turned toward the road to see Ennis Hunter and his dog, Dover. In a previous life, Ennis had been an engineer, but after an automobile accident, where he'd incurred brain damage, he'd never been quite the same. Now, all he did was walk around Honey Hill in overalls all day.

Dover reached Lunden before Ennis did. "Hey, boy," she said.

Dover was a brown, scraggly mutt with one eye, wiry fur, and teeth that protruded from the bottom and made him look like a smiling piranha. While Dover wasn't the most attractive dog, Lunden somehow found him extremely adorable. Maybe because she always rooted for the underdog. Despite his dirty coat, Lunden played with him as if he were the cleanest K9 in town.

Dover's tail wagged with so much force his entire body shook. People could learn a lot from a dog. Mainly, how to be happy despite hardship.

Ennis finally made his way to her. "Dover sure does like you, Mayor. Probably because you're always so nice to him."

"He's such a good boy," Lunden said in a happy voice similar to one you used with a child who'd just eaten all his veggies.

"Are you going to see Ms. Shugga?" Ennis asked.

Lunden came to a full stand. "Ms. Shugga died, Ennis. Remember?"

Ennis donned a perplexed expression, then scratched his head vigorously. "Yeah. Yeah, I remember. I forget things sometimes. Granny says it's because of the accident." He frowned. "But I remember now. Ms. Shugga always gave Dover doggy biscuits and me cookies. And she always treated me normal, even though I'm a little weird. I forget things sometimes and get confused too easily." He glanced down at himself. "And I only like wearing overalls."

"Ennis, you're not weird. You're . . . unique. And you're perfect just the way you are. Overalls and all. Besides, normal is boring. Who wants to be a plain ole horse when you can be a unicorn?"

Ennis flashed a troubled expression. "I'm a unicorn?"

"No. It's just a figure . . ." Her words trailed off when Ennis looked dismayed. "You're a person. A very nice and kind person."

Ennis's smile grew again. "So are you, Mayor. And you're going to find happiness soon, because you deserve it."

Lunden pushed her brows together. Why had he said that?

"Well, we have to go now, Mayor. Me and Dover have to finish exploring."

"All right. Be safe, okay? You too, Dover," she said, rubbing the top of the dog's head.

Lunden watched them both limp away before heading toward the house. She stopped shy of the stairs when she heard music playing, an upbeat instrumental set to what sounded like a violin. She followed the pebble-lined pathway toward the back of the house, arriving just as Quade emerged from the swimming pool.

Lunden froze next to an oversize flowering bush. Unnoticed, she stared wide eyed as Quade cranked the music higher, then reached for a towel, draped it over his head, and scrubbed it dry. Droplets of water slowly rolled off his chiseled frame. When heat swirled in her stomach, she didn't fight it. Heck, she couldn't fight it. His appearance had her brain a scattered mess right now.

The sun hit him at the perfect angle, causing his smooth, dark skin to glisten like a freshly polished Cadillac, fully loaded with all the features. Her inquisitive eyes took in every solid inch of him. The muscles that rippled in his arms with every move he made. His pecs, formed with such precision they could have been hand sculpted by a master ceramist. The defined six-pack that suggested he had very little body fat. Of course, she could see that simply by looking at him. Her gaze followed the fine line of hair that disappeared underneath his waistband to the—Lunden gasped, her eyes widening and jaw dropping.

"Dear . . . God in heaven," she mumbled to herself.

The wet blue fabric of his swim bottoms clung to one impressive bulge at his crotch. Apparently, not all men suffered from cold-water shrinkage. A second later, something occurred to her. What if he *had* experienced shrinkage? That would mean . . . she swallowed hard, pushing all thoughts of the size of his penis from her head.

Still oblivious to her presence, Quade continue to dry himself. Lunden's entire body hummed with pure delight. He was absolutely magnificent. Watching him like a lion did a gazelle it was preparing to pounce on, she found herself imagining his hands moving over her body with the same slow, tender care he used to trace the towel over his own.

Lunden's nipples beaded and ached inside her bra. Her internal temperature rose, sending a wave of heat rippling through her entire body that finally settled all its energy between her legs. Her core pulsed with an intensity she hadn't experienced in a very long time. Tightening her thighs did little to subdue the throbbing. She needed a release so desperately her hands trembled.

Balling her fists, she closed her eyes and took several deep, cleansing breaths. *Get yourself together, girl. You're here to apologize, not lust over Quade Cannon. Any woman would have reacted the same way. You've had your moment; now pull it together. He's just like any ordinary man. Nothing special. He has a goal, and so do you. Now focus on that.*

The pep talk helped a lot. A smile curled her lips.

You've got this. Just take a few more deep breaths and focus.

Opening her eyes, she yelped and stumbled backward. With the music playing, she hadn't even heard him approach. "What are you doing?" she said to Quade, who was standing inches from her.

"I think I should be the one asking the questions. You're the one hiding behind a bush in my yard."

He folded his arms across his chest, causing his muscles to flex. Lunden's eyes traveled to the mounds of his arms.

"Are you stalking me?" Quade asked.

Her gaze snapped up. "I most certainly am not."

"Then what are you doing here? And if it has anything to do with this place"—he swept a long arm toward the house—"you're wasting your time. My mind is made up and there's no changing it."

"Well, if you must know, I came to . . . to, um, apologize." *See, that wasn't so hard to say.*

Quade's brows furrowed like he was expecting her to yell, *Just kidding!* and run off.

Lunden saw an opportunity and took it. "But since you brought it up—"

Before she could finish her thought, Quade sighed heavily and stalked away. *How rude.* Instead of reacting to his curt response, she reminded herself why she'd actually come here. To apologize. They could reach an understanding about the inn later.

Quade stood at the edge of the pool, his back to her. When she walked up behind him, he didn't even acknowledge her presence. She fought the urge to shove her hands into his back and send him splashing into the water. Mostly because she wasn't sure she could handle seeing him all wet again. Squaring her shoulders, she said, "I apologize for the way I reacted at the meeting. You had a right to be heard. That's all I wanted to say."

Quade released something that sounded like a mix of a humorless laugh and a disgusted scoff.

Coming to stand beside him, she said, "Is there something you want to say?"

Quade whipped his head toward her, his lips parting as if he were about to say something, but a beat later they closed and he looked away again. "Thank you for the half-assed apology. You can leave now."

Half-assed apology? Instead of making a volatile situation worse, Lunden started away.

"There's really nothing else you want to apologize for?" Quade said.

Rejoining him, and with a gentle, noncombative tone, she said, "I won't apologize for voicing my opinion about the inn. I had a right to be heard, just as you did."

Quade's expression hardened. "But you didn't have a right to—" He stopped abruptly, his jaw muscles flexing.

"I didn't have a right to what? To stand up to you? Since you're the big-city hotshot, I was supposed to bow down to you, right? *Ha!*"

"You didn't have the right to make me feel like shit over something I had no control over," he said. "I . . ." His words trailed off, and he shook his head. "Just leave."

When he walked the length of the pool, Lunden was on his heels. "Not until you explain—"

Quade whipped around. "I don't owe you an explanation."

Stunned by his quick motion and stone-cold tone, she lost her footing, toppled over, and swan dived into the pool like a drunken mermaid. Quade reached for her, only to lose his footing and fall in, too, making a splash right next to her.

"Are you okay?" Quade asked, his tone much softer than before.

Lunden brushed clumps of soaking wet hair out of her face. When Quade came into view, she scowled. "You did that on purpose."

Quade barked a laugh. "Are you serious? It's *my* fault you nose-dived into the pool?"

"Yes! You practically pushed me when you whirled around like a lunatic, causing the wind trajectory to change and . . ." Her words dried up. A second later, she burst into laughter, and so did Quade.

"Changed the wind trajectory?" he said. "Really?"

Well, it was possible. His energy was as powerful as any turbine. And boy, was she feeling the force of him now with them standing so damn close, practically toe to toe. His close proximity had her both anxious and exhilarated.

"I probably look like a wet dog," she said, pushing her fingers through strands of sopping-wet hair, unsure why she cared how she looked in front of him.

"You look beautiful," he said. "But you always look so beautiful."

Lunden's lips parted, but nothing filtered out because, honestly, she didn't know exactly—or even partially—what to say. While it was rare—practically unheard of—she was lost for words. Her brain dried up fully when Quade's head slowly inched forward like he intended to . . . kiss her?

Stunned, she couldn't budge, could hardly breathe. Oddly, she wanted his lips to touch hers. God, was she insane? *Yes!* Yes, she was. She'd gone from wanting to kill him five minutes ago to wanting to kiss him now. *Totally insane.* But her brain wouldn't process the command to pull away, flee this potentially disastrous situation. Instead, she closed her eyes in anticipation.

Her heart pounded in her chest, her breathing became ragged, and her skin burned so hot she was surprised the pool water hadn't started to boil. Quade Cannon was about to kiss her. But the craziest part . . . she was about to allow him.

🐝

Quade wasn't sure what was happening. Actually, he was. He was about to kiss Lunden, and he was powerless to stop himself. But he really didn't want to. Something intensely powerful drew his mouth toward hers, like metal to an industrial magnet. Judging by her closed eyes and puckered lips, she held no objections. He just hoped it wasn't a ploy for her to bite off his tongue.

Just before he could experience what he knew would be heaven, a loud splash forced him and Lunden apart. *What the . . . ?* He turned to see a one-eyed dog paddling toward them. *Where the hell did you come from?* A second later, a tall, medium-built man in overalls, a white

T-shirt cut off at the sleeves, and well-worn work boots hobble-ran in the direction of the pool.

"Oh Lord. I'm so sorry, Mayor. I guess Dover still had your scent. That dog has one fancy nose," the man said.

"Ennis?" Lunden said, appearing startled and nervous at his presence.

Ennis, Quade said to himself. Who was he, and what was he doing in Quade's backyard? The man's face scrunched as if he were trying to figure out a difficult problem in his head.

"Mayor, why are you swimming in the pool with your clothes still on?" Ennis asked. "Did you forget your swimsuit?"

Lunden waded to the edge of the pool, the dog splashing after her. "I'm not swimming. I accidentally fell in when . . ." She glanced over her shoulder at Quade, then back to Ennis. "When I tripped. Quade—Ms. Shugga's nephew—jumped in to help me."

Ennis looked at Quade. "You're Ms. Shugga's nephew?"

Quade nodded. "Yes."

"Ms. Shugga's dead," Ennis said.

"Yes, she is," Quade said.

"She was nice. I miss her chocolate chip cookies. They were always hot and tasted real good. Sorry Dover interrupted when you were about to kiss the mayor. He don't know nothing about boyfriend-and-girl-friend stuff."

"We're not boyfriend and girlfriend, and we weren't about to kiss," Lunden said, urgency lacing her tone. "Quade was, um, helping me."

Obviously, there was something a little mentally wrong with Ennis, but even he didn't appear convinced by what Lunden had just said. They weren't boyfriend and girlfriend, but they'd definitely been about to kiss. Quade cursed Ennis and the dog for ruining the moment.

"Oh no. Did you hit your lips on the way in?" Ennis asked.

Quade couldn't help but snicker, which earned him a severe scowl from Lunden. Obviously, she found no humor in the situation.

"More like my head and shook some of my good sense loose," she said.

"Same thing happened to me," Ennis said. "Folks say I'm a good egg, just a little scrambled. Reckon you're scrambled now, too, Mayor. Come on, Dover. Get out of there. We have to go."

The dog seemed to be having way too much fun to follow the command. While Dover resembled a wet rat, something about the homely animal was adorable. Maybe it was the way he appeared so carefree and happy.

Lunden sliced through the water, headed toward the stairs. Clearly, she had no intention of finishing what they'd started. A feeling of despair settled inside him. Who knew where the kiss would have led. Possibly to an end of his eight-month sexual drought.

Yeah, yeah, yeah, he said to the little voice chirping in his head. He'd said there would be no bedding the locals. But sleeping with Lunden could be considered a civic duty. His way of making Honey Hill a better place. One stroke at a time. A happy mayor meant a happy town, right?

"Lunden, wait," Quade called out. "Your—"

Without giving him the courtesy of eye contact, she said, "I have to go, Quade."

"—shoe." He fished the sexy-looking, sparkly silver heel from the water. *Dammit.* So much for fulfilling his civic duty.

CHAPTER 9

The busier Lunden attempted to be, the less effective she became. She just couldn't concentrate. Why? Because Ennis had been right. She was one scrambled egg, and Quade Cannon was to blame. The man had plagued her thoughts ever since she'd swan dived into his pool and had nearly allowed him to kiss her several days ago. *Thank you, universe, for sending Dover to intervene. What was I thinking?*

That you wanted him to kiss you, a tiny voice chirped.

And she had.

For no other reason than that she'd wanted to feel his warm mouth against hers. Wanted to remember how it felt to be kissed, desired. Wanted to relive those breathless seconds following the parting of mouths. Wanted to feel the aftereffects of kiss-swollen lips. Wanted—no, *needed*—to know that somewhere deep inside, the passionate woman she once was still existed. But could the last have been achieved by a simple kiss?

The question got Lunden to thinking even harder. If Ennis and Dover hadn't appeared and her and Quade's lips had actually touched, where would it have led? Would she have had the willpower to walk away if he'd invited her into his bedroom? While she told herself she would have never allowed it to even get that far, honestly, she wasn't sure.

Lunden shifted papers around on her desk. Whatever spell he'd temporarily cast on her had worn off. And with the grace of God, she wouldn't succumb to it again. Infatuated women lost sight of their goals. She wouldn't allow that to happen to her. *Again.*

She thought about all the dreams she'd held pre-Hunter—her ex-husband. Oh, she'd planned to conquer the world, one boardroom at a time. Then love had happened, spiraling her completely out of control, then shattering her into a thousand pieces. "Never again."

A tap on her door drew her from the dismal place she went every time she thought about her life with Hunter. One beautiful thing had come from their union that helped her smile every day. Zachary. And he made up for every unfulfilled dream.

"Yes," Lunden said, pulling her keyboard closer to at least appear busy.

Rhonda, her admin, entered. "Sorry to disturb you, but you have a visitor."

Lunden's brows furrowed. Last time she'd checked, her calendar was clear. "Visitor?"

Before she could inquire any further, Quade appeared. The daunting presence of the man—wearing jeans, a green polo shirt, and that drop-your-panties smile—snatched her breath away.

"I hope I'm not intruding," he said.

Of course you are. She kept the snide remark to herself. "Of course not. My door is always open to any Honey Hill resident. Thank you, Rhonda."

Rhonda smirked, nodded, then shut the door.

"What are you doing here?" Lunden asked.

"Well, Cinderella, I wanted to return this."

When he held up her shoe, she experienced a prickle of embarrassment. Thank God he'd returned it. Now her favorite pair was complete again. Lunden stood and rounded her desk. "Thank you." When she reached for the shoe, Quade pulled it back.

"Have lunch with me," he said.

Was he asking or demanding? Lunden pushed her brows together, then allowed them to relax when the muscles in her forehead started to hurt. Why in the world would he believe she'd have lunch with him? Then it hit her. Did he expect them to pick up where they'd left off? Of course he did. "Sure," she said. "Let me just grab my purse." The only thing that would give her more pleasure than getting her shoe back would be the look of disappointment on Quade's face when he realized there was no way she would allow their lips to almost touch again.

A faint look of surprise spread across Quade's face, like he'd expected her to say no, and then he passed her the shoe. Seconds later, they exited her office.

"Rhonda, I'm headed to a business lunch." Because business was the only thing she and Quade had to talk about. "Can I bring you back something?" Lunden ignored Rhonda's accusatory smirk, as if *I'm headed to lunch* could be translated as *I'm going to give and get head.* Maybe that was Quade's motivation, but certainly not hers.

"I brought my lunch today, but thank you," Rhonda said. "Would you like me to reschedule your two o'clock?"

"That won't be necessary. I should be back in plenty of time," she said, letting Quade know this wouldn't be an all-day outing. Stepping into the hallway, Lunden ran into Dick.

"Mayor. I was just coming to see you. I needed to chat with you before the meeting this afternoon," he said. His gaze slid to Quade. Pushing his glasses up his shiny nose, he offered his hand. "Richard Dickerson."

Quade accepted his hand. "Quade Cannon."

"Ah, the new owner of the inn," Dick said. "Well, welcome to Honey Hill. I understand you'll be selling the property."

When Tricky Dick's eyes twinkled, Lunden wanted to poke him in both.

"That's the plan," Quade said.

Lunden ground her teeth but kept her commentary to herself. Undoubtedly, Dick was running the numbers in his head. One thing she could say about him, he always put the town's financial health above all else. Even town landmarks. What was it with men? Was everything a business transaction?

"I'm the town's financial manager. If you have any questions, any at all, don't hesitate to call my office."

Quade accepted the business card Dick had plucked from somewhere. "Financial manager, huh?"

Dick's chest pushed out a bit when he said, "Yes, sirree." Lunden nearly laughed.

"You should join us for lunch," Quade said.

Dick looked just as surprised as Lunden was sure she did. Maybe she'd gotten it wrong. Maybe Quade hadn't intended to seduce her. Unless he was into threesomes. The thought of such a thing made her shiver. The idea of the third party being Richard Dickerson knotted her stomach.

As far as looks went, Dick wasn't a bad-looking guy, just . . . not her type. Besides, Quade didn't strike her as a man who liked sharing. He would want it all for himself. When a skin-prickling heat rushed through her, she chastised her rebellious body. Maybe Dick *should* join them after all. *For lunch. Strictly for lunch.*

"Thank you for the invite, but I must decline," Dick said. "Maybe next time. Speak to you after lunch, Mayor."

Quade gave a single nod, and they were off again.

"Since you know the town better than I do, where would you like to eat?"

"There's a new Chinese restaurant just outside of town I've been wanting to try. If you're okay with that?"

"Ashamed to be seen with me in town, huh?"

"If that were a concern, I wouldn't have accepted your invitation at all, right? Several people have seen us. I'm sure most of the town knows we're together by now. Well, not together, but . . ." She sighed. "You know what I mean."

"I guess," was all he said.

While Lunden had downplayed Quade's suspicions, to an extent, what he'd suggested was true. In Honey Hill, perception outweighed actual intent. If they'd gone to the diner, they would have been under constant scrutiny. Instead of everyone seeing the mayor having an innocent lunch with a constituent—as she'd done countless times before— they would see it as much more. She could see the headlines now. *Mayor Cozies Up with Town's Newest Arrival.*

At his vehicle, Quade held the door open for Lunden, then closed it once she was settled in the seat. *A gentleman.* As he rounded the front of the vehicle, she scrutinized the interior of the luxury SUV. If an automobile was an extension of its owner, this one suited him well. Impressive to the eye and designed for durability. What did her Prius say about her?

On the drive, Lunden promised herself that no matter what transpired, she'd keep her cool.

A short drive later, they arrived at Star China. The first person they encountered once they entered the restaurant was Hilary Jamison, the worst person they could have run into. So much for dining on the low.

As usual, the woman wore enough layers of makeup to classify her as an oil painting. Her pink blouse was unbuttoned low enough to give anyone who cared to see a distasteful peek of cleavage. She wore a short, dark-gray skirt, so tight it would probably unravel at the seams if she bent over. The woman loved attention and usually got a lot of it. However, Quade didn't appear intrigued.

"Good afternoon, Mayor," she said, a twinkle of mischief in her mail-order green eyes.

"Hilary," Lunden said dryly.

Lunden didn't care much for the conniving woman. When Lunden had decided to run for mayor—actually, more like had had running decided for her by Ms. Shugga—her opponent had been the incumbent, Roberta Jamison—Hilary's grandmother. Unlike her granddaughter, Ms. Roberta was a pleasant woman—the only one in the Jamison clan—but in her time served, she'd done little beneficial for Honey Hill and even less for its residents. Booting her out of office had been a necessity. At least, it had been according to Ms. Shugga. Not many had believed Lunden held a snowball's chance in hell of winning, but when she had, Hilary's already existing grudge had grown.

The contentious woman flung her long blonde weave over one shoulder, then set her gaze on Quade. "Quade." Her menacing eyes gobbled him up whole. "Nice to see you again."

"Hello," Quade said.

Hilary stepped a little closer to him. "We didn't get to finish our conversation at the picnic. I wanted to tell you that if you needed someone to show you around town, I'm your woman."

His and every other man's in a hundred-mile radius, Lunden thought.

"Honey Hill has a lot of nooks and crannies to explore," Hilary said.

Shameless. Disgusted by the woman's obvious come-on, Lunden said, "I'll let you two talk."

"I promise not to keep him too long," Hilary said, batting her fake eyelashes. "I'm sure you two have important *business* to discuss." She half smirked, half sneered.

"Actually, I'm good," Quade said. "Our esteemed mayor has graciously agreed to show me around town. Isn't that right, Mayor Pierce?" A hopeful expression flashed across his face.

Lunden smiled. "Yes."

Quade donned a look of relief.

"However, if you would prefer Hilary—"

"It was nice seeing you again, Hilary," Quade said, cutting Lunden off midsentence.

A beat later, he rested his large hand on the small of Lunden's back and urged her forward. His touch sent a shiver through her entire body.

"Bye, Hilary," Lunden said.

"That woman makes me uneasy," Quade whispered.

For good reason. Hilary was cunning, sneaky, and not to be trusted.

When they settled into one of the red booths, the waitress took their drink orders—Diet Coke for Lunden, a bottled water for Quade—then moved away.

Lunden perused her menu, teetering between sesame chicken and General Tso's. When she noticed Quade hadn't bothered to even crack his open, she said, "You already know what you're getting?"

"I'm not getting anything," he said.

Confused, she said, "I thought you liked Chinese."

"Oh, I love it."

Lunden lowered her menu. "So what's the problem?"

"Their sanitation grade. It's a seventy-five."

Was he serious?

The waitress returned with their beverages. Now Lunden understood the bottled water. Initially, she'd assumed he had something against tap water.

"Are you ready to order?" the young woman asked.

"Can you give us a couple more minutes?" Lunden said.

"Sure." She walked off again.

"So you're one of those people who scope out the sanitation grade the second you enter a restaurant, huh?"

"No."

Lunden gave him a look, and he laughed.

"Okay, yes. But for good reason. Two words. Food poisoning. Trust me, it's no fun. Their sanitation grade is seventy-five. I've been to greasy spoons with higher scores. And didn't you say this place just opened? They should at least be in the nineties."

Lunden laughed. "There could be a hundred reasons why."

"You're right. *Salmonella. E. coli.* Rat droppings."

"*Wow.* I would have never guessed you suffered from cibophobia."

"I don't have a fear of food. I have a fear of getting sick from it. Food. Poisoning," he reemphasized.

Honestly, it surprised her Quade knew what the word meant. She only knew the term because it had been an answer to a *Jeopardy* question. "Well, I'm hungry, and I'm ordering."

"Order whatever you like. It's all on me."

He was probably hoping she'd get sick. For spite and to prove a point. Luckily for her, she had a stomach of steel.

The food arrived piping hot. So that she wouldn't feel awkward while she enjoyed her lunch, Quade appeased her by requesting a handful of fortune cookies, individually wrapped and sealed for freshness. They made small talk as Lunden ate her fill of the Mongolian pepper steak with onions and peppers and shrimp fried rice.

"Was it good?" Quade asked after Lunden pushed her plate away.

"Delicious."

He slid a fortune cookie toward her. "Dessert."

After unwrapping, she broke the cookie in half to get to the fortune. She read it aloud. "'Wouldn't it be ironic if you were wrong?'" Lunden slid it to Quade. "I think this one is meant for you." She claimed another cookie, cracked it open, and read, this time silently. *Welp, no more fortunes for me.*

"What does it say?" he asked.

"Nothing." Before she could react, Quade plucked the paper from her fingers.

As he scanned the strip, his brow arched. *"Hmm."* He eyed her. "'Plan for ultimate pleasure.' Interesting."

Though it was a lie, she said, "I plan to swing by Rylee's bakery for cupcakes after work. Nothing brings pleasure like her baking."

Quade gave her a lopsided smile. Something told her she didn't want to know what was running through his mind.

"Last cookie," he said.

"It's all yours."

Quade chuckled. "'An all-consuming blaze will be kindled by an unexpected spark.'" He placed the paper down. "That's scary."

Silence settled between them a moment. Quade wanted something. It was time she found out what.

"Why did you invite me to lunch, Quade?"

"I needed to talk to you about something."

"If it's about what happened in your pool—"

"Nothing happened in my pool. You fell in. I helped you."

Lunden wasn't sure whether she should feel relief that she didn't have to discuss their near kiss or anguish that he'd summed it up as nothing. "Right," she said.

"I want to talk about the inn," he continued.

That surprised her. He hadn't wanted to broach the subject before. What had changed? Had spending time at the inn reminded him of the great times he'd shared with Ms. Shugga there and changed his mind about wanting to sell it? A glimmer of hope blossomed inside her.

"Upon its sale, I've decided to make a sizable donation to Honey Hill in my aunt's name. To be used in any way you deem necessary."

Well, the glimmer hadn't lasted long. Lunden's smile dimmed. *Sizable donation?* Was he serious? Did he believe money would make her more accepting of what he was trying to do? "I see. That's certainly . . . generous of you." She took a sip from her glass.

Quade reclined against the cushion. "There's no winning you over, is there?"

"The inn means more to me than a 'sizable donation.' And it should mean more to you as well."

Quade looked away.

"The memories made between those walls . . . are they not enough to touch something inside of you? You once told me there was no happier place on earth for you than the inn." To her recollection, this was the first time she'd alluded to anything in the past. Specifically something that involved the two of them. Until now, it hadn't been necessary to travel down memory lane with him, because they were no longer two kids in puppy love. But maybe the memory was potent enough to soften him a bit.

"I was a kid, Lunden. Nothing back then was real."

Lunden's head jerked with shock at his words. *Nothing back then was real?* She tried not to get her emotions involved but failed. While it should have had little effect on her, his dismissal of what they'd shared had hurt. Collecting herself, she said, "I see." She eyed her watch. "I really should get back to the office."

Quade reached across the table to touch her hand, but she snatched it away.

Drawing his arm back, he said, "Lunden, I didn't—"

"Don't do that," she said. "Don't backpedal. Own your words. You said them. Own them." She slid from the booth. "I'll wait for you outside. I need some fresh air. I'm feeling a little queasy. Maybe I should have listened to you about the sanitation grade." She forced a smile, then moved away. She'd known it had been a mistake to come here with him.

CHAPTER 10

Quade watched Lunden hurry toward the exit. *That went well.* He washed a hand over his head. *Own your words.* She had to know he'd get the significance of the statement. Memories plagued him as he waited for the waitress to bring the bill. One moment more than any others.

I love you. He'd said those words to Lunden seconds before entering her for the very first time. He'd meant them, but when he'd thought he'd spooked her, he'd tried to clean it up. *I mean—*

She'd cut him off. *Own your words,* she'd said. *You said them. Own them.* That time, she'd regarded him with a look of affection. Today, she'd given him one of disappointment. Both equally powerful, but for different reasons.

Nothing back then was real. How had he allowed the words to slip from his mouth? Especially when his feelings for her had been the realest thing he'd ever known? The fortune cookie had been right about sparking a fire.

After paying the bill, he joined Lunden at his vehicle, opened the door for her to get in, and closed it once she had. "You feeling any better?" he asked, sliding behind the wheel, not truly convinced she'd felt ill. Just sick of him.

She didn't bother to face him when she said, "Yes, thank you."

The drive back to her office was a quiet one. Once they arrived, Lunden was out of the vehicle before he'd popped it into gear. Clearly, she was eager to get away from him.

"Thank you for lunch," she said.

"You're—"

She closed the door.

"—welcome."

Two steps forward, ten steps back. That seemed to be the rhythm they danced to. Since it was still early and he didn't have shit else to do, he decided to swing by the hardware store to speak with Randy Pitman about Aunt Shugga's bees, since Sam Whitman, who was currently in Alabama helping his sister as she recovered from double knee surgery, wouldn't be available for a while. *His* bees, he corrected himself. "I own bees." He laughed. Never in a million years could he have ever imagined this one.

When he arrived at the hardware store—a large space that had anything and everything one could need—he was told Randy was at the barbershop. Since he was there, Quade picked up a few things before heading to his next stop.

Quade had seen a lot of interesting things since arriving in Honey Hill, but a horse tied to a light post and standing in a parking space outside the barbershop had to be the most peculiar thing he'd seen thus far.

The animal was gorgeous. Dark-brown shiny coat and a luscious mane. Whomever it belonged to took great care with its appearance. "Hey, horsey." When the creature glanced at him, it smiled, showing rows of large white teeth. "What the . . . ?" Quade shook off what he'd just witnessed and made his way inside the barbershop before the animal started talking.

The first thing he heard when he entered through the doors was, "All I'm saying is a wise frog never jumps over a unicorn."

The walls rumbled from the laughter. What conversation had he just walked in on that brought forth such words of . . . *wisdom*? The energy was so electrifying in the shop that Quade started to laugh, too, despite having no idea why or what he was laughing at.

An older gentleman with chestnut-brown skin, a spit-shined bald head, and a salt-and-pepper goatee swiveled toward Quade. "Welcome to Senior's," he said through laughter. "I'm Senior."

"Quade?" Canten said, lounging in one of the five barber chairs. "Come on over and join the show."

"Sheriff," Quade said, offering his hand, then moving across to shake Senior's.

Two more older gentlemen sat at a well-worn chess table. The scene inside the shop reminded Quade of when he used to visit the barbershop with his father as a child. The worn leather chairs. Pictures of Ali and Martin Luther King Jr. on the walls. Dated wallpaper. Checkerboard flooring. And lots of laughter.

"I hope you like being entertained," Canten whispered, then slouched down in the chair and covered his face with his wide-brimmed hat as if he was about to take a nap.

"Don't mind these fools," one of the men at the table said, not bothering to look up from the board and the only one in the shop not laughing.

"That's Sly," the gray-haired man sitting across from him said.

Was this the grumpy Sylvester Ms. Jewel had referred to when he'd walked her home? Probably, because the man looked stone faced and ornery.

"Sly just mad 'cause we talking about the one good ball he has left."

Quade hoped by *ball* the man was referring to a basketball, a baseball, even a golf ball.

"Go to hell, Clem," Sly said. "Don't be hatin' on me 'cause I was adventurous in my yoot."

It took Quade a second to figure out *yoot* meant *youth*.

"Adventurous in your youth? Fool, you lost your ball three years ago. You were sixty-four. And it wasn't no damn adventure. It was a late-stage midlife crisis. This fool thought he could run with the bulls down in that yonder Met-see-co."

Quade chuckled at the way Mr. Clem pronounced Mexico.

"Those tequila shots will get you every time," Senior said.

More laughter rang out.

"Bad knees. Bad back. Rickety hip. And this fool thought he could outrun a mad bull," Clem said.

"You better be glad a ball is all you lost. You could've lost your manhood," Senior said.

"He would have never even known it was gone," Clem said, amusing himself.

Still studying the board, Sly said, "Fool, I'm hung like a mighty python."

Of course, this brought on more laughter. Even Sly, who hadn't cracked a smile since Quade had arrived, chuckled.

Three things Quade had learned about the men in the short time he'd been here: They seemed pretty tight with each other. Two of them loved the word *fool*. They were all funny as hell.

"Just 'cause it slithers, too, you can't call a worm a snake," Clem said.

"Go to hell, Clem. But before you do, checkmate."

"Don't mind these clowns," Senior said, through laughter. "What brings you by here? You need to be freshened up?"

Quade hadn't intended on getting a haircut, but since he was here . . . "If you have time," he said.

Senior stood, then popped the empty chair with a white towel. "Sit on down."

Quade did. "I'm also looking for Mr. Randy. They told me at the hardware store he was here."

"Randy's in the crapper. The fool is lactose intolerant but eats hoop cheese like it's going out of style. He'll be in there for at least another twenty minutes or so," Clem said.

"*Flush,*" Senior, Clem, and Sly yelled in unison.

"Go to *h*," came from the back.

"Randy don't cuss," Clem said to Quade. "Whatchu want with him, anyway?"

"Mind your own business, Clem," Sly said. "This youngster don't want you all in his."

"It's okay," Quade said. "I was told Mr. Randy could help me with beekeeping at the inn."

The faces in the room grew somber. "You Shugga nephew, huh?" Sly said more than asked.

"Yes, sir." Quade gave an inward groan. *Here come the condolences.*

"You really gon' sell the inn?" Sly said.

"Yes, sir."

Quade guessed neither of the men supported the decision by the glances exchanged between them, but no one voiced objections. Unlike Lunden, they apparently respected the fact that it was his decision to make.

"Shugga sho is missed around here. She was a fine woman. A fine woman, indeed," Clem said. "Conroy ain't been himself since she passed."

Quade's brows bunched. "Conroy?"

"There you go running your mouth again, Clemmons. Always in somebody else's business. You worse than Lady Sunshine. You two would make a good couple," Sly said.

"First of all, Lady Sunshine couldn't handle all of this thunder," Clem said. "Second of all, Conroy is my brother. His business *is* my business. Third of all, ain't no secret around Honey Hill that he had a thing for Shugga." The man's expression turned sad. "Just never got around to telling her. Time. It moves forward even if we don't." He shook his head slowly, a pitiful expression on his face.

"You and Lady Sunshine the reason there ain't no secrets around here," Sly said.

"Those two bicker like an old married couple. Conroy owns the sign shop," Senior said, answering the question Quade had originally asked. "A good man."

All the others agreed. Quade made a mental note to visit the sign shop. He wasn't sure why; he just felt like he needed to meet the man who'd held a secret torch for his aunt. Had she known? Of course she had. Women could sense when a man cared about them. Like most women, Shugga had probably wanted Conroy to take the lead and make the first move.

"Is he snoring?" Clem asked, head pointing to Canten.

Quade eyed Canten, his fingers interlocked across his chest. Yep, he was definitely snoring. Obviously, the man could sleep through anything.

"Let my son rest," Senior said. "He was up half the night helping over at the Silverdale farm. Those feisty alpacas got out again."

"One of those monsters got in my backyard once," Clem said. "When I tried to shoo it away, the damn thing spit on me."

"It probably felt threatened by all that ugliness," Sly said.

"Go to hell, Sly."

They all laughed.

Another thing Quade had noticed: Clem and Sly seemed to enjoy sending each other to hell.

"If it comes back, I'll invite y'all over for alpaca burgers, 'cause I'm cooking it," Clem said.

"I'll pass," Senior said.

"Me too," Sly said.

Canten's radio chirped, and the man bolted forward like he'd been tased, his hat falling to the floor.

"Sheriff, you there?" boomed through the speaker in a deep southern drawl.

Canten pressed the button of the radio attached to a loop on the shoulder of his shirt. "Go, Gunter."

"You might want to get out to Old Man Patterson's farm, sir. Brutus is up in the tree again, making a god-awful squawk. Old Man Patterson says you're the only one who can get him down 'cause he likes you. He also said you should hurry 'cause the others are meowing, which he said means it's gonna rain and that peacocks don't like water."

Peacocks? Quade had been sure the man on the radio had been talking about a cat.

"Ten-four. Headed that way," Canten said, standing and stretching.

"Why is the peacock in the tree?" Clem asked.

"I bet Ennis's dog got after it again," Sly said. "That damn dog 'bout as crazy as his owner."

"All right, now, Sly," Senior said. "You know it ain't no ill talk about Ennis allowed in my shop."

Sly grumbled and brushed Senior's words off.

"How does a peacock get in a tree?" Clem asked.

"He flew up there," Canten said.

"Peacocks can fly?" all four men asked in unison.

"Not far, but yes," Canten said. "Dover likes terrorizing Old Man Patterson's bevy."

"His Bevy? Clem, you didn't tell us Old Man Patterson had a girl-friend," Sly said.

Clem put a hand on his hip. "How the hell was I supposed to know that?"

Canten shook his head, apparently exhausted with the men. "Bevy is not a woman. It's a family of peafowl." Obviously, he witnessed the confusion on their faces. "Peacocks are the males, peahens females, and peachicks are the babies. All of them together are peafowl."

"How the hell do you know so much about them birds? Did they make you take a peacock—pardon me—peafowl course at the academy?" Clem said.

Canten bounced his index finger against his temple as he headed toward the exit. "Knowledge is power. Later."

"That's my boy," a proud-looking Senior said.

A second later, Canten was gone. Several seconds after that, Quade saw him trot by on the horse. The sheriff rode a horse. Damn, he really was in the country.

"Somebody better tell that boy he keep riding that horse around town, Sly ain't the only one who's gon' have only one good ball," Clem said.

"Now don't you put that in the universe, Clem. I want grandbabies," Senior said.

"You might be getting them. Rumor has it he's dating that pretty lil thing over at the diner," Clem said.

"So is half the town," Sly said.

"He's not dating anybody," Senior said. "It's hard for him."

Quade didn't have to wonder long what Senior had meant by the comment.

"My son lost his wife a few years back. Gun violence. Thirty years old." Senior shook his head. "It's tough losing the woman you love. But he'll be all right."

Quade could hear in Senior's voice that he was concerned about Canten.

After a quick trim-up, Senior convinced Quade to try a hydrating facial. The man rubbed some kind of cream into his skin that smelled amazing, like pound cake, then placed a warm towel over his face. Quade came close to falling asleep too. When Senior removed the towel, Quade could see and feel the difference in his skin. Whatever this stuff was, it was amazing.

The sound of the toilet flushing reminded Quade why he was here. Mr. Randy had been in the bathroom so long Quade wondered if the man had fallen asleep.

"A piece of advice," Senior said. "You're going to want to find someone else to help you. Don't get me wrong, Randy is good, but slow as ice-cold molasses."

"At everything," Clem added.

"Mmm-hmmm," hummed Sly. "You see how long he was in the bathroom, don't you? Just slow."

"I tried Sam Whitman, but he's out of town for a while."

"Why don't you ask the mayor? I'm sure she'd be happy to help. She loves that inn. And she's the best beekeeper in town," Senior said.

Wait. Lunden is a beekeeper? The woman really was a superhero. Damn if he didn't learn something new about her mighty powers every day. But would she agree to help him? Something told him no. *Hell no,* to be more accurate.

CHAPTER 11

Several hours after her contentious lunch with Quade, Lunden sat around a table with people she actually enjoyed, like Zeta Deane, the town's attorney and her friend. Dick, the town clerk, and several other key department heads were also present. These were the men and women Lunden most depended on to help her keep Honey Hill running at its finest.

Usually, she enjoyed their biweekly collaborating sessions, but today she just wanted the meeting to be over. Why? Because she was still reeling from her lunch with Quade. The negative energy had her feeling crappy. How could he actually have believed money would or could sway her?

Because he doesn't know you, she told herself. And even when he had, it hadn't been real, according to him. The admission had hurt her far more than it should have. Mostly because it had been real for her. One of the realest things she'd ever known in her life. Even as a *kid,* she'd known without a doubt that she loved Quade Cannon. Now, she knew he really hadn't felt the same. Regardless of what he'd whispered in her ear way back then. *Just empty words.* After all these years, why did any of this still matter? Because she had a propensity for living in the past.

"You okay, Mayor?" Russ Povartie from public safety asked.

Snapping back to reality, she forged a smile. "Yes. I think I ate too much at lunch." Definitely too much grease, because her stomach was performing somersaults. And it wasn't because of a stupid sanitation grade.

"Where'd you two end up going?" Dick asked.

"The new Chinese restaurant just outside of town," she said.

"The one with the low sanitation rating?" someone from public works asked. "The score is something like a sixty."

Someone gasped.

Someone else groaned.

Someone actually gagged.

Lunden shook her head at the antics. Was she the only one not obsessed with sanitation ratings? "Their grade is a seventy-five. *Still* passing," she reminded them.

This started an open dialogue about the horrible things found in restaurant kitchens. From roaches and rat droppings to mold and used condoms. The mental visuals made her stomach rumble even more.

Taking a sip from her water glass, she said, "Can we please get back on track so we all can get out of here?"

The room quieted, and they continued. A half hour later, Lunden dismissed everyone. All except Zeta.

Once the room had cleared, Lunden turned to her friend. "Any success?" she asked.

Zeta laughed. "Not yet, but I'm still working on it."

Lunden released a sound of exasperation. "Well, couldn't we just toss him out of it? Claim it as eminent domain or something?" Now she sounded like Dick.

"There are no grounds for eminent domain. He's not a scum land-lord trying to force his tenants out by making the property unlivable. As far as we know, there's no illegal activity taking place, and it's not abandoned."

"Ugh."

"He has to hold on to the inn for six months, right?"

Lunden massaged her eyes. "Yes." Which gave her a very small window.

"Then we have six months."

The woman sounded a lot more confident than Lunden was.

Zeta stood, lifted the planner from the table, and moved toward the door but stopped shy of leaving. Turning, she said, "For the record, my money's on you. Lord knows when you're determined to do something, there's no stopping you."

"Did you just call me stubborn?"

"*Passionate* sounds better. Love you, girl. Talk later," Zeta said.

"Bye," Lunden said. She closed her eyes and massaged her temple. Maybe she should consider Ms. Jewel's advice. But what in the hell could she show Quade in Honey Hill that would convince him not to sell the inn and to abandon millions of dollars? *Nothing,* she told herself. *We're screwed.*

Quade thought he was dreaming, but when he realized his cell phone was actually ringing, he blindly fumbled for it on the nightstand, knocking over a glass of water. *Shit.* He squinted as his eyes adjusted to the glowing numbers on the clock: *2:47.* Who the hell was calling him at this ungodly hour in the morning? This had better not be a tipsy Pryor calling to say he'd found the woman of his dreams . . . again.

"Hello?" Quade answered, his mouth dry and voice croaky.

"Quade?"

The tiny, shaky voice at the opposite end garnered Quade's full attention. Judging by Zachary's wobbly tone, something was wrong. He swung his legs over the side of the bed and planted his feet on the icy, wet floor. "Zachary? What's wrong? You okay?"

114

"I can't get my aunt Rylee on the phone, and my mom is really sick." He sniffled. "I'm scared. Can you please come over?"

In a matter of seconds, Quade was on his feet, padding across the floor to his dresser. "I'll be there in five minutes. Is your mom awake?" he asked, fighting to slide into a pair of gray sweatpants while simultaneously keeping the phone to his ear.

"Yes. She says she's okay, but I know she's not. She keeps throwing up."

Throwing up? Was she pregnant? It was morning. She was sick. It was a plausible conclusion. After yanking a black T-shirt over his head, pulling on a pair of socks, sliding into his running shoes, and grabbing his keys, he was out the door.

He intentionally kept Zachary on the phone, because he could hear the distress in his voice. A short drive later, Quade whipped into Lunden's driveway, popped the SUV into park, darted out, and sprinted across the yard. "I'm here. Open the door for me."

"Okay," Zachary said.

The phone went dead. Zachary's soft footsteps against the hardwood grew closer and closer. When the door swung open, Quade's heart sank at the sight of Zachary's red-rimmed eyes. The navy-blue-and-red pajamas peppered with bicycles he wore were the happiest thing about him at the moment. Zachary slid the back of his hand across his cheek, then rushed him, tossing his short arms as far around Quade's waist as they would go.

"Thank you for coming, Quade."

"Dude, what are friends for?" When Zachary backed away, Quade knelt to be at eye level with him. "Everything's going to be okay, I promise."

Zachary nodded, his top lip quivering. Quade could tell he was trying to put on a brave face, but he saw the fear in his eyes. "Where's your mom?"

Zachary swung his arm toward the hallway. "In the bathroom in her room."

Quade returned to a full stand and followed Zachary into the master bedroom—a large, cozy room with a king-size bed, decorated in earthy tones—then into the master bathroom, fashioned with similar hues.

Lunden sat on the floor, her back to them and arms draped around the toilet as if she were giving an old friend a hug. Her head rested on one of her arms. She wore a black tank top and hot-pink, polka-dot boy shorts underwear. While he would be the first to admit that this was ill timing, he couldn't help but admit how damn sexy she looked with half her ass cheek peeking out from under the stretchy fabric. And had it been under different circumstances, it would have been arousing as hell. Oh, she was going to freak when she saw him.

"Mom?" Zachary's voice was low and cautious.

"I'm okay, son," she said. "Go to bed. You have school in the morning."

"Quade's here to help you," Zachary said.

"*Quade?*" she mumbled to herself as if she hadn't fully comprehended what Zachary had just said. A beat later, her head rose, and she glanced over her shoulder.

Her hair was an unruly mess, and her eyes were tired looking and red, like she'd enjoyed one too many glasses of wine. If she held any objections about his presence, she didn't voice them, simply dropped her head back onto her arm.

No snide remark.

No eye roll.

Not even a hiss.

Damn, she really must be sick.

"What are you doing here?" she finally said, her voice weak and raspy.

"Zachary called me. He's worried about you."

"I'm fine, Peanut. I just need a hot shower, that's all," she said.

This time, Zachary didn't protest the pet name.

"Quade can help you. Right, Quade?" Zachary said.

While Quade didn't have a problem helping Lunden into the shower, he seriously doubted she would be open to the idea. "If—"

"I can do it myself," Lunden said, attempting to push herself to her feet.

Quade rushed forward and caught her when her arms wouldn't support her efforts.

"Mom!" Zachary said, his tiny voice trembling.

"I'm just a little dizzy."

"I'm taking you to the hospital," Quade said, scooping her into his arms. Clearly, not everything had made it into the bowl, because the front of her shirt was splattered. In an effort to not be insensitive, he didn't react to the rancid smell of vomit wafting off her, despite his churning gut.

"No," she said.

Quade wasn't sure if she was protesting his lifting her into his arms or the trip to the hospital.

"I just need a shower," she repeated.

More like a hose down. He lowered his voice to a whisper so as not to frighten Zachary any more than he already was. "Lunden, you can't even stand by yourself. Why are you so damn stubborn, woman?"

"I'm not going to the hospital." She made a futile attempt to free herself but gave up after one and a half wiggles.

"Zachary, can you run to the kitchen and get your mom some water?" Quade said.

"Yes, sir."

When Zachary left the room, Quade eyed Lunden. "You don't want anyone to find out you're pregnant? Is that why you don't want to go to the hospital?"

Lunden's weak eyes widened. *"Pregnant?* I'm not *pregnant.* You have to have sex to be pregnant, and I'm definitely not getting—" She stopped abruptly. "Oh God! Put me down!"

"So you can fall on your ass and terrify your son even more?" he asked.

"No, so I don't—"

A beat later, she vomited on his shoulder. Quade dry heaved and stumbled backward until he bumped into the counter, but he somehow managed not to drop Lunden. The smell made him heave again. Luckily, he hadn't eaten, because there would have been a mess inside that bathroom.

When Lunden motioned as if she was going to throw up again, he hurried her back down by the toilet. It was a false alarm.

Zachary reentered the room, carrying a glass of water filled to the brim. "I got—" He stopped, his face contorting into a tight ball as he eyed Quade's shirt. *"Eww.* Gross."

Quade wholeheartedly agreed. After carefully removing his shirt, he tossed it into the sink. It would definitely have to be burned. Turning the faucet on full blast, he cupped several handfuls of water and splashed himself. Using the creamy yellow soap sitting on the counter, he lathered until he no longer smelled like vomit, instead now like lemons. When he eyed Lunden again, she jolted as if she'd been caught peeping through a keyhole. Her eyes darted away from him and toward Zachary.

"Tell Quade good night, son, then go to bed. I'll be okay."

"Pinkie promise?"

Lunden managed to hold out her pinkie. When Zachary hooked his around it, she said, "Pinkie promise. I love you so much. Sleep well." She blew him an air kiss.

"I love you too. Feel better, okay?"

Lunden flashed a wobbly smile. "I will."

Zachary set the water on the counter, covered his nose, and gave Quade another hug. "Thank you, Quade," he said through his fingers. Lowering his voice, he added, "Don't leave her alone, okay?"

"I won't," Quade whispered.

Zachary rushed from the room, and Quade couldn't blame him.

"Sorry I threw up on you," Lunden said. "But in my defense, I told you to put me down."

"You probably could have led with *I'm about to hurl.*"

"I'm sorry Zachary troubled you. I'm fine. Really."

"You don't look fine."

"Gee, thanks."

Quade rested against the counter. "I didn't mean it like that."

A brief silence played between them.

"I'm surprised you came," Lunden said.

"Yeah, well, kids don't usually call me crying at two in the morning. I figured it was an emergency."

Lunden's brows furrowed. "He was crying?"

Quade nodded. "He was really worried about you."

And truth be told, so was he.

CHAPTER 12

While the room might have spun and Lunden's stomach might have lurched, the sight of a shirtless Quade crossing in front of her was a balm to her system. His chest was like a skillfully sculpted masterpiece. All solid muscles and defined abs. Surely the man had at least one flaw. It wasn't his body, that was for sure.

Shamelessly, she'd ogled him while he splashed water on himself at the sink and had been caught. The infraction had been worth it. The way the water glistened on his chocolate skin should have been a crime. But how did you sentence someone for being too damn sexy?

Her brows knit when Quade moved to the bathtub and turned on the water. "What are you doing?" she asked.

"Running you a bath. There's no way you can take a shower without me joining you to hold you upright."

He paused for a moment as if allowing her the opportunity to respond. She refused to dignify such a ridiculous comment, so she remained silent.

Quade continued, "And since you're so determined for water to touch your body, a bath will have to do. I'll help you get undressed and—"

Apparently, confrontation was recharging, because she perked up a bit. "You already think I look pregnant with my clothes on. I'm definitely not letting you see me naked." Not that she was sheepish about her body. Her frame was a divinely constructed temple. Besides, if that were the case, she would have been mortified by his seeing her in her current attire. Her hang-up was the fact that he was essentially a stranger.

"I thought you were suffering from morning sickness, which was a perfectly logical conclusion. It's morning. You're sick. But now I know that's not the case because you're not having sex."

She narrowed her eyes the best she could. "Excuse me? How do you know I'm *not* having sex?"

"Because you told me. Right before you puked on me, remember?"

Oh yeah. She had let that slip. "Whatever," she said.

"Want to talk about it?" Quade asked.

This man was relentless. "Why would I want to talk about my sex life with you?"

"Moral support?"

Lunden managed a flimsy laugh. "You are . . . one unique bird."

"Thank you," he said.

It wasn't as much a compliment as it was an insult, but she didn't challenge him.

"If it's any consolation, I'm not having sex either."

It was not. Lunden knew his situation was strictly by choice. There were at least five women she knew of who would slither from their marital beds right now if Quade came calling. "Well, give it time."

Quade laughed, a sound so sexy she almost forgot how horrible she felt. "I hate to say I told you so, but I did point out the low sanitation grade at that Chinese restaurant yesterday."

"It was not the Chinese food," she said, despite believing it had been responsible for making her sick. However, she wouldn't give Quade the satisfaction.

"Of course it wasn't," he said. "You ready to get undressed?"

"That would be a no."

Quade rested his hands on his hips and cocked his head to the side. "You're acting like I haven't seen you naked before."

"Um, I was fifteen, and everything was in its rightful place."

His eyes did a slow crawl down, then back up her body. "By the looks of it, it still is," he said.

Lunden gave a humorless laugh. "Your slick tongue talked me out of my panties when I was young and dumb. It won't happen again."

Quade's head snapped back in apparent shock. "My slick tongue?" He chuckled. "*Wow.* I'm offended by both your sullied opinion of me as well as your blaring lapse of memory. As I remember it, *you* were the one who damn near ripped my clothes off that stormy Saturday in July."

Okay, maybe he was right, but she refused to admit it. Instead, she said, "Whatever," feeling kinda sentimental about the fact he could recall the time frame of their first time. Still, his *nothing was real* comment haunted her and devalued the memory.

Things got quiet between them for a moment.

"Lunden, about what I said at the restaurant . . ." His words trailed off. "*We* were real. And while I know it means nothing to you now, it hadn't been my choice to never return to Honey Hill. Not being able to see Shugga anymore was awful."

The fact he hadn't mentioned her bothered Lunden more than it should have.

Quade continued, "But being unable to be with you devastated me. Getting over you was rough. You were my best friend, my first love."

Lunden willed the tears stinging her eyes not to fall. "Why didn't you call, write, something, anything?" she said before fully processing her thoughts.

"I tried. When I got caught phoning Shugga, I got into so much trouble. When I got caught trying to call you . . ." He paused a moment. "I got into worse trouble."

Lunden could tell he wanted to say more, but he didn't. "I'm sorry," she said, unsure why she'd apologized, other than that it felt necessary.

"So am I," he said. "I thought about you. All the time. I even considered hitchhiking back here." His expression turned sad. "But my mom needed me." A teeny sliver of light brightened his features. "I looked you up on social media once."

He'd looked her up? "Why didn't you reach out?"

Quade chuckled. "Honestly, I was afraid. With the way things ended between us, I wasn't sure you would want to hear from me."

There had been so much lingering hurt that she would have probably instantly blocked him had he contacted her.

Silence fell between them.

Since he was giving her truth, she decided to dish a little of her own. "I cried for you until I was numb. I convinced myself that everything you'd told me had been a lie." Especially the part about his loving her, but she kept that to herself. "I just assumed you'd gotten what you wanted and dismissed me like I was just some quest you'd wanted to conquer."

"I get why you could have thought that, but you had to know how I felt about you."

"All I knew then, Quade, was how it felt to have my heart ripped from my chest. Getting over you was rough for me too." And had affected her more than she was ever willing to admit to him. Because of the rejection and abandonment she'd felt, she'd refused to allow another man complete access to her heart, including her ex-husband.

"I'm so sorry, Lunden. I wish things could have been different."

So did she. Maybe she wouldn't be so cynical about love.

Lunden hadn't realized until now how much she'd needed to have this conversation. As strange as it sounded, it felt as if a burden had been lifted from her shoulders. One she'd chosen to carry all these years. "It means something," she said, referring to his opening comment. "You telling me this means a lot. Thank you."

Quade turned away and removed the bottle of honey-almond-lavender bubble bath from the shelf. He popped the cap, took a whiff, then poured a capful into the tub.

"Why are you wasting my bubble bath? That stuff takes forever to make."

Quade's brow shot up. "You made this?"

She managed a nod.

He took another whiff. "It smells amazing." His gaze slid back to the shelf. "You made all of these?"

"Yes."

"The candles too?"

"All of it."

Quade studied the bubble bath label, then smiled. He never glanced up when he said, "Still love sunflowers, I see."

The logo she used for her handmade skin-care products and line of hand-poured soy candles was a bridge adorned by sunflowers. "Always," she said.

Lunden regretted the single-word reply the second it slipped past her lips. When Quade eyed her, she looked away. Clearly, her response recalled the same memory for him that it had for her. One she would much rather *not* have remembered at all.

Quade turned off the water and closed the distance between them. "If it makes you feel any better, I'll close my eyes," he said.

He grinned.

She growled.

Since she was fairly certain he had no plans of giving up, she gave in. "You don't have to carry me. I can walk." She didn't need the shock of being in his arms again disrupting her system any further. "Just help me up. *Please.*"

When she was on her feet, Quade steadied her, then rested his hands on either side of her waist and guided her to the tub. His tender touch caused her skin to prickle. She gasped when he hooked one arm around her waist. Startled by the move, she said, "What are you doing?"

"Helping you," he whispered in her ear.

His warm breath tickled the side of her neck. "I—"

"Don't argue with me, woman. Let's just get it done," he said. "You've had a long night. You need to rest."

The tender manner in which Quade handled her defused her. He used his free hand to help her lift the shirt over her head. The simple activity felt as if she'd dragged a five-hundred-pound bag of flour from one side of the room to the other, despite Quade doing most of the work. When it came to removing her underwear, again Quade took the lead, helping to slide the fabric down her body.

Lunden blamed her beaded nipples on an imaginary chill in the room. Truthfully, the feel of Quade's hot, hard body brushing against hers had her nerve endings all firing at once. Under different circumstances . . . *No! No, no, no. Under no circumstances. None at all.* Under zero circumstances would she have enjoyed this.

"Close your eyes and turn around. I have it from here," she said.

"Lunden—"

"Close them and turn around."

Quade sighed heavily but did as she instructed. Lunden lowered herself to the side of the tub, swung one leg over the lip, then slid into the water with a splash. Not with the grace of a mermaid. More like the blunder of a drunken seal.

"You okay?" Quade asked, his back still to her.

"Yes," came out in a moan as she sank down into the perfectly heated water, relaxed her head back, and closed her eyes. She inhaled a lungful of the fragrant bubble bath, the lavender relaxing her. This was far better than a shower. Of course, she wouldn't tell Quade this.

Opening her eyes, she said, "You can—" She stopped abruptly when she discovered he had moved from standing by the tub to sitting on the closed toilet seat, his elbows resting on his thighs, fingers locked, head bowed. Her eyes glided over his strong shoulders, down his muscular arms, and to his long fingers. Then there were the gray sweatpants that, alone, demanded attention. Something fluttered in her stomach.

Ugh. Stop it, Lunden.

Returning to her previous position—head back, eyes closed—she said, "You don't have to sit there. I'll call you when I'm ready to get out." She knew it was the only way to persuade him from the room.

"Who was she?" he asked in an uncharacteristically tiny voice.

"Who?" Lunden asked.

"My aunt."

Lunden's head slowly rose, and she eyed Quade, who still hadn't looked up. His leg bounced slightly, like he was nervous. Why did mentioning Ms. Shugga always seem to have a disconcerting effect on him?

"She was a lot of things to a lot of people. Friend. Confidante. Protector. She opened her home to anyone. For Ms. Shugga and so many more, the inn wasn't just a place to spend a night or two. It was a safe haven for many. She had a way of piecing together the broken and making them feel whole again." Lunden lost herself for a moment, unshed tears burning her eyes. When she floated back to reality, Quade was staring at her. Their gazes only held a second or two before he lowered his eyes to his fiddling fingers. She continued.

"Ms. Shugga gave people fresh starts, purpose. All without asking for a single thing in return." Lunden laughed. "She was habitually happy. Now that I think about it, I'm not sure I ever saw her unhappy, especially when Gladys Knight played. She loved her Gladys."

Though his head was bowed, Lunden could see the hint of a smile on Quade's face, but it slid away just as quickly as it had formed, as if good and bad were battling in his head and bad had won out. A second later, he bolted to his feet.

"You'll call for me when you're ready to get out?" he asked.

Confused by his abruptness, she nodded. A second later, he was gone.

Quade dropped down onto Lunden's bed. Lunden probably thought he was crazy from the way he'd rushed from the room. Hell, maybe he was. But listening to how his aunt had been so many things to so many people, had helped anyone who'd crossed her path, yet she'd never once reached out to him . . . hurt. What had he done so wrong to force her from his life?

Collapsing back on the mattress, he eyed the ceiling. She'd obviously felt guilt or shame over her actions. That had to be why she'd left him the inn, right? What other reason could there have been? It didn't matter. What was done was done. The inn was his now to do with what he wanted. And he planned to sell it.

The sound of splashing water drew him from his thoughts. He came up on his elbows, his ears perking. "You okay in there?"

"Peachy," Lunden said.

Convinced she wasn't in distress, he eased back again. Yawning, he closed his eyes, just for a second. When Quade cracked them open again, Lunden was angled across the bed, fast asleep. He eased forward. Had she called for him to help her from the tub? Probably not.

The moonlight penetrating through the blinds washed Lunden in an angelic glow. A lavender throw covered her lower half. She snored, but not like a grizzly. More like a cute and cuddly kitten. Delicate and adorable.

The clock on her nightstand read 4:18. He should have gotten up and gone home, but since he'd promised Zachary he wouldn't leave his mom, he eased back down instead and closed his eyes again . . . just for another second.

This time, it was daylight when Quade cracked his eyes open a second time, and only because Zachary lightly tapped his shoulder. Zachary still wore his pajamas. In a whisper, Quade said, "Hey, dude. You good?" Zachary nodded, his smile wide and bright. Quade swore he was the happiest kid he knew. Not that he knew many kids.

"I have to be at school by eight fifty-five, or I'll be tardy," he said.

"School?"

Zachary nodded excitedly.

Quade glanced over at Lunden. She was sleeping so peacefully he hated to disturb her. He could handle getting the kid to school, right? He'd gotten himself to work for years without problem. "I can take you to school."

Zachary pumped his fist. *"Yes!"* he said in a teeny voice. "I'll get ready." A second later, he darted from the room.

Quade wished he had Zachary's energy at seven in the morning. So as not to disturb Lunden, he inched from the bed. She didn't budge. After taking a step, he stopped and looked down at himself. He definitely couldn't show up in the carpool line shirtless. That would fuel some interesting dialogue. Luckily, he had a spare in his SUV.

Clueless about what actions he should be taking, Quade stood in the hallway. Was he supposed to help the kid get dressed? He ran a hand over his head. Trekking to Zachary's room, he tapped two knuckles against the bedroom door. "Knock, knock," he said, entering the empty room.

Zachary popped out of the bathroom, his mouth foaming with toothpaste. "I'll be out in a minute, okay?" he said around the red-and-blue toothbrush sticking out of his mouth.

"Do you need my help with anything?"

"No, sir. I got it." Zachary disappeared back into the bathroom.

"Okay." Quade spotted the blue-and-white striped polo shirt and jeans neatly folded on the desk, along with a pair of white socks. Instead of lingering in the room, he used the guest bathroom to relieve his bladder, then peeped in on Lunden and chuckled. She hadn't moved an inch. Bracing himself against the doorjamb, he watched her sleep. Even with her hair strewed all over the place and her mouth wide open, she was beautiful.

Quade flinched when Zachary tapped him. *Damn.* This kid must have been a ballerina in a previous life, because he was hella light on his feet. Quade placed his index finger over his lips, then led Zachary into the kitchen. "You're looking sharp, kid."

"Thank you."

"Did you wash your face?" he asked, because that was what he'd seen parents do on television. And since he was kinda, sorta acting as one right now, it seemed appropriate.

"Yes, sir."

"Behind your ears?" Again, something else he'd seen on television.

"Yep."

"Good. What about under your arms?" That one he hadn't heard but figured it couldn't hurt to ask. Did six-year-old boys even get musty?

Zachary bent over in laughter as if Quade had told the best joke he'd ever heard. "You're funny, Quade."

Quade scrubbed a hand over Zachary's head. "Do we need to pack you a lunch?"

"No. I eat lunch at school. But my mom usually makes me breakfast."

Breakfast? Okay, he could handle breakfast. "What does she usually give you?"

"Bacon, eggs, grits, toast, and orange juice."

Quade massaged his forehead. "Wow. Bacon, eggs, grits, toast, and orange juice, huh?" *Whatever happened to a bowl of cereal, oatmeal, or cream of wheat?*

"But I like cereal better."

Okay, cereal he could do. Of course he couldn't bow to defeat. He shrugged. "Well, if cereal's really what you want."

Zachary nodded, and Quade blew a sigh of relief. Burning down their house in an attempt to fry bacon was not how he'd wanted to start his day.

Quade grabbed two bowls from the cabinet, figuring he'd fill the empty hole in his stomach too. "Now you're sure you don't want bacon?"

"I'm sure."

When Quade slid the bowl of frosted corn cereal in front of Zachary, the kid scrubbed his hands together as if he were about to dig into a porterhouse steak. Who got this excited over a bowl of cereal? *Zachary.*

After they'd both gotten their fill, Quade peeped in on Lunden, who was still fast asleep. He jotted down a quick note in case she woke before he returned, placed it on the counter, then headed out the door.

Ten minutes later, Quade pulled behind a silver minivan. "We're here." He wasn't sure what the procedure was, whether he was supposed to just idle here or walk Zachary inside. "Do you need lunch money?" While he didn't have his wallet with him, he always kept a spare hundred-dollar bill in his glove box.

"No."

A short, stocky brunette moved toward his SUV, wearing a smile so wide Quade was surprised she hadn't cracked the corners of her mouth.

"*Yoo-hoo.* Good morning," she sang out.

"That's Mrs. Holmes. She's nice, but she talks a whole lot. And she laughs funny." Zachary opened his door and hopped out. "Thank you for bringing me to school, Quade. I like riding in Josie."

"You're welcome, little man. You have a good day, all right?"

"I will. Can you give my mom a kiss for me when she wakes up? She's going to be sad I didn't give her one."

Quade massaged his stubble when he had a vision of Lunden socking him in the jaw for trying to kiss her. "Uh . . . sure."

"Bye, Quade. I'll see you later, okay?"

Quade pulled away from the curb before Mrs. Holmes got a chance to interrogate him. On his way back to Lunden's, Quade decided to swing by the bakery for coffee and pastries in case Lunden wanted something and didn't feel like cooking bacon, eggs, and grits. He smiled, liking the idea she took the time to prepare Zachary a full breakfast before school. His mom had done the same when he was that age. *Fuel for the day,* she used to say.

Arriving at the bakery, Quade pulled into a space and ducked inside. He spoke to several folks as he made his way to the counter. "Good morning,"

Rylee turned toward him, her eyes briefly lowering to his shirt. Probably wondering why he wore a white button-down shirt with sweatpants. "Hey. Good morning. How are you?"

"Good, thanks. You?"

"Great. What can I get for you?"

"Two large coffees and . . ." *What would Lunden like?*

"Might I suggest cinnamon buns," Rylee said. "They're popular. Along with the cream-cheese-filled and glazed croissants."

Call him crazy, but he had a sneaking suspicion Rylee knew exactly where the pastries were headed.

"Great. I'll take four of each."

As Rylee filled the box, she said, "How are you liking Honey Hill?"

"It's . . . okay. Getting better, I guess."

"Not one for small towns, huh?"

"That obvious?"

Rylee slid the box toward him, along with the coffees. "Be careful. This place has a way of growing on you. On the house," she said. "Consider it a welcome-to-town offering. Enjoy."

"Thank you." He gathered the goodies and headed out of the shop. Sliding behind the wheel, he thought about Rylee's warning. *Be careful. This place has a way of growing on you.* He chuckled. *Fat chance.*

CHAPTER 13

The world slowly came alive around Lunden as she drifted awake. She rolled onto her back, her eyes fluttering open. She closed them when the bright light pouring through the blinds intensified the throb in her head. This was the first time she'd suffered a hangover without consuming a drop of alcohol.

Debating whether she had enough energy to climb out of bed and drive Zachary to school, she lay there, listening to the hum of the air conditioner, birds chirping outside her window, a stray car passing by. God, what she wouldn't give for a couple more hours of sleep.

Sleep! Quade!

Summoning what little energy she could, she sat forward. Her eyes swept the foot of her bed. No Quade. When had he left? And why hadn't he woken her? She eyed the clock. "Eight thirty? *Shit!*" Adrenaline gave her just the boost she needed to vacate the bed. "Zachary?" She called him a second time when he didn't respond. "Zachary. Wake up, son." She rarely had to wake him. The kid had a built-in alarm clock. And speaking of alarm clocks, why hadn't hers sounded? Well, she didn't have time to waste figuring out whether she'd even activated it.

When she rushed into his room, it was empty. The bathroom too. Panic set in. Hurrying into the kitchen for her cell phone, she spotted a scribbled note on the counter. *You were snoring pretty good. Didn't want to wake you. Taking Z to school. Q.* "I don't snore."

Lunden's head whipped toward the door when it opened. Quade ambled in, a bakery box in one hand, a beverage tray cradling two large coffees in the other. While he wasn't making any fashion statements in the button-down shirt and sweatpants, at least he wasn't shirtless.

"Hey," he said. He placed her keys on the table by the door. "I grabbed your keys so that I could get back in. I didn't want to leave the door unlocked while you were asleep. I hope that was okay."

"It's fine," she said.

"How are you feeling?"

"Pretty much how I'm sure I look." Which had to be like a blazing-hot mess. She raked her fingers through her hair, not that she thought doing so would improve much, then felt a pang of embarrassment when they got stuck.

"For a woman who spent a good chunk of the night by the toilet, you look fine."

"Thank you," she said. "I'm impressed. You said it with such a straight face." Quade stared at her in a way that made her self-conscious.

"I brought breakfast. Cinnamon rolls. Cream-cheese-filled and glazed croissants."

"My favorites. Wait, did you tell Rylee those were for me?"

Quade flashed a confused look. "No."

"Good."

"Mind if I ask why?"

"Why what?"

"Why you would care whether or not Rylee knew these were for you."

"I don't," she said. "I'm not sure I can stomach anything right now, but don't let that stop you. I know you have a sweet tooth."

Quade eyed her in a way that suggested he knew exactly what she was attempting to do: divert the conversation. Instead of calling her out, he simply smiled and said, "I should get going. I could use a hot shower and sleep. Your snoring kept me up all night."

He'd spent the night? Duh. Of course he had. How else would he have been able to take Zachary to school? "I don't snore. I purr. Like a kitten."

"If by *kitten* you mean a drunken lion, then I agree."

Lunden laughed. "Ouch," she said, kneading her temple. "Don't make me laugh. I have a throbbing headache."

"Sit down. I'll get you something. Do you have any acetaminophen?"

Easing into a chair at the table, Lunden pointed to a lazy Susan on the counter. With pill bottle in hand, Quade shook two out and passed them to her, along with one of the coffee cups. "Take it with this. Coffee will help the acetaminophen work better."

"Really?" She'd never heard such a thing before. Considering the source, of course, she was skeptical.

"Trust me," he said, obviously seeing the skepticism on her face.

Well, he hadn't murdered her in her sleep. That was a good sign. She guessed she could trust him with her well-being one last time. Popping the pills, she took several sips from her cup. "Happy?"

"You will be once your headache is gone in record time."

"Thank you for making sure Zachary got to school . . . and for last night. I owe you."

"I'm ready to collect."

Well, that was fast. "O . . . kay. So what do you want?" she said, almost afraid of his response.

"You."

Lunden choked on the coffee and had a coughing fit. "E-excuse me?" she sputtered out between hacks.

"You," he repeated. "Actually, your time. I need to hire you."

Still as confused as she had been seconds before, she said, "Hire me? Hire me to do what, exactly?"

"To help me learn beekeeping. It was one of the stip—" He stopped abruptly, as if he'd been about to reveal too much. "I could really use your help."

She eyed him a moment. "No." To her surprise, his expression remained relaxed. Not a single flinch in his brow, twitch of the lip, or wrinkle across the forehead, as if he'd expected her to decline.

"I understand," he said, standing. "I hope you feel better soon." He turned and moved toward the door.

Pushing her grievances aside, for now, she said, "You don't have to pay me. I'll help you for free." It was the least she could do, considering all he'd done for her in the last twenty-four hours. Yet something deep down told her she would regret this.

Quade was still in disbelief over the fact Lunden had actually agreed to help him. But here she stood on his patio, on a glorious Saturday afternoon, schooling him on the ins and outs of beekeeping. The dos, the don'ts, and the maybes.

A smile curled one side of his mouth. Call it intuition, but he knew she would eventually warm up to him. That Cannon charm never failed. Or it could just be she thought she owed him. Which she didn't. Regardless, they were here, and she hadn't once looked as if she wanted to kill him. *Progress.* Sadly, she hadn't looked as if she wanted to kiss him either. He wasn't sure why that bothered him so much.

He refocused on her spiel, but all the terminology sounded foreign to him. *Honey supers. Brood boxes. Swarms.* And on and on and on. He didn't complain, though, because he enjoyed watching her glossy lips move. The woman in front of him now looked vastly different from the one he'd peeled away from the toilet over a week ago.

"You love this, don't you? Talking about bees."

"I enjoy it, yes. I don't think people understand how important they are. They pollinate nearly everything we eat, they're great for the environment, and, of course, they produce delicious honey. Unfortunately, colonies are vanishing at alarming rates."

She sounded like a *save the bees* infomercial. "I love honey," he said. The muscles in his stomach tightened as an image of drizzling the sticky, sweet substance all over Lunden's breast and then licking it off flickered through his head.

"Earth to Quade," Lunden said, snapping her fingers in front of his face.

"Hmm?"

"Did I lose you? You looked like you were a thousand miles away."

Refocusing, he said, "Nope. I'm right here, right now, ready to learn. Teach me."

After another half hour of absorbing information he knew he'd never use again in his life once he left Honey Hill, they left the patio and headed toward the cottage, where, according to Lunden, Shugga kept the equipment. She would know.

On the way, Lunden quizzed him. "What's the one thing you don't want to do?"

"Agitate the bees," he said like a star pupil.

"Why?"

"Because they will become aggressive."

"And what happens when they become aggressive?"

"They sting."

"Huh. You were paying attention," she said. "Let's get you suited up."

Quade stopped. "Wait. Suited up? Why would I need to be suited up?"

"So you would prefer to interact with thousands of bees without the proper protection?"

"I would prefer not to interact with them at all."

Lunden laughed. "How do you expect to tend to your bees if you're afraid to go near them? Telepathy?"

"Now hold on. I'm not afraid." Lunden gave him a look. "I'm not. I just thought we'd work me up to it."

"I just spent the last hour working you up to it." She slapped his chest twice. "Put on your big-boy briefs. It's game time," she said, walking off. "Coward," she mumbled just loud enough for him to hear.

"Did that feel like the chest of a coward?" he said.

She ignored him.

As they entered the cottage, broken glass crunched under their feet. Lunden knelt to pick up a rock, then glanced toward the broken windows, her brows furrowing.

He'd been meaning to have someone come out to fix the windows the misfits had shattered, just hadn't gotten around to it. Before she started to ask questions, he diverted her attention. "Wow. There's a lot of stuff in here." And there was.

Several oversize stainless steel pot contraptions lined one wall. Lunden described them as motorized honey extractors. She pointed out several pieces of equipment: frames, smoker, hive tool. She moved to a storage bin, unlocked it, and removed an all-white bodysuit made of what looked like thick canvas. A second later, she passed it to him.

"What am I supposed to do with it?" he said.

"Put it on."

Quade shook it on the off chance something had made its home inside, then slid into the ridiculous-looking outfit. "Jesus, this thing is hot. Feels like I'm at hot yoga."

"You do yoga?" Lunden asked, her brows arched.

"Yes," he said. "It's a mind, body, and spirit workout. Don't knock it till you've tried it."

Lunden flashed her palms. "I'm not judging. Do what makes you happy," she said, passing him what looked like a round safari hat with an attached veil that encased the entire piece.

Again, he made sure it was free of anything that flew, crawled, jumped, or slithered.

"You're not the outdoorsy type, huh?"

Quade couldn't help feeling Lunden's words were more of an insult than an observation. "Never really had much time for the outdoors," he said.

"Right." She handed him a pair of thick gloves made out of heavy cotton material. "Put these on."

The more pieces that came, the more Quade began to suspect Lunden was making him wear all of it simply because she could. "Hat, suit, gloves. All of this seems like a bit of overkill," he said.

"The hat and veil protects your head and face. The suit, your torso. Gloves, hands. It's cumbersome, but it's better with all of it than without. Lessens your chances of getting stung."

Quade pushed his brows together. "Wait. *Lessens?* You mean to tell me that with all of this stuff on I could *still* get stung?"

"Yes. Nothing's a hundred percent guarantee. Such is life."

God, he was disliking beekeeping more and more by the second. While he stood in the full-body getup, Lunden slid into a white jacket. And it looked vented. Her head covering resembled a fencing hat. That was exactly how he looked, like he was about to go fencing. Something told him that would have been much safer. Lunden didn't even pull out gloves for herself. "Why aren't you in full-body protection?" he asked.

"Because I know what I'm doing."

Okay, he'd give her that one, because she certainly knew more than he did about this. "How'd you learn all of this, anyway?" he asked.

"Ms. Shugga. She was a certified master beekeeper and a great teacher."

Quade looked away. "So when do we get the honey?"

"Mid- to late July," she said. "That's the fun part. Well, that and bottling. Ms. Shugga used to make bottling like a big party. She'd have food, drinks, music. Most of the town showed up to help, even the kids. Though they just really like the honey straws." She glowed as she talked about all of it.

"You really like this bee stuff, huh?"

"Yes. It's therapeutic."

He could think of far better ways to soothe his soul. Yoga, chocolate cake, sex. Swimming, a nap, sex. Jazz, a hot bath, sex. Sipping a smooth cognac, sex, and sex.

"You ready?" Lunden asked.

No, he wasn't, but he refused to say it. That damn male ego. "Let's do this."

Quade had thought Lunden had exaggerated when she'd said thousands of bees. She hadn't. But thousands looked more like millions, all flying and buzzing around them, capable of an attack at any moment. Being here launched him completely out of his comfort zone. Lunden, on the other hand, looked perfectly within her element. Watching her soothed him a bit. Still, he didn't trust these tiny killers.

"Luckily, they're pretty docile right now," she said. "Midday is a good time to work your hives. The forager bees are usually out." She nudged him. "Don't stand in front of the hive's entrance. It blocks any returning bees' path."

"Forager bees?" Quade asked.

"Worker bees who venture outside the colony to collect water, nectar, pollen. They come and go multiple times a day, collecting and depositing."

Lunden schooled him about the queen, who led the colony and laid the eggs, and how without one in the colony, it would eventually die off. She talked about the worker bees—all females—and their function: taking care of the younger bees and the queen, cleaning and expanding the hive, and foraging and scouting for new hive locations, if necessary. Then the drones, the male bees—they couldn't sting, which made him happy—whose primary job was to mate with the queen. Being a drone sounded like the perfect gig until Lunden told him they died immediately after mating because their dicks were violently ripped off. It made him cringe.

"You said they were docile," Quade said. And hopefully, they stayed that way. "How do you know?"

"Their buzzing. Listen. You hear how it's a low, steady hum?"

Tuning out the other sounds of nature and the flow of the creek several feet away, he listened.

Lunden continued, "When bees feel threatened, you will hear a change in their buzzing. It'll become more intense, letting you know they're agitated. They're telling us to clear out of their space because we're making them uneasy. If that doesn't work, they'll bump into our veils and release pheromones that'll alert other bees to impending danger."

"Why do they go for the veil? Why not the body?"

"They're reacting to the carbon dioxide."

"Violent little creatures," Quade said.

"They're just protecting their homes. Instead of guns, they have stingers. They don't want to sting you because they'll die. But they're willing to make that sacrifice to keep the hive and their queen safe. It's kinda remarkable."

"What happens after they bump us?" Quade asked.

"We're not going to worry about that, because we're going to keep our bees calm. This will help."

She lifted something that looked like an old-school coffee percolator, but with a spout instead of a lid. "What is it?"

"A smoker. You fill it with paper and/or dried leaves, then puff the smoke over the hive. They can't detect the danger pheromones other bees may be releasing. Thereby keeping them docile. And that's what we want while we're invading their home."

Quade stood back several feet as Lunden explained the components of the hive. The three boxes on the top were called honey supers, where bees stored their honey. The box on the bottom was called a brood box and was where the queen laid her eggs, up to three thousand per day. The number astonished him.

"Okay, we're ready to open them up and inspect," Lunden said. "You can watch me do several; then you can try."

"Um . . . maybe I should just watch this go-round."

"This is just like the time I crossed the creek but you were too afraid to. Even though the water barely covered your ankles." She laughed.

Quade remembered that day very well. Even thinking about it now gave him pause. He'd been petrified when she'd crossed the easy-flowing water, had refused to cross himself, then had stomped off angrily when she'd kept trying to encourage him to do so.

Lunden continued, "You wouldn't even get in the pool that summer."

"I'd seen a neighborhood kid drown in a pond before coming to Honey Hill that summer." A knot formed in his stomach just thinking about it. Watching someone lose their life had been awful. The trauma of it remained with him to this day.

Lunden's expression turned somber.

Quade looked off into the distance. "Staring at that water, all I could see was Ernest Haywood thrashing in that murky water like a hooked fish. Then he was gone." He eyed Lunden again. "I couldn't bring myself to step into that water. I took swim lessons after I left Honey Hill that summer. While you hadn't admitted it back then, I saw the disappointment in your eyes at my cowardliness when you looked at me. I told myself I never wanted you to look at me like that ever again."

"I . . . don't know what to say, Quade," she said.

"There's no need to say anything. It was a long time ago."

"Maybe I was disappointed a little, but not for the reason you think. I'd spent my entire allowance buying stuff for a picnic I'd set up on the most perfect knoll. I was disappointed you wouldn't get to see it. I had all your favorites. Even licorice. Yuck."

"Why didn't you tell me?"

"You weren't exactly in a listening mood." She neared him. "Why didn't you tell me? It seems as if you kept all the important stuff happening in your life away from me. It was almost like you didn't trust me with the information."

"I told you everything, Lunden. You were my best friend."

"You didn't tell me your father had passed."

This time, he didn't know what to say. She was right. He hadn't told her. Partially because he hadn't wanted to talk about it. Mostly because he couldn't talk about it. Mainly because he hadn't handled it well. Ultimately, he'd wanted to protect her by not pulling her down into the dumps with him. "I'm sorry." Though apologizing now seemed useless.

She shrugged. "Like you said, it was a long time ago. Let's get to work."

He nodded, because what else could he do?

After getting the smoker going, Lunden passed it to him with instructions on what to do with it. "When I say *smoke*, press the bellows a couple of times. And keep it fueled. The last thing you want is no smoke with agitated bees." It was a lot of pressure. But he was a master griller—self-proclaimed, of course. For sure if he could keep coals lit, he was confident he could keep this thing going.

Lunden used something that resembled a mini back scratcher to pry open the top of the hive, stuck down by something called propolis. She described it as a compound bees produced from the sap of trees that apparently helped to heal wounds and fight bacteria.

"Smoke," she said.

After he released a couple of puffs inside, Lunden closed the lid for several seconds, then removed it completely, placing it on the ground.

"Come look inside."

Was she serious? She really wanted him to hover over an active beehive? If he didn't know any better, he'd think Lunden *wanted* him to become a pincushion. A second later, he abandoned the idea. She'd never been the malicious type. After cautiously approaching, he peered inside. Eight frames hung snugly in place.

"Give it a little more smoke," she said.

He did as told, listening for any variations in their buzzing. Yes, he'd been taking mental notes. Using the tool again, Lunden moved slowly to loosen one of the frames, lifted it, and rested it on the box. Covered in hundreds of bees, it was impressive.

"Is that honeycomb?" he asked.

"Yes." She pointed to one of the workers. "See the pollen on their hind legs? It's called a pollen basket. These beautiful ladies are hard at work making delicious honey. See right here?" She pointed to a section capped over with wax. "Honey."

"I can't wait to taste it," he said.

They continued inspecting the hives, making sure the queen in each was healthy and laying eggs. They were also on the lookout for pests and disease. On the last hive, Quade gained a boost of confidence and volunteered to inspect it. Mimicking what he'd learned watching Lunden, he successfully worked his first hive.

"Look at you. You're a pro now," she said.

"I had a great teacher."

"Thank you. We're done. I know you're ready to get out of that hot suit, so replace the top cover and let's head back."

Just as Quade dropped the lid in place, Lunden touched his ear and buzzed. Adrenaline kicked in. He swatted furiously at the veil, while Lunden bent over in rib-cracking laughter. Amused, he laughed, too, until realizing he'd apparently given access to a few unwanted visitors.

"*Lunden . . . Lunden*, they're in my suit!"

"What?" she asked through laughter.

"*They're in my suit!*" He danced around as if the ground were on fire and he were attempting to keep his feet from frying. "*They're in my suit!*" he said, his tone going an octave or two higher. "*Oh God! Ouch!*

Ouch!" He clawed at the suit when he felt a stinging pain on his chest, neck, shoulder. "They're stinging me! *Shit.* Call them off!"

"I'm not the honeybee whisperer," she said. "Stop moving. You're agitating them."

Stop moving? Was she serious? How did she think that was even possible when he was getting eaten alive? "That's like telling water to stop being wet."

Lunden dosed the swarm around him with smoke, allowing him to make a safe escape. He charged toward the cottage. "I'm never going near those . . . those . . . flying hell demons again."

Lunden jogged up next to him. "Don't be like that. Stings are a part of beekeeping. Every beekeeper, experienced or not, gets stung."

He stopped and whipped toward her. "Yeah, well, I'm not a beekeeper."

"Well, you are for the next several months. Let's get you undressed so we can take care of those stings," she said, walking off like she'd just claimed an undeclared victory.

Maybe she had.

CHAPTER 14

Lunden wasn't sure what she'd been thinking when she asked Quade to remove his shirt so that she could tend to his stings. Sitting on the couch while trying her best not to stare at the impressiveness of his torso was torture. She should have worn gloves, because every time her finger smoothed ointment across his bare flesh, blood rushed to all her sensitive parts.

Had she really thought she could handle seeing this man shirtless . . . again? Hadn't she learned her lesson the first damn time? Apparently not. In her defense, she'd reasoned that since he wasn't wet, it would have no effect on her. Wrong. So wrong.

Gliding the tip of her finger across one of the welts on his skin, Lunden could feel his eyes on her. She prayed he didn't witness the slight tremor in her hands.

"You've changed," he said.

Her gaze never rose. "It's been twenty years, Quade. I would hope so." Some of the change voluntary, some involuntary. Lessons had been learned with both.

He continued, "But you're still the same, too."

This brought her eyes up to meet his. "How so?"

"You're still a nurturer. Regardless of how you feel about someone, you still help them. I know I'm probably your least favorite person in town. Yet here we are. Thank you, by the way."

Lunden smiled a little. "You're welcome." When she noticed the strange look on Quade's face, she said, "What?"

"I was hoping you were going to tell me that I *wasn't* your least favorite person. You really do hate me, huh?"

"*Hate* is such a strong word. I don't hate you. I don't hate anyone. We're just . . . different. But that's no reason to hate someone. Dislike them a little, yeah. Hate, never."

Quade chuckled. "I guess I should feel honored. You simply dislike me, not hate."

"I mean, you're okay at times."

"Just okay? Woman, I came to help you in the wee hours of the morning. You vomited on me. Does that not at least get me a toe into the friend zone?"

"Oh, you want us to be friends? Interesting."

"It would be nice to have at least one while I'm here."

"You do have one," she said.

"Thank you."

"Zachary," she said. "Next time, don't piss off the bees."

"That's cold. For the record, Zachary's my *best* friend. I need a regular friend."

"I'm sure you have plenty of friends waiting for you back in Charlotte."

Quade pushed his brows together. "How do you know I lived in Charlotte?"

"Ms. Shugga mentioned it a time or twenty. That woman was really proud of you. Her big-city nephew. Out there conquering the world."

When Quade lowered his head, Lunden rejoined him at the table. Unsure what came over her, perhaps motherly instinct, she placed a finger under his chin and tilted his head up. Something flashed between them. It sent volts of electricity pulsing through her entire body. He must have felt the vibration, too, because a bemused expression slid across his face.

Allowing her hand to fall away, she rested it in her lap, closing it into a fist to subdue the tingle. In a gentle voice, she said, "Why do you get so sad whenever I mention Ms. Shugga?"

Quade stared at her a long moment, as if debating whether to reveal any little piece of himself to her. She would understand if he chose not to. They weren't the inseparable fifteen-year-olds they'd once been. Quade dragged his nails across his denim-clad thigh over and over again, like he was scratching an itch. Did he even know he was doing it? If she had to guess, no.

He finally broke his deafening silence. "Out of the blue, I get a call that I'd inherited an inn from an aunt I was told had died years ago," he said.

Remembering all Lady Sunshine had revealed to her flooded Lunden with compassion for him. When she took his offending hand into hers, Quade lowered his gaze to their connection. A second later, his fingers tightened around hers, as if human contact was exactly what he needed at that moment. And for once, she didn't regret touching him.

He continued, "All these years . . ." His words trailed off. "All these years, I thought she was dead. It's what my mother told me." He shrugged. "I don't know why she'd tell me such a lie, but she did. The worst part is I'll never know why. Everyone keeps telling me how proud my aunt was of me, which means she knew all about me but never *once*, not *once*, reached out to me."

Pain was present in his tone, but Lunden also noted a hint of something else. Brokenness, possibly. In an effort to soften the rigid atmosphere, she said, "Maybe she had her reasons."

"Like what? What force could have been powerful enough to keep Shugga from doing exactly what she wanted to do?"

Lunden looked away. One thing everyone had known about Ms. Shugga was that once her mind was set on something, not even gale-force winds could stop her.

"My point exactly," he said, releasing her hand, standing, and walking over to the window and staring out.

She didn't take it personally. The situation had to both hurt and anger him. He seemed intently focused on something on the other side of the glass. The only thing she could guess was the old sycamore tree in the distance.

"I didn't know her, Lunden. Not anymore. Everyone keeps tossing condolences at me that I don't deserve. I'm confused, angry, hurt. I have so many questions that I'll never get the answers to."

She closed the distance between them. "Maybe I can answer some of them for you."

Quade whipped toward her. "Can you tell me why my aunt didn't care enough to reach out to me, even after my mother's—her sister's—death? She had to know, right? She knew everything else. Can you answer that for me?"

Her lips parted, closed, parted again. Would telling him violate her zipped-lip pact with Lady Sunshine if she didn't reveal her as the source? Didn't he have a right to know? She would have wanted someone to tell her, no matter how troubling hearing it would be. He was desperate for answers, ones she could give him. But should she? Was it just best in this situation to let sleeping dogs lie? God, she was so torn about what to do.

"What is it?" he asked.

"Nothing. It's getting late, I should probably get going." She turned and started away.

"Lunden?" His words dripped with sorrow. "Please."

Lunden inhaled deeply, then released the slow stream of air. "It—" Her voice cracked, and she stopped. Clearing her throat, she continued. "It was your mother."

Quade's footsteps drew near until he was standing right behind her. "My mother? What about my mother?"

Quade listened as Lunden recounted a story she'd been told. How his mother and Shugga had argued about his well-being. How his mother had promised Shugga she'd never see him again. How Shugga had gone to see his mother on her deathbed. How his mother had demanded someone who had been one of the most important people in his life never contact him.

He swallowed hard to push down the bile burning the back of his throat. His heart banged against his rib cage. The air in the room became almost too thick to breathe, causing his head to swim. When Lunden made a move to touch his arm, he pulled away.

"I don't believe you," he said, despite having no reason not to. Sure, they'd had their issues—still had issues—but Lunden had no reason to lie to him, especially about something like this. Regardless, it was mentally easier to refute her claim than to accept it.

"I understand," she said in a tender voice.

"Whoever told you this has it wrong. My mother would never . . ." He stopped shy of claiming what his mother wouldn't do, because he clearly hadn't known her at all.

"Quade, I didn't mean—"

"You didn't mean to what, Lunden? Upset me? You didn't. I'm fine. *Peachy.*" He tossed his hands into the air. "None of this matters, anyway, true or not, because once I off-load this place, all of this"—he slapped his hands together as if he were knocking off flour—"will be nothing but an ugly memory."

The tender expression never left her face. It would have been better had fire sparked in her eyes and she shot flames in his direction. He deserved to be singed for the juvenile way he'd just reacted. But what was the proper way to respond when the walls seemed to be crashing down around you?

Lunden pointed over her shoulder. "I should go. I promised Zachary I'd take him to the arcade. That kid loves his games. And pizza." She turned and moved away. Stopping, she faced him. "Quade, if you need to—"

"I'm good," he said. "Enjoy the arcade." God, he detested what he saw in her eyes. Pity. There was no need to pity him. He was fine. And he would continue to be fine. None of this bothered him at all. None of what he'd learned mattered.

Sadness plagued her features. "Okay," she said and continued out the door.

The second the front door clicked shut, Quade dropped down onto the sofa, leaned forward, and rested his elbows on his thighs. Interlocking his fingers, he lowered his head. A second later, warm tears streamed down his face, the same way they had the first time he'd lost Shugga. Only this time felt much worse, because it felt as if he'd lost his mother a second time too. "Damn this place," he whispered to himself.

CHAPTER 15

Lunden hurried to her vehicle, debating whether she'd done the right thing by telling Quade what she knew. The sheer amount of pain she'd witnessed in his eyes had her thinking that maybe she should have simply kept her mouth shut. In the moment, telling him had seemed like the lesser of the two evils. Now, after seeing the tortured look on Quade's face, she wasn't sure.

The second she slid behind the wheel, she groaned. In her urgency to leave, she'd neglected to grab her keys. *"Dammit."* For a moment, she seriously considered walking home to retrieve her spare instead of venturing back inside. "Stop being a wuss."

She made her way back to the door and knocked twice. Quade didn't answer. After another round of unanswered raps, she let herself in. Entering the sitting room, she had a feeling he knew she was there, but he didn't acknowledge her. "Sorry for barging in. You didn't answer. I forgot my keys," she said.

Quade washed a hand down his face. "It's fine," he said, his voice cracking with emotion.

Lunden's heart broke when she realized he had been crying. She was halfway across the room before she even realized her feet had been uprooted. Moving in silence, she positioned an ottoman directly in front of where he sat, then took a seat. Quade never glanced up, and she didn't attempt to get him to do so. When more tears streamed down his cheeks, she used a tender touch to wipe them away.

"Why would she do that, Lunden?" he asked, his red-rimmed eyes rising to meet hers. His usually steady tone now rattled with emotion. "I know why, but . . . why?"

Lunden assumed he was referring to his mother. Of course she couldn't know what had gone through his mother's mind, but she offered the best explanation she could. "Mothers are extremely protective of their children, Quade. We don't want anyone telling us what's best for them. Whether they have a valid argument or not. Most mothers never want to think we're failing our children. If I had to guess, your mother feared losing you to someone else."

"She was my mother. I was her son. No one could have ever come before her. I loved her with my entire heart. I still do, despite how she's hurt me."

"I'm sure she knew that. And I don't think her intent was to hurt you. Either of you."

"Then why would she keep us from each other? My mother had a chance to make this right, but she chose to maintain this deception."

"Maybe she was afraid you would hate her for what she'd done."

"I could have never hated her. She was all I had. I had no one to lean on when she died. Did it ever occur to her that I would be all alone? That I could have used Shugga in my life? I was a young man forced to maneuver the world alone. By the grace of God I managed, but . . ." He blew out a heavy breath.

"Where was your stepfather?" It seemed like the man was not an active part of Quade's life. Since it wasn't relevant, Lunden hadn't mentioned Lady Sunshine's telling her his mother had married his father's best friend. But with her asking about the man, he had to know, or at least suspect, she knew.

"I don't want to talk about him," he said, a hardness present in his tone.

She didn't push. His tone, coupled with the look of disdain on his face, told her all she needed to know. That they weren't close. Despite being curious, she respected his decision to keep that part of his life private.

Quade's eyes lowered to the floor and stayed there awhile. His tears had dried up, but she could tell he was still hurting. His usually squared and confident shoulders were now slumped. This news had broken him, and it was all her fault.

"I'm sorry," he said, still studying the floor.

Confused, she said, "For what?"

"Dragging you into my drama. Thank you for listening."

Lunden offered a delicate smile. "We're friends, right? And that's what friends do. Listen. Plus, you were there for me when I needed you."

"Finally, you admit you needed me."

She sliced a hand through the air. "*Pssh*. I just said that to make you feel better."

They shared a laugh.

"You know what else friends do?" Lunden said.

"What?"

"They cheer each other up when they're down, so you're coming with me," she said.

"I don't think I'd be very good company."

"You'd be amazed by the healing power of Whac-A-Mole. Plus, you'd absolutely make Zachary's day. For some reason, that kid really likes you. I don't get it."

Quade barked a laugh. "You should go ahead and admit it. I'm growing on you."

Lunden was about to come back with some snarky remark when Quade stood, drying up her words. He continued to talk, but she hadn't heard a word. Why? Because her face was on a level with his crotch. Something naughty captured her brain, and she found herself fantasizing about unbuttoning his pants and pushing them—along with his underwear—over his hips, then taking him inside her mouth. In her head, a chorus of his moans of pleasure played over and over, causing the space between her legs to awaken and her nipples to bead inside her bra.

A reel of him taking her against the wall—delivering long, powerful strokes—played in her head. Shamelessly, and definitely uncharacteristically, she cried out for more. And he gave it to her. She sucked her bottom lip between her teeth and bit down so hard it snapped her back to reality.

"Uh-oh, you're groaning. Are you having second thoughts?" Quade asked.

More like thoughts of seconds, when she shouldn't even be daydreaming about firsts. Damn this man and the things he did to her mind and body. She'd be doggone if he got her soul. Her eyes did a slow crawl up his torso, his bare chest intensifying the ache of need between her legs. "No." Though she should have been. She stood. "You should probably put on a shirt first. Don't want to be cited for indecent exposure." Her gaze trailed downward, then shot up quickly. "Definitely should put on a shirt."

Quade's full lips curled slightly, as if he could sense the desire swirling inside her. She was sure he'd had plenty of practice recognizing the signs. In Charlotte, she bet women constantly threw themselves at him. No doubt he'd caught his fair share of them in both hands.

"I'll wait for you outside. I need to let Rylee know I'm on the way." And to warn the woman not to read anything into it when Quade showed up with her to get Zachary. When she started away, Quade captured her hand.

The sensation that shot up her arm made her gasp. His touch was like a pair of jumper cables and her body a drained battery, now fully recharged because of his handling. The second the two made eye contact, it jump-started a wave of longing inside her. Why did this man have such an effect on her, dammit?

His expression was so gentle and his brown eyes so tender they snatched her breath away. When he pulled her closer to him, she didn't resist. They stood in toe-to-toe silence for what felt like several lifetimes. In actuality, it had been no more than ten seconds or so. Alarm lit her like a firecracker. If he tried to kiss her again, there was no Dover to intervene, and she knew with 100 percent certainty she wouldn't be able to pull away on her own. What made this even more troubling was that the need to feel his mouth against hers was too great to deny.

"Thank you," he finally said.

"You're welcome." Needing to derail this fast-moving, destructive train of lust, she added, "But we'll see how thankful you are when I whoop your ass in air hockey."

Quade arched a brow. "Oh, did you just issue a challenge, Ms. Pierce?"

"Why, yes, I did, Mr. Cannon."

"Competitive, huh?"

"I like to think of it as confident in my abilities."

He studied her. "I accept your challenge, Ms. Pierce, but why don't we make it a little more interesting. Say, a small wager."

Oh, she was going to enjoy taking his money. "I should warn you, I haven't lost an air hockey battle since my senior year of high school."

"Which means it's probably going to hurt twice as much when I slaughter your winning streak."

Lunden arched a brow. *Cocky.* She was going to enjoy taking him down a few notches. "As for this small wager, what did you have in mind? And please make it worth my time and effort."

He crossed his arms over his chest, then massaged his chin in a way that was way too sexy. She had to turn away before the sight of it—along with the way the muscles bulged in his arms—made her melt into a puddle at his feet. "If you win, I'll foot the entire bill for the community pool. Construction to begin immediately."

She'd been under the assumption they'd be playing for $10 or $20, not something that cost over $20,000. And why would he wager something so pricey? Then it hit her. Ms. Jewel had told him about her efforts toward getting a community pool installed. Still, it didn't explain why he would make such an extravagant offer. Unless . . .

Lunden's suspicions kicked into overdrive. Was this an attempt at taking her focus off saving the inn and diverting it toward the pool construction? While her idea of this being some kind of bribe seemed far fetched, Quade was a man, and she didn't put anything past them.

Clearly, he could afford it, or he wouldn't have made the suggestion, right? And it was his money. If he wanted to gamble with it so recklessly, who was she to object? Removing the cost from the budget would certainly make Dick happy. Plus, it would teach Quade a lesson. "That's acceptable," she said. "And if you win, what equally grandiose gift are you proposing for yourself?"

"You."

Since she'd been here before, his declaration didn't faze her. The last time he'd said it, he'd needed her help with the bees. What did he want from her now? Confident in her abilities, she would agree to anything he proposed, because he didn't stand a chance against her at air hockey. Her not-so-guilty pleasure.

She played when she was happy.

She played when she was sad.

She played when she was frustrated.

Had played a lot after her divorce, pretending the puck was her ex-husband and the slot a bubbling trough of lava. Yeah, this probably made her certifiable, but it had brought her such wicked delight.

"Attend the jubilee with me?"

She stood corrected. Agree to *almost* anything. "You're attending the jubilee?" That surprised her, because being social didn't seem to be a priority for him.

He chuckled. "Ms. Jewel. I swear I can't seem to say no to that woman. It's like she works some kind of mind voodoo on me every time."

Yep, that sounded like Ms. Jewel. The woman had a gift for persuading folks to do things they hadn't even been considering. Maybe that was why she and Ms. Shugga had been such good friends. Ms. Shugga had possessed the same powers of persuasion. Uneasy, Lunden shifted her weight from one foot to the other. "You . . . want me to be your . . . *date?*" They didn't even like each other.

Quade became overly fidgety, rubbing the side of his face, his neck, then the length of one arm. "No. No. I know you would never agree to that. Well . . . I guess I kinda am asking that. But not, like, in a romantic way or anything." He gave a shaky laugh.

Lunden bit back her amusement. Quade's behavior reminded her of the first time he'd asked to kiss her when they were young. Despite wanting nothing more, she'd shaken her head, just to see how he would react to being told no, putting into practice one of the many bits of wisdom her father had given her on one of their countless fishing outings: *A boy who respects a girl will respect the word* no *without question.*

Quade had simply eased his hands into his pockets and lowered his head, as if he'd been, in some way, embarrassed that he'd asked. In response, she'd angled her head and pressed her lips to his. Once his visible shock had worn off, he'd rewarded her actions with the most gentle, soul-stirring first kiss imaginable. She'd fallen in love with him in that beautiful moment.

The memory warmed her from the inside out. *God, and to think I almost kissed him in the pool.* No way could she allow his lips to ever touch hers. Just in case.

"So what do you say? Will you be my nondate?" Quade asked.

Standing here waiting for Lunden to respond had Quade's stomach in knots. He couldn't recall the last time he'd felt so anxious. And why? It wasn't like it would be a real date. Lunden would simply be running interference for him. It would be just like they were teammates. Yeah, that was the perfect description. Teammates.

"Why?" she finally said.

"Why what?"

"Why do you need a nondate for the jubilee? Or a date at all, for that matter? Excuse me, *nondate*."

Quade couldn't determine if she was being sarcastic or serious when she emphasized *nondate*. "Because I always end up feeling like a piece of meat at these types of functions. You'll simply be running interference. It'll be like we're teammates." Wow, that had sounded so much better in his head.

"You're an attractive man. Women are drawn to you. *Some* women, I suppose. I mean, I guess," she said, stumbling over her words.

"Well, you're definitely a woman. Are you drawn to me?"

"Absolutely not. You're not my type."

The comfort and ease with which she delivered the words could have convinced someone else of her disinterest. Not him. He'd witnessed the teeny flicker of lust in her eyes every time her gaze crawled over his body, but he understood her need to deny it. It probably mimicked his own. No attachments. Especially one that wouldn't last past his temporary stay in Honey Hill. "Perfect," Quade said. "I won't have to spend all night fighting you off me."

Lunden barked a laugh. "If only you could be so lucky."

"If only," he said nonchalantly. "So shall we shake on it?"

Lunden's gaze lowered, and his followed. Damn. How could he have not realized before now that they were still holding hands? Maybe because touching her felt so natural.

"I think we already have," she said, easing her hand from his. "I'll wait for you outside."

He nodded and watched her walk away. Ten minutes ago, he'd been ready to set fire to the world over all he'd learned; now he was headed to an arcade? It didn't make sense, but he didn't debate it. When they were younger, Lunden had always had a way of distracting him when he'd needed it most. That clearly hadn't changed. And he'd certainly needed to be distracted now.

After volunteering to drive, Quade followed Lunden to her place to park her vehicle. Their next stop was the bakery to pick up Zachary, who'd hung with Rylee while Lunden had been on bee duty. *Those damn bees.* His chest still stung where those tiny bastards had brutalized him.

The look of accusation that shone on Rylee's face when he and Lunden entered together didn't go unnoticed. The unspoken words exchanged between the two told Quade Lunden would have a lot of explaining to do later.

"*Quade!*" Zachary said, appearing from the back, rushing toward him, and hugging his tiny arms around his waist.

Quade wouldn't call himself kid friendly, but he couldn't deny it— he liked this one.

"Hey, what am I, mincemeat?" Lunden said.

Zachary hurried to his mother and gave her an even bigger hug. "I missed you," he said, looking up at Lunden with loving eyes.

"I missed you too," she said, kneeling and squeezing him tight.

Quade loved watching these two together. It reminded him so much of his relationship with his mother at that age. The beautiful memories it brought forth helped to dilute the ugly ones still in the forefront of his mind. He shook off the dismal feelings fighting for his attention. "Z, I hope you don't mind me tagging along with you guys to the arcade."

"We're going to have so much fun," Zachary said, his expression full of elation.

"Um, Lunden. Before you guys leave, I really need to show you something. In the back," Rylee said.

Quade knew that was code for *I need every detail.*

"I'll be right back," Lunden said.

"We'll wait for you in the vehicle," Quade said.

Lunden gave a nod.

By the time Quade and Zachary had made the short walk to the SUV, Zachary had covered fifteen different subjects. After Zachary climbed into the back seat, Quade helped him buckle in, then leaned against the vehicle and waited for Lunden.

"Quade?"

"What's up, little man?"

"Are you and my mom boyfriend and girlfriend?"

Where had that come from? "Um . . . no. We were a long time ago. When we were kids." Why in the hell had he volunteered that? "We're just friends now." For some reason, the distinction made Quade smile a little. They were making progress. While it hadn't been his motivation, maybe forging a friendship would make it easier for Lunden to accept his plans for the inn. Once she realized he wasn't some money-hungry creep, she would actually put her support behind the sale. However, something told him he had a long way to go with convincing her of either.

Zachary's expression dimmed. "Oh." A second later, he added, "Would you be her boyfriend if she wanted you to?"

You're killing me, kid. "I . . . don't think your mom is looking for a boyfriend." And he wasn't looking for a girlfriend.

"I heard her tell my aunt Rylee that sometimes she gets lonely and that maybe she should start dating again."

Quade made a mental note to never say anything he wouldn't want repeated if Zachary was anywhere in the vicinity. This kid was more informative than the nightly news. "Really?" Quade said.

Zachary nodded. "And she also said she was afraid to be hurt again." Zachary flashed a look of confusion. "Does having a boyfriend or girlfriend hurt?"

Quade chuckled. "It can. If you're not careful." *But even when you're careful, it can still mar you.* He could attest to that.

"Like riding a bike," Zachary said. "You can get really hurt if you're not careful."

Kids made things seem so simple. "Something like that," he said.

"I fell off my bike once and skinned my knee. My mom put a Band-Aid on it, and it healed." Zachary looked as if he was processing something in his head. "I know. Maybe if you put a Band-Aid on my mom's hurt, she wouldn't be afraid to date you because you helped her heal."

Stunned speechless, all Quade could do was stare at Zachary. How was he supposed to respond to that? Luckily, he didn't have to, because Lunden now strolled toward them.

"Sorry to keep you two waiting," she said.

"No worries." He opened the door for her, closed it once she was in, then made his way around the vehicle, Zachary's words still ringing in his ears like midday church bells. Curious, he wondered, *What does Lunden need healing from?*

CHAPTER 16

The smell of popcorn and grease greeted them as they entered Glassen's Arcade and Games, making Lunden's stomach growl. She hadn't eaten anything since breakfast. Voices of dozens of excited kids, teens, and adults, along with dings, chimes, and winning bells, filled the air. Like on most Saturdays, the place buzzed. The atmosphere instantly filled Lunden with a childlike giddiness.

Just as Lunden had expected, all eyes settled on them the second they moved through the doors. *This should give them something to talk about for the next week or so.* She shuddered at the thought of how the story would morph into a hundred different versions as it burned its way through town. Ignoring the quizzical stares, Lunden carried on the same way she would have had she been strolling along Main Street—greeting people and donning a vibrant smile.

"Mom, can I go say hello to Mr. Glassen?" Zachary asked.

"Yes," Lunden said.

A second later, Zachary took off.

"Mr. Glassen owns the arcade. Zachary likes him because he always sneaks him chocolate," she explained to Quade.

"Um, why is everyone staring at us?" Quade asked.

"Because they're trying to decide whether we're just friends or if we're sleeping together." Of course, they would automatically jump to the latter. As long as she knew the truth.

Quade's head snapped back in surprise. "Wow. Okay." He washed a hand over his head. "So are you okay with being here with me? I don't want to make things uncomfortable for you."

Lunden found Quade's consideration refreshing. She wasn't used to a man actually putting her comfort before his own. She folded her arms across her chest. "Sounds to me, Mr. Cannon, that you're attempting to weasel your way out of our deal. You scared?"

"Woman, I ain't never scared. Let's grab a table."

They settled into one of the few available booths situated around the perimeter of the large room. Sarah Jane, a redhead with a face full of freckles, took their food and beverage orders, then ambled off.

Quade scrutinized the room. "This place looks nothing like I remember."

"A lot can change in twenty years."

Quade tilted his head slightly and eyed her in the most peculiar way. "Yes, it can."

"About today . . . I know it was rough. Are you okay?"

"You made it bearable."

Unfortunately, she'd also been the one who'd made it uncomfortable. "Anytime you want or need to talk—"

"You're here to listen?" he said, finishing her thought.

"Actually, I was going to say the pastor's door is always open, but I guess I can leave mine cracked for you." Playfully, she rolled her eyes heavenward. "That would be the godly thing to do, right?"

Quade chuckled. "That's cold."

"I'm kidding. I'm kidding. Seriously, if you need to talk . . . I'm here."

"Thank you, Lunden. That means a lot."

For a long, draining moment, their gazes locked tight. When Quade's eyes lowered to her mouth in a slow, steady manner, a warming sensation blossomed in her cheeks and traveled down her entire body. "So w-what—" She paused and cleared her throat. "What are your plans after Honey Hill? Will you return to Charlotte? I know you must be homesick." Really, all she wanted to discuss was the inn, all the reasons he shouldn't sell, but she decided to shift her train of thought. At least for today. Tomorrow would be a different story.

Quade's gaze returned to her as he rested his forearms on the table and interlocked his fingers. His shoulders slumped a bit as if something had deflated him. "Truthfully, I don't know." A perplexed expression distorted his features. "Have you ever felt like you were supposed to do something but had no idea what? Like there was a journey you were supposed to be on, yet you had no idea where you were headed or why?"

Lunden nodded. "Yes, I have." Her journey had led her here, to Honey Hill, and she'd never been happier. She chose to keep that to herself, because she didn't want Quade thinking she was trying to sway him.

"What did you do?"

"I got quiet and listened," she said. Advice Ms. Shugga had given her. Quade looked as if her answer stunned him. Regardless of what he probably thought, she was capable of listening. When she wanted to, of course.

"Did it help?"

"Yes."

Sarah Jane returned with their drinks, informed them the kitchen was running behind, then moved away.

"So there's no one waiting for you back in Charlotte?" Lunden took a long swig from her Mason jar filled with sweet tea, chastising herself for asking something so personal. But since she'd be working alongside him, wasn't it her right to know whether some jealous girlfriend could potentially show up at her door?

"Not anymore," he said, his eyes stern on hers.

"What happened?"

"I did," he said.

Lunden pushed her brows together. "What does that mean?"

"She cheated. I would love to place all the blame on her, but honestly, I have to shoulder some of it."

Confused, Lunden said, "How are you in any part responsible for a bad decision she chose to make?" She accepted absolutely none of the blame for her ex-husband's philandering. It had been a choice he'd made over, over, and over again, not one she'd led him to. She'd been a good wife. Scratch that. She'd been a *great* wife.

"I buried myself in my work. Neglected her, our relationship. Apparently, she needed more than I gave and found it in someone else's arms."

"I'm sorry."

"Why? It wasn't your fault. You didn't make me a workaholic or her cheat."

True. "Are you still a workaholic?" she asked, taking another sip from her glass.

Quade barked a laugh. "I don't even have a job, so no."

Lunden choked on her tea and coughed ferociously. Recovering, she said, "You're unemployed?" not bothering to mask the shock in her voice. How did he plan to pay for a pool, with good intentions? Was this why he was so determined to off-load the inn? He needed the money?

A part of her softened a little. She understood struggle all too well. She'd arrived in Honey Hill with a toddler on her hip and the clothes on her back. Nothing else. Not even hope, because she couldn't even afford that. If it hadn't been for Ms. Shugga and the inn . . . well, her life would be much different now.

Ms. Shugga had built him up to be this great success. Had it all been a lie? Quade certainly played the part well. Luxury vehicle. Fancy clothing. But was it all just for show? Plagued with questions, all she could do was stare at him. Hadn't he been a big shot corporate man back in Charlotte? Had he drunk or gambled all his money away? Blown it on a lavish lifestyle and expensive women? Lunden just couldn't figure it out. Especially the part where a man with no job would offer to pay for a pool he probably couldn't even afford.

Quade wanted to laugh at the expression on Lunden's face. Did she have any idea how easy she was to read? Right now, she was wondering how in the hell he would pay for a pool without a job. Did he tell her he was far from destitute? *Nah.* "Maybe I can get a job in town. Do you know anyone who's hiring?"

Lunden jerked as if she'd been deep in thought. "Um . . . yeah. Yes. Mr. Conroy at the sign shop is looking for someone to help around the place. I believe it's only part time, though."

That was perfect. He'd needed a reason to connect with the man. Now he had one. "Sounds good. I'll check it out."

Zachary bounded toward the table. "*Quade! Quade!* Do you wanna shoot some hoops with me?" he asked, bouncing up and down with excitement.

"Heck yeah," Quade said, sliding from the booth.

"You can come, too, Mom, if you want."

Lunden smiled softly. "No, you two go ahead. I'll call you once the pizza arrives."

"Can I have some money for tokens?"

"I got it," Quade said, resting his hands on Zachary's shoulders.

"You don't have to do that," Lunden said, fishing inside her purse for her wallet.

"I insist," he said, moving away before she could mount a protest.

Quade passed Zachary one of the plastic buckets sitting atop the token machine, directed him to place it under the chute, then inserted a hundred-dollar bill into the slot. Zachary's eyes marveled at the number of coins being deposited into the pail. On their way to the hoop machine, they stopped to play several games.

First, Whac-A-Mole. Lunden had been right: this was a great stress reducer. From there, they ventured to the Skee-Ball machines. Lastly, a dancing game that Zachary was insanely good at. Quade, not so much. The multicolored flashing floor threw him off. That and the fact he wasn't the best at dancing; however, oddly, he liked to do so.

"You'll get better with practice," Zachary said as he stuffed a rope of tickets the machine had spit out into his pockets. "My mom's not that good either. She's better than you, though. So is my aunt Rylee. My friend Benjamin is better than you too."

As they moved toward the hoop game, Zachary listed several more people who were better at the dancing game than Quade.

"Is there anyone in town I'm better than?"

Zachary appeared to be contemplating the question. "Arielle."

Finally.

"But she's only one and doesn't really know how to dance yet. But she'll probably be better than you too," he said, then burst into laughter.

Quade jostled him playfully. "You've got jokes, huh?"

Zachary laughed some more.

"Okay, kid, let's see whatcha got," Quade said, inserting tokens into the machine.

Quade's head snapped back when Zachary made more than half of the shots he took. While Quade could have easily made all his shots, he chose to give Zachary the win. Zachary jumped up and down and spun around. For a second, Quade thought he would drop into a split like James Brown.

"Can we play again?" Zachary asked, hope shiny in his eyes.

"Of course."

Quade happened to glance over at their table to see Lunden chatting with an impeccably dressed, tall, caramel-toned man. When Lunden tossed her head back in laughter, he wondered what had been so funny. Was that a pang of jealousy he'd felt? Nah, because that wouldn't make sense.

"It's your turn," Zachary said.

Pulling his attention away from Lunden, he squared up for his shot. "Who's the man your mother's talking to?" he asked nonchalantly.

Zachary glanced across the room. "Oh, that's her husband."

"Her what?" Quade said, simultaneously releasing the ball and turning toward Zachary.

Things moved in slow motion. From Zachary's eyes widening in shock—or fear—to him covering his head and yelling, "Duck!" to Quade blindly facing forward and getting clobbered square in the nose by the rogue basketball that had apparently bounced off the rim.

He grabbed his nose, then winced from the pain. *"Shit!"* he said far louder than intended, drawing the attention of half the room. *"Oooh,* he said a bad word," came from somewhere near him. Quade saw stars as he pulled his hand away to see his fingers covered in blood. It made him queasy. He managed to focus on Lunden, who now stood in front of him, pushing napkins to his nose.

"He's okay," Lunden said, responding to the numerous questions of concern. His head swam as she led him to their booth.

"You know, if you were afraid to play me, you could have just said that. This was a bit much, don't you think?" she said.

"I would laugh if it didn't feel like my face was about to slide off."

"Yeah, that tends to happen when you use it to stop a basketball."

"Quade, are you okay?" Zachary asked in a tiny voice.

"I'm good, little man."

"What happened?" Lunden asked.

"I took my eye off the ball." *When Zachary told me you were talking to your husband.* But he kept that part to himself. This was what happened when you attended to other people's business.

When he slid into the booth, Lunden instructed him to lean forward and pinch his nostrils shut. It hurt like hell, but he did so.

"Let me take a look."

Quade glanced up to see a plump older gentleman with salt-and-pepper hair, tawny skin, shiny black glasses, and a smile bright enough to eclipse the sun.

"I'm Doc Vickers," he said. "Bet you thought I was some crazy person trying to play around with your nose, didn't you?" He gave a hearty laugh that tickled Quade.

"Quade Cannon."

"Oh, I know who you are. Everyone in town knows who you are," Doc Vickers said.

"Doc's the best practitioner in the county," Lunden said, giving the man an affectionate smile.

Had he been Aunt Shugga's doctor? No, she'd probably had a specialist. But maybe he'd diagnosed her. "It's nice to meet you," Quade said.

Dr. Vickers cupped Quade's chin and turned his head to the left, to the right, then smiled. "Having difficulty breathing?"

"No."

"Good. Well, it's not broken, but you're going to have some wicked soreness, bruising, and probably swelling tomorrow. Take a couple of pain relievers and ice it for up to ten minutes every one to two hours or so. You should be back to new in no time. However, if you experience a headache, confusion, dizziness, ringing in your ears, nausea, vomiting, slurred speech, head to the hospital. You could have a concussion."

Dr. Vickers sounded like one of those new drug commercials where the side effects seemed to outweigh the benefits. "Thank you, Doctor," Quade said.

"Just call me Doc. Everyone else does," he said, then moved away.

"I'm sorry you got hurt, Quade," Zachary said, a pitiful look on his face.

"It's not your fault, Z. I'm sorry I ruined your day at the arcade."

Zachary grinned. "You didn't."

Lunden washed a hand over Zachary's head. "Kiddo, you can play some more until the pizza comes if you want."

"Are you coming, Quade?" Zachary asked.

"I think I'm going to sit this one out, but go and have fun with your friends. You have a ton of tokens to use."

"I'll win a lot of tickets so I can get you and my mom a prize."

"Sounds good to me," Quade said, then held out his hand for Zachary to smack.

"Be careful," Lunden said as Zachary darted off.

"Okay, Mom," he called back.

Lunden slid in across from him. "Seriously, are you okay? You can leave if you want. Zachary and I can walk home. It's not that far."

"Come on, now. Do you really think I'm going to allow you two to *walk* home?" Quade said, checking the napkin to make sure his nose had stopped bleeding. "Plus, we still have some unfinished business, remember? Give me a few minutes and I'll be good. Unless you're trying to back out. In which case you forfeit and I win."

"Fine."

"Fine, what?"

"I forfeit."

Quade narrowed his eyes on her. "Why?"

"You've already been brutalized once. It feels wrong to put you through that a second time. You've had enough excitement for one day, don't you think?"

Yes, he did. Something told him her forfeiting had less to do with his injury or hard day and more to do with the fact she thought he couldn't hold up his end of the deal. The imaginary angel perched on his shoulder urged him to come clean, but that little devil flew over from his opposite shoulder, drop-kicked it off, and persuaded him to keep quiet, because he wasn't to blame for her assumptions. Made sense.

Still, he didn't feel 100 percent comfortable with the deception. For his peace of mind and to balance things, he said, "Under one condition."

"Which is?"

"You have Z's birthday party at the inn. I know he really wants a pool party, and I have a pool. Friends help friends out, right?"

Lunden tilted her head and studied him. "I take it you haven't been around many kids."

Quade pushed his brows together. He hadn't, but her assessment made him curious. "Why do you ask?"

"Because anyone who had would not invite dozens of sugar-high kids into their home. But condition accepted," she said.

The evil grin that spread across her face made him nervous. Maybe he should have reconsidered the invitation, but this was for his main man. So he was willing to sacrifice his sanity for a few hours to make the kid happy. How bad could a roomful of six-year-olds actually be? Besides, he had several weeks to prepare.

CHAPTER 17

After all the excitement, buzzing, ringing, dinging, and banging at the arcade, Lunden needed time alone. While she loved to be around people, she also loved moments like these. Lounging on her deck, a mug of hot orange-passionfruit-jasmine green tea in hand, with nothing but the sounds of nature. Staring off into the darkness, she marveled at the fireflies lighting her backyard. It brought back memories of her youth.

A euphoric feeling washed over her as she recalled how she and Quade used to lie in the meadow and watch as hundreds of lightning bugs floated around them. *What in the heck was I thinking, lying on the ground with spiders, snakes, and only God knows what else?* She laughed at her foolishness. Youth made you so naive. There was absolutely no way in hell she would do anything like that today. Honestly, she kind of missed that girl.

The one who'd tossed caution to the wind.

The one who'd lain in fields with bugs.

The one who hadn't been afraid to live life to the fullest.

In her defense, she was a mother now, which required her to be mindful of her actions. Granted, these days she took mindfulness to the extreme, to the point of being boring. *I'm boring.* When had this happened?

By no means could she have ever been considered the life of the party, but she hadn't exactly been a wallflower either. Until now. Maybe she needed a little recklessness in her life. Something to jump-start her stagnant existence. Or someone. She balked at the image of Quade that flashed in her head. "Nope. Absolutely not," she mumbled to the part of her brain that had apparently thought putting him there had been a good idea.

"Mom?"

Zachary's tender voice sounded behind her. "Hey, sweetie. Everything okay?"

"I can't sleep," he said, climbing into her lap.

As hard as he'd played at the arcade, he should have been dog tired. Apparently, the five-minute catnap he'd gotten as Quade had driven them home from the arcade had recharged him. It always brought her joy when he nestled in her lap like this and rested his head on her shoulder. If he could only stay this size forever. "Did you have fun tonight?"

"I had the best time. I like Quade. He's fun."

"He likes you too."

"Mom?"

Uh-oh. If history was any indication, Zachary was about to ask a question suited for someone well beyond his six years. Odds were she'd have to research it and get back to him. The kid asked the darnedest things. He was so intuitive for his age. *An old soul,* Ms. Shugga had always said, then praised her for raising such a sharp-witted young man. "Yes?"

"When I asked Quade if you were boyfriend and girlfriend, he said you used to be. Why did you break up?"

The air seized in Lunden's lungs. *Oh God. He asked Quade what?* "Why did you ask Quade if we were boyfriend and girlfriend?"

Zachary giggled. "I don't know."

"You don't know, huh?" She tickled him, and he laughed uncontrollably. Settling, she hugged him to her chest. "Quade used to come to visit Ms. Shugga every summer. One summer, he stopped coming."

"Did he call you and break up?"

"No."

"Did he write you a letter?"

Again, she said, "No."

Zachary glanced up at her, his tiny face a ball of confusion. "If he didn't call you or write you a letter, that means you're still boyfriend and girlfriend."

Lunden laughed. "It doesn't work quite like that, son. You'll understand when you're older and you get a girlfriend."

"Girls. Ew, yuck!"

"Hey, I'm a girl," Lunden said.

"You're my mom."

"Yes, I am." She stared into his innocent eyes. Sliding her finger down his nose, she said, "I love you more than anything in this world."

"I know, and I love you too. *This* much." He spread his tiny arms as far apart as he could.

Maybe she'd made some bad decisions and some wrong turns in her life, but she'd gotten it right with Zachary. "Are you excited about your birthday?"

He nodded rapidly. "Yeah, yeah, yeah."

"Guess what?"

"What?"

"You're having a pool party." She pretended to cheer.

His eyes widened with excitement. "I am?"

Lunden nodded. "Quade's letting us use the pool at the inn."

"Quade's the *best*. Can I call him to say thank you?"

"It's late. He's probably asleep now. And you should be too," she said, slapping his thigh. Maybe she would check in on him tomorrow. A call, of course. It was the least she could do, since she was the reason he'd been at the arcade. Oh, he was going to hate her tomorrow. Who nearly knocked themselves out playing indoor arcade basketball? "Peanut?"

"Mom," he dragged out. "I'm almost seven. I'm too old for that kiddie name."

Said the almost-seven-year-old curled up in her lap. She flashed a sad face.

"Okay, you can call me peanut, but not in front of people, okay?"

"Fine. I'll call you Zachary Chandler Griggs."

"You only say my name like that when I'm in trouble," he said.

True.

"Mom, why don't we have the same last name?"

"Well, after your father and I divorced, I decided to go back to my maiden name. My name before I married your father," she said for clarity.

"Can I go back to my maiden name?" Zachary asked.

Lunden chuckled. "Sweetie, you don't have a maiden name."

"I want your same last name."

"Why?"

"Just because. Can I?"

"We'll see."

Zachary slapped his small hand across his forehead. "Oh boy. That means no."

She laughed. "It does not." But probably. His father would have to sign off on the change, and she had no desire to wage that war. He'd actually pitched a fit when she'd changed her name. She could only imagine his reaction if she told him she was changing Zachary's. Not because he truly cared but because it would, somehow, be a slap to his ego. On the other hand, he might not care at all. It wasn't like he was all that present in their son's life, which was a-okay with her. "Okay, my big boy, what do you want me to call you?"

His face lit up. "Z."

"Let me guess, because Quade calls you Z?"

"Yes. But it's also cool."

"Yes, it is. Just like you."

"You are too. The coolest mom *ever*."

Oh, he knew how to make her feel special. Out of the blue, Lunden recalled Zachary apologizing to Quade at the arcade. "Son, how did the ball hit Quade?" The last time they'd visited the arcade, Zachary and one of his little friends had knocked over a pitcher of soda, clowning around with the balls. Had Zachary tossed the ball at Quade and Quade was covering for him?

Zachary shrugged. "I don't know. He wasn't paying attention, I guess. He asked who you were talking to. When I said your husband—"

Lunden pushed her brows together. "My husband?"

"Mr. Obi. I heard Aunt Rylee call him your work husband."

Ah, now it makes sense. Jutsen Obi was like her work husband. Anytime she needed help moving something, figuring out her PC, or killing a bug, she called Jutsen, the town's IT guru.

Zachary continued, "When I told Quade he was your husband, his head whipped around really fast, and his eyes got really big. Like plates. And then the ball said *bam*"—he smacked his hands together, startling her—"right upside his face. And then he cursed really loud. And then you came running really fast."

Lunden bit back her laughter. Her son was nothing if not animated. "Oh," was all she said, too tickled to say anything else. She could see how that could have taken Quade by surprise. There she was with him—but not exactly with him, she clarified to herself—yet talking to her quote-unquote husband. Yeah, she bet that had been a shocker. But had he really thought she'd be out and about with him if she had a spouse? Why hadn't he asked her about Jutsen? *Because he doesn't care, silly.* And why should he?

Zachary lowered his head back to her shoulder. "Mom?"

"Yes, son."

"Was Quade supposed to be my dad?"

The inquiry took her by surprise. Where in the hell had that come from? And why did this kid keep coming up with this stuff? Still, she pondered the question. At fifteen, she'd held no doubt Quade was the person with whom she was destined to spend her life. He'd witnessed her flaws, vulnerabilities, insecurities. Yet he'd loved her still.

For a long time, she'd held on to the possibility of their finding their way back to each other, until the chance of its happening no longer seemed plausible. She'd done the one thing her mother had always cautioned her against. She'd lost hope. In the process, she'd lost a piece of herself, too, because at one point Quade had been everything to her.

"So was he, Mom?" Zachary asked.

"Yes," she whispered, the word gliding off her tongue as if it were covered in oil.

"I knew it."

Lunden felt Zachary smile against her chest, but she frowned. In that moment, she was forced to face an uncomfortable truth. A teeny part of her still felt . . . *something* for Quade. Not enough of it to damn herself, but just enough to rattle her a bit and caution her to be careful.

Quade was jolted from the best dream he'd ever had in his life when his cell phone bubbled—as he described it—indicating an incoming video call. Only one person used this method of communication with him. *Pryor.* The man always had the worst timing. This moment was no exception.

Quade placed a hand between his legs to adjust himself. The painful erection told him just how into the dream he'd been. It had been so real, in fact, he swore the taste of Lunden's essence still lingered on his lips. Every delicious drop of her he'd managed to claim before being rudely snatched from their artificial encounter.

No doubt the dream had been prompted by the considerable amount of time they'd spent together the day before. The bees. The arcade. They'd been intimately close on both occasions. His dick throbbed as he remembered how Lunden's fingers had glided ever so gently across his chest as she'd tended to his stings. Then there had been the delicate care she'd taken with him at the arcade when he'd gone a round with the basketball. *A lover's touch.* He chastised himself for the foolish thought. *A mother's touch* was more accurate.

"It's nine a.m. on a Sunday morning, Pryor. This had better be good." Quade winced from the pain he felt from moving his mouth. Next time, he'd mind his own damn business. Why had it even mattered who Lunden had been chatting with, anyway? He had no stake in her personal life. A second later, his brain shifted gears. Why had Zachary called the man Lunden's husband? Curiosity ravaged his thoughts.

"What in the *hell* happened to your face?" Pryor said, squinting at the screen and practically yelling through the phone.

Quade snapped back to reality. Making the image of himself larger on the screen, he flinched at the sight. "Shit."

Discoloration spread across the bridge of his nose and partially under his left eye. Luckily, there wasn't much swelling he could see.

"Okay, who whooped your ass and why? And please don't tell me it was over a woman."

Quade couldn't fault Pryor for his suspicions, because it most definitely looked as if he'd been in a brawl. "Spalding," Quade said. "Or it could have been Wilson. I'm not sure."

"Oh, hell no. They jumped you? I'm on my way to Honey Hill right now."

Quade appreciated his friend's dedication. Obviously, it hadn't registered to Pryor that these were names of basketball brands. "No one jumped me. It was an accident with a rogue basketball. But by all means, please come. I could use a familiar face."

"Small-town living weighing on you already? You need a distraction to help the time pass."

"I agree. I'm going to get a job."

"Well, that's one way, but not exactly what I had in mind."

If he knew Pryor—and he did—sex was what his friend was thinking of. "Weren't you the one who told me if I slept with someone here, all the town would know?"

"Yes, but surely Honey Hill has at least one or three women capable of discretion. What about the mayor? Politicians are good at harboring secrets. Plus, you two have history."

Quade barked a laugh, then regretted the painful move. He could see it now, proposing a no-strings-attached relationship to Lunden, simply because they had history. Their history was why such a thing would be a horrible idea. To this day, he'd never experienced the same intimate satisfaction with any woman that he'd experienced with Lunden. Something about that made him even more standoffish when it came to Lunden in that way. In theory, it could be the ideal arrangement, because they'd established early on that neither of them was having sex; unfortunately, bedding Lunden didn't align with his goals, and bedding him probably didn't align with hers either.

Arguably, his face now was probably nothing compared to what it would look like if he were foolish enough to even suggest such an arrangement to her. He already suspected it was taking all she had to be as kind to him as she was currently being. He pushed his brows together. A little too kind, if he thought about it. Which, in his experience, always meant one thing . . . "The mayor's up to something," he said. A second later, he brushed his words off. "Or maybe I'm just being paranoid," he added, despite believing the opposite. But it was possible. God knew he had the right to be suspicious of any woman in his life. *But Lunden is not exactly in my life,* he reminded himself.

"We both know your gut never lies," Pryor said. "It's kind of spooky. So what do you think she's up to?"

Quade shook his head. "I'm not sure. But whatever it is, it has everything to do with the inn." *That*, he was 110 percent sure of.

"What are you going to do?"

Quade pondered the question a moment. "Keep her close." The strategy he'd use for any enemy. Only Lunden didn't quite feel like a foe. More like . . . a complication. One who continuously worked her way into his dreams.

CHAPTER 18

After convincing her they should visit Quade instead of calling him, Zachary practically dragged Lunden to the front door of the inn. Since they had been out and about anyway, it hadn't been a big deal. Zachary had seemed overly eager to come here, which made her wonder whether she should be concerned with Zachary's fascination with Quade. What would happen when Quade left Honey Hill? She seriously doubted the man would return to visit. For whatever reason, Zachary obviously held an attachment to him. One that appeared to be growing.

Lunden halted Zachary, then knelt to eye level with him. "Hey. You do know that Quade's only in town for a little while, right? That he'll be leaving eventually and not coming back?"

"I know. But we have to make him feel at home while he's here. That's what Ms. Shugga would have done. She always said to make people feel at home."

Well, she couldn't argue with that, could she? "I can tell you really like him. I just don't want you to be sad when he leaves."

"I won't be, Mom." He tugged at her hand. "Come on."

"Okay, okay. In and out, remember? We have to get to the strawberry patch before it gets packed."

"Okay."

Zachary rang the doorbell, and they waited for Quade to answer. Lunden turned toward the road when a horn honked.

"Afternoon, Mayor," came from the passing vehicle.

Great, Lunden thought, tossing her hand up to wave at Minnie Dempsey, head of the usher board at church. It was one thirty now. By two fifteen, half the town would know she'd been spotted on Quade's doorstep. One would think with her being the mayor, she'd be shielded from town gossip. Unfortunately, that wasn't the case. Oftentimes, it seemed she became more susceptible to it.

"Hey, Qu—*whoa!*"

Hearing the uncertainty in Zachary's voice made Lunden turn away from the road. *"Whoa!"* she said, echoing Zachary. "I mean, um . . ." She bit at the corner of her lip. It looked like Quade had been on the losing end of a bar brawl.

Quade chuckled. "Don't worry. I already know it looks bad."

"It's . . . not *that* bad," she said, massaging the space between her neck and shoulder. It was bad. Real bad. Like, the kind of bad where he should have been somewhere lying down with a bag of frozen peas on his face.

Quade stepped aside and allowed them to enter. When Lunden passed, he leaned in close and whispered, "You're a horrible liar," in her ear.

The feel of his warm breath against her neck made her shiver. Well, he had her there. For a politician, she sucked at stretching the truth. However, she was capable of telling a humdinger when absolutely necessary.

"I think you look cool, Quade," Zachary said. "Like a superhero who's been in a fight with the bad guy. It looks like you lost, though. But that's okay. My mom says losing builds carrier."

Lunden bit back her laughter at Zachary's pep talk.

Quade washed a hand over Zachary's head. "Your mom's right. It does build *carrier.* Is she always so smart?"

Zachary nodded.

When Quade eyed her and winked, she found something about the move ultrasexy, despite his jacked-up appearance. "I hope we're not intruding. Zachary wanted to stop by and personally thank you for allowing us to use your pool for his birthday party."

"Yeah. Thank you, Quade." Zachary wrapped his arms around him. "You're awesome."

"So are you, kid."

"We're on the way to pick strawberries," Zachary said. "Do you want to come? Can he, Mom?"

Lunden froze from the shock of Zachary's totally unexpected invite. Now she knew why he'd been so eager to come here instead of calling. Oh, he was slick. He definitely had some of his father in him. Honestly, she should have suspected he would invite Quade to join them. They were best buds, after all. At least according to the two of them.

Quade didn't strike her as someone who was the least bit interested in strawberry picking, which told her he would only be willing to tag along for Zachary's benefit. Her gaze lowered to Zachary's glowing face. "I'm sure Quade wants to rest."

"Actually," Quade said, "I could use some fresh air. Give me a minute."

Good Lord. With the amount of time they were spending together, you would think they were sleeping together. When Quade disappeared up the stairs, Lunden eyed a visibly thrilled Zachary. Lowering her voice, she said, "Why did you invite him?"

"Because he's lonely," Zachary said.

Lonely? What would make Zachary say that? Before she could inquire any further, Quade descended the stairs, wearing a dark-green ball cap that shadowed his features. The hat matched his shirt in the same shade. Dark jeans and dark-brown high-top sneakers completed his outfit. Some men could wear anything and still look enticing. *Nope, not enticing. Not enticing at all.* More like a thorn in her side.

"We should get going," Lunden said.

"Can we take Josie?" Zachary asked.

Josie? Who is Josie?

"Sure. If your mom says it's okay," Quade said.

Obviously, she was the only one in the dark about this Josie character. "Who's Josie?" she asked, looking from Quade to Zachary.

Zachary and Quade eyed each other, then laughed as if they'd both been told a joke.

"What's so funny?"

"Josie is Quade's car," Zachary said.

Of course he would name his vehicle. She rested her hands on her hips. "And what's wrong with my car?"

"It's kinda small, Mom," Zachary said.

"Yeah, and I'm kinda big," Quade added.

Seriously, she made an effort at keeping her thoughts PG-13, but she failed miserably. Based on what she'd seen of Quade in his swim trunks, *big* was a perfect descriptor. *Jesus.* What was wrong with her? She morphed into a horny adolescent anytime she got near this man. Retraining her thoughts, she parted her lips to protest Quade driving, but when she considered the strawberry patch was an hour's drive away, she clammed up. It would feel good to be a passenger. "Well, since I'm outnumbered"—she sighed for effect—"I guess Josie it is."

Lunden had to admit Quade's vehicle was a lot more comfortable than hers. She eyed him as he slid behind the wheel. "Are you sure you're okay to drive? I can drive, if you like. I'm sure I can handle Josie."

"I'm good. Plus, nobody drives Josie but me," he said.

"Fair enough."

An hour later, they arrived at Hobgood's Strawberry Farm. As usual, the parking lot teemed with vehicles. Quade whipped Josie into the first available space they spotted. The way he maneuvered the oversize vehicle into the tight spot was impressive.

The scent of peppers and onions greeted her the second she stepped out of the vehicle, causing her stomach to growl. Luckily, it couldn't be heard over the sounds of the passing cars. She couldn't wait to sink her teeth into an italian-sausage hoagie, an ear of corn, and possibly a turkey leg. And she planned to wash it all down with a huge lemonade. Poor Quade. He'd have to watch her eat it all, because she seriously doubted he would eat here.

They lucked out and scored one of the stone picnic tables closest to the play area.

"Mom, can I go to the playground?"

"Don't you want to eat first?"

"I'll eat later," he said, bouncing up and down with excitement.

"What are the rules?"

Using his fingers, he ticked them off one by one. "Don't talk to strangers. Play nice with others. Stay where I can see you and you can see me. And let you know if anyone bothers me."

"Perfect," Lunden said. "Have fun. And try not to get too dirty."

"Yes, ma'am. I'll see you in a little bit, okay, Quade?"

"Okay. Be careful, little man," Quade said.

"I will," Zachary said, taking off. Once he made it to the play area, he looked back and waved.

Both Lunden and Quade waved back.

Quade clapped his hands together. "Well, I'm starving. Let's eat."

"Wait. You're going to eat here?" Lunden questioned, her brows knitting.

"Don't look so shocked. Besides, they have a score of one hundred and one. That's like an A-plus. It was the first thing I scoped out."

"Of course it was," she said. "You are a unique bird, Mr. Cannon."

"Thank you. Now, what can I get you?"

Lunden reached into her purse and pulled out a fifty-dollar bill. "How about you tell me what you want, and I'll get for you this time," she said.

Quade massaged the side of his face as if he'd been slapped. "Put your money away. I got it."

"Fine." She eased down. "Then I don't want anything," she said.

Quade eyed her a moment. "So you're telling me if I come back with an italian-sausage dog, a turkey leg, fries, corn, nachos, you're not going to eat any of it?"

"Nope." Her stomach growled, even louder this time. She hadn't eaten since breakfast and had skipped out on the meal they served after church because she'd planned to stuff her face here. Now her stubbornness had pinned her in a corner.

"You really do like getting your way, don't you?" Quade said. He shook his head. "Fine." Plucking the fifty from her fingers, he said, "What do you want, woman?"

After she'd happily rattled off her order, Quade started away but stopped. Backtracking, he rested his hand atop the table, then leaned in as if he were about to kiss her. Her heart skipped a beat, and the air seized in her lungs. But instead of planting his soft lips against hers, he positioned them close to her ear.

"For the record, you're not going to always get your way," he whispered.

Their mouths were so close when he pulled away that if she had breathed, their lips would have grazed. When he moved away, she swallowed hard, then blew out a long, steady breath to regulate her overheating system.

As Lunden waited for Quade to return, she surveyed her surroundings, homing in on a young woman sitting several tables away. Lunden followed her focus right to Quade. The woman ogled him as if he were a perfectly roasted turkey at Thanksgiving dinner. She gobbled him up with her eyes. A second later, she said something to the other ladies at the table, and they all shifted their attention in his direction. The way another one of the captivated women gyrated in her seat suggested the comments being made were sexual in nature.

Lunden's gaze slid back to Quade. His long, sturdy legs were slightly apart, and his strong arms crossed his chest. The man dripped with confidence. She could understand their fascination. Who wouldn't appreciate a specimen like that?

While he might have been a nuisance, he was surely something nice to look at, even if she couldn't touch. Back in the day, when he was a younger, shorter, skinnier, big-eared version of his current self, she'd still found him attractive. Some things never changed, but it was a good thing others did. Like her schoolgirl infatuation with him, which definitely no longer existed.

She allowed her harmless appreciation to linger on him a moment longer, her inquisitive eyes raking over him. She bet he was amazing in bed. Those sculpted arms holding on tight. Those large hands touching all the right places. Those delicious-looking lips kissing all the perfect spots. That mouth exploring every heated inch. Yeah, she was convinced he could deliver a woman massive pleasure.

The gobbler who'd been gawking at Quade approached him, snapping Lunden out of her lustful stupor. The big-breasted woman looked as if her thin frame would topple over if a strong wind blew through. Too bad they were experiencing calm weather. Undoubtedly, the bold woman had seen them arrive together. Yet there she stood, approaching a man who, for all she knew, was there with his significant other. *Trifling.*

Lunden continued to watch the unfolding scene. The strawberry redhead tilted her head slightly, smiled, and twirled a lock of hair around her finger, batting those ridiculously long fake lashes as if she had something in her eyes. *Pathetic.*

Granted, it had been a long time since Lunden had flirted with a man, so no doubt she was out of practice, but was this how women were doing it nowadays? When Quade said something to her, Lunden perked her ears as if doing so would allow her to hear the conversation taking place between them. Not that she truly cared.

Feeling the heat of eyes on her, she turned to see the gobbler's friends eyeing her, smirks etched on their heavily made-up faces. *Ah.* So making her jealous had been their plan. Youthful ignorance. *Too bad, ladies.* She definitely wouldn't get jealous over a man who wasn't hers. Lunden waved, turning their faces to stone. Obviously, it hadn't been the reaction they'd been expecting. Her days of fighting over a man had ended with her divorce. The only people she fought for now were Zachary, herself, and the residents of Honey Hill.

Ignoring them all, she turned her attention to the playground. Zachary pushed a little girl with bouncy afro puffs on the swing. *So much for "ew, girls."* A tiny smile touched her face as Ms. Shugga's voice played in her head. *That one is going to break a lot of hearts,* she'd said. Lunden hoped not. She was determined to raise her son to treat women right.

No sooner did she have the thought, another little girl with long, swinging braids tapped Zachary on the shoulder, said something to him, then took off running. A beat later, he took off after her. Afro Puffs didn't appear too pleased with losing her swing pusher; however, her annoyance didn't last long, as another little fellow took Zachary's place and her elation returned. Oh, if adult life were that simple.

"Miss me?" Quade asked, rejoining her at the table.

Lunden pushed her brows together. "Oh, you were gone?"

"Ouch."

Quade placed the overflowing tray of food down, then lowered himself down next to her. Practically so close their thighs touched, warming her entire right side. With all the available space at the table, why did he have to sit so near? And why did he have to smell so damn good?

"I see you met a new friend," she said, regretting the words as soon as they'd escaped her mouth. By no means had she wanted him to think she'd been watching them. Even if she had been.

"Ah. Jessica," Quade said. He eyed Lunden. "Jealous?"

"*Ha!* Of Jessica Rabbit?"

Quade's brow furrowed. "Jessica Rabbit?"

"*Who Framed Roger Rabbit.* The movie." When he continued to wear a confused expression, she said, "Don't tell me you've never watched *Who Framed Roger Rabbit.*"

He shook his head.

"That's sad. Well, maybe you and *Jessica* can watch it together. She looks like she might be into animation." Okay, so now she was sounding a little jealous. To divert the conversation, she said, "This italian sausage looks amazing. Plenty of onion. Just like I like it."

"She asked if we were dating," Quade said nonchalantly, freeing his foil-wrapped turkey leg.

Lunden briefly eyed the malicious women, who, surprisingly, no longer seemed interested in them. "I bet she was extremely happy when you told her no." Though she kind of wished he'd said yes, just so she could witness the look of disappointment on their paint-palette faces.

"Actually, I said yes," he said, biting into the meat. "Man, this turkey leg is delicious."

Lunden whipped her head toward him. "Why did you do that?"

Quade shrugged. "For fun, I guess. I have this weird sense of humor sometimes. Oh, I also told her you did this to my face when you found me talking to another woman. You should have seen the way she scurried off."

Lunden gasped. "Quade Cannon. I can't believe you did that. They probably think I'm some jealous and deranged madwoman who belongs on an episode of *Snapped.*"

"Do you care what they think?" he said.

"No."

"Good." Quade placed his turkey leg down and wiped his mouth. Shifting toward her, he said, "Lunden . . . before we go any further, I have a confession."

The seriousness of his tone and sternness of his expression filled her with concern. What was it now?

※

Quade stared at Lunden, curiosity written all over her face. He thought he might have seen a hint of concern as well. She brushed an invisible piece of hair from her face. Was their charged connection making her uneasy? He could feel the waves of energy pass between them; she obviously could too. He'd be a liar if he said they didn't have some serious chemistry, but he'd be a damn fool to act on it.

"So are you going to tell me, or what?"

He snapped out of the trance he'd fallen into from staring at her. God, he swore she got more beautiful by the day. "I hope you won't look at me differently," he said.

Lunden's posture stiffened slightly. "W-what is it, Quade?"

For dramatic effect, he allowed several more seconds of silence to play between them before finally saying, "I've never been strawberry picking." By the dazed expression she displayed, it wasn't exactly the kind of confession she'd been expecting.

Lunden rested a hand on her chest. "Oh my God. I thought you were about to tell me . . ." Her words trailed off. "Heck, I have no idea what I thought you were about to tell me." She tossed a fry at him. "Jerk. You intentionally made me think you were about to tell me something sinister."

Quade laughed when she jostled him playfully. "It's not my fault you like jumping to conclusions."

"I don't jump to conclusions."

Quade arched a brow. "Really?"

"Name one time I jumped to a conclusion."

Truthfully, he could recall several, but he chose to go with the most recent. "The arcade."

Lunden's brows knit. "The arcade?"

"Yes. When I told you I didn't have a job, you jumped to the conclusion that I was broke."

"I—"

"And don't try to deny it," he said, cutting her off before she could. "You don't have much of a poker face."

"I didn't jump to any conclusion. I simply . . ." Her words dried up. "Okay, maybe I did."

"For the record, I'm not destitute. Far from it, actually."

"Oh, so that means you're not selling the inn because you have to; you're selling it because you *want* to."

Oh no, he was not traveling down this road. Things were going too good between them. While he knew they would eventually return to sparring over the inn, it wouldn't be today. "May I have a bite of your italian sausage?"

Lunden stared at him. The impassive expression on her face told him she was well aware of what he was attempting to do—change the subject. He expected a confrontation, but instead, she slid the hoagie toward him. "Don't eat it all," she said, reaching for his turkey leg.

Quade took a hearty bite. "Man, this is good."

"I told you," Lunden said around a mouthful of turkey leg. "And so is this. *Mmm.*"

He ignored the way the sensual sound rang in his ears. "I can tell."

"For the record," she said, taking another bite of what apparently *used* to be his turkey leg, "it doesn't shock me you've never been strawberry picking, Mr. Harvard Business School."

He chuckled. "You know, you seem to know a lot about me, Ms. Pierce."

"Like I said, Ms. Shugga talked about you all the time."

For the first time, the mention of his aunt didn't cause him anguish. In fact, he smiled. Something about learning the truth had somehow freed him.

"Well, since you know so much about me, it's only fair I should know a little something about you too."

"You do know a little about me. You know I'm mayor of a charming small town that I love. I have an adorable son who is the absolute core of my universe." She tossed a glance toward the play area. "I'm divorced."

Quade snapped his fingers. "That part I'm a little confused about."

"How so?"

"At the arcade, someone said the man you were talking to was your husband."

"What man?"

She played clueless, but he suspected she knew exactly the man he was referring to. He played along. "Tall, brown skinned, beard, kind of stylish." He stopped when he noticed the peculiar way Lunden eyed him. Like she found something strange about the fact he could recall all those details. Maybe it was strange.

"Wow, you remember all of that about him, huh?"

"I'm a stickler for details. Plus, I have an eidetic memory."

"*Ah.* Jutsen." Her brows furrowed. "And who did you say told you this, again?"

One side of his mouth lifted into a smile. "I don't reveal my sources."

"Well, your source was right. He's my husband."

Quade stopped chewing, confused as hell. "Wait—"

"*Work* husband, that is," Lunden added, enjoying yet another chunk of his—make that *her*—turkey leg. "Jealous?"

"*Ha!* Of *Jutsen? Psh.* He's no threat." *Shit.* Why had he made it sound as if he were pursuing her in some way? That was definitely not the case. If Lunden had any objections to what he'd stupidly said, she didn't voice them.

"You weren't in church today," Lunden said.

"Yeah. I didn't want to field a lot of questions about my face. About us."

"There is no us," she said.

Quade ignored the rather pointed way she'd responded. As if she'd wanted to make absolutely certain he wasn't confused about their . . . association. She could be assured he wasn't. And to make sure she wasn't confused, he said, "You don't have to do that."

"Do what?"

"Constantly clarify what we are—or aren't, in this case. I'm not interested in you. I'm only here temporarily, remember? I'm not seeking a relationship. So you don't have to worry."

"I wasn't, because I'm not interested in you or a relationship either. So I guess neither one of us needs to worry. There's no chance of you falling for me and absolutely no chance of me falling for you, so it's all good. Perfect, even."

The way she said it—with finality—almost made him want to make her fall for him. Just to prove to her he could.

"I imagine falling for you would be a replay of my marriage," she said, followed by a scoff. An actual scoff.

"Well, that must mean your union was truly beautiful." He said this in hopes of her opening up about her marriage. The way Ms. Jewel had made it sound, it had been awful. But in true Lunden fashion, she gave him little insight.

She pushed her tray away as if the mention of her past had snatched her appetite away. "Beauty is in the eye of the beholder, isn't it?" A beat later, she stood. "I'm going to check on Zachary."

Lunden moved away, leaving him sitting there alone. His eyes performed a slow crawl down her body, stopping to appreciate her magnificent ass in those red shorts, reminding him of a ripe and juicy strawberry. Too bad he couldn't sink his teeth into it. Then again . . . since she wanted to play Ms. Untouchable, maybe he should show her just how exhilarating his touch could be. He'd always loved a good challenge. Proving to her she wasn't as impenetrable as she thought could be fun in so many tantalizing ways. Something told him he could spend hours between those thighs and still not get enough. The thought stirred him below the waist.

His perusal continued down to her long, shapely legs. *Those legs.* Sexier than any model's he'd ever seen. A vision of them wrapped around his waist, as he took her against the wall, filtered into his thoughts. When he closed his eyes, the scene played like a movie in his head. Her eyes pinned closed. Lips parted just enough to allow her moans to escape. Soft, sweat-slickened skin glistening under the glow of the chandelier. Hips rocking against him as she met his every stroke.

Switching course, he pulled out of her and lowered to his knees. When he circled his tongue around her clit, she called his name, over and over again. *Quade . . . Quade . . .*

"Quade?"

The low whisper of her calling his name was so clear it was like she was actually standing inside his head. "Say my name again," he mumbled to himself, getting way too into his fantasy.

"Quade? Are you okay?"

He was better than okay. "I'm perfect."

"Then why are you moaning? People are staring."

"Because it tastes so—" *Wait.* He pushed his brows together. What did she mean, people were staring? The images in his head deteriorated, shattering into a thousand shards of glass, then floated away. When his eyes popped open, Lunden, Zachary, and several strangers were staring at him, confused expressions on their faces.

"Is he having a heatstroke? Should we call 9-1-1?" an old lady with wiry gray-blue hair asked.

This sparked a conversation about heatstrokes among the onlookers and who they knew who'd had one.

"Are you okay, Quade?" Zachary asked. "First you were rocking back and forth like you were on a hobbyhorse; then you started saying 'mmm, mmm, mmm' like you were eating my mom's honey pie."

Embarrassed that he'd actually been acting out the things playing in his head, he intentionally coughed ferociously, hoping it would give him a few moments to concoct a plausible story.

"Give him something to drink. He needs hydration," the same concerned elder said.

He waved his hand through the air. "I'm fine," he said.

Lunden held his straw to his lips. "Sip."

He did.

Once he'd consumed enough, he said, "Thank you," then set his focus on the crowd, which was clearly waiting for a more extended explanation than *I'm fine*. "I got stung by a bunch of bees yesterday. Maybe the venom is still in my system."

They eyed him like he'd grown a second head. Several mumbled among themselves.

"I also got hit in the head with a basketball," he added. This garnered him some sympathy. He stood. "Thank you for the concern. I'm fine now." He gave Lunden a *let's get out of here* look that, thankfully, she interpreted correctly.

Moments later, they moved in the direction of the strawberry field.

"Are you sure you're okay?" Lunden asked.

"Yes. I think I dozed off. I didn't get much sleep last night." Which wasn't a complete lie. He'd tossed and turned most of the night because she wouldn't get out of his damn head.

Quade couldn't tell whether she believed him or not. Well, he guessed if you ignored the part where he'd answered questions in his *sleep*, the explanation was plausible. "Hey, look." He pointed across the way. "They're selling baskets of strawberries over there. Wouldn't it be easier to buy 'em?"

"Where's the fun in that?" Lunden captured his hand. "Afraid of getting these manicured nails dirty?" Her fingers slid across his open palm. "Oh gosh, we definitely wouldn't want you to get these baby-soft hands scuffed up."

"You love taking jabs at me, don't you? Just like when we were young." Of course, back then, when she'd given him a hard time, it was because she'd had a crush on him. A second later, Lunden released his hand, apparently remembering the same thing.

Zachary moved ahead of them, jumping, spinning, and entertaining himself. The carefree life of a kid.

"He's great at entertaining himself. Don't you wish you could travel back in time?" she said, eyeing Zachary. "When there was not a single care in the world. The only thing that concerned you was how late you'd be allowed to stay out to play with your friends."

"Yes, I do. Do you have plans to give Z a little brother or sister one day?"

Lunden looked alarmed. "Did he say something to you?"

Quade shook his head. "No." She eyed him as if she didn't believe him. "Seriously, he hasn't."

She finally turned away. "All that kid talks about is being a big brother. Coincidentally, he does have a little brother, but he rarely sees him."

Apparently, her ex had gotten remarried, and they'd had a kid. "How much of an age difference is there between them?"

"Two months."

Quade stopped walking. "Wait. How is he two months younger than Z?"

"Because my ex-husband didn't value the sanctity of our marriage."

"Oh," was all Quade said before starting to move again. "I'm sorry to hear that. That had to be tough."

"He'd done a great job of hiding his second family until the child's mother showed up at my doorstep to tell me my then husband should be with her and *their* child."

"What did you do?"

"I gave him to her. I left him that night and never looked back."

"Good for you. That had to take a lot of courage."

Lunden eyed him as if she wanted to say more, but she didn't. Honestly, he couldn't believe she'd shared this much with him.

"Do you have kids?" she asked.

"None that I know of," he said. When Lunden whipped her head toward him, pinning him with a narrow-eyed gaze, he held up his hands in mock surrender. "I'm kidding. No, I don't have kids. Parenthood is not for me."

"Interesting," she said.

"That I don't have kids or that parenthood is not my thing?"

"Both. You're so good with Zachary; it seems like you have experience."

"My best friend has nieces and nephews. They're like my family too. So a little experience, I guess."

"Why are you against parenthood?"

Quade thought about the numerous times he'd been told by his stepfather how worthless he was. How he would ruin any life he touched. So far, the man had been right. "Don't think I'd be any good at it."

"We all think that until we become parents. And then actually discover we *aren't* any good at it." She chuckled. "At least, not at first. But like with anything, you keep working at it until you finally feel like you have some sliver of an idea of what you're doing. Once, I was doing ten things at once and accidentally filled Zachary's bottle with french-vanilla coffee creamer instead of milk. He'd scarfed down half the bottle before I realized it. I was convinced I was the worst mother ever."

"Well, you seem like a natural now. Zachary is a great kid. Well rounded and so happy. I can tell you're doing a fantastic job. He's lucky to have you."

"Thank you, but I'm the lucky one. It's hard being a single mother, but I wouldn't trade it for the world. If it wasn't for Zachary . . ." Her words trailed off. "That ray of sunshine gave me the strength I needed to keep going, every single day. Him and Ms. Shugga."

A second later, tears ran down Lunden's cheeks. She turned her back to him. "I'm sorry."

Quade rested his hands on her hips, then rotated her to face him again. When she glanced up at him, her cheeks streaked with tears, something tugged at his heartstrings. "What are you apologizing for, Lunden? You don't have to wear a suit of armor around me. You don't have to be hard all the time."

"Are you guys coming?" Zachary asked from a distance.

"Being soft gets you gobbled up and spit out. Trust me, I know." She wiped away the rest of her tears, stepped out of his hold, and donned a brilliant smile. "Of course we are," she said, instantly reverting to her old unbreakable self.

In that moment, Quade knew Lunden had given him a glimpse of herself that he was sure not many people got the opportunity to witness, a vulnerable side that she kept tucked away like old Christmas lights. But since she was running a town, he guessed that was necessary to an extent. And why would she trust him, of all people, with this side of her? Whether she'd said it or not, he knew she didn't trust him. And honestly, who could blame her? He was threatening her way of life.

CHAPTER 19

Lunden hated the way she'd broken down in front of Quade, but she'd had a moment. Thinking about her past. Thinking about Ms. Shugga. It had all become so overwhelming, but she was okay now. As she started away, Quade captured her hand, thwarting her escape.

"Hey," he said.

Plastering a smile on her face, she turned to face him. His unmistakable look of compassion took her breath away. It had been a long time since a man had eyed her with so much concern. Regaining her composure, she said, "Yes?"

"What was that?" he said.

"Nothing," she said, widening her smile and pulling away from him. He didn't stop her this time.

For the next half hour, they moved from row to row, picking strawberries. Every time Lunden glanced up, Quade was watching her, studying her. Probably trying to figure out whether she'd start bawling again. He had nothing to worry about. The moment had passed.

Turned out he didn't have an issue getting his hands—or clothes—dirty, since they spent most of the time on their knees. Or more likely, he was simply pretending to not have an aversion for her benefit.

Men.

"Are you having fun, Quade?" Zachary asked from several rows over, collecting strawberries with a friend he'd made.

"Tons. Thank you for inviting me."

Zachary grinned and returned his attention to the plants.

"You're not that good of a liar either," Lunden whispered.

"I'm better than you."

She didn't doubt that for one minute.

"And I am actually having fun," he said.

Lunden plucked a strawberry. "Have you tried one?"

Quade's face contorted. "*No.* They're dirty."

"Funny. I don't remember you being so sensitive." She rubbed the fruit back and forth on her shirt. "A little dirt won't hurt you," she said, then bit into the flesh. "*Mmm.* Delicious. Sweet and juicy." Lunden knee walked until she was directly in front of him. "Try it," she said, holding the strawberry inches from his mouth.

Quade wrapped his large hand around hers. "I don't think so."

When she attempted to fly it into his mouth like an airplane, like a mother did with a fussy eater, they struggled playfully, falling over into the dirt.

"Whoa," Quade said, attempting to brace the impact.

Lunden landed on her back and Quade half on the ground, half on her.

Rolling with laughter, she said, "First the pool, now the dirt. You love knocking me off my feet, don't you?"

Through his own laughter, Quade said, "Like you said, a little dirt won't hurt you."

"You two are silly," Zachary said, apparently unfazed by their current situation.

Sobering, Quade came up onto his shoulder. The way he stared down at her stilled her. Something deep, dark, and daunting danced in his eyes, a look far more menacing than she'd witnessed in them at the pool. It was arousing as hell. His jaw muscles flexed as if he was clenching his teeth. His breathing was deep but steady, unlike hers. Quick and ragged. Rattled, she said, "W-we should probably get up before someone reports us for lascivious behavior." She laughed clumsily.

Quade's stone-faced expression didn't flinch. A beat later, his upper body lowered closer to her as he reached across and removed the strawberry she was still holding between her fingers. He brought it to his mouth and bit into it.

"*Mmm*. Delicious. Sweet. Juicy."

Fixated on his mouth, she mumbled, "Told you."

Quade held the remainder against her lips. "Bite."

When she sank her teeth in, juice ran over her lip. Quade used the pad of his thumb to wipe it away. The moment was so sexually charged her nipples beaded inside her bra. Parts of her throbbed, while others trembled. If ever she'd wanted to be kissed by a man, it was now. And she hated herself for the potent desire coursing through her.

Before her brain could process her next move, Quade was on his feet. He offered his hand for her to take. When she did so, he pulled her to her feet in one swift, powerful motion. After dusting herself off, she collected her pail. "I, um, think we have enough strawberries," she said, then walked off, reminding herself she had a plan that didn't include falling for Quade Cannon.

A week later, Lunden rested her hip against the metal prep table inside the kitchen at Rylee's bakery and looked on in amazement as Rylee expertly worked a tube of lavender icing onto an anniversary cake. The things this woman could do with buttercream were sheer magic. "You are so good at that," she said.

Rylee stopped and glanced up at her. "*Great,*" she corrected. "But of course I don't want to toot my own horn."

"Of course," Lunden said, laughing.

"It's Friday. Why aren't you at the town hall?"

Lunden popped one of the chocolate-dipped strawberries Rylee had prepared into her mouth. Doing so reminded her of the trip she,

Quade, and Zachary had taken to the strawberry farm close to a week ago. Mainly the moment when Quade had fed her a strawberry. She placed two fingers to her lips, the memory sending a shiver up her spine.

"Are you okay?" Rylee said.

Lunden gave a wobbly laugh. "Yes. I'm on my way to the community center to look at the jubilee decorations. I wanted to stop by to see my bestie first, whom I haven't seen in a couple of days and have missed dearly. If that's all right with you?"

Rylee smiled but didn't look up from her task. Lunden envied the woman's laser-sharp focus. Not just with the cake but with everything. Nothing rattled Rylee. Well, almost nothing. The sheriff had a way of throwing her off balance.

"And my nephew? Where is he, with Quade?"

Lunden stopped chewing. "No? Why would he be with Quade?"

Rylee didn't answer, simply smirked. Another thing she was good at: communicating without actually communicating.

"For your information, he's at Senior's, getting a haircut for the jubilee tomorrow. He didn't want me to wait there for him. Apparently, he's old enough to wait at the barbershop alone. God, he's growing up too fast."

Rylee changed the icing color and piped a yellow flower onto the side of the cake. "Sounds to me like it's time to have another one."

"I think virgin birth ended with Mary."

"Well, perhaps Qu—"

Lunden jabbed a finger at Rylee. "Don't you dare say it."

"Say what?" Rylee asked sheepishly. "It wasn't like I was going to suggest Quade impregnate you or something."

Lunden rolled her eyes to the ceiling. "*Ugh.* Like I told you before, Quade and I are *just friends.*" Besides, according to Quade, he didn't want kids. Which was why, even if by some foolish chance she wanted something more with him, it wasn't an option. She wanted another child. Maybe even two.

This time Rylee claimed a green bag of icing and adorned the flowers she'd created with leaves. "For two people to only be *friends*, y'all sure do spend a lot of *family* time together. The apiary at the inn. The arcade. The strawberry patch. Plus, he's helping you organize Zachary's birthday party. *And* he's escorting you to the jubilee tomorrow?"

"I—"

"*Oh, wait,* I left out the Chinese restaurant," Rylee said.

Okay, Lunden could see how the combination of events could be misconstrued. However, she could assure her friend nothing was percolating between her and Quade Cannon. Gaining Quade's trust was all a part of her plan. "And each occurrence was platonic, including the strawberry patch." Despite how sizzling hot things had gotten between them.

"And speaking of the arcade—"

"I didn't say anything about the arcade," Lunden said.

"—I hear you two looked awfully cozy, especially when he was attacked by that basketball." Rylee snickered. "Seems as if everything's attracted to him. Bees, balls . . . bullheaded mayors."

"You are absolutely unbearable at times. We're just friends," Lunden reiterated.

"We're friends. You two are something else entirely. You just haven't seen it yet. Can you tell me with a straight face you're not attracted to him?"

Lunden slid her eyes away. Rylee knew her too well, so lying was pointless.

"No need to respond. I see the way you two look at each other. There's something there," Rylee said.

"An attraction to someone is a far cry from wanting to be with them," Lunden said.

"Yeah, but that's how it starts."

Ignoring Rylee's comment, Lunden said, "I have a master plan."

Rylee stopped work and glanced up at her. "Master plan?" Her brows bunched. "What master plan would that be?"

"The way I figure it, Quade's not invested in the inn or Honey Hill; therefore, he couldn't care less about either. If I can make him remember how much he used to love them both, then maybe he'll be less apt to sell it."

"Hmm," Rylee hummed.

Okay, so the strategy was a long shot, but she was willing to do whatever needed to be done to thwart Quade's plans to sell the inn. She at least owed it to Ms. Shugga to try. What Lunden didn't share with Rylee was the alternative plan she was cooking up with Zeta, because Lunden knew her friend well enough to know she wouldn't approve. However, the way it was looking, that plan wouldn't pan out either. Zeta hadn't found one single thing that could help her.

Rylee eyed her for a long moment before finally saying, "You should just sleep with him. I'm sure that'll conjure a lot of sentimental memories." Then she returned to her task.

On second thought, *almost* anything. "I'm being serious, Rylee."

"So am I. Didn't you tell me he was unemployed? And what do unemployed people want? Money. If he needs money and selling the inn is the only way for him to get it, you're going to need to do more than show him the town. You're going to need to show him a nipple. A butt cheek. Some cleavage. Something more enticing than a few buildings and magnolia trees."

Lunden couldn't hold back her laughter. "You get on my nerves."

"Yeah, but you love me. *And* . . . you know I'm right."

"According to Quade, he doesn't need the money, but I'm sure the lure of millions of dollars has to hold some appeal." Selling wasn't the only option for him to make money from the inn. Once it was up and running again, it would generate great revenue just as it always had. Maybe not millions, but decent money. For him *and* the town.

Rylee came to her full height, placed the icing-filled bag on the table, and removed her gloves. "Sweetie, does Quade strike you as a man who would be satisfied operating an inn? Those confident, corporate-type brothers love a challenge. And Lord knows you're a challenge. It turns them on. Why do you think he's so drawn to you? Other than your strikingly good looks and charming personality, of course."

"Remind me again why we're friends," Lunden said.

"Because I love you and will always have your back," Rylee said, hugging Lunden playfully.

"You're getting icing all over me," Lunden said but didn't pull away from her friend's affection, because she needed it.

"Am I interrupting?"

Lunden and Rylee both turned their focus toward Canten, who was standing at the door.

"No," Rylee said.

While Rylee had denied it before, the way her eyes lit up when they landed on Canten told Lunden one thing: she was in love. Studying Canten told her Rylee wasn't the only one. She prayed they made their way to one another.

"Mayor," he said.

"Sheriff," Lunden said.

"Rylee."

"Sheriff. Shouldn't you be out fighting crime?"

"Can't do it on an empty stomach, and I'm starving," he said.

"I'm sure I have something around here that'll satisfy you."

Lunden's brows arched. *Good comeback, Ry.* Canten's gaze silently lingered on Rylee as if he was entranced. A smile touched Lunden's lips. It was only a matter of time for these two. She decided to help them along on their journey by giving them some alone time. Glancing at her watch, she said, "*Wow.* Would you look at the time. I have to go. I need to swing by Lendell's shop before I pick Zachary up. He's working on a project for me. I'll call you later, Ry. Bye, Sheriff."

Lunden wasn't sure if either one of them even noticed she'd left the kitchen. To the detriment of her mind and body, she remembered the sentiment of feeling like the only two people in the room. Like if the world were to end at that very moment, it wouldn't matter, because you were with the one person who had the uncanny ability to make even death feel secondary.

For her, such a sensation had only ever been experienced with one person, but she refused to think his name. But as if the universe demanded she acknowledge him, her phone rang, and his name flashed across her screen in big, bold letters. Quade Cannon. *Okay, universe, I'll grant you that one.* But she got the last laugh when she sent his call straight to voice mail. Maybe she had to acknowledge him, but she didn't have to talk to him until she wanted to. And there was nothing the universe could do about that one. Satisfied with her claimed victory, she grinned, dropped the phone into her purse, and continued toward the exit.

For whatever reason, Lunden felt light as air as she floated through the bakery, speaking to the many patrons enjoying Rylee's creations. Today was going to be a good day. Scratch that—a great day.

"The universe will always get its way."

The words stopped Lunden dead in her tracks. She whipped her head toward Agnes Wexler, owner of the Dancing Planet Books and Gifts store. If you needed sage to rid your space of evil, crystals to balance your chakras, or tarot cards to get a glimpse of your past, present, or future, Agnes Wexler's new age shop was the place to go. The middle-aged woman reminded Lunden of actress Blythe Danner, if Blythe Danner had a mess of rainbow dreadlocks and a dozen moon, sun, and star tattoos or held weed-smoking parties she cleverly disguised as ceremonial cleanses.

"What did you say?" Lunden asked, her tone even and steady, despite the uneasiness rumbling in her stomach.

Agnes boasted a wide smile. "The universe will always get its way. It's what Estella writes at the end of each of her blog posts. And she's right."

Leather-wearing, Harley-riding, sixtysomething Estella Donahue owned the town's nighttime-attire shop. In addition to the more traditional pieces like robes, pajamas, and gowns, the shop also offered more risqué items kept in a separate area in the back of the store: role-play costumes, crotchless bottoms, and a collection of pleasure items. Or so Lunden had heard. While many whispered about the bawdy side of the store, no one ever really admitted to seeing it firsthand.

In addition, Estella ran a surprisingly popular blog, *The Untamed Kitten*, tasked with keeping the inquisitive folks of Honey Hill in the know. However, to Lunden, it usually read like a cyber version of gossiping. And just like she handled Estella's blog, Lunden chose to pay her universe assertion no mind.

Over the past week, Quade hadn't been able to stop thinking about Lunden and their time together at the strawberry patch. Who would have ever thought he could actually enjoy himself playing around in the dirt? To be honest, he'd enjoyed himself a little too much. And that bothered him, because he wasn't in Honey Hill to enjoy himself. He was here to conduct his business and leave.

He sat forward, rested his elbows on his legs, and interlocked his fingers in front of him, remembering how close he'd come to kissing Lunden after they'd toppled over onto the ground. He'd wanted to kiss her so bad it had ached. It'd taken everything inside of him to pull away. He massaged the back of his neck. Maybe escorting Lunden to the jubilee wasn't such a good idea after all.

"Actually, it's a horrible idea," he said aloud.

Making a rash decision, he lifted his cell phone off the table, pressed the speed dial location associated with Lunden, and waited. When she answered, he'd simply tell her something had come up and he couldn't make it to the jubilee, thereby canceling their arrangement. That should make her happy. It wasn't like she really wanted to go with him anyway. If he had to guess, she'd only agreed because she'd felt sorry for him.

After several rings, the call rolled into voice mail. Since this wasn't the type of thing he wanted to do via message, he hung up before the beep with intentions of trying again later. After checking his watch, he grabbed up his keys and headed out the door for the barbershop. But first, he wanted to swing by the screen printing shop.

Ten minutes later, Quade walked through the doors of Honey Hill Screen Printing. No one manned the front of the store, but Quade assumed someone was here because the door was unlocked, plus several large embroidery machines worked away in a corner of the store. The noise was deafening. A beat later, an older gentleman appeared from the back, his attention trained on a ring of swatches. Because he held such a strong resemblance to Mr. Clem, Quade assumed this was Mr. Conroy.

"Hello," Quade said over the roar of the machines.

Mr. Conroy's head snapped up, and he dropped the ring to the floor. He removed his ear protection. "Good Lord, son, you trying to give me a heart attack?"

Quade quickly moved to pick up the swatches. "I'm sorry. I didn't mean to startle you." He came to a full stand in front of Mr. Conroy and passed him the ring.

Mr. Conroy eyed him strangely. "You're Shugga's nephew," he finally said.

"Yes, sir."

He stared at Quade a couple of seconds longer before visibly shaking himself out of some sort of daze. "Sorry it's so loud in here. I'm working on baseball caps for the fire department's baseball league. The caps will be the only thing that look good out on the field, because the team—to put it kindly—sucks. Still, I'll be right there, along with the rest of the town, watching and cheering them on. What can I do for you?"

"I hear you may be looking for some help around here."

"You're looking for a job?" Mr. Conroy asked, appearing surprised by the inquiry.

"Yes, sir. I'm no good at sitting around and twiddling my fingers. Since I'm here for the next several months, I figured I'd occupy my time."

"Follow me," Mr. Conroy said.

The man led Quade into a small room housing stacked cardboard boxes, wire shelving, tons of thread, and several jugs of liquid. A four-top table with worn brown-leather chairs sat in the middle of the room. Mr. Conroy directed Quade to one, then took a seat himself.

"You have any experience with screen printing?" Mr. Conroy asked.

"No."

"How about embroidery?"

Again, Quade said, "No."

"Have you ever used a heat press or done sublimation?"

Quade chuckled. "No, but I'm a quick study."

Mr. Conroy scratched his wiry salt-and-pepper beard, the sound mimicking sandpaper rubbing against wood. A perplexed expression spread across his face. Quade suspected the man was attempting to figure out why in the hell someone with no screen printing experience would come to a screen printing shop looking for a job.

"Well, I could use some part-time help around here to do some of the heavy lifting. Reckon I can teach you how to run the machines. I don't offer health insurance or benefits. And I can't afford to pay you much."

"That's fine," Quade said.

Mr. Conroy studied him a moment, then extended his arm. "Welcome aboard."

A short time later, Quade arrived at Senior's. Just as he approached, the door opened and Lunden and Zachary strolled out. She looked stunning, even in a simple yellow T-shirt, black shorts, and sandals. In those colors, she reminded him of a sexy honeybee.

"Quade!" Zachary said, hugging him.

"What's up, Z? Looking good, little man," Quade said, running a hand over his freshly cut hair.

"Thank you," Zachary said. "Mom, there's Joshua and his mom. Can I go and say hi?"

"Yes," she said. "But stay close."

"I will." A second later, he took off down the sidewalk.

"What are you doing here?" Lunden asked.

"Haircut and shave. Senior has this face cream that smells like cake. The stuff is *amazing*."

Lunden smiled. "Lemon, vanilla, and honey from your bees. And you're right. It is pretty awesome. One of my biggest sellers."

"*You* made that?" Why wasn't he surprised?

"Yes," she said, folding her arms across her chest and beaming with pride.

The move caused her breasts to swell slightly. It was all he could do to keep from staring. Swallowing hard, he said, "Really?"

"Why do you sound so surprised?"

"I'm not. Well, I guess I am. But not for the reason you think. You're a mother, mayor, and entrepreneur, creating these incredible products. I don't know how you find the time to do it all. You amaze me."

"Thank you," she said softly.

For several moments, they eyed each other in comfortable silence.

"Sorry I missed your call earlier. I was, um . . . I was in a meeting. About the jubilee," she added.

Aww, she's so cute when she lies. "No worries," he said.

"Did you have questions about tomorrow? Or was it something else? You weren't calling to cancel on me, were you?"

"No. I mean, yes. I mean . . ." *Get it together.* "I was calling because I was curious about what color you were wearing tomorrow. That's what I wanted." *What in the hell are you saying? Just tell her the truth. You can't make it. Simple as that, then walk away.* "I . . . wanted to make sure we coordinate."

"Oh. Well, what color do you plan to wear?" she asked.

"Black. I'm wearing black."

"I see. I think black still goes with anything," she said, "so we should be okay."

"Yeah, you're probably right." Quade glanced inside the barbershop. Senior and Mr. Clem eyed them through the glass. No doubt he would be the target of their chiding banter.

"Seven o'clock?" Lunden said.

Shifting his attention back to Lunden, he said, "Hmm?"

"Do you want to pick me up around seven? Or I can meet you at the community center, if you prefer."

Last chance to back out. "Seven works." *Idiot.*

"Perfect. I should let you get inside. I think Senior's waiting on you," Lunden said, then smiled and walked away.

Watching her move away—the rhythmic sway of her hips causing him to bite into his bottom lip—gave him a thrill he couldn't explain. Actually, he could explain it. It was akin to those moments you were undressing a woman with the full knowledge that, within seconds, you would be sliding deep inside her to enjoy the fine art of lovemaking.

Shaking off the longing thrashing around inside him like the storm-ravaged sea, he entered the barbershop. "Great afternoon," he said.

"I bet it is," Mr. Clem said. "Even from here, I noticed that twinkle in your eyes, chatting with the mayor."

"I think I noticed a little something too," Senior said, directing Quade into his chair.

"I don't know what you're talking about. There was no twinkling. We were just having a friendly conversation. Nothing more."

"Well, that's too bad. Mayor's a good one. Long overdue for some happiness," Mr. Clem said. He pressed his index finger into his chin. "Come to think of it, I can't remember the last time I saw the mayor with a gentleman caller."

Gentleman caller? Quade chuckled at Mr. Clem's choice of words.

Mr. Clem returned to playing a solo card game. "Though with how that ex-husband of hers treated her, guess no one can blame her for keeping her guard up."

Stiffening in the chair, Quade said, "How did he treat her?" hoping his inquiry didn't sound overly eager.

"Not good, son. Not good at all," Senior said, reclining Quade back.

Mr. Clem made a sound of disgust. "Turned out he was just as worthless as the rest of the scoundrels in that family. Whole clan was good for nothing. Even down to the dog. A bunch of crooks and bullies. Honey Hill was a much better place when they all packed up and left."

"More like was run out of town," Senior corrected. "Unfortunately, not before that eldest boy could sink his claws into Lunden. Never knew what she saw in him."

"Grief," Mr. Clem said. "Makes you vulnerable. After losing her brother, I think she just needed to feel something other than sadness. Though I suspect it hadn't turned out quite like she'd expected."

"Lex died?" Quade said. That explained why Lunden had no pictures of him displayed at her place.

"Mmm-hmm," Senior and Mr. Clem hummed in unison.

"Nasty motorcycle accident up in Raleigh. Someone going the wrong way slammed head on into him. Died instantly."

"Damn," Quade said. He could only imagine how hard Lunden had taken it. Those two had always been close.

"That bastard she married used her grief as his way in. I know she regretted the day she ever laid eyes on him." Senior shook his head. "Some men just don't know how to treat a good woman."

Getting past the impact of the news of Lex's death, Quade asked, "How did he treat her?" a second time.

"He was insecure," Clem said. "That's why he treated her that way. Made himself feel strong by making her feel inferior. Signs of a weak man."

"You got that right," Senior said.

"How did he treat her?" Quade repeated a third time, hoping this go-round someone would respond to his question; however, the knot in his stomach told him he probably wouldn't like the answer. From the various tidbits about Lunden's life he'd gathered in passing, he already suspected her marriage hadn't been a good one. But just how tumultuous had it been?

"Word is—" Mr. Clem stopped abruptly. "Oh, I shouldn't be telling the mayor's personal business."

Now the man wanted to be mindful of other folks' personal business?

"Though . . . I reckon it ain't no harm in telling you what the rest of the town already knows. Seeing how you're one of us now," Mr. Clem said.

Quade wouldn't go quite that far, but if it got the man to talk, he'd own it for now.

"What you think, SR?" Mr. Clem said.

"I think it doesn't matter what I think. You're gonna do what you want anyway," Senior said, smoothing the cream over Quade's face.

"He moved the mayor to Texas." Mr. Clem paused. "Or was it Virginyee? Now that I think about it, it could have been Alabamer."

Quade didn't care if it was Virginia or Alabama. He just wanted the story. "They left Honey Hill for someplace else," Quade said, prompting the man to continue.

Senior chuckled, making Quade do the same.

"It was Texas, for sure," Mr. Clem said. "Course, it could have been anywhere, I suppose. He was one of those shifty types. Just like his daddy. Always moving from one place to another. I had an uncle like that. Just couldn't stay in one place for too long."

Mr. Clem had that in common with his uncle, because the man couldn't seem to stay on subject for too long.

"Good Lord, Clem. If you gonna tell the story, tell the story. We'll be here all afternoon waiting on you."

Thank you, Senior, Quade said to himself.

"Anyway," Mr. Clem said. "While that good woman was busy making their house a home, raising their son, and cooking his meals, he was out chasing anything in a skirt. Even heard he had a baby outside the marriage. Course, I don't know how true that is."

Quade shifted in the chair. While he knew the latter to be a fact, he didn't confirm it. When he opened his eyes, Senior stared down at him. By the look on his face, Senior knew the truth as well.

"Reckon she got tired of his trifling ways, 'cause she left him," Mr. Clem said.

Quade blew a sigh of relief, thankful Mr. Clem hadn't mentioned anything about Lunden's ex being physically abusive. Nevertheless, it sounded as if he'd been emotionally and mentally abusive, which was equally devastating in his experience.

Mr. Clem sighed. "Poor thing had a toddler, not a cent to her name, and no place to call home."

Quade could relate. At least to the *no place to call home* part.

Mr. Clem continued, "She'd sold her parents' place before moving away, but in Honey Hill, we look after one another. That buzzard had broken her spirit. But like she'd done with so many others, Shugga wrapped her and that boy in a cloak of love. Welcomed her into the inn. Gave her a job. Helped her get back on her feet. Your aunt was something special. Helped anyone who walked through her doors and expected nothing in return. She was an intuitive woman. Knew what people needed before they did."

Senior hummed in agreement.

Now Quade understood why Lunden was so hard, so headstrong. She needed to prove to herself that she was no longer the broken woman she'd been in her marriage. Well, the woman he'd spent time with was not in pieces. She was whole.

A whole lot of strength.

A whole lot of passion.

A whole lot of tenacity.

And a whole lot of temptation.

CHAPTER 20

Lunden laughed at Rylee frantically waving a hand in front of her face. The dramatic woman acted as if it were a hundred degrees. June in Honey Hill was typically smoldering, and while it was warm, it wasn't scorching . . . yet.

"Please remind me again why we're walking to the salon instead of driving? No one loves walking around town as much as you. Well, excluding Ennis and his dog."

Lunden ignored Rylee. The woman had been complaining since they'd left the bakery. "It's a beautiful day. *Perfect* day, actually." She closed her eyes and inhaled a lungful of fresh air. This was one of those rare days when everything had gone right from the moment she'd climbed out of bed. She really hoped it would continue.

"Would that have anything to do with you spending the evening with a certain tall, dark, and deliciously handsome hunk?"

Lunden's eyes popped open. "No. In fact, I almost have a notion to call and cancel."

"And what about your *master plan*? To get him to fall in love with the town, you have to actually spend time showing it to him. Or a nipple," she added.

"For the last time, I'm not showing Quade Cannon any of my naked body parts."

"We'll see," Rylee mumbled loud enough for Lunden to hear.

Things fell silent between them, but only for a few seconds.

"We nearly kissed," Lunden said.

Rylee stopped walking. "*Again?* You two put the *slow* in *slow burn*. But when you two finally do kiss . . . *man!* It's going to be chart topping, especially with all this built-up sexual tension."

Lunden didn't dwell on this because there would be no kissing. No more touching. No more paralyzing eye contact. No more too-close-for-comfort moments. She had to play it smart going forward. *No losing sight of the goal.*

They continued to move.

"When and where this time?" Rylee asked.

"The strawberry patch." Lunden recalled the intense look of desire that had been present in Quade's eyes and exhaled a long, steady breath.

"*What?* That was like a week ago. Why are you just now spilling this tea?"

"Because I wanted to forget," Lunden said.

"Are you sure?" Rylee asked.

"Of course I'm sure. I know when I want to kiss someone, and I don't want to kiss Quade Cannon," she snapped.

Rylee flashed a palm. "Okay. Calm down. You don't have to take my head off. I get it. You don't want to kiss him."

"Only I do," Lunden said in a defeated voice. "I wanted to kiss him when I fell in the pool. I wanted to kiss him at the strawberry patch."

Rylee eyed her with a look of sympathy. "Not to be insensitive, but how exactly does your plan work when anytime you two are together, you nearly kiss?"

"I haven't worked out all the kinks yet."

"Maybe you should. Kiss him, I mean. Once you've gotten it out of your system, perhaps you'll be able to focus."

Lunden parted her lips to vehemently protest but reconsidered. What if Rylee was right? What if all she needed to do was kiss him to extinguish whatever this was lingering between them? But what if she liked it?

Nope. She wouldn't like it. She wouldn't allow herself to like it, because she didn't like him. Not like that anyway. So what if she was a little attracted to him? So was every other woman under fifty in Honey Hill. Heck, even some women over fifty.

"I have to tell you something," Rylee said.

This snapped Lunden from her thoughts. Oftentimes when Rylee had to tell her something, it wasn't good. She stopped and turned toward Rylee, who hesitated to face her. "What did you do?"

Rylee flashed a tortured look. "I may or may not have *accidentally* let it slip to Lady Sunshine that you were attending the jubilee with Quade."

"Ry!"

"I know, I know. I'm sorry. She stopped by the bakery this morning. One question led to another, and before I knew it, I was singing like a canary. *Ugh.* She gets me every time."

Lunden rolled her eyes heavenward. Now she couldn't cancel. If she showed up tonight alone, the first thing people would assume was that Quade had stood her up. While she didn't care what anyone thought . . . but actually, apparently she did, since she was worried about being seen alone.

"Are you mad at me?"

Lunden forced a faux scowl but laughed a second later. "No. Everyone would have known the second we walked in together anyway." She'd just wanted to avoid a bunch of beforehand inquiries. With any luck, Lady Sunshine hadn't mentioned it. As they continued their stroll toward the salon, she said, "I wonder if a certain baker would be so chatty if a certain mayor hinted to Lady Sunshine that the aforementioned baker was sweet on a certain sheriff?"

Rylee's eyes widened. "You better not."

"May . . . your? Yoo-hoo, May . . . your?"

Lunden groaned, instantly recognizing the contentious southern drawl as that of Herbert Jamison. Spouse to her predecessor, grandfather to her nemesis, and headache waiting to happen. Plus, the only person in the state who couldn't pronounce *mayor* normally. Forcing a smile, she turned to face him, gasping at the sight of the short, stout, balding man wearing a short-sleeved plaid shirt—fluorescent orange—yellow striped knickerbockers, walnut-brown tube socks pulled to his knee-caps, and pecan-colored sandals. For the individual who owned the town's menswear shop, he surely wasn't representing the business well.

"What the—"

Lunden elbowed Rylee to silence her. "Mr. Herbert? What can I do for you?"

"Might I have a moment of your time?" he said. His swamp-green eyes slid to Rylee. "Alone?"

"I'll catch up with you at the salon," Lunden said to Rylee.

Once Rylee walked off, Mr. Herbert said, "I would like to voice my objection toward this ridiculous crusade you're on in regards to the inn."

That was no surprise. Since she became mayor, the man hadn't supported a single initiative she'd introduced. When she'd voiced the need for a community center, he'd countered with concerns about litter, of all things. When she'd pushed to expand the food pantry, he'd claimed it would cause an upsurge of rodents with all the extra food "just sitting around." Then there was the pool. The ornery man had made it sound as if anyone who so much as dipped a toe in would drown.

Mr. Herbert only supported the things that would directly benefit him. He had no true love for the inn or Honey Hill as a whole, she suspected, despite having lived here all his life. After Ms. Shugga had endorsed Lunden for mayor, Mr. Herbert had conjured up some ridiculous belief that Ms. Shugga had been out to get him. Lunden had clearly become the enemy by association.

"Thank you, Mr. Herbert. I'll keep that in mind," Lunden said.

Ignoring her dismissal, Mr. Herbert continued, "I think it's high time we welcomed more upscale accommodations with all the modern amenities. That will bring tourists and their dollars to this . . . hapless town."

Lunden had been taught to always respect her elders, but Mr. Herbert was about to test her resolve. Folding her arms across her chest, she said, "Duly noted."

"My Roberta had plans to do just that before she was pushed out. She had vision."

"*Voted* out," Lunden said. And her so-called vision had nearly bankrupted the town.

Mr. Herbert hiked his knickerbockers. "Excuse me?"

"Mrs. Roberta wasn't *pushed* out."

He waved her off. "Tomato, tomahto."

"Like I said, Mr. Herbert, I've noted your concerns. Ultimately, I'll do what I believe is in the best interest of the town and its residents, which is what I was elected to do. Regardless, I do appreciate your input. As always, it's of such value. Now, if you will excuse me . . ." She offered a smile, then walked away.

Lunden could hear the laughter coming from the salon before she reached the door. As she passed the glass, she noticed all five chairs inside Happi Curls were occupied except the one Lunden hoped Happi was holding for her. She didn't want to be here all day.

As soon as she stepped through the door, the sour mood the interaction with Mr. Herbert had put her in was erased. She loved her visits here. A dedicated safe space to discuss anything and everything under the sun without the fear of being judged or ridiculed. And oh, if these walls could talk.

"Hey, Mayor," several of the ladies said in unison as she walked in.

"I thought I was going to have to save you from Hypocrite Herbie," Happi said, using the name she called Mr. Herbert behind his back.

Happi sashayed toward Lunden wearing a form-hugging sleeveless black maxi dress that hung down to her ankles and accented her curvaceous figure. Her sapphire-blue hair was fixed into a messy bun atop her head. The color perfectly complemented her flawless mahogany skin.

"Come on and sit down and tell us all about it."

Happi draped a leopard-print salon cape around Lunden's neck, fastening it a smidge too tight. Lunden ran an index finger between her skin and the fabric to loosen it. "As always, he has an issue."

"Forget Herbie. I'm talking about you and that *fine-ass* Quade Cannon. I hear you two are a thing now. How's he in bed? I bet he's dynamite."

Several of the women voiced their support.

"No, we're not a thing. And I have no idea how he is in bed," Lunden said. By the way the other women eyed her with raised brows and skeptical stares, they didn't believe her.

Happi combed through her hair. "You two are going to the jubilee together, right?"

Lady Sunshine strikes again.

When Lunden sent a narrow-eyed gaze at Rylee, occupying one of the salon chairs opposite her, Rylee mouthed, "Sorry."

"Yes, we are. But only as friends," Lunden said. "*Just* friends," she reemphasized.

Happi hummed, "Mmm. I had a friend like that once. The things that man did to my body were probably illegal in several states."

The room exploded with laughter.

Lunden groaned. "It's not that kind of friendship."

"Girl, it should be. Have you seen the size of his feet?" Happi asked.

Yes, she had.

Happi continued, "You better make it that kind of friendship. In fact, friendships with benefits are the best."

Not that Lunden was seriously entertaining this foolishness, but she said, "How so?"

"The only thing you two expect from each other are mind-blowing orgasms."

The other women sounded their agreement in a chorus of *mmm-hmm*s and *oh yeah*s. Lunden had mind-blowing orgasms. Granted, they were via her trusty vibrator, but still . . . an orgasm was an orgasm, regardless of how it was achieved. However, she did miss non-self-induced climaxes.

"You haven't used that honeypot in a while. I know it probably has cobwebs on it by now."

Lunden gasped. *"Happi!"*

"I'm just saying."

"Well, could you say a little less? And for your information, I experience plenty of orgasms. Thank you very much."

"Honey, I'm sure that bumblebee vibrator you got from Estella's secret room can't hold a candle to the pleasure that sinfully delicious Quade Cannon could deliver."

Well, Lunden couldn't argue with that. But she had no plans to find out.

🐝

Quade arrived at Lunden's place at exactly six forty-five that evening. Not too early and definitely not late. But before he could ring the bell, his cell phone rang. After fishing it from his pocket, he said, "What's up, Pryor?"

"We have a new player in the game. The Danbury Group out of Mississippi. Just got off the phone with one of their representatives. They're offering *eight* million for the inn. Almost double any of our current offers."

The Danbury Group. Quade had never heard of it. While the offer thrilled him, it also concerned him. No company shelled out this type of money without plans for a huge return on its investment. As it stood, the inn would never generate that kind of revenue to recoup such a lofty price tag. So what were the Danbury Group's plans?

"So should I schedule a site visit?"

"No," Quade said, descending the stairs.

"No?!"

Quade understood Pryor's reaction, but he needed a minute to sit on this. While this was certainly the type of big fish they'd hoped to snag, he guessed a part of him wanted to make sure it wouldn't consume the guppies. "Not just yet. Let's talk about this later." He checked his watch. "I'm about to be late."

"That's right. You have a date," Pryor said.

"It's not a date."

"If you say so. Any signs of misdeed from your Lady Fair?"

Quade eyed the house from the yard. "No. And trust me, I've been watching. In fact, she hasn't even mentioned the inn lately. Strange, right?"

"Definitely interesting," Pryor said. "But maybe she finally realized it's in her best interest not to intervene."

"Yeah, maybe," Quade said, unconvinced.

"Or," Pryor dragged out, "there could be another reason altogether."

Quade was afraid to ask but did anyway. "And the reason?"

"Lady Fair's falling for you, and the inn is now secondary. You two have been spending *a lot* of time together. She wants to have your big-headed babies."

"Bye, Pryor," Quade said with a laugh and ended the call. Shaking his head, Quade mumbled, *"Ridiculous,"* as he climbed the steps again. When he rang the bell, Zachary answered the door. The little dude looked debonair in a black suit, white shirt, and African-print bow tie with an asymmetrical pattern in yellow, green, orange, and black.

"Hey, Quade. How do I look?"

"Sharp, kid. Real sharp."

They slapped palms.

Quade followed Zachary farther inside the house.

"My mom's coming," he said. "She wants to look perfect."

For me? The thought swelled him with pride.

Zachary lowered his voice. "She looks *really* pretty. You should tell her that, okay?"

In an equally muted tone, Quade said, "I will." Because he had no doubt she did.

"You wanna see a card trick?" Zachary asked once Quade was seated.

"Sure."

"Okay. Be right back."

Zachary darted down the hall. A second later, he returned with a deck of cards. Standing directly in front of Quade, he shuffled the cards—dropping half on the floor. After retrieving the ones he'd lost, he fanned them out with his hands and told Quade to pick one. He did.

King of hearts.

"Okay, put it back in," Zachary said.

Once he did, Zachary shuffled the deck again, losing several cards just as he had before. Instead of fanning them this time, he plucked one out and flashed the three of spades at Quade.

"Is this your card?" he asked, his bright eyes wide with hope.

"Wow! How'd you do that?" Quade asked. Since he hadn't actually answered yes or no, it couldn't exactly be considered lying to the kid. Merely encouraging him to continue to hone his skills.

"Magic," Zachary said. "Wanna play again?"

Before Quade could respond, Lunden appeared, sucking the air completely from the room with her stunning appearance. Quade stood, his eyes glued to the woman before him. Every inch of her was . . .

"*Magnificent,*" he said absently.

Lunden's hair was in an updo. Tiny curls framed her face, which was lightly made up. Her cranberry-tinted lips held his attention far longer than they should have. His eyes trailed down to her exposed shoulders in the dress he just now realized matched Zachary's bow tie. Her skin shimmered as if it had been spritzed with fairy dust. And speaking of that dress . . .

The colorful fabric hung from her frame like the *Mona Lisa* hung on the wall of the Louvre Museum in Paris, commanding just as much attention. This woman was a sheer masterpiece. The dress was cinched at the waist with a black leather belt, highlighting the impressive curve of Lunden's hips. The material cascaded to her ankles in the back but stopped just below her knees in the front. She'd completed the ensemble with a pair of three-inch open-toed sparkly gold stilettos. The footwear was almost as sexy as that dress. *Almost.*

"I told you she looked pretty," Zachary whispered.

"Yes, she does," Quade said, unable to take his eyes off her.

Lunden flashed a low-wattage smile and shifted her weight as if his scrutiny made her nervous.

"You look nice," she said in a tiny voice. If the way her eyes slowly crawled over him was any indication, she'd understated her appreciation.

"Thank you," Quade said.

"And you look . . ."

"Magnificent?" she said.

"I'm not sure that's actually a powerful enough description."

"Flattery will get you . . . maybe one dance," she said.

Quade chuckled. Definitely a fast song, because he wasn't foolish enough to let this woman into his arms. Not looking like this. Not when his entire body craved nothing more than intertwining with hers. A different time, a different place, a different woman.

CHAPTER 21

Lunden didn't want to stare, but damn, Quade looked . . . *magnificent* too. Had she ever seen a man wear a suit so well? *Nope.* Whoever had tailored—because it fit him too well to be off the rack—that black suit should be arrested as an accessory, because he or she was assisting him in the commission of one hell of a crime.

"Are we ready?" she asked.

"I am," Zachary said, bouncing up and down.

"Me too," Quade added.

A beat later, they were out the door.

"It's such a nice evening. Do you mind if we walk? It's not as far as it might seem," Lunden said.

"I don't have a problem with it, but"—his eyes lowered to her feet—"you want to walk in *those* shoes?"

Lunden laughed. "Believe it or not, they're actually really comfortable."

Quade shrugged. "Let me grab something out of my vehicle. I'll be right back."

A moment later, he was.

"I got you something," he said, popping the lid of a plastic container.

Lunden gasped when he removed a wrist corsage. As odd as it sounded, she'd never received one before. Not even at her senior prom, when her absentminded date had forgotten it. "It's beautiful," she said, admiring the two small sunflowers adorned with greenery and black ribbon. Now she knew why he'd wanted to know what color she would be wearing.

"I hope it's not too dorky."

She extended her arm. "It's perfect. Put it on me?"

Once he slid it onto her wrist, he said, "It looks great on you."

Lunden eyed the adornment. "Yes, it does. Thank you. That was very thoughtful of you."

"Hey, Z," Quade called out to Zachary. "Come here a second."

Zachary ran toward them. "Yes, sir?"

Quade opened a second container. "I have something for you."

"You do?" Zachary asked, his eyes dancing with excitement.

Quade knelt to Zachary's level and pinned the single sunflower boutonniere, which matched her corsage, to his lapel.

"Gotta have a boutonniere," he said. "You're going to be the classiest kid in the building."

"Way cool," Zachary said. "Look, Mom. It's just like yours."

"I see," she said.

"This is the best night ever. Thank you, Quade," he said, hugging him. "I can't wait to show my friends. I bet none of them have a boot a deer."

Lunden covered her mouth and chuckled. When Quade returned to his full height, she said, "Where is your *boot a deer?*" Of course, he didn't need one to stand out. He was doing a grand job of that already.

"I don't like wearing them. I'm afraid of getting stuck by the pin," he said. "Flashbacks. The last time I had blood drawn, the lady didn't know what she was doing, and I nearly blacked out."

Something told her he'd given his boutonniere to Zachary to wear. "Why'd you have blood drawn?"

Quade eyed her, an amused expression on his face. "Kind of nosy, aren't you?"

"I figured, since you're always in *my* business, it was okay to get into yours."

"I got tested," he said. "Three times, actually. I needed to make absolutely certain the first two tests were correct."

"Tested for what?"

Quade chuckled. "Everything. I wanted—needed—to make sure my ex's reckless behavior didn't expose me to anything," he said. "She didn't, by the way."

"I remember those visits," Lunden said. "I made them a few times after my divorce. That last negative result felt like I'd gained a new lease on life."

"Look at us, adulting when it comes to maintaining our good health."

"Shouldn't we have been able to trust the people who'd claimed to love us with our most precious commodity?"

"Yes," Quade said.

"I thought so," she said.

As they continued toward the community center, Lunden took the opportunity to reintroduce Quade to Honey Hill. The more he knew about the town, the more likely it would grow on him. At least, she hoped so. Enough for him to not want to sell the inn. "That's the treasured Galloway Oak Tree. Rumored to be six centuries old. The old tale is that the blood of slaves has kept it thriving all these years." Lunden liked to believe the care the town showed it played a part too.

"Six hundred years? I bet that tree has some stories to tell," Quade said.

She pointed out the Van Lé Pier House, which was now a museum but had once served as the town's medical center back in the early 1800s. "It was run by a descendant of one of Honey Hill's founding families."

Quade eyed her. "You're just a wealth of information, huh?"

"Goes along with being mayor." She was about to tell him about the albino squirrels that had recently made Honey Hill their home when his arm jetted out and kept her from walking any farther. "What are you doing?"

"Don't move," he whispered. "Just stay here. I'll grab Z."

Confused, she said, "Huh?" She followed the direction his eyes were trained.

"It's a peacock," he whispered.

"I know what a peacock is," she said.

"They're territorial."

Lunden laughed. "That's Presto. He's harmless. Just roams the town at will. We typically just let him be. Sometimes Dover will get him riled up, and they chase each other up and down the street. It's quite entertaining."

Quade chuckled. "This town."

"I know, right? Great, isn't it. Kinda grows on you after a while."

"Mmm," was all Quade said.

He wasn't convinced now, but he would be, if she had anything to do with it.

"Watch this," Lunden said. A second later, she made a whistling sound. Presto fanned out his large, patterned plumes in an impressive display, then turned in a slow circle as if to model his majestic appearance.

"Wow," Quade said.

"Breathtaking, right?"

"Yes. Not the most beautiful thing I've seen today, but a close second."

When Lunden glanced up at him, he eyed her and winked, then refocused on Presto. After the angelic bird strutted off, they continued moving. Quade bent and plucked something from the grass.

"A dandelion," he said. He held it close to her mouth. "Make a wish."

She eyed him strangely. A second later, she closed her eyes and logged her wish. That this man would stop making it so easy for her to like him.

❋

Quade experienced a tightening in his gut when Lunden's painted lips puckered as she blew onto the dandelion. He swallowed hard and ignored the urge to kiss her. Would the temptation ever cease?

"Come on, guys," Zachary called out ahead of them, waving them forward.

"What did you wish for?" Quade asked.

"If I tell you, it won't come true," she said.

As they strolled along, Quade was glad Lunden had suggested they walk. He'd gotten to see a bit more of the town and experienced a peacock without getting mauled, or whatever peacocks did to their prey.

Booming music greeted them as they neared the building. When he opened the door for Zachary and Lunden, Rick James's "Super Freak" poured from inside. Oh, this was going to be an interesting night.

"Just act normal," Lunden said as she passed by.

Just act normal? How else would he act?

The first thing Quade noticed as they moved through the door was the mass of people on the floor, dancing their hearts out. The second—the gorgeous decorations. Sunflowers, hay bales, and Mason jars gave the space a country-rustic feel. Now he understood why the women at the flower shop had suggested he go with sunflowers for Lunden's corsage. Of course, he would have chosen them anyway, because they were still her favorites. The third thing Quade noticed was all the eyes plastered on them.

"Why does it seem like the entire room is staring at us?" he asked, though he doubted he should be surprised. They tended to garner looks whenever they were out together. Which seemed to be an awful lot, now that he thought about it. Strangely, spending time with Lunden and Zachary felt . . . normal, making it that much more abnormal.

"Because they are," she said, giving a wave to several folks.

Following Lunden's lead, he nodded and waved as they made their way through the crowd. Some of the faces of the people who greeted him were familiar; others weren't. Man, he hated crowds. And this one was particularly cumbersome, with everyone watching him like a duck they were preparing to roast.

"Hey, Ms. Shugga's nephew."

Quade turned toward the familiar voice. "Ennis? How you doing?" As usual, the man wore a pair of overalls. Only this time they were paired with a white shirt, black tie, and black suit jacket. While he stood out like a cardinal in snow, he looked sharp.

"Good. I'm good. I'll see you later," he said, then walked off.

"Mom, can I go dance with my friends?" Zachary asked.

Permission secured, he darted toward the dance floor. This was probably a good song to invite Lunden onto the dance floor on, because it wouldn't require them to get too intimately close; however, since they'd just arrived, she probably wanted to make a few rounds first.

Spotting the sheriff, Senior, and Mr. Clem at a table, Quade decided to go over and speak. "I'll be right back," Quade said over the music.

"Everything okay?" she asked.

"Yes, I see a few people I want to speak to."

"Should I keep an eye on you? Run to your rescue if the vultures start circling?"

"Something tells me no one's brazen enough to approach me. They know their mayor is a spitfire." Before walking away, he leaned in close to her ear and whispered, "First dance is mine."

Pulling back, she studied him a moment, nodded, smiled, and moved away. Typically, he would have watched until she disappeared, but he didn't need anyone witnessing him drool.

"Gentlemen," Quade said, approaching the table.

"I heard the rumor, but I refused to believe it until I saw it with my own eyes," Mr. Clem said. "Now, I've seen it and still don't believe it. How you woo the mayor so quick?"

"Reckon that was a little more than a twinkle we saw," Senior said.

"Don't let these OGs give you a hard time. They're just mad they're sitting here alone," Canten said.

"And you're sitting right here with us, Sheriff," Mr. Clem shot back.

They all laughed.

Taking a seat, Quade said, "Just old friends on an innocent outing. Nothing more. I think she felt sorry for me. Newcomer and all," he added to better support his claim. "Just doing her mayoral duty."

The men went silent for a moment, each staring at him. A beat later, they burst into laughter again. This time at him. He waved them off.

For the next little while, Quade talked, laughed, and learned more about the residents of Honey Hill than he needed to know. Like the old man who'd gotten drunk, painted his horse apple green, and ridden it through town buck naked. Like someone they called Mystic Blu because they swore the woman could predict the weather. And Tangelo Brown, who walked around in a tinfoil hat because he was afraid aliens were trying to read his thoughts. None of whom were in attendance tonight, which could have potentially made the night even more interesting.

"You better get out while you can," Mr. Clem said. "Once Honey Hill gets you, it gets you."

"I think I'm immune," Quade said.

"Same thing I said," Senior said, "fifty-some years ago. You've been warned."

Even over the music, Quade recognized Lunden's laugh. His eyes swept the crowd, spotting her standing with a group of women. As if sensing his eyes on her, she glanced in his direction. A tiny smile touched her lips, and he reciprocated.

"Mmm-hmm," Clem hummed.

"What?" Quade said.

"I looked at a friend like that once. Wound up spending the next forty-seven years with her."

Luckily for Quade, he had no desire to get married. Ever. He'd almost made that mistake once. Deciding he'd been tortured long enough, he said, "If you will excuse me, gentlemen—I, for one, am not here alone and should probably see if the mayor needs anything," taking a good-humored jab of his own.

"Damn. She's got you whipped already?" Mr. Clem said.

More laughter.

"They're just jealous. Go handle your business," Canten said.

Quade made it halfway across the room before someone snagged him by the arm.

"Well, hello there."

Quade recognized the voice but for the life of him couldn't remember her name, so he went with the usual, Blondie. "Good evening," he said.

"Oh, you don't have to be so formal," she said, fiddling with his lapel.

Quade's eyes briefly lowered to her offending hand, then met her hungry gaze again.

"You sure do seem to have the eye of every female in here on you, but I can definitely see why. You sure do know how to wear a suit."

"Thank you." Looking past her, his gaze connected with Lunden's. The second it did, she turned away as if not wanting him to know she'd been watching his interaction.

Blondie glanced over her shoulder, apparently noticing his focus wasn't on her. Smirking, she inched closer to him. "I see you escorted our illustrious mayor this evening. Her idea or yours?"

With furrowed brow, Quade eyed her silently.

She brushed her own words off with a fake laugh. "Can't fault her for wanting to spend the evening on the arm of the most handsome man in Honey Hill. Our mayor is certainly determined. Most women in town will do whatever they have to do to get what they want," she said, biting the tip of her manicured nail and running her eyes up and down his frame again. "From what I hear, a lot of them want you."

What was she saying? Had she heard the mayor wanted him?

"Excuse me, dear," Ms. Jewel said, interrupting the borderline-aggressive woman's spiel. Threading her arm through Quade's, Ms. Jewel continued, "I need to borrow this handsome gentleman a moment. Do you mind?"

"Actually, we were—"

"Thank you, dear," Ms. Jewel said, cutting Blondie off midsentence, then guiding him away.

"Thank you for that," he said.

"Might I offer a little unsolicited advice?"

Quade had an idea he would get it whether he welcomed it or not. For kicks, he considered saying no but said, "Absolutely," instead.

"Now I know you're a man with needs, but stay far away from that barracuda. That child . . ." She shook her head. "Always going after whatever man's not nailed down and some that are. Just a trifling-ass excuse for a woman." Ms. Jewel patted his forearm and smiled warmly. "Pardon my language."

"You don't have to worry about that." No matter how desperate he got, Blondie would be the last woman he'd turn to. "She's not my type."

"Something told me she wasn't. And speaking of the mayor . . ."

One thing Ms. Jewel was not, and that was subtle.

"I haven't seen you two on the dance floor yet. I know I'm old, but I do believe it's still customary for a man to dance with his date at least once."

"Oh, this isn't a date. I think the mayor felt sorry for me and agreed to come with me." The same line he'd used with the men. Ms. Jewel didn't appear to buy it either. While everyone seemed convinced otherwise, this wasn't a date. Why was that so hard to convey?

Ms. Jewel glanced up at him. "Did you ask her here?"

"Yes, ma'am."

"And you escorted her here, right?"

Again, he said, "Yes."

She laughed. "It's been a long time since I've been on a date, but that sure does sound like one to me. But if you say it's not, I reckon it's not. You young folks sure do tickle me," she said, giving a laugh. "I need your help with something," she continued, winding him through the crowd.

After Ms. Jewel filled him in on her plan, he smiled. "I'd be honored to help."

It wasn't a surprise Ms. Jewel led him to Lunden. He spoke to the ogling women before extending his hand to Lunden. When Michael Jackson's "Don't Stop 'til You Get Enough" played, he deemed it a good time to ask Lunden to dance. "Care to show me what you got on the dance floor, Mayor?"

"I would love to," she said, allowing him to lead her away. "Oh my God. Thank you for that. They all but had us married with a house full of little Quadettes."

He laughed. "Same here."

"Apparently, people don't think a man and woman can mingle without sleeping with each other."

"That's some twisted logic," he said. "Because I definitely don't want to sleep with you."

"Exactly. And you absolutely know I don't want to sleep with you either."

"See. A man and a woman can coexist without sex."

Lunden and Quade danced through several songs. Not only did she impress him with her moves, he was equally enthralled by the fact she could move so effortlessly in those shoes. At one point Zachary joined them, and they all danced together. Honestly, this was the most fun Quade had experienced in a while.

"Are you tired?" he asked.

"No. I have at least five more songs in me."

Just as the words escaped her mouth, Marvin Gaye's "Got to Give It Up" faded, replaced by Haley Reinhart's rendition of "Can't Help Falling in Love." That was his cue to leave the dance floor. Apparently, Lunden's too.

"I, um, guess we should take a break," she said.

Quade was poised to agree until he saw Blondie moving toward them. He all but snatched Lunden into his arms. "I thought you had at least five more songs in you." He breathed a sigh of relief when Blondie diverted her direction.

"I didn't mean it literally," Lunden said.

"Too late. We're already moving."

With Lunden's body pressed so intimately close to his, he thought about an array of things—baseball, horses, even honeybees—all in an effort to avoid an awkward erection. How would he explain that away? The heat they generated, her scent, the way she stared into his eyes, drove him insane. Subconsciously, he hugged her a little closer to him.

Lunden gasped softly. "I should go check on Zachary," she said but made no moves to free herself from his arms.

Quade glanced past her briefly. "He's fine. I can see him."

Lunden narrowed her eyes at him. "Hilary's stalking you, isn't she? That's why you're holding me captive."

I'm holding you because you feel so damn good in my arms. Of course, he didn't dare say that aloud. Instead, what came out of his mouth was, "Guilty."

And as if Lunden had conjured the woman, she materialized out of nowhere. Quade didn't acknowledge her presence.

"Mind if I cut in?" she asked.

Without looking at her, Lunden said, "Yes."

Blondie made a funny sound, mumbled something under her breath, then walked off.

"I owe you," he said.

"Running interference was part of our deal, right?" she said.

"You don't seem to particularly care for her. Why?"

"I don't have a problem with her. She has one with me."

"What happened between you?"

For the first time since she'd been in his arms, she looked away briefly.

"My ex-husband. They dated on and off in high school. Apparently, she had still been in love with him when we started dating. If I knew then what I know now, she could have had him."

So this was why Blondie kept trying to garner his attention? It was an attempt to spite Lunden. "How long have you been divorced?"

"Almost four glorious years."

"His loss," Quade said. And someone else's gain. He wasn't sure why imagining Lunden with another man troubled him. Actually, he *was* sure, but he refused to give life to the possibility.

CHAPTER 22

For the first time in a long time, Lunden allowed herself to have fun. Authentic fun. And with the most unlikely source. Her eyes searched the space, her gaze landing squarely on Quade, who was standing across the room, chatting with Canten and Sebastian. Three of the most handsome men in Honey Hill.

Thinking about the way Quade had held her in his arms—close, tight—caused a wave of heat to ripple through her. The sensation had made her legs wobbly. For a moment, she'd actually thought they would betray her. That would have given everyone something else to talk about. She could see the headline now: *Mayor Melts in the Arms of One of the Hottest Men in Town.*

"He's got the seat of your panties wet, doesn't he?"

Lunden snapped back to reality at the sound of Happi's voice. "My panties are as dry now as they were when I slid into them. And they're going to stay that way."

"Judging by the way you two looked on that dance floor, not for long. If that man would have so much as blown on you, you would have had an orgasm."

Happi and Rylee both burst into laughter.

Ugh, Lunden loathed the accuracy in that statement. "Both of you make me sick," she said, laughing a little herself.

"Lu, you two were looking awfully cozy out there. But my favorite part was watching you, Quade, and Zachary hold hands and dance in a circle." Rylee made a sappy face. "Like one big happy family. It was beautiful to watch the way you smiled."

Not wanting to admit she'd liked that part, too, Lunden said, "All a part of the plan."

Rylee smirked. "Uh-huh."

Happi's brows banged together. "Plan? What plan?"

Rylee pressed her fingers into her chest and sounded a faux gasp. "The mayor didn't tell you about her brilliant scheme?"

Happi shook her head.

"It's not a *scheme*," Lunden said. "It's a plan."

"My apologies," Rylee said. Eyeing Happi, she continued, "The mayor *plans* to expose Quade to the town, make him fall in love with it, and hopefully prompt him to change his mind about selling the inn."

Happi looked back and forth between Rylee and Lunden as if waiting for someone to say more. When no one did, she said, "That's the dumbest thing I've ever heard. You better expose that man to your vagina. That'll get the job done and in half the time. Judging by the way he looks at you, the only sight he's interested in seeing is one that consists of you lying naked underneath him, moaning. *Quade! Oh, Quade. Right there*," she mocked.

Rylee and Happi high-fived.

Lunden swatted at Happi, then surveyed to make sure they didn't have any extra ears listening. "Will you stop it? It's not that kind of party. I'm only here with him tonight as a courtesy. To keep these lust-driven women from gobbling him up." She slid her gaze across the room and landed on him again, appreciating the view. She drank him in and absently said, "Quade and I are . . . mere acquaintances. Two people with opposing views on the same matter. My one and only goal is to sway him over to my side for the well-being of Honey Hill."

"I get it," Happi said.

This drew Lunden's attention. Finally. Someone who understood her motivation.

"In fact," Happi continued, "when I watched the two of you on the dance floor, wrapped in each other's arms, lovingly staring into each other's eyes, I said to myself, *Aww, look at those mere acquaintances.*"

Lunden gave up. She just couldn't with these two.

"Uh-oh, looks like duty calls," Rylee said, directing her attention across the room.

Lunden frowned. "That damn woman is relentless," she said, watching Hilary approach Quade's group. But before she could intervene, the music lowered, and Ms. Jewel's commanding voice boomed through the speakers.

"On behalf of the planning committee, we'd like to thank each and every one of you for coming out tonight. As always, the floral sisters did a fantastic job of transforming the room. Give them a round of applause." Once the rapturous appreciation ended, Ms. Jewel continued, "None of this would have been possible without our other volunteers, all of you, and . . ." She paused. "Our esteemed mayor. Where you at, child? Come on up here."

Well, Quade was on his own. She made her way to the front, and Ms. Jewel directed Lunden to stand beside her. Lunden's brows furrowed. "What's going on?" she whispered.

"We're giving you your flowers while you're still here," Ms. Jewel said. "We thank you, Mayor. For all the effort you put into running our little ole town. For the way you fight for it, for us. For your willingness to do whatever it takes to get the job done. Oh, the ancestors would be proud. You are our hometown hero, and you deserve this."

A second later, Quade appeared, carrying a beautiful diamond-shaped crystal piece that he passed to Ms. Jewel.

"Thank you, son," Ms. Jewel said. "On behalf of the men and women of Honey Hill, we present you with this year's Heroes Award."

Lunden accepted the brilliant piece, admiring it as if it truly were a diamond. "I . . . don't know what to say," she said.

"Yeah, right," came from the audience.

The room filled with laughter.

Lunden gave a short speech about how much she loved Honey Hill and how honored she was to be celebrated this way and how she'd always protect the people and place she loved. Ending her speech, she said, "I dedicate this award to Ms. Shugga. The woman who . . ." She paused to gather herself. "The woman who showed me my story wasn't finished. Without her I wouldn't be here." Lunden's voice cracked when she said, "Thank you." After leaving the podium, she went to stand next to Quade. "Did you know about this?"

"A little birdie may have told me something earlier," he said. "Congratulations."

"Thank you. Did a little birdie tell you anything else?"

"Like what?" he said, a quizzical expression on his face.

Lunden smiled. A second later, the lights dimmed and the projection screen lowered. "This is for you," she whispered.

The worry lines in his forehead deepened, but he didn't ask any questions, simply slid his attention to the screen. Lunden observed him as the compilation video of Ms. Shugga she'd commissioned Mr. Lendell to create began to play to the backdrop of Gladys Knight. When the first image flashed across the screen, Quade's shoulders stiffened. Lunden wondered whether this had been a good idea after all. But the more images of Ms. Shugga—with him as a boy, with his mother, with his father, with townsfolk—transitioned to music across the screen, the less rigid his posture became. And by the time the short video wrapped, tears ran down his face, but not sad ones, judging by his smile. It stunned Lunden that he wasn't bashful about showing such emotion, because most men she'd encountered were.

"We love you, Shugga," came from multiple directions in the crowd, followed by howls, cheers, claps, and whistles.

Quade washed a hand down his face, then pulled Lunden into his arms right there in front of everyone. Sounds of compassion swirled around them.

"Thank you," he whispered in her ear, "for reintroducing me to my aunt."

Lunden hugged him back. "You're welcome."

The jubilee drew to a close shortly after the video. Lunden provided some closing words and joined Quade at their table. Zachary was fast asleep, stretched out between two folding chairs. Quade stood and hoisted him into his arms, and they all headed toward the door.

"What are you feeding this kid?" Quade asked.

"I can get the car," Lunden said, feeling bad about his having to tote Zachary all the way home.

"I'm not letting you walk alone in the dark," Quade said.

Lunden stopped moving and eyed him. "Not *letting* me?"

"Mayor Pierce, I prefer you not walk home alone. Is that better?"

"Much. Let's go."

A few steps into their journey, Lunden regretted walking. She hadn't planned to spend most of the evening on the dance floor with Quade. She stopped to remove her shoes. "My feet are a little upset with me."

"I thought you said those shoes were comfortable."

"They are when I don't spend four hours on the dance floor. Thanks to a certain Quade Cannon."

"I'm sorry," he said. "Want to get on my back?"

Lunden laughed. "I'll pass, but thanks just the same for the offer."

"Suit yourself, country girl."

"Country girl?"

"No one in the city walks around barefoot."

"I'll accept that label."

A brief silence fell between them.

"The video . . . ," Quade said. "Thank you again. It brought back some great memories. I'd somehow forgotten all about the truck my dad and I were rebuilding. He purchased it as a gift for my mother. They were watching a Christmas movie, and she commented she wanted a Christmas truck. That was all it took. Coincidentally, someone around here was selling a 1948 Ford F1 pickup. Dad jumped on it." His expression turned somber. "We never got to finish her. Noel, my mom named her."

"Well, since you have some time on your hands, maybe you can finish Noel now."

Quade flashed a puzzled expression. "What do you mean?"

Obviously, he hadn't ventured into the garage. "It's still in Ms. Shugga's garage. Your garage, I mean."

"Really?"

She nodded.

"Wow. I . . . I hadn't looked in there yet. Wow," he said again.

"You okay?" she asked, noting the sorrowful look on his face.

He smiled. "Yeah. Yeah, I'm good. I have a job. At the screen printing shop. A few hours a day, a couple of days a week."

Lunden didn't miss how he'd effectively changed the subject. "Good for you. You'll like Mr. Conroy. You two should get along fine."

Quade adjusted Zachary in his arms.

"Do you want me to carry him the rest of the way?"

"I got him. Clearly, this kid can sleep through anything."

"When he's out, he's out," Lunden said.

"Were they dating? My aunt and Mr. Conroy?"

How did he . . . ? The barbershop. "Officially, no. But I do believe they cared deeply for each other."

"Hmm," was all he said.

"Finally," Lunden said, reaching her driveway.

"Tired of me already?" Quade asked.

"No. Just tired."

Inside, Quade placed Zachary in his bed, then went up front. Lunden undressed Zachary, then tucked him in. Before leaving the room, she watched him sleep for several seconds. No one swelled her heart like this kid. Joining Quade up front, she said, "Can I get you something? Wine, a beer, water? It's no trouble." She'd come a long way, because she remembered a time when she would have wanted to drown him in the liquid.

Quade ran a hand over his lips and pointed over his shoulder. "It's getting late. I should get going."

When he inched closer to her, it unnerved her a bit. His masculine scent intoxicated her. If he tried to kiss her this time, she would let him. Like Rylee had said, she should just go ahead and get it out of her system. Afterward, she'd be able to get back to normal. A normal that didn't include constantly fantasizing about Quade.

Instead of planting a kiss on her lips, he pressed a kiss to her forehead. A surge of energy traveled through her entire body. How could such an innocent act have such an impact?

"Thank you for tonight," he said, turning to leave.

Only he didn't move forward. He stood there as if waiting for someone to escort him to the door.

"Everything okay?" she asked in a delicate voice.

Before she even processed he'd moved, Quade pulled her into his arms and kissed her so hard it felt as if she'd transitioned through space and time. When she returned to her body, a fire hotter than anything she'd ever felt before seared her insides. His strong arms wrapped around her, and her trembling hands inched over his rock-hard muscles, sending her body spiraling into an even more erratic tailspin. The kiss was extraordinary. It both sated and starved her. All at once. Energized and drained her, simultaneously. Brought her pure joy and sadness.

The more Quade gave, the more she wanted—needed. Moans of pleasure flowed from her mouth and into his, where he swallowed them whole. Just when she thought a kiss couldn't get any better than this, he proved her wrong. Deepening the delicious assault on her mouth plummeted her into a black hole of sexual insanity. In this delusional state, if he'd asked for her body, she would have freely given it to him. Every. Damn. Inch. But just as fast as the kiss had started, it ended.

Quade pulled away and stared at her, his chest rising and falling with the same intensity as her own. Was he waiting for her to make the next move or debating whether he should? She parted her lips to say . . . hell, she had no idea what to say, so she closed them.

"Good night, Mayor," Quade said.

A second later, he was gone. And it was probably for the best. Rylee had been wrong. So, so wrong. Kissing him hadn't ended one problem; it had simply created another.

Sliding behind the wheel, all Quade could think about was that damn kiss. He wasn't sure what had gotten into him, but he'd been powerless to stop it. The second his mouth had latched onto Lunden's, he'd known he was in trouble. She'd become like a battery that had jump-started his entire body. Had she given him just a sliver of an indication that she'd wanted more from him, he would have given it to her.

He'd made the right decision by leaving, but that still didn't stop him from regretting not hoisting her into his arms and carrying her to the bedroom. His dick twitched at the missed opportunity. He shook his head. How in the hell would they face each other again after that kiss? A kiss that had nearly taken him to his knees.

Cranking the engine, he sat there a minute before pulling away. Just in case she came running out of the house to stop him like he'd seen in the movies. Unfortunately, the only movement he caught was Ennis walking down the road with Dover. *What the hell is he doing out this late?*

Quade pulled out of Lunden's driveway and rolled down his window. "Ennis? You need a ride?"

"No, Dover enjoys our midnight strolls."

"Hey, Dover," Quade said, when the curious dog sniffed around the SUV.

"When he wiggles his body like that, he's saying hey," Ennis said.

"Well, you two be safe."

"We will," Ennis said, walking off.

The first thing Quade did when he arrived at the inn was look inside the garage. Sure enough, there sat Noel in all her weathered glory. A mess of emotions flooded him. Moving closer, he ran his hand over the peeling seafoam-green paint. "Hey, girl. Remember me?"

Quade smiled as he recalled the way his mother's eyes had lit up when his father had had the clunker towed to the inn. She'd darted off the front porch, sprinted across the yard, and leaped into his arms. They'd kissed like he'd just returned from war. Sadness replaced Quade's elation, and he backed out of the building.

Inside, he shrugged out of his jacket and slung it over the banister, loosened his tie, and unfastened the top buttons of his shirt. He prepared a stiff drink, downed it in one gulp, then poured a second. After moving into the living room, he dropped down onto the couch and kicked out of his shoes. Reclining his head, he stared at the picture hanging above the fireplace. A dandelion losing its pappus. If he had an actual dandelion right now, his one wish would have been that Lunden stood in front of him, naked. Before he got the opportunity to enjoy the full impact of the visual, his doorbell rang.

Quade bolted forward. *Could it . . . ? Nah.* Placing his glass down, he moved to the front of the house and pulled the door open. "Ennis? What's up?"

"There's a light shining in your vehicle."

Quade squinted toward Josie. *Damn.* He'd left his interior light on. "Thanks, Ennis. I'll take care of it."

"You're welcome," Ennis said and walked off.

After taking care of the light issue, Quade decided to call it a night. When he was halfway down the hall leading to his bedroom, the doorbell rang again. Backtracking, he pulled the door open, curious about what Ennis wanted this time. "Lunden?" He stepped aside. "Come in." His brow furrowed. "Everything okay? Where's Zachary?"

"Everything's fine. Rylee's watching him for me," she said.

Quade trailed Lunden into the living room. Inside, she scrutinized the space as if she'd never been here before. Quade crossed his arms over his chest and watched her. The heart-stopping dress she'd worn earlier had been replaced with a comfortable-looking sleeveless black dress that swept the floor when she walked. From the moment he'd opened the door, he'd known why she'd come, but would she admit it or simply expect him to act?

Lifting his glass from the table, she took a sip, then held it out to him. Closing the distance between them, he accepted the glass and downed the remainder. A drop or two remained in the bottom of the glass. He collected it with his thumb, then dragged it across Lunden's bottom lip. When her lips parted and her tongue grazed the pad of his thumb, it awakened a beast inside him, but he didn't unleash it on her. He placed the glass back on the table, then returned to a full stand in front of her.

"I'm not going to walk around town holding your hand. I'm not going to fall in love with you. I don't even want a relationship," she said.

"What do you want, Lunden?"

"You," she said. "I want you. But only for one night."

In a million years, he'd never imagined those words coming out of her mouth. But . . . there they were, and he damn sure planned to fulfill them.

CHAPTER 23

Apparently, kissing Quade wasn't the only thing Lunden needed to get out of her system. And while she was absolutely certain she would regret her reckless behavior tomorrow, tonight . . . this was what she wanted. *He* was what she wanted.

Quade didn't appear shocked by her forwardness. Like he'd known all along what she wanted. But of course he had. She'd shown up at his doorstep close to midnight and hadn't come for a cup of sugar.

"I thought you didn't want to sleep with me," Quade said.

"I don't plan to do any sleeping," she said.

Quade's brow arched in what she took as surprise. He studied her long and hard. Why was it taking him so long to make his move? He wanted her. She could see the raw desire blazing in his dark, daunting gaze. Here she was, giving herself to him. So what was he waiting on?

He took a step closer to her. "You're going to regret this tomorrow."

"I'm—"

He pressed a finger to her lips, silencing her. "You are," he said. "Maybe I will too. But let's save our regrets for tomorrow. Tonight . . . tell me what you want, what your body needs, and let me give it to you."

She nodded, his words arousing her even more. The mere thought of him doing everything she wanted him to do to her electrified her entire body. A second later, he snaked a hand behind her neck and pulled her mouth close to his, but he didn't kiss her.

"I don't hold hands. I couldn't give less of a damn about love. And I'm done with relationships," he said.

"Well, then tonight sounds like a win for the both of us."

A beat later, Quade crashed his mouth to hers, kissing her with a raw, untamed passion that made her delirious with need. A steady, low moan escaped as his tongue wildly sparred with hers. Gathering the slinky fabric of her dress between his fingers, he broke their mouths apart just long enough to lift it over her head, revealing the fact she wasn't wearing a bra or panties.

Quade flinched, as if her nakedness startled him. "Wow."

"Just thought I'd save you a little time," she said.

"Thank you for being so considerate."

When he hoisted her into his arms, her legs instinctively wrapped around his waist as he carried her to the sofa and eased down with her in his lap. Their mouths joined again in an exhilarating kiss. Quade ran the tips of his fingers along her spine, causing her to quiver.

Reluctantly, Lunden pulled away from his tantalizing lips. She didn't break eye contact as her trembling fingers fumbled to unbutton his shirt. Once she'd unfastened the last button, she glided her hands up his smooth, hard chest and over his strong shoulders until the fabric fell away. She angled her head, leaned forward, and planted light kisses from the crook of his neck to the space below his earlobe, nipping it playfully.

In one swift motion, Quade had her on her back. His mouth hovered inches from her, but he didn't kiss her. Why was he teasing her like this? Growing impatient, she lifted to meet him, but he pulled away. One side of his mouth lifted in a devious smile.

"I told you you weren't going to always get what you wanted," he said.

A second later, Quade stood. Panic gripped Lunden. Was he rejecting her? She'd seen the primal desire blazing in his eyes. He wanted her just as much as she wanted him. Realizing he'd only stood to undress—not to end things—Lunden breathed a sigh of relief.

Lunden watched in gleeful anticipation as Quade unfastened his pants and inched them off his narrow hips, along with the designer boxers he wore. Her lips parted and a shallow breath escaped as she took in every inch of him. His body hadn't been the only thing to experience a growth spurt.

"See something you like?" he asked.

"Maybe. Come a little closer so I can get a better look." Lunden wasn't sure where all this confidence was coming from, but she embraced it. Maybe it stemmed from the fact that she felt comfortable with Quade. Not at the same level she had when they were younger, but enough to be at ease with him.

Quade wagged his index finger back and forth at her, dropped to his knees beside the sofa, and lowered his head between her legs. Warm, gentle kisses peppered the inside of one thigh, making her shiver with anticipation the higher his lips climbed. When he claimed her core, she cried out in pleasure.

Eyes clamped shut, she concentrated on all the wonderful sensations flowing through her. She wasn't sure what oral black magic Quade was working on her, but it felt so damn good. Better than anything she'd ever experienced before. His tongue—alternating between firm and lithe—swirled, licked, flicked her into submission.

Quade took his time tasting her, exploring her. Each pass over her clit, kiss to her folds, weakened her resolve more and more. The fluttering sensation in her lower stomach told her she wouldn't be able to hold back much longer.

Lunden splayed her fingers, clenched the sofa fabric between them, and willed her body to hold out just a little longer, but the buildup was too much. Pain traveled through both her feet from curling her toes so tight she thought she'd break one. When Quade suckled her swollen bead between his lips, it spelled her doom.

She held Quade's head in place. *"Right there. Right there."* He gripped her hips and pulled her closer to him. No longer able to resist, she exploded with an orgasm so powerful, she screamed. Literally screamed. No doubt she'd frightened off any wildlife for miles.

Her heart banged in her chest. Blood whooshed in her ears. Every muscle in her body seized. "Oh my—" A second release gripped her before she'd come down off the first, snatching both her breath and ability to speak. She'd never come two—"oooh, God"—make that *three* times back to back. Who knew such a thing was possible?

A second later, she collapsed down on the sofa, her body still feeling the aftershocks of the earthquake Quade had caused to rip through her. When Quade scooped her into his arms, she rested her head on his shoulder. "Where are we going?"

"To the bed. I don't want to break the legs on the sofa," he said.

Something about the declaration recharged her. She crashed her mouth to his. They kissed all the way to the bedroom. Placing her feet on the floor, he walked her backward until her back met a wall. Resting hands on either side of her face, he kissed her like her mouth held the key to life. Quade broke their mouths apart but continued kissing her along the jaw, down her neck, over her collarbone, and back up to her ear.

"Are you on birth control?" he whispered.

"Yes," she practically moaned back. Despite not having sex, she'd continued with the pill to regulate her cycles.

Quade kissed his way back to her mouth, pecked her gently, and pulled away, causing her eyes to open.

"Do you trust me with your body?" he asked.

The tenderness she witnessed in his eyes made her want him even more. "Yes."

Placing his hands behind her thighs, he lifted her body and pinned her against the wall. They kissed again. Only this time it wasn't ravenous. It was gentle, sweet. She whimpered when he teased her opening with the head of his dick, right before slowly inching inside her as if giving her body time to conform to him.

Quade released a guttural sound, a mix between a grunt and a growl. His strokes started long and slow but quickly grew hard and fast. Their harmonies of moans, cries, even curses, coupled with the sound of smacking flesh, filled the room. If she'd known being with him would feel so damn good, maybe she would have reconsidered limiting them to one night. Then again, one night was for the best, because nothing that felt this fantastic could be good for her.

Quade was about to lose his mind. The second he slid inside Lunden, it released a flood of memories. The past came rushing back. This moment was reminiscent of their first time, only a million times greater. He was no longer a shy kid, fumbling around and trying his best to make her feel how much he loved her. And he hadn't stared into her eyes and whispered *I love you* as he'd entered her. Love wasn't a factor now. This was only sex. Damn good, mind-blowing, just-what-he-needed sex. While he'd never been one unable to separate sex and feelings, their intimacy felt so familiar it rattled him.

He slammed back to reality when Lunden dug her nails into his sweat-slickened flesh, causing his back to sting. Oddly, it aroused him even more. He was already doing all he could do to keep it together, so he didn't need one more thing dragging him to the edge.

Being inside Lunden, no barrier between them . . . it was enough to drive a man wild, evident by his growls. He was determined to take his time with her, to fully and thoroughly enjoy their one night together, plus ensure she reveled in it too. But she was making it damn hard. Not only did he want it gratifying, he wanted it memorable. Every time she saw him from this night forward, he wanted her body to quaver just a little, recalling how he'd made her feel. This was purely ego talking.

One thing he hadn't counted on—actually, several things: her feeling so damn good, feeling so damn familiar, being so damn wet, and fitting around him so damn perfectly.

"Dammit, woman, you should have warned me," he said through gritted teeth.

"About what?"

"You," he said.

Getting too close to his breaking point, Quade pulled out of her.

Lunden's protest was immediate. "*No, no, no.* Not yet. Don't stop yet," she pleaded. "Why are you torturing me?"

What she didn't know, couldn't possibly know, was that by denying her, he also tortured himself. But it was a sacrifice he was willing to make, because if she was only giving him one night, he needed to make the most of it. Kissing her objections away, he carried her to the bed, eased her down, then flipped her onto her stomach. Blanketing her body with his, he eased back inside her, moving with unhurried, steady strokes. Positioning his mouth near her ear, he whispered, "Do you regret ringing my doorbell tonight?"

"No," she said without hesitation. "Not for one second," came off a moan.

"Good." He nipped her lobe. "Do you like the feel of me inside you?"

A beat or two passed before she said, "No. I . . . I love it."

He snaked a hand between her legs and massaged her slowly, delicately. "Does this feel better than your vibrator?"

"So much better. So much better," she repeated.

Every time she pressed the cold, hard device between her legs, he wondered if she'd think about him. His tongue lapping up all her essence. His fingers moving gracefully between her thighs. Would doing so make her come harder, faster, multiple times, as she'd done earlier? Taking his hand away, he came up on his knees and gripped her hips.

Still, he kept his strokes slow and steady. "Tell me how you want it, Lunden. How you need it," he said.

"Harder," she said. "Faster. Harder and faster. Please."

He gave her what she wanted, hiking her hips and driving in and out of her like a madman. Lunden's ass jiggled each time he plowed into her. When she clawed at the mattress, he knew she was just as close to shattering as he was.

"Oh . . . my . . . God, Lynx. I'm about to . . ." Her words dried up.

Lynx. Hearing the pet name Lunden had given him years ago—because he'd been solitary and mysterious and had distinctive ears, *just like a lynx cat,* she'd said—knocked him off his game, but only momentarily.

After a couple more strokes, Quade's body betrayed him, sending him careening off a cliff of pure pleasure. His head lashed back, and he roared a sound so primal he barely recognized his own voice. The release gripped him with such force it was hard to breathe. He swore he'd shot a part of his soul into Lunden. His body collapsed down, half on her and half on the mattress.

Several minutes passed before Quade could speak, but when he did, he said, "Ready for round two?" Because he'd be damned if he let her get away without experiencing her again. Even if something told him it would be to his own detriment.

CHAPTER 24

Lunden was usually attentive when she joined one of Ms. Jewel's Saturday teas, but truthfully, she hadn't heard a word any of the ladies had said since they'd settled on the front porch of the purple Victorian. No matter how hard she tried to focus, her brain always journeyed back to one event. Her night with Quade. Butterflies fluttered in her stomach when she thought about it.

Two weeks should have been enough time for her to have purged it from her system, right? So why in the hell was it still lodged so prominently in her head, as if it had just happened the night before? *Because how in the hell does one forget a night like that?*

Quade had given her body exactly what it had needed and so much more. In return, she'd given herself to him in a way she'd never given herself to her ex, opened up in a way that now terrified her to recall. She'd never felt so . . . uninhibited in the bedroom. What had come over her? She smiled softly. *Tell me how you want it, Lunden. How you need it.* He'd come over her.

Lunden absently fiddled with the bumblebee charm on her necklace. *Lynx.* She'd actually allowed the name she hadn't spoken in years to slip past her lips. Like she'd had a choice. Not when Quade had been in complete control of her mind and body.

Her initial assessment of his performance capabilities in the bedroom had been spot on. He was a phenomenal lover. The woman who captured his heart and gained access to his body anytime she wanted it was going to be one lucky individual. She reconsidered the *captured his heart* part when she recalled him saying he was done with love. Actually, his exact words had been *I couldn't give less of a damn about love.*

Apparently, his ex's infidelity had cut him to the core. She, of all people, understood that kind of hurt. You never wanted to believe the person you loved the most could be the one who hurt you the worst. But while she'd been battered and scarred by love, too, she wasn't at the point of giving up on it completely. But it sounded as if Quade was.

Granted, she didn't see herself falling in love anytime in the near future, but one day. Maybe. But if she ever risked it all again and sacrificed her heart, she would make damn sure she got it right this time. Thanks to her ex, she now knew exactly what she didn't want. Since there weren't any viable prospects in Honey Hill, it was possible she'd never fall in love again. Especially if leaving was a requirement. This was her home, and she would never leave it again.

"I miss sex."

The words snagged Lunden from her thoughts, and she eyed Ms. Harriet in shock. She wasn't sure how she felt about hearing the woman—old enough to be her grandmother—talk about sex.

"*Sister,*" Ms. Bonita said with an eye roll.

"What? It's true. But not just any sex. I miss that head-over-heels-in-love sex. Not that hot-in-the-loins mess y'all young folks are into," Ms. Harriet said. "Though I spect I'd settle for that right about now."

"Lawd, Harriet, you have an orgasm at your age, you liable to go into cardiac arrest," Ms. Jewel said.

"Well, then I reckon I'd better find me a doctor or paramedic, so if I flatline, they can jump-start me."

The porch shook with laughter.

Once things settled, Ms. Bonita lowered her voice to a whisper. "Have y'all ever been in Estella's secret room?"

"Bonita, why are you whispering?" Ms. Jewel asked in an equally muted tone.

"'Cause she thinks the squirrels will hear her and go and tell Pastor," Ms. Harriet said.

More laughter.

"And you know I've been there," Ms. Harriet said. "Heck, I signed up for her rewards program. A couple more visits, and I'll get a free bumblebee vibrator."

At the mention of the bumblebee vibrator, Lunden choked on her sweet tea and coughed ferociously. All eyes landed on her.

"I see someone already owns one. Tell the truth: Is it any good? I can't be wasting my time on a dud," Ms. Harriet said.

Lunden's cheeks burned under the older women's scrutiny. "Um . . . I don't . . . I mean . . ." Truthfully, it used to bring her great pleasure. Now, she couldn't quite find the right spot. She blamed Quade for throwing her system out of whack.

"Don't be ashamed, child. We all have tickled our own petal once or twice," Ms. Jewel said.

"Speak for yourself, Jewel," Ms. Bonita said.

Ms. Jewel and Ms. Harriet eyed Ms. Bonita with a *do you actually think we believe that* look. Honestly, Lunden could see Ms. Harriet visiting the room, but not Ms. Bonita. While they were sisters, their personalities were worlds apart. Ms. Harriet had traveled the globe, while Lunden believed Ms. Bonita had never left Honey Hill.

Ms. Bonita took a sip from her glass. "Well, maybe once or twice," she said with a smirk.

Lunden's eyes bulged, then slid toward Rylee, whose brows touched the sky. Apparently, Ms. Bonita wasn't as straitlaced as originally thought. *An in-the-closet freak.* Lunden laughed to herself.

"Ms. Harriet, what is head-over-heels-in-love sex?" Rylee asked.

"I'm glad you asked," Ms. Harriet said.

Before she started, Ms. Harriet reached over and fished a flask from her pocketbook, unscrewed the top, and poured a finger or two into her glass. She offered some to the others. Like true southern ladies . . . they all accepted. Taking a sip, Lunden was surprised that whatever Ms. Harriet had given them hadn't eaten through the glass.

"There are different stages of sex," Ms. Harriet continued. "There's the *he'll do* sex. You don't really like him, but you need some. While it's hit or miss, it can be fun."

Lunden recalled her college years. She'd experienced this type, once or twice.

"Then there's the *I can work with this* sex. You might have to direct him, but all in all, he's okay in bed."

Lunden had been there too.

"Lastly, there's the *this fool has been marked by the devil* sex."

"*Marked by the devil* sex?" they said in unison.

Ms. Harriet nodded. "Yes. You gotta watch out for him. Sex so good he'll have you cashing in your retirement and pursuing him around the globe." Ms. Harriet gazed off, starry eyed. "*Mmm.* Good times."

Ms. Bonita placed a hand on her hip and pinned Ms. Harriet with a narrow-eyed gaze. "Sister, is that why you needed to borrow five thousand dollars that one time? You told me you needed your car fixed."

Ms. Harriet smiled. "Well, he did have my motor purring like a kitten," she said.

Rylee spit a mouthful of tea across the porch.

"You lied to your own sister," Ms. Bonita said.

"I'm sorry, sister. The devil made me do it."

Even Ms. Bonita had to laugh at that one.

Ms. Jewel shook her head. "No wonder you been divorced five times. You wore those poor men out."

"I was good at sex, just no good with love," Ms. Harriet said.

"Except with Theodore," Ms. Bonita said. "You loved him, and good Lord in heaven knows that man loved you."

Sadness shadowed Ms. Harriet's features. "Theodore," she said, more to herself than to them. A gentle smile touched her face. "The one who got away."

When Ms. Bonita rubbed her sister's arms, Ms. Harriet perked up. "Well, this is the perfect lead-in to that head-over-heels-in-love sex. Love, true love, can feel like an out-of-body experience. Like monstrous waves crashing inside you. There's no pain, just pure pleasure. It feels like you're connecting on a chemical, even cellular level. It's so intense that it changes you. You feel him. Everywhere. Like he's injecting himself straight into your veins. You reach the highest high. At that moment, he's your world and you're his. And combined, you're perfect. Absolutely perfect."

Lunden refused to believe she'd experienced this with Quade, though a lot of what Ms. Harriet described, she swore she'd experienced. But love didn't exist between her and Quade. Just lust. Changing her train of thought, Lunden desperately wanted to ask questions: Who was Theodore? Where was he now? How had he gotten away? But she didn't.

Ms. Harriet looked from Rylee to Lunden. "If you ever experience that kind of connection with someone—and trust me, there'll be no mistaking it—don't let it get away. Fight for true love. Always. Because love is love and there's a lot to go around, but a love that fills your soul is hard to be found."

The women were quiet for a long while, each lost in her own thoughts. Lunden considered Ms. Harriet's poetic words. She couldn't imagine ever being so in tune with another person. Such a bond sounded . . . paralyzing.

"What do we have here?" Ms. Harriet said.

The click-clack of hooves hitting pavement drew Lunden's attention toward the road.

"Well, would you look at that," Ms. Harriet said.

Oh, she was looking. Hard.

Ms. Harriet continued, "The good Lord was just showing off when he made those three."

Lunden drew a slow, shallow breath. While all the men nearing them—mounted high on horses—were attractive, her gaze locked on the one who'd kept her up into the wee hours of the morning ravishing her body.

Even from this distance, Quade's presence made her tingle all over and her cheeks heat. *Pull yourself together!* she demanded of her body.

"Oh, to be young again," Ms. Bonita said.

"Who needs youth. Experience is the better teacher," Ms. Harriet said. "And I can sho nuff school them."

"On what, the proper use of Bengay?" Ms. Jewel said.

They all laughed.

As a show of fortitude—or maybe it was the liquor—Lunden stood. "Excuse me," she said, then walked toward the road to greet the men. She needed to at least *pretend* Quade's presence had no effect on her. Thankfully, Rylee followed suit, giving her added confidence.

"Hey, fellas," Lunden said.

"Mayor," they said in unison.

Lunden's gaze settled on Quade. Everything about him was attention grabbing. The black cowboy boots he wore. The dark denim jeans that hugged his powerful thighs. The plain black T-shirt that exposed his strong arms. The black-and-white bandana tied around his neck. That black Stetson hat. Definitely that hat.

Jesus, you look good.

Canten and Sebastian were similarly dressed, but neither was as delightful on her eyes as Quade. Lunden fought her attraction to him, but man, was it potent. This pull she felt right now scrambled her thoughts. And for a moment, she fantasized about sleeping with him again, but she swiftly kicked the idea aside. There were so many reasons why it couldn't happen again, but the main one was this: She didn't need sex clouding her judgment. No matter how good said sex had been. She needed to think about what was best for the town, not herself.

"Where are you guys headed?" Rylee asked. "Looking all royal on those horses."

"Giving Quade the deluxe tour around town," Canten said.

Lunden's plan was definitely not working as well as it had in her head. For one, she'd avoided Quade for the past couple of weeks. For two, it would be kind of hard to focus, showing him around town, when all she could think about was their night together. Thinking about it, she reasoned it didn't specifically have to be her who exposed Quade to the town. Maybe it was best Canten and Sebastian did it. That whole male-bonding thing. If Quade formed a bond with them, this could sway him, right? Why did it feel like she was grasping at straws here?

While Rylee entertained Canten and her brother, Lunden chatted with Quade. "So you're a cowboy now, huh?"

Quade shrugged. "When in Rome."

"The hat looks nice on you."

Quade gave her a low-wattage smile, then touched the brim of the hat. "Why, thank you, pretty lady," he said, then winked.

Lunden laughed at his poorly executed country accent. The horse nuzzled her, and she rubbed its head.

"She likes you," Quade said.

"Of course she does. Burgundy is my horse."

"Your horse, huh? No wonder she's such a smooth ride," Quade said.

Lunden went still from the hidden innuendo in his words. As she eyed him, her lips parted slightly to release a tiny breath. The dark, daunting, hungry look in his eyes mimicked one she'd witnessed before. When he'd taken her against the wall. A jolt of awareness shot straight to her core. "W-well, not actually mine, but she and I have a bond. Don't we, girl?"

A second later Lunden took a step back as if fearing Quade would jump off the horse and take her right there in Ms. Jewel's front yard. Or, more accurately, feared she'd snatch him off the horse. Either way, it was best to have some distance between them. "I . . . um . . . should probably let you get going." She snapped her fingers. "Oh, I've been meaning to call you—"

"Really?" he said, cutting her off midthought.

The cynicism in his words wasn't lost on her. A pang of guilt for intentionally avoiding him hit her. "Busy," she whispered. "Planning Zachary's party." It wasn't a whole lie, but obviously enough of one to draw a look of disbelief from Quade. Continuing, she said, "That's what I needed to talk to you about."

"I see," was all he said.

From experience using those two words, she knew there was something more he wanted to say. Was he salty with her for not calling him? If so, why? It wasn't like they were an item and needed to check in with one another. They'd spent one hell of a fulfilling night together. It wasn't like he'd reached out to her either. Simple as that. There was that word again. *Simple.* When would she learn it did not belong in any sentence pertaining to Quade Cannon? This man was far from simple.

"Swing by tonight," he said. "Around seven. We can talk then. If that's what you want to do."

If that was what she wanted to do? Was he proposing they do more? Folding her arms across her chest, she eyed the ground briefly, then looked back at Quade. "Sure," she said but had no intentions of going. Alone with him again? She didn't need that kind of temptation in her life. And with Zachary away on a weekend field trip, she couldn't even use his presence as a buffer.

Quade pulled the bandana over his face, leaving only those hypnotizing eyes exposed. Giving her a single nod, he trotted off. *Whew, Lord, please give me strength.* Rylee came to stand beside her as she watched them ride away.

262

"Um, Mayor, remind me again how your brilliant plan is going," she whispered.

"It's still in motion," Lunden said. "Thank you very much." She just wasn't sure what direction it was headed.

Quade laughed to himself. Did Lunden even realize she always eyed the ground when she lied? He'd known from the minute she'd said, "Sure," she had no intentions of coming by. That was probably a good thing, because he couldn't make any promises that he wouldn't try to get her in his bed again. After their mind-blowing night together, he'd be a fool not to at least wish for such euphoria again.

"Are you going to ask him, or am I?" Sebastian said, drawing Quade's attention to him.

Canten shrugged. "None of my business," he said.

Sebastian waved Canten's words off before turning to Quade. "Spill, man," he said.

Confused, Quade said, "Spill what?"

"What's up with you and Lunden?"

Quade chuckled. "Nothing, man. We're just friends."

"That's good to hear, because I intend for Lunden to be my wife," Sebastian said.

Quade shifted on the horse, the news hitting him in the chest with the force of an angry gorilla. Unexplainable jealousy coursed through him. "Your . . . your wife? I didn't realize you two . . ." His words trailed off; he refused to give them a label. If Lunden was Sebastian's, she certainly didn't act like it. Especially when she'd been in his bed. Quade's shoulders stiffened, and a tension headache formed behind his eye.

Sebastian eyed Canten, and they both burst out laughing. Quade scrutinized them like they'd grown extra heads.

"I'm just messing with you, man," Sebastian said through his laughter. "Lunden is like my sister. You should have seen the look on your face. Are you sure you're just friends? That look in your eyes, I thought you were about to tackle me and the horse." Sebastian laughed some more.

"I'm going to have to agree with Sebastian on that one," Canten said. "I thought I was going to have to restrain you."

All three men laughed some more.

Again, Quade said, "It just took me by surprise, that's all. Lunden and I are just friends." At this point, he'd said those words so frequently lately that he was starting to feel like a record on repeat. Pryor had been right about the small-town thing. People were constantly in your business.

Sebastian continued, "If any more sparks had flown between the two of you, Ms. Jewel's house would have went up in flames."

Canten laughed. "It is pretty obvious you two have some serious chemistry happening."

Damn, had his and Lunden's vibe been that evident? He had to admit something had taken hold of him the second he'd seen her sitting on Ms. Jewel's porch. And when she'd walked toward them, her hair fashioned into braids on either side of her head, lips glossy, skin glistening, he'd been drawn to her like a caged animal to freedom. All he could envision was her naked body underneath that yellow jumper. And it called out to him.

"We're not trying to get in your business, man," Canten said. "Whatever is or isn't happening between you two is your business. It's just good to see Lunden smile again, that's all."

Sebastian agreed.

"Now, we came to ride, so let's see who can keep up," Canten said, galloping off.

Later that evening, Quade got a good shock. He hadn't expected Lunden to show up at his place, but he was pleasantly surprised when he opened the door and there she stood, looking and smelling as wonderful as usual. He invited her in, and a sweet, floral scent filled his nose as she walked past him and into the living room. His appreciative eyes fixed on her ass in a pair of navy-blue shorts.

"Why did you look so surprised when you opened the door?" she asked.

"Because truthfully, I hadn't expected you to actually come. You looked a little . . . hesitant earlier."

She turned to face him. "I was," she admitted.

Quade folded his arms across his chest and studied her for a moment. "Why?"

"I wasn't sure being alone with you was such a good idea."

Quade pushed his brows together. "I don't understand."

"I . . ." Her words dried up, and she gnawed at the corner of her lips as if whatever needed saying was difficult for her to relay. A beat later, she said, "Never mind. I should go."

Hurrying past him, Lunden moved toward the front of the house. He was on her heels. When she opened the door to leave, he reached above her and pushed it closed.

"Say whatever it is you need to say, Lunden. I'm a big boy. My feelings won't—"

"I want you," she blurted out. "I haven't wanted a man the way I constantly want you in a long time."

"I want you too," he said.

Lunden's shoulders slumped. "Us wanting each other is a bad idea, Quade."

He turned her to face him. "Says who?" he said, his mouth slowly moving inches from hers. "Says who?" he repeated, capturing her mouth in a heady kiss that made him feel as if he were floating. Until this moment, he hadn't realized just how much he'd missed this mouth. This intimacy. This woman.

Quade curled a hand behind her neck, then tangled his fingers in her hair. He kissed her harder, deeper. His manhood swelled inside his pants, and all he could think about was the moment he would bury himself deep inside Lunden. The thought made him ache with need.

Lunden's vigor matched his as they kissed one another like reacquainted lovers who hadn't tasted the sweetness of each other's mouths in a very long time. Her soft moans only aroused him more. Kissing her was good, but he wanted—desperately needed—more. Before he could make his desires known, though, Lunden broke their mouths apart.

They eyed each other in charged silence, her haunted gaze saying far more than anything that could come out of her mouth. Translating the look on her face, he took a step back. A second later, she was gone.

CHAPTER 25

It wasn't supposed to happen like this. All Lunden had wanted to do was save the inn. Instead, she'd fallen for Quade. As a result, the town would suffer. *She* would suffer. Massaging the tension in her neck, she chastised herself for allowing this to happen.

Children's laughter swirled around her, which helped to free her from her own thoughts. She would have put money on today being awkward. Money she would have lost, because from the moment she'd arrived at the inn two hours ago to set up for Zachary's party, Quade had treated her no differently than at any other time, despite how she'd left things. Unresolved. She appreciated him for not harboring a grudge. Maybe he had realized she'd made a good point.

Watching him run around with Zachary and his friends made her smile. She didn't understand why he couldn't see himself as a father. He seemed so good with kids. When he tripped and landed in the grass, she laughed right along with him. Zachary offered his hand, and Quade took it. But instead of getting up, Quade pulled Zachary down with him. The sound of Zachary's laughter warmed her heart. He was going to be heartbroken when Quade left.

The afternoon moved along without a hitch. The kids, and some adults, enjoyed several hours in the pool. Lunden thanked God that

Quade hadn't gotten in. She wasn't sure she could have handled watching other women salivate over him.

After the pool, they enjoyed a spread. While she'd been prepared to have food catered in, Quade had volunteered to cook on the grill, something he loved doing, he'd said. He'd gone all out with hot dogs (pork and beef), burgers (beef, turkey, and veggie), rib eye steaks, sausages, corn (just for her, he'd said), and several more items.

When Lunden went inside to start cleaning, she felt Quade behind her before ever seeing him.

"You don't have to do that," he said.

"I'm not going to leave you to clean up this mess. You've already done so much. Thank you again. I'm not sure who had more fun in the pool, the kids or the adults."

Quade walked over to the sink and rested his backside against the counter. "Why didn't you get in?"

"And mess up this hair?"

He chuckled, a smooth sound. "It looks nice, by the way. All those tiny curls. I bet it took all day."

"Not really."

Lunden laughed to herself. With all the pointless small talk, they sounded like two adolescents just learning how to talk to the opposite sex. "You know, if you really wanted to do something, you could dry while I wash."

He held his hand out for the towel. "Let's do this."

The dishwashing took far longer than it should have, but it was intentional. She enjoyed talking and laughing with Quade. The stories he told about him and his *other* best friend, Pryor, had her cracking up. He told her about the stresses of his old job and his plans to go on a journey. He didn't elaborate on what kind of journey, and she didn't ask.

Unfortunately, this journey meant he definitely intended to leave Honey Hill. While she'd purposely avoided mentioning the inn, now seemed like an appropriate time to bring it up. Who knew, maybe he had a little more consideration for what the inn meant to the town. Turning toward him, she said, "Quade—" She stopped abruptly, the sounds of a commotion outside drawing her attention.

"What the . . . ?" Quade tossed the dish towel down and hurried away.

Lunden was on his heels. Several kids were frantically pointing toward the creek, their words unintelligible. Motherly instinct kicked in, prompting Lunden to scan the yard. When she didn't see Zachary, her pulse rate kicked into overdrive, and her heart banged against her rib cage. "Where's Zachary?" she half cried, half panted.

A second later, Quade took off toward the creek. A feeling of dread lodged firmly in her stomach as her wobbly legs carried her after him. She'd told Zachary a thousand times to stay away from the creek. The jagged rocks and uneven bed made it dangerous. *Please, God,* she kept repeating over and over again.

At the creek, Quade slid down the embankment as if he were sliding into home base. When Lunden arrived to see Zachary facedown in the water, she released a bloodcurdling scream and half slid, half tumbled down into the water.

"Call 9-1-1," someone screamed.

Without skipping a beat, Quade scooped Zachary's tiny frame into his arms and carried him out of the water. Blood trickled from a gash on Zachary's forehead. Lunden could barely see through her tears.

Zachary's eyes fluttered open. "Quade?" His tone was fragile and low. "I fell and hit my head."

"Don't worry. I got you now, buddy. You're going to be okay."

Zachary's tiny voice was music to Lunden's ears. "Peanut?" Her voice cracked with emotion.

"*Mom.* That's a little kid's name. I'm seven now."

Lunden had never been more thankful in her life to hear his protest than she was at that moment.

Later that night, Quade drove Lunden and Zachary home from the hospital. While the rain had held out for Zachary's party, it unleashed its fury now. Rain fell in sheets, and he could hear the thunder in the distance. What a day.

Every ten seconds, Lunden tossed a glance into the back seat at the sleeping Zachary. While he'd been required to get twelve stitches, it could have been a lot worse. He thanked God it hadn't been.

Lunden eyed him, and he eyed her back. "What?"

"Thank you, Quade. Thank you so much," she said.

He wasn't sure what she was thanking him for, but he accepted it. "You're welcome."

Arriving at her place, Quade scooped Zachary out of the back seat and carried him inside to his bedroom. The kid didn't flinch when he placed him in the bed. Quade wasn't sure what they'd given him in the hospital, but he was knocked out, snoring and all.

Both he and Lunden stood at his bedside, staring at the snoozing Zachary, for a long while. Zachary might not have been his kid, but when he'd seen him in the water, motionless, Quade was sure he'd been just as terrified as Lunden had been. He'd thought for sure Zachary had drowned. It had brought back horrible memories. As he'd raced toward him, the fear had been almost paralyzing.

Lunden walked out of the room, but he stood there a little while longer. "I'm glad you're okay, kid," he whispered. Lunden paced inside the kitchen, arms hugged around her body, her head tilted back. "Hey, you okay?"

With tear-filled eyes, she shook her head and said, "No." A tear slid down her cheek. Surprisingly, she didn't turn her back to him like she had at the strawberry patch. "What if . . . ?"

Quade swiped the pad of his thumb across her cheek. "Don't," he said, resting his hands on her shoulders. "Don't torture yourself. Z's fine. A little banged up, but fine. And that's all that matters."

She nodded and forced a smile. It was obvious she was doing all she could to hold it together. When her bottom lip trembled, Quade pulled her into his arms and held her tight against his chest. Seconds later, she bawled. Her body went limp against him.

"I got you," he said. Scooping Lunden up, he carried her into the bedroom. Kicking out of his shoes, he crawled in the bed with her trembling body still clinging to him. Laying her down, he nestled his chest close against her back and draped a protective arm over her body.

After about ten minutes, her body relaxed. For a minute, he thought she'd fallen asleep.

"He's all I have in this world," she said.

At least she had Zachary. He had no one to love the way Lunden loved Z. For the first time ever, that saddened him. "Your world is fuller than you think. You have friends who adore you. A town that cherishes you. A son who loves you more than the sun and moon combined. You're lucky, Lunden. Far luckier than you know. Far luckier than most."

"Blessed," she said. "Not lucky."

He supposed she was right. "Do you want me to leave so you can get some rest?"

Still air passed between them.

"No," she finally said.

Her answer brought him far more joy than it should have. "I'm here for as long as you need me."

The room grew quiet, just the sounds of the rain and thunder pouring in. Being so close to Lunden was absolute torture to his entire system. Yet he didn't budge one hair while every warm inch of her called out to him. This was the truest test of willpower he'd ever experienced.

"Have you ever had stitches?" she asked.

"Yes."

"The scar on your back? Below your shoulder blade?"

"Yes," he said again.

"What happened?"

A knot formed in the pit of his stomach. "I fell."

"How?"

"How?" he said, repeating her. "Oh, I . . . tripped."

"You're lying," she said plainly.

How could she know that? "What makes you think that?"

"You repeated the question in an attempt to buy yourself time to think of a plausible explanation. I watch a lot of crime TV."

Clearly. Quade shifted slightly, uncomfortable thinking about the incident. "My stepfather pushed me into a glass table when I challenged him for yelling at my mom." Even though he hadn't voiced it back then, he'd believed the man when he'd said it had been an accident, and so had his mom. Still, it had only fueled Quade's hatred for him more.

Lunden rotated until they were facing one another. Sadness showed on her face.

"I'm sorry," she said.

"Don't be. Pain is the price you pay for love, right?" And like Lunden was for Zachary, Quade's mother had been his world, and he would have done anything to protect her.

She didn't respond immediately, simply stared at him. "Your stepfather . . . he sounds like a horrible man."

"He was." When he'd passed, Quade had attended the funeral. Not to mourn but to make sure he was really dead. "I hated him, and he hated me too. For simply existing. I think I reminded him too much of my father. And when he finally came to the realization my mother would never love him the way she loved my father, he turned cold and bitter."

"I hate you went through something like that," Lunden said, genuine compassion in her tone.

"I got away from him as soon as I could. College."

"Is that where you met your ex-girlfriend?"

"Fiancée," he admitted. "We were engaged."

Something flickered in Lunden's eyes. "Wow. Engaged?"

"Yes. And no, we met years later. Through mutual friends."

A soft smile touched her lips. "So you thought she was the one."

He scratched the side of his head. "Um . . ."

"Uh-oh. Doesn't sound like you did, so why did you propose?"

"I had a plan. I had the career. Logically, family was the next step. She was the woman I thought fit into that plan."

Lunden chuckled. "Fit into your plan? You make her sound like a cupcake on a points-based diet. Did she fit into your heart?"

"I cared for her," he said, hating how shallow he sounded.

"You were willing to vow forever to a woman whom you didn't love?"

"My mom married a man she didn't love. Just so she wouldn't grow old alone."

"Is that why you proposed? So you wouldn't grow old alone?"

"No. I had a plan," he said.

"Plans don't work. Trust me, I know. They get derailed by life, happenstance, feelings—" She stopped abruptly. "Marry for love, Quade. Don't deny yourself the chance at true happiness."

"Did you marry for love?"

"For what I thought was love, yes. Turned out I was wrong. But I don't regret any of it, because that union gave me my most precious gift."

"Would you do it again?" he asked. "Fall in love, I mean."

"I really don't think I have a say. Love is not something you plan. It just . . . happens."

Quade parted his lips to speak, but a ferocious clap of thunder rattled the house, and lightning illuminated the room. A second later, the power went out, leaving them in pitch darkness.

Lunden fumbled with something on the nightstand. Moments later, the room lit with the soft glow of candlelight. The scene was ultraromantic.

"Should I go check on Zachary?" he said. It would give him the opportunity to reboot his system.

"Trust me, if he was awake, we would know. He dislikes storms. Plus, whatever they gave my baby at the hospital has him knocked out. But thank you for always looking out for him. I know he's going to miss you when you're gone."

"Will his mother?" Quade said, then chastised himself for allowing the words to slip past his lips. "I don't know where that came from. You don't need to—"

"Yes," she said. "Something tells me I will."

As if he were no longer in control of his actions, his mouth was on hers, kissing her with all the built-up desire inside him. His body revved to attention. And just when he thought he'd get to satisfy the ache inside him, she pulled away just like before. Only this time, when she looked into his eyes, it wasn't confusion he saw. Something told him she knew exactly what she wanted.

Lunden rolled out of bed, then crossed the floor and closed and locked the door. After returning, she straddled him. "I desperately need to feel something besides fear tonight," she said.

Quade was eager to oblige. He wasted no time removing her shirt and bra. The sight of her plump breasts and taut nipples caused his hunger for her to grow. There was nothing gentle about the way he sucked one of her nipples between his lips, but her moan suggested she didn't mind. Equal attention was given to the opposite.

In a blur, they undressed one another. When he made a move to put her on her back, she protested. Straddling him again, she angled her hips and effortlessly slid him inside herself. They both released sounds of pleasure.

Lunden rode him slow and steady, staring past his eyes and into his soul. His hands slid up her rib cage and cupped her breasts. He loved the way they spilled from his hands. Sitting forward, he took a nipple into his mouth again and teased it with his tongue. She whimpered when he slid a hand between them and circled a finger against her clit.

Her tempo grew clumsy, but he didn't want her to come just yet. "Hold on for me," he said. He kissed his way to her mouth. Tangling his fingers in her hair, he gently pulled her head back and licked the length of her neck. "I love being inside you," he said against her skin. She rocked in his lap, fast, hard, wild. Gripping her ass, he drove in and out of her, losing more and more control with each powerful thrust.

"Oh God," she said, dropping her head onto his shoulder. "What . . . are you doing to me?" she whispered.

"Making you feel something," he said, flipping her onto her back in one swift motion. Gripping the back of the headboard, he plowed into Lunden as if he were trying to split her in half.

"Yes!" she cried out. "Yes! Don't stop. Please don't stop."

Tears streamed from the corners of her eyes, but he obeyed her and kept pounding away. Finally, Lunden's back arched off the mattress. Her mouth opened wide, but it was as if whatever sound was trying to escape had gotten stuck in her throat. Her body trembled underneath him. The feel of her muscles contracting around him milked him dry. He came so hard both his hearing and sight became impaired for a short time.

Collapsing, he snatched in breath after breath. Angling his head, he stared at Lunden, and she stared back at him. He reached over and wiped the wetness from her face, then gathered her into his arms.

"You're going to ruin me for any other man," she said into his chest.

"Good," he said, but the idea of another man between her thighs filled him with a lot of emotions, mostly jealousy and strife.

CHAPTER 26

Lunden loved honey-harvesting time. Quade would finally get to witness firsthand the fruits of all his hard labor. She looked on like a proud sensei as he cautiously removed the frames from the super. Clearly, he was far more comfortable now than when he'd first started. And he actually appeared to enjoy it.

"Wow, this sucker is heavy," he said, holding the honeycomb-covered frame so that she could brush the bees away.

"All of that delicious honey. Wait until we extract it," she said. "Fresh honey is so delicious."

"I bet it doesn't taste as good as you do," he said with a wink.

Lunden attempted to bite back a smile. Since Zachary's accident a couple of weeks ago, she and Quade had spent almost every night together. While she'd originally fought her desire for him, after Zachary's accident, she'd realized that life could change in the blink of an eye and was too short not to fill it enjoying the things you wanted. And she wanted Quade. Even if their clandestine affair was only temporary.

Instead of thieves in the night, they were more like lovers in the night, with Quade always leaving her place before Zachary woke or her leaving his before the sun rose. They had the perfect arrangement. No commitments. No expectations. No regrets. The zeal of a new relationship, without the headaches. They simply enjoyed their time together. A win-win for them both.

Several hours later, Lunden and Quade had the frames extracted and multiple pounds of honey straining. She dragged her finger across one of the spent frames, then licked the sticky sweetness off. "Mmm," she hummed. "That's so good. Want some?"

Quade flashed a roguish grin. "All the time," he said.

"Stop it," she said, hiding a smile. "I'm talking about the honey." However, if Zachary hadn't been riding around the yard, she would have given Quade all he could handle. She loved having sex with him. Somehow, he knew exactly when, where, and how to touch her. The man sometimes knew what she needed before she did. She also loved the way he couldn't seem to get enough of her.

Quade frowned. "If that's all you're offering." He captured her hand and singled out the finger she'd just used, slid it across the frame again, then sucked it into his mouth. His brows arched. "That is good. I'm looking very forward to discovering how it tastes spread over you." He snagged the fabric of her apron and pulled her to him. "Make sure you save a bottle for personal use."

"It's your honey," she said.

"I like the sound of that."

Quade kissed her gently, then pulled back and stared at her. "What if—"

"Hey, Mom. Hey, Quade," Zachary said, entering the honey cottage.

Lunden broke away from Quade. "Hey, son. What's up?"

"Are you bottling honey for the summer market yet?"

In two weeks, Honey Hill would hold its annual summer market, which took place every August. Local shop owners packed the square to showcase their businesses. There was food, music, dancing, and prizes. The event drew a crowd each year. Lunden was glad Quade had agreed to stick with Ms. Shugga's tradition of selling the honey they collected and donating the proceeds toward their outreach programs.

She cradled Zachary's cute face between her hands. "Not yet. Are you going to help?"

He nodded excitedly. "Yeah, yeah."

The only reason he was so excited was that he loved licking all the honey spillage off his fingers.

"How's the bike holding up?" Quade asked, rustling a hand over Zachary's head.

To Lunden's surprise, Zachary hadn't been as attached to his old bike as she'd suspected, because when Quade had surprised him—surprised them both—with a new one for his birthday, Zachary had dropped the old one like a bad habit and hadn't touched it since.

"It's the best bike in town. All my friends want to ride it, but I'm afraid they won't give it back."

"If they steal your bike, they're not your friends, right?" Quade asked.

"No, sir! Friends don't steal from each other."

"That's right." Quade held out his hand, and Zachary smacked it.

The two clowned around a bit before Lunden tasked Zachary with organizing the Mason jars they would use to bottle the honey. When he walked away, she faced Quade. "What were you going to say," she asked, "right before Zachary entered? What if what?"

"What was I going to say?" he said.

Lunden knew whatever followed would be a lie.

Quade continued, "Oh, I was going to say, what if we ordered pizza. I'm starving."

She eyed him a moment. By the look on his face, he knew she knew he wasn't being truthful. But instead of pressing him, she said, "Sure, pizza sounds good."

"I'll make the call," he said.

Before he walked off, she noted something behind the weak smile he flashed her. Distress. Questions plagued her. What had just happened? What was going on with him? Why had he lied to her? And what was it he'd changed his mind about saying?

✳

Quade watched Lunden sleep, as he did most mornings he woke up next to her. Whether he wanted to admit it or not, something had changed between them. Grown. Blossomed. At least it had for him. He no longer saw the woman whose bed he casually shared most nights. Now, he saw the woman he actually wouldn't mind waking up to every morning. This complicated things.

A couple of weeks ago, he'd almost asked her, *What if I decided to stay in Honey Hill?* Even now, he wasn't sure where the question had even come from, but when he'd stared into her eyes, it had materialized. He knew her current stance on relationships—it was the same as his—but could that change for her? Clearly, it had for him, if he was pondering whether there could be a future for them.

Unfortunately—or fortunately, he wasn't sure yet—before he could get the question fully out, Z had walked in. It had spooked him. Even from the grave, his stepfather still haunted him. He peppered himself with questions: What if the grouch had been right? What if he was more like him than he realized? What if Zachary grew to hate him just as he'd hated his stepfather?

Quade ground his teeth. *No. I'm nothing like that bastard. I would be good to them.* Far better than Lunden's ex had been. He knew that for sure. The man his mother had married had taught him one valuable lesson . . . who *not* to be.

Wait. Quade pushed his brows together, recalling his own words. Had he called himself a stepfather? And without a single second of hesitation? There was only one way to gain such a title. Was he thinking marriage? And without an ounce of fright? What in the hell had this town done to him?

He couldn't believe he was admitting this, but he could actually see himself calling Honey Hill home. Oddly, he'd fallen in love with the town. And some of its residents. But he wouldn't make any sudden moves. He had to wait to see what his gut told him.

Eyeing the clock, he realized he needed to leave. Zachary would be up soon. Hiding their nonrelationship from him was important to Lunden. Quade understood why. That kid told everything. Quade also needed to get home, showered, and dressed, since he'd told Mr. Conroy he'd come in early to help him finish heat pressing the shirts for the summer market, which started later this morning. If there was one thing Honey Hill liked, it was its celebrations.

Quade liked working with Mr. Conroy. Every day, the man had a different story to tell him about Shugga. They were so vibrant Quade actually felt as if he truly knew his aunt again. While Mr. Conroy hadn't admitted to being in love with Shugga, the glint in his eyes whenever he talked about her told Quade he had been. Talking about her had been beneficial for them both.

Quade kissed Lunden's shoulder, up to her neck. She squirmed a little. "Wake up, sleepyhead," he whispered in her ear. "I have to go."

She whimpered. "Already? What time is it?"

"A little after five."

She groaned. "I have to get up soon too. To help set up for the market."

"I'll be there to help as soon as I can get away from the shop," he said.

"Don't rush, I can handle it." She smirked. "On second thought, do rush. Seeing you will give me energy."

"Flattery will get you anything you want," he said.

"Promises, promises."

"Give me a kiss," he said.

Lunden protested, "No, I have morning breath." She pushed him away. "Go. I'll make up for it tonight."

Quade kissed her forehead. "I'm holding you to it."

Minutes later Quade crept from the room. He hadn't made it five steps before he heard . . .

"Hey, Quade."

Quade froze. *Shit.* What was this kid doing up so early? Turning, he said, "Z. What's up?"

The kid was all grins. "Nothing."

"I stopped by early to drop something off to your mom," he said.

Zachary's grin grew. *"Quade,"* he dragged out. "I know you spent the night again."

Again? Apparently, they'd been made. Curious, he said, "How?"

"Because when I get up for water, I hear you and my mom talking and laughing. She laughs *a lot* when you're around. I think you make her really happy. I think she makes you happy, too, because you don't look sad all the time anymore."

Don't look sad all the time anymore? He'd looked sad all the time before?

"Does she make you happy too?" Zachary asked.

Quade eyed Lunden's bedroom door. "Very."

Zachary's eyes widened. "Does that mean you're going to stay here forever and ever now, instead of leaving?"

"Maybe," he said. Lowering his voice, he added, "But let's keep that between us men, okay?"

"Okay, Quade. It'll be our secret. Best friends keep each other's secrets all the time, and they can't tell anyone."

Quade fist-bumped Zachary. "I'll see you later, okay?"

"Yep."

Quade started to the door but stopped. "Z, don't tell anyone you saw me, okay? That's our secret too." However, he seriously doubted their association was much of a secret around town.

Zachary gave him a thumbs-up. "I won't," he whispered.

Quade eyed Zachary for a moment, smiled, then headed for the door. Yeah, he'd be a great stepfather.

"Quade," Zachary said, running up to him and throwing his arms around him. Pulling away, he said, "I'm glad my mom's plan worked."

Plan?

Zachary was about to say more, but Lunden's bedroom door opened, and she moseyed out. Oblivious to their presence, she headed toward the kitchen.

"Hey, Mom?"

Lunden sent an urgent glance in their direction. Her eyes widened, and her mouth fell open.

"He already knows," Quade said.

Lunden pinned Quade with an accusatory look.

"He hears us talking and laughing."

Zachary giggled, then covered his mouth with his hand.

Lunden wagged a finger at him. "Have you been eavesdropping at my door?"

"No. I hear you when I get water."

Lunden popped him on the bottom playfully. "Go take your bath. I'll fix breakfast."

"Okay. Bye, Quade," he said, then took off down the hall.

Peeping back around the corner, he pushed his finger to his lips. Quade nodded. When Lunden looked in his direction, Zachary took off again.

"I can't believe he knows and never said anything," she said.

"I'm just as surprised as you." Because, again, the kid told everything.

Lunden wrapped her arms around his waist. "I brushed my teeth. I'll take that kiss now."

Quade kissed her forehead. "I have morning breath," he said. Lunden eyed him strangely, as if she knew something was off. "I'll see you later, okay?"

Her arms fell to her sides, and she nodded. "Okay."

On the trip home, in the shower, as he dressed, and during the drive to the shop, all Quade could think about was what Zachary had said. *I'm glad my mom's plan worked.* Early on, his gut had told him Lunden was up to something. Was this plan it? If so, what were the details of said plan? Obviously, it had something to do with the inn, but she hadn't shown much interest in its future lately. At least, not like before. Letting it go for now, he moved through the doors of the screen printing shop. He didn't know what was up, but he sure as hell intended to find out.

Mr. Conroy was already hard at work. The man was like a workhorse that never stopped. Quade respected his work ethic. "Good morning," he said.

"Morning. Got some bagels in the back if you're hungry."

"I'm good, but thanks." He didn't have much of an appetite for food, only for answers.

"What time did you get here?" Quade asked.

"A little after five," he said, changing the needle on one of the embroidery machines.

"You should have told me. I could have gotten here earlier." To Quade's surprise, he truly enjoyed working here. He'd caught on fairly quickly and could run most of the equipment without difficulty. It was amazing how soothing watching a design stitch out could be.

"I'm used to rising with the chickens. Been doing it for years."

"Love it too much to retire, huh?" After forty-some years of running this place, Quade would have thought the man would be eager to spend his glory years doing nothing. Or maybe Mr. Conroy was like him, no good at doing nothing.

"Couldn't before. But I might be able to soon, thank God." He looked around the space. "I love this place, but I'm tired, son. These old bones need to rest." Mr. Conroy shuffled through the pile on the counter, then passed Quade a letter. "Got this here letter in the mail. Say they want to purchase my shop."

Quade instantly recognized the company name. *The Danbury Group*. What were they up to?

"Haven't phoned them yet, but I will on Monday morning."

Quade made a mental note to call Pryor to see what he knew about this.

"Why don't you start on the rest of those market shirts, and I'll finish up these special-order embroidery shirts."

Quade nodded and went to work. A bit after nine thirty, he pressed the last vinyl cutout. Mr. Conroy had told him screen printing them would be much faster, but since he'd be donating them, he'd opted for the more economical version. Either way, the yellow shirts with *Honey Hill's Summer Market* pressed in white on the front looked great, if he did say so himself.

The front door chimed, drawing both Quade's and Mr. Conroy's attention. Quade groaned when Blondie strutted through the door, dressed in white from head to toe.

"Good morning," she said, removing her designer glasses.

Both men returned the greeting.

"Mr. Conroy, my grandfather sent me for his invoice."

"Got to write it up. I'll be right back," he said, disappearing to the back.

Quade had seen Mr. Conroy's invoicing system, if you could call carbon copies a system. It would take him forever to handwrite the order. Which meant he was stuck entertaining Blondie.

"I wouldn't have taken you as a blue-collar man," she said.

"I'm full of surprises," he said, busying himself folding the shirts.

"I just bet you are," she said, her eyes swallowing him whole. "Word on the street is that you and the mayor are keeping close company."

Quade arched a brow, though he wasn't truly surprised. "Really?" was all he said. By the shaken expression on her face, she'd hoped he would have denied it. But why? She didn't stand a chance.

"Funny," she said, biting at the earpiece of her sunglasses.

"What's that?"

"You strike me as being too smart to fall for the woman scheming to steal his property right from under his nose." She shrugged. "But I guess lust is a powerful thing."

Quade stopped folding. "What are you talking about?"

He didn't have to ask twice. Blondie seemed eager to share what she knew.

"One of my nail clients works at the town hall. She happened to overhear a phone conversation between a town official and Lunden."

Clearly, she intended on blocking her source, making whatever information someone had obtained through eavesdropping less credible in his opinion.

"I won't bore you with all the filler. Long story short, Lunden asked a town official to find a way to block you from selling the inn. By any means necessary."

When she rested a hand on his arm and flashed what he assumed was supposed to be a look of sympathy, he casually pulled away from her touch.

"She plans to confiscate your property. The mayor is good at taking things that don't belong to her." A brief sneer replaced her look of constipation. "But don't worry, she's no good at holding on to them."

For a second, Quade considered the source of the information—a woman who clearly disliked Lunden. But then he recalled Zachary's comment from earlier about some plan. Was it true? Had Lunden played him?

He didn't get it. He didn't get any of it. They'd shared things with each other, gotten . . . close. Or at least he'd thought so. Had it all been a part of her plan? Sure, he and Lunden had never quite seen eye to eye on the inn, but would she . . . ? His thought trailed off.

Damn. Well, now he knew why the inn hadn't come up much lately. She'd been scheming on the low. *Wow.* He'd pegged her as a lot of things, but never sneaky. Quade's jaw clenched. Clearly, Lunden wasn't the person he'd thought she was. Unfortunately, she'd turned out to be just like the rest.

His gut hadn't lied. Lunden had been up to something, all right. Manipulating him. This entire time had been nothing but a ruse to get him to drop his guard. Sadly, it had worked.

CHAPTER 27

Lunden checked her watch again. The tenth time in the past hour. Three thirty. She scanned the sea of faces in the square. Where was Quade? Surely he should be at the market by now. Worried, she tried his phone a fifth time. Her concern for his well-being alerted her to just how much she'd grown to care for him. The man had made it too damn easy to fall for him, but she wasn't complaining. Or maybe she was, just a little, because she hadn't wanted to fall for him. But the heart wanted what the heart wanted, and as much as she hated to admit it, hers wanted Quade.

Again, her call rolled into voice mail. "Where are you?" she mumbled to herself, opting not to leave another message.

"Did you say something?" Ms. Jewel asked, packaging another jar of honey.

"No, ma'am," she said, forcing a smile and easing her phone into her back pocket.

Another half hour ticked past with no sign of Quade. Lunden was poised to jump into her vehicle and go in search of him. It had been a long time since she'd fretted over anyone other than Zachary. Why was she so concerned? Quade was a grown man who could take care of himself. Too bad she couldn't shake the feeling that something was . . . off. She recalled the odd way he'd responded that morning on his way out the door. Had Zachary's catching them spooked him?

And speaking of Zachary . . . Lunden smiled when she spotted him by Rylee's table, passing out samples. She was sure he would consume twice as many as he gave out. Zachary wasn't the only person she spotted. *Mr. Conroy.* Leaving the reins to Ms. Jewel and the other volunteers, she hurried over to him. Uncharacteristically, she didn't stop for small talk with the several folks who attempted to engage her. She simply spoke and kept it moving. Finally making her way over to him, she said, "Mr. Conroy?"

He turned toward her. Flashing a wide smile, he said, "Mayor. Great day for the market."

"Yes, it is. Mr. Conroy, I was wondering if Quade was still at the shop."

Fine lines crept across his forehead. "Quade? No, he's been gone about three, four hours now."

"By chance, do you know where he was headed?"

"Why, no. No, I don't." He snapped his fingers. "But you can check with Herbert's granddaughter. She came into the shop, and they chatted for a long while. Maybe she knows."

"Hilary?" she said.

"Yes. I can never remember her name."

Lunden got a sinking feeling in the pit of her stomach. "Thank you," she said and walked off. Approaching Rylee's table, she said, "Ry, do you mind keeping an eye on Zachary a couple of minutes?"

"Sure." Her brows creased. "Everything okay?"

"Yes. I'll be back shortly," she said. After directing Zachary not to move from the spot he was in, Lunden headed toward her vehicle.

"*May . . . your*, might I chat with you a moment?"

Dammit. She did not have time for Mr. Herbert's foolery right now. Plastering on a smile, she turned. "Mr. Herbert, I'm kinda in a hurry—"

"This won't take long. I just wanted to say I hope you have no intentions of trying to block us from selling our personal properties to the Danbury Group. Whether you know it or not, many of us are eager to sell. Myself included. I've spoken with their representative, and the offers are legit. Of course, there are contingencies. This is why you can't—"

Lunden held up her hand. "Wait, Mr. Herbert. I have no idea what you're talking about. Someone is trying to purchase your business?"

"Yes. Well, I'm sure they just want the property, but yes." Mr. Herbert fished a letter from the pocket of his purple seersucker pants and passed it to her. "Surely, I thought you knew." He smiled as if he was satisfied he knew something she didn't.

As she perused the letter, Lunden's concern shifted. Sure enough, this company wanted to purchase Mr. Herbert's shop. "And you said others received a similar letter?"

"Yes," he said.

Lunden would bet her life savings this had everything to do with the inn. But why hadn't she heard about this before now? Did Quade know about this? "May I borrow this?" she asked.

"Yes, I have copies."

By the way he informed her he had copies, Lunden wondered if he expected her to burn the letter or something. "Thank you," she said and started away.

"*May . . . your,*" Mr. Herbert called out.

Huffing, she turned again. "Yes, Mr. Herbert?"

"Myself and others would appreciate no interference from outside sources," he said pointedly before strolling off.

Quade's car was parked in the inn's driveway. After pulling in behind it, she made her way to the door. *Keep your cool, Lunden. Instead of biting into him, lead up to the letter.* It appeared as if her knocks—more like bangs—would go unanswered until the door crept open.

Quade didn't greet her with his usual enthusiasm—pulling her into his arms and smothering her lips with his. That was probably a good thing, because she might have bitten his tongue off.

"Hey," she said. "Is everything okay? I was expecting you at the market."

"I decided not to come. I needed to get some things in order here. The buyers for the inn will be visiting soon."

Aha. That was definitely no coincidence. "Buyers," she said. "I see. So you still intend to sell?"

"That has always been my intention," he said. "Oh, wait, you thought your plan had worked? Tell me, Lunden, what was this plan, exactly? Wait, let me guess. Coax me into your bed, gain my trust, get me to fall for you in hopes that it would keep me from selling the inn?"

Lunden's mouth fell open, but no words escaped. Did he truly believe she would use her body that way? Did he actually think the reason she'd slept with him was to sway him? "Quade—" He walked off, leaving her on the porch. She trailed him inside. "Let me explain."

He whipped around to face her. "Did you have the town lawyer scheming up ways to keep me from selling a property that is rightfully mine?"

Well, when he said it like that . . . "Yes, but—"

"Then there's nothing left to explain," he said and continued into the living room. "I guess Hilary was right. You will do whatever needed to get what you want."

The fact that he quoted anything Hilary had said burned her up, but she kept her cool. "When I first learned you wanted to sell the inn, yes, I was prepared to do whatever I could to stop you. But I never, *never* slept with you with the intention of making that happen."

"And I'm supposed to believe you because you're so honest, huh? Every single day you smiled in my face, knowing all along you were stabbing me in the back." He shrugged. "But hey, I shouldn't even be surprised. Every woman I've ever cared about has deceived me. Why would you be any different?"

His words pulled at her heartstrings. Not only the deception part but the suggestion that he cared about her.

He moved to the bar and poured himself a drink but didn't consume it. With his back to her, he said, "Get out, Lunden. And this time . . . stay out."

The hardness in his voice coupled with the cold words broke her heart, but there was no time for pity. Yes, she'd been deceitful, but so had he. "Let me guess the name of your buyers," she said. "The Danbury Group, by chance?"

Quade folded his arms across his chest in a defiant manner. His silence confirmed her suspicions.

"You are unbelievable. You stand there condemning me for being dishonest for a good cause, yet you deceived me for what, money?"

"I didn't deceive you, Lunden. My intentions have always been to sell the inn. You deceived yourself by thinking that would change."

Lunden wanted to be offended by his words, but she couldn't be, because he was right. His goals had never changed. And because she'd allowed feelings to get in the way, hers had. As a result, she'd screwed herself and the town. "You're right," she said. She turned to leave but stalled. Facing him again, she said, "When I shared your bed, it was not to bamboozle you. I wasn't looking for an advantage. I didn't have any ulterior motives. I was there because I wanted to be. I wanted to be," she repeated. "I was there because I wanted *you*."

Quade's shoulders visibly relaxed, and the hardness in his face softened.

Lunden continued, "Don't you ever devalue or disrespect me again by equating me to nothing more than a whore." She walked off but stopped again. "And just so we're clear, when I smiled in your face, you smiled back. All of the time knowing your parasites intended on bleeding the town dry. Guess I'm not the only one holding a knife. Despite what you believe, I never once used mine, but I can still feel yours between my shoulder blades."

This time, she left, and there was no turning back. Quade had said something to her once, and he'd been right. Pain was also the punishment for love.

Quade wasn't sure what it was about the inn's patio that gave him clarity. Actually, he was sure. The sycamore tree. Every time he lounged here, his eyes couldn't move away from the massive growth. Silly as it sounded, it was like the grand branches and leaves watched over him. It gave him serenity, focus. And in his current centered state, all he could roll around in his head was, *Quade Cannon, you're a damn fool.*

It had been two weeks since he'd last seen Lunden, and instead of forgetting about her, he couldn't stop thinking about her and how much he missed her. Which made him a damn fool. It pissed him off that he couldn't get her out of his head. She'd lied to him, deceived him, sneakily plotted to take the inn; yet his heart still longed for her. The soft, sweet sound of her voice. Her gentle touch. Her warm body next to his.

What the hell was wrong with him? Why was it each day, her absence affected him more than the day before? Hell, he even dreamed about her most nights. He missed Zachary too. Almost as much as his mother. That kid had grown on him. They both had. Since he hadn't seen Z, Lunden had obviously given him a stern warning to stay away.

Quade could have come up with a thousand reasons why he couldn't get Lunden out of his system, but the only true cause—as painful as it was to admit—was that he'd fallen in love with her. And that angered the shit out of him. He didn't like feeling this helpless, this vulnerable.

"You okay over there, man? You're gripping that beer bottle like it did something to you."

Damn, he'd almost forgotten Canten was there. He'd stopped by under the pretense of seeing if he wanted to go riding, but Quade suspected he'd actually come by to check on him. Since the incident with Lunden, he'd gone MIA from town. He hadn't been hiding, just wasn't sure who he could trust. For all he knew, the whole town could have been in on her scheme. Including Canten. Had Canten been privy to her plans? Worse, had he been a part of them? He and Sebastian had welcomed him into their circle with open arms. Had it all been a ploy to earn his trust? Despite their kindness, their allegiance was with Lunden, not him.

"Did you know?" Quade said, sliding his gaze from the tree to Canten.

"Know what?" Canten said.

"About Lunden's scheme to take the inn?"

"Oh, that. Initially, no. But when Pop received the letter about selling his shop, and I questioned it, I heard about what her plan *had* been."

Quade wondered why he'd emphasized the word *had*.

"Out of curiosity, how did you find out?" Canten asked.

"Hilary Jamison," Quade said, finally remembering the woman's name. But who could forget the name of the woman who'd hipped you to the fact you were being played?

"Mmm."

"What does that mean?" Quade asked.

"Nothing. Just . . . I'm not sure I'd take Hilary's word on much. Especially anything where Lunden was involved. There's bad blood there."

This wasn't news to Quade, but Lunden hadn't gone into great detail about the reason, other than it had to do with her ex. Maybe he should hear it from Canten. "What kind of bad blood?" he asked.

Canten paused a moment, as if he was debating whether to share any information with him. "Hilary used to mess around with Lunden's ex before they were a thing. Nothing serious, at least on his part, but Hilary was in love with him. Then him and Lunden started dating. Hilary's held a grudge ever since. Plus the fact Lunden unseated her grandmother as mayor. All I'm saying is I'd think twice about listening to anything that came from Hilary. Her intentions are rarely good ones."

What Quade didn't share with Canten was that Lunden had practically admitted it to him. Well, kind of admitted it. He hadn't actually let her fully explain herself. But there hadn't been a point. The notion she'd even attempt something so despicable had been enough for him. And to think she wanted him to believe her sleeping with him hadn't been part of her ruse.

"It doesn't matter. In a few weeks, I intend to sign the paperwork, and I'm out of here."

"Mmm," Canten hummed.

Again with the *mmm*. "Something on your mind?"

"Nothing. Just . . . honestly, your leaving kind of surprises me. I got the impression Honey Hill had grown on you. You seemed . . . I don't know, happy here."

"I never planned on staying," he said, intentionally not addressing his other comments. Mostly because the place *had* grown on him, and he *was* happy here. At least, he used to be. Now, it only reminded him of all the deception he'd faced in his lifetime. It never seemed to end.

"I get it," Canten said. "Shucks, I never planned on becoming sheriff. Hell, I wasn't even supposed to be in Honey Hill. My life was in the big city. Then my wife died, and there was no other place I wanted to be than right here. As crazy as it sounds, the amount of peace I found here told me I'd been brought back for a reason. That I'm right where I'm supposed to be."

Quade studied Canten. "Well, I know exactly what brought me here, and it has nothing to do with divine intervention." More like an overzealous aunt.

Canten swigged his beer. "Truthfully, a lot of us thought Ms. Shugga would have left the inn to Lunden."

"I wish she had. It would have made my life far less complicated."

"Your aunt had an odd way of doing things, but they always seemed to work out. It was like she had a vision no one else could see, but it was what was needed. Like she had a sixth sense or something."

Things got quiet between them.

"Quade, I don't have any insight into what Lunden did or didn't intend to accomplish, but I can say with a hundred percent certainty that the Lunden you met when you first arrived to town isn't the same Lunden you know now. That's because of you, brother. Just talk to her. Work whatever this is out, because frankly, we miss watching you two pretend you're just friends."

Quade chuckled. "Were we that bad?"

"Yeah, you were."

"Well, I bet we could pull it off now," he said.

Canten flashed a somber expression. "You two should at least talk. If you still . . ." His words trailed off, and he looked past Quade, his brows furrowing.

Quade eyed Zachary, who he saw moving toward them. The troubled look on his face filled Quade with concern. Standing, he said, "Z, what's wrong?"

Zachary stopped, then forcefully pushed the bike toward him, causing it to bang to the ground. "Here's your stupid bike back. I don't want it. And we're not best friends anymore. Best friends don't tell each other stories."

Tell stories, kid-speak for *lie*. What did Zachary think he'd lied about? What the hell had Lunden told him? "Z, what are you talking about?"

"You said you liked my mom, but you don't. You said you were going to stay here with us, but you're not."

"Z—"

"Don't call me Z!"

Quade flashed his palms. "Okay. Let's just talk. Man to man."

"I don't want to talk to you. Ever again. You used to make my mom laugh all the time. Now she only cries. She doesn't think I know, but I hear her at night." Tears streamed down his face. "And when I ask her what's wrong, she says nothing. But I know what's wrong. You broke her heart, and you broke mine too. I . . . I . . . I hate you, Quade."

A second later, Zachary ran off. Quade wanted to call after him, run after him, but neither his mouth nor his feet would move. Once the moment of paralysis passed, he eyed Canten. The man's usually stern face was drenched with sympathy.

His tone was soft and low when he spoke. "Hey, man, I'm sure—"

"He meant it," Quade said. And it tore him apart inside.

CHAPTER 28

Over the past two and a half weeks, Lunden had learned something about herself. Her creative juices flowed when her life was in shambles. There were hundreds of bath bombs, dozens of candles, and countless tubes of flavored lip gloss to prove it. Her inventory was well stocked, yet she continued to churn away. Staying busy kept her mind off *him*.

During the day when she thought about Quade, it filled her with rage. How could he ever believe she would have used what they'd shared so maliciously? And how could he believe anything Hilary's trifling behind had to say? God only knew what she'd told him. And whatever she'd told him, Lunden was sure she'd put her twisted spin on it. She had a notion to march over to Hilary's nail salon and rip her a new one. No, she refused to let the barracuda know she'd won.

Nighttime was a totally different story. What she felt then was unbelievable sadness, because despite all that had happened between them, she missed him. She banged one of the candle jars down with a little too much force, causing the beeswax inside to slop over the edge. *Dammit.* Why was she incapable of compartmentalizing her feelings like normal people?

Recalling Quade's words tugged at her heartstrings with the same potency as when he'd originally said them: *Every woman I've ever cared about has deceived me. Why would you be any different?* She blinked back the unshed tears stinging her eyes. Hurting him hadn't been her intention, and doing so was one of the things she regretted the most. That and the effect all of this was having on Zachary.

The blinding light that usually shone in his innocent eyes had definitely dimmed, and he'd moped around for the past week. Undoubtedly because she'd told him he could no longer see Quade. The order hadn't been out of retaliation. She'd been attempting to protect Zachary's feelings. Maybe she'd made the wrong call. She was doing a lot of that lately.

The one thing no one could deny was the fact all her actions had been done for the betterment of the town. The letters received by nearly all the business owners in town filled her head. They couldn't afford to turn down the amount of money the Danbury Group was offering. Nor should they. She sighed. What would become of Honey Hill?

Her cell phone vibrated against the table. Zeta's name flashed across the screen. Making the call active, she said, "Hello?"

"I know it's taken me a long while, but I finally did it. I finally found something that will prevent Quade from selling the inn."

Lunden was speechless for a moment. "Really? How?"

Lunden listened as Zeta explained something called a run-with-the-land covenant put in place generations ago, which stipulated the inn had to remain in the Caldron family line. At such time as there was no descendant available, ownership would be offered to the town of Honey Hill for an insanely low purchase cost.

"Wouldn't Ms. Shugga have known this?" Lunden asked.

"I don't know. The information was buried so deep in the archives, honestly I'm surprised I found it. You wanted ammunition that would save the inn. Now you have it. How do you want to proceed?"

Before Lunden could respond, her other line beeped. When she checked the screen, concern set in. "Zeta, it's Zachary's teacher calling. I'll call you back. Do me a favor and keep this between us, okay? *Strictly* between us." While Zeta had sworn she hadn't said anything to anyone else about what Lunden had asked her to do, Hilary had found out somehow. Lunden needed to make sure that didn't happen again, especially with this information.

"You got it."

Clicking over, Lunden said, "Hey, Perri. Is everything okay?"

"Hey, Mayor. That's what I wanted to ask you. Zachary hasn't been himself the last few days. I'm a little concerned. He's always the life of the classroom. Now, he barely speaks. When I ask him what's wrong, he says it's nothing."

Lunden couldn't tell Perri what she suspected was ailing Zachary. Instead, she offered, "Thank you for letting me know, Perri. I will talk with him as soon as he gets home."

"He's not home yet?" Perri asked.

Lunden checked her watch. Four o'clock. She'd lost track of time. Zachary should be home by now. He usually popped in to let her know he'd arrived. "I've been in my workshop. I'm sure he's inside. I didn't realize what time it was."

Ending the call, Lunden hurried inside. Zachary was curled up in his bed. This kid never took naps. Maybe he was sick. "Zachary, sweetie, is everything okay?"

"Yes, Mom. I'm just tired," he said, not bothering to face her.

Lunden eased onto the bed. "Ms. Perri called. She said you haven't been yourself."

Silence.

She rubbed his side. "Do you want to talk?"

More silence.

"Zachary? Please tell me what's going on."

When he burst into tears, she turned him to face her. "What's wrong?" Her heart raced. "Did someone do or say something to you?"

"No."

"Then what's going on?" She was so anxious she nearly started crying herself.

"I . . . I told Quade I didn't want his stupid bike, but I did. And I told him we weren't best friends anymore, but he's my bestest friend ever. Then I . . . I . . . told him . . ." He started sobbing harder. "I told him I hated him, but I don't hate him, Mom."

Lunden was so confused. She'd just seen Zachary's bike in the yard. Why had Zachary told Quade he hated him? Why had he ended their friendship? Instead of asking questions right now, she focused on consoling her son.

"Do you think Quade hates me?" Zachary asked in a shaky voice.

She held him at arm's length. "Absolutely not. He could never hate you. You're one of his favorite people."

"Is that why he brought my bike back? I left it at the inn because I was mad at him, but the next morning it was in the yard again."

Well, that answered one of her questions. "That's exactly why he brought it back." She popped the tip of his nose with her finger. "Because you're his best friend."

"I don't want him to leave," Zachary said, wiping his eyes.

Lunden held him close. "Neither do I, son. Neither do I."

Zachary reared back to look at her. "Will you take me to apologize?"

Lunden recalled Quade's words to her. *Stay out.* "Sweetie, I don't think it's a good idea that I take you. But you can go this one time," she said.

"Please, Mom, please. I have to apologize before he leaves. You have to take me. Please take me."

Quade walked the property with representatives from the Danbury Group: Emily Bastille, a tall, no-nonsense brunette—whose personality matched the severe black pantsuit she wore—and her assistant, a timid young man named Chad or Chase or Chris. Quade wasn't sure, because the woman had called him all three. For the life of him, he couldn't explain why he felt so conflicted. This was what he wanted. To off-load the inn and get the hell out of Honey Hill.

"This place will do just fine," Emily said.

"Glad to hear this," he said.

Emily rested her hands on her hips. "Once we bulldoze all those trees, we should be able to accommodate dozens of lakefront condos. It'll be marvelous."

Quade's head snapped back. Lakefront condos? "There's no lake," he said, stating the obvious.

"There are no condos either," she said. She eyed him. "But there will be. Lots of them," she added, then walked off.

A lake wouldn't be so bad. It'll give the bees another water source. And condos . . . jobs. Landscapers, customer service reps. Plus, it would expand the inn. Allowing more visitors. In turn, generating more revenue for the town. It'll be good.

Emily turned to . . . Young Man C. "Remind me to phone Broderick Davenport. Write it down."

YMC flinched when Emily spoke, then jotted something in his notebook. Broderick Davenport? Why did the name sound so familiar to Quade? After giving it a second's more thought, he had it. Davenport, an ex–pro golfer, now built world-renowned golf courses. "You're adding a golf course?" It was more a comment than a question.

"Not just *a* golf course"—Emily half smiled, half sneered—"*the* golf course. One that will attract players from all over the world."

A golf course of that magnitude in Honey Hill? "That sounds . . . ambitious," he said.

"Ambitious is what I do best," she said.

Again, he considered the benefit to the town. Tourism dollars. Jobs. Golf. But he also thought of the negatives from such a venture. Crowds. Tournaments. Traffic. Loss of the small-town feel. But hey, that wasn't his problem.

Emily lowered her designer glasses and squinted off into the distance. "What is that?"

Hadn't she ever seen beehives before? "Beehives. I'm sure you'll have a restaurant. Fresh honey would be a great addition. They produced close to a hundred pounds of honey this season." Just saying it filled him with pride, as if he'd done something special to cause it to happen. The time he and Lunden had spent at the hives—talking, laughing, clowning—flashed into his head. He shook the intrusive scene away.

"Locate a bee-removal company," Emily said to YMC.

"Wait," Quade said. "You can't get rid of the bees. This is a farming town. The local farmers depend on their pollination for their crops." He rattled off everything he'd learned from Lunden, along with what he'd learned in the books he'd read about protecting the bee population.

Emily looked bored or annoyed. He couldn't really decipher which.

"*Used* to be a farming town," she said, walking off.

Used to be? What the hell did that mean? So he asked. "What do you mean by 'used to be'?"

"As in once was, but no longer. By the time it's all said and done, the Danbury Group will not only own this property—we'll own the town. Several businesses and residents are already eager to sell their properties. Who says everyone doesn't have a price?"

Residents? So they weren't just snatching businesses. They were acquiring homes too? "What exactly—"

Emily cut him off. "We'll definitely need to demolish the house," she said, eyeing the inn. "On second thought . . . we can possibly make it the foyer for the new-and-improved facility. Write that down, Carl."

"It's, um, actually Billy, ma'am."

Emily scowled at him, and his eyes lowered to the notepad. Starting off again, she stood directly in front of the sycamore tree. "Well, this is an interesting monstrosity. Once we cut it down, maybe we can use the wood to make something beautiful. Benches, perhaps. Or maybe—"

"No," Quade growled. All the time he and Shugga had spent under this tree, *their* tree, laughing, talking, crying, came rushing back.

Emily whipped toward him. "Excuse me?"

"The tree stays." In that moment, he understood why Lunden had fought so hard for the inn, for Honey Hill. "But you can go."

"You can't renege on our deal. You signed a letter of intent."

Which he knew was not legally binding. Giving him the right to change his mind if he chose to do so. And he did. "Good day, Ms. Bastille."

Quade walked off before she could respond. Inside, he snatched up his keys and headed for the door. When he yanked it open, he was stunned to see Lunden and Zachary standing there. A feeling of pure euphoria washed over him.

Lunden's gaze was set on Emily, stalking across the yard with Billy in tow, while Zachary's was fixed on the ground. "Hey," he said to them both.

"Hey, Quade," Zachary said, his voice tiny, still studying the ground as if he was afraid to look at him.

Lunden's eyes slid to him, the impact of their connection nearly toppling him over. Of course they hadn't been able to hide the fact they were more than friends, because their supercharged chemistry wouldn't allow for it. Even now, it was as present and potent as it had always been. Lunden felt it too. He could see it in her eyes. *I've missed you,* he wanted to say, but he kept his words to himself.

"Is this a bad time?" she said.

"No." He stepped aside. "Come in." Once inside, he closed the door behind them. The sweet floral scent trail Lunden left in her wake was like an aphrodisiac. "Can I offer you something to drink?"

"No, we won't be long. Zachary told me what happened the other day," she said. "He asked me to bring him here to apologize."

When Zachary's head slowly rose, tears were running down his face. The sight was like a gut punch. Quade knelt in front of Zachary. "What's up, little man? Why the tears?" Quade wiped them away.

"I love my bike. It's the coolest bike ever. And I love when you call me Z. And you can call me that, because you're still my best friend. I've never had a best friend before, and you're the bestest best friend ever. You don't treat me like a kid. And you're lots of fun. And you play games with me. And you make my mom laugh a lot." Tears streamed down his face again. "I didn't mean it, Quade," he said, sniffling several times. "I don't hate you. I love you. And my mom does too."

Quade's eyes rose when Lunden gasped. Something told him that his foyer was the last place she wanted to be.

CHAPTER 29

Lunden couldn't breathe. Had Zachary really just told Quade that she loved him? What had the child been thinking? How would she get out of this one? Collecting her composure, she gave a wobbly smile. "Son, I, um, don't love Quade."

"Uh-huh, Mom. I heard you tell Aunt Rylee. You said you love him, but you didn't mean to fall in love with him."

Dammit. That was exactly what she'd told Rylee. Zachary's eavesdropping was out of control. Her gaze briefly settled on a dazed-looking Quade. "I don't love him," Lunden said. At the moment, denial was her only recourse.

"You do, Mom, and he loves you too. He looks at you all googly eyes. Nicholas looks at Ms. Perri googly eyes, and he's in love with her too. But he's only eight, and Ms. Perri is real old. Like twenty-five. But he tells her he loves her every single day. But she doesn't say it back because she's an adult and he's a kid. If you say it to Quade, he'll say it back to you. Because you two are adults."

Lunden sighed. "Zachary—"

"Tell him, Mom. Please. Tell him, and he might not leave. You said you don't want him to leave."

Dear God in heaven. Would he ever stop rolling this bus over her? "We have to go, Zachary."

"But, Mom—"

"*Now*, Zachary!"

Instantly, she regretted raising her voice at him, but this wasn't a conversation she wanted to continue. Tears ran from Zachary's eyes, and with her emotions all over the place, they ran from hers too. She turned her back to them and wiped them away, chastising herself for not having better control.

"Z," Quade said, "I need to talk to your mom a second. There's ice cream in the freezer. Chocolate. Your favorite."

"Can I, Mom?" he said, his voice barely a whisper.

Lunden nodded.

Zachary started away but stopped. "I didn't mean to make you cry, Mom. I just want you to be happy again. And Quade makes you happy. I know he does," he said with conviction.

Lunden couldn't speak, so she simply nodded, knowing Zachary's intentions had been good. Quade was so close to her now that she could feel the heat from his chest on her back. Why had she come here?

"Is what Z said true, Lunden? Did you tell Rylee you were in love with me?"

Pulling herself together, she turned, overwhelmed by his closeness. "Was that the buyer I saw leaving?" she asked.

"Yes. And I—"

"There's something you should know. About the inn," she said, cutting him off.

Quade folded his arms across his chest. Fine lines ran across his forehead. "Okay."

Lunden's lips parted to tell him what Zeta had told her earlier, but nothing would come out. She couldn't tell him. She knew how it felt to feel caged, stuck between a rock and a boulder. And while Quade had hurt her, she couldn't box him in. If he wanted to sell the inn, she wouldn't be the one to stand in his way. She'd make sure Zeta reburied what she'd found. "I just wanted to tell you that I have no intentions of standing in your way. This place is rightfully yours. You should be able to do with it what you choose." Had she really just blown her opportunity to save the inn?

"Thank you for that," he said. He studied her long and hard. "This plan you had . . . I want to hear it from you."

She slowly shook her head. "It doesn't matter anymore. You believed the version you were told. Let that be enough."

"It's not. I *need* to hear it from you," he said.

Oh, so now he wanted to listen to her? What had prompted this? *Fine.* "I wanted to make you fall in love with Honey Hill. Simple as that. I thought doing so would encourage you to change your mind about selling the inn. In the event it didn't work, as a contingency, I sought a way that would force you not to sell. I never considered how unfair I was being to you." She shrugged. "Or maybe I didn't care. I wanted what I wanted. For Honey Hill to remain exactly as it has always been. I was wrong. Change is inevitable."

"You resented me for inheriting the inn."

"Yes," she said honestly. "At first. But then I got to know you. Personally. Intimately. I grew to like you, despite how hard I fought against it. Somehow, I allowed my feelings to get involved, which kept me from accepting the truth."

"Which is what, exactly?"

"That someone like you could never be content living in small-town America, running an inn."

Quade's gaze lowered to the floor.

Zachary reappeared. "I finished my ice cream."

Lunden put on her game face as she always did. "Hey, kiddo," she said, batting back tears. "You ready to go?"

"Yes, ma'am. I'll see you around, Quade."

The amount of distress Lunden witnessed in Quade's eyes told her he wanted to say more. Something was holding him back. What?

"Bye, Z," he said, his tone uncharacteristically soft.

Lunden couldn't bring herself to say goodbye. At least without more tears, making herself look even weaker, so she gave a warm, genuine smile and said, "I wish you the best, Quade Cannon." At the door, she stopped. "Zachary, go ahead. I'll be right there," she said. Once he walked off, she backtracked to Quade and took his hand into hers. After pausing a moment, she used her index finger to trace three numbers into his palm, 1-4-3, then walked away again. With each step she took, she willed him to stop her. He never did.

When Lunden and Zachary returned from Quade's, Zachary went straight to his bedroom without a single word. Apparently, he needed some time apart from her. Understandable, so she didn't push him to talk. Instead, she retreated back into her workshop rather than moping around the house.

Before Lunden knew it, two hours had passed. She decided to finish up labeling the last of the candle jars before heading inside to prep dinner.

"Knock, knock."

Lunden glanced up to see Rylee entering.

Rylee's eyes widened as they swept the room. "*Whoa*. You have been busy."

"Inspiration struck," she said.

"It's me, Lu. I know you better than anyone in this town. Which is how I know it's not inspiration behind this explosion of product."

"Ry, I really don't—"

Rylee cut her off midthought and closed the distance between them. "You are one of the most outspoken, strongest women I know. You fight for everyone around you. Why not fight for yourself? Instead of pouring all your feelings into these candles, pour them out to Quade."

"—want to talk about this now," Lunden finished.

"You are in love with this man, Lunden. Why are you running from this?"

Lunden slammed the glass jar down so hard it cracked. "Because I'm scared, Rylee. I'm scared," she repeated.

"Of what?"

"Of being the weak woman I once was."

"Weak? There's not a damn thing weak about the Lunden Pierce I know. Nothing."

"There is when you still want a man who's made it clear he doesn't want you. I swore I would never be that woman again, Rylee. The one trying to hold on to a man who doesn't want to be held."

Rylee smiled gently. "Loving someone doesn't make you weak. The heart wants who it wants. We can't always control that."

Lunden sighed. Maybe she could have had she tried harder. "For once, I just want to be the one someone can't live without. I want to be someone's everything, their purpose, their . . . forever."

Rylee hugged Lunden. "You will get your happily ever after. I promise."

Lunden knew Rylee couldn't promise something like that, but she loved her for trying to make her feel better. While she and Quade had only been friends with benefits, it felt as if he had abandoned her all over again. The emotions she'd experienced years ago were the same ones she experienced now. Only this time, the hurt was far more potent, because this time Quade had had a choice, but he hadn't chosen her.

Quade usually traveled straight home after work, but today he planned to make a pit stop by Ms. Jewel's. He'd agreed to help her with a few tasks around the house. While he still wasn't sure about the rest of the town, his gut told him Ms. Jewel had had no part in Lunden's plan. Heck, could he even trust his gut anymore? It had told him it was safe to drop his guard for Lunden. Look how that had turned out for him.

When he recalled the last time he'd seen Lunden a week ago, his hand tingled. The three numbers she'd traced into his palm had him so damn confused. Had he made the right decision by letting her walk away? *Yes,* he told himself a second later.

It was obvious they weren't meant to be. He preferred the city; Lunden enjoyed small-town living. Though he understood the appeal. Honey Hill was . . . soothing. Thinking back, he couldn't recall one time in recent years he hadn't felt stressed to the point of breaking. Until he'd come here.

Another point to support his claim: Lunden had a child. "Zachary," he said with a smile. For a moment, the kid had actually had him believing he could be a good father. *He deserves better.* But Zachary had really grown on him. Maybe because Quade saw a little of himself in him. The kid was definitely a risk taker. Evident by the many times he had shown up at Quade's house in the past, even after admitting he wasn't supposed to be there. Not lately, though. That saddened him. He missed both Zachary and his mother more than he felt comfortable acknowledging.

Quade slid behind the steering wheel. When he cranked the engine, Gladys Knight's rendition of "I Hope You Dance" poured from the speakers, causing him to instantly think about Aunt Shugga. Instead of pulling away from the curb, he relaxed against the seat and enjoyed the angelic sound. Something Mr. Clem had said once filtered into his thoughts. *Shugga knew what people needed before they did.* He glanced heavenward. "If you know what I need, please show me. I'm lost."

Pulling away, he thought about his final point as he drove to Ms. Jewel's. He wasn't a family man. Who had time for visits to strawberry patches, kiddie birthday parties, town jubilees? And who wanted to wake up next to the most beautiful, tenacious, smart, compassionate woman every single morning for the rest of their life? Who needed those kinds of challenges?

Quade put the vehicle in park and froze. It only took him a second to realize that instead of driving to Ms. Jewel's place, he'd driven to

Lunden's. Her back was to him, and she was pulling weeds from her flower bed. Obviously she had in earbuds, because she hadn't looked in his direction. Or maybe she did know he was there and just didn't care enough to give him her attention.

"How did I—" He stopped when another Gladys Knight song played: "Best Thing That Ever Happened to Me." Staring at the radio, he fell back against the seat, a little stunned and spooked.

Something willed his gaze. When he looked up, Lunden now stood, staring in his direction. The second their eyes connected snatched his breath away. Well, he guessed he couldn't burn rubber out of here now. He killed the engine and exited. Standing arm's length from her, he said, "Hey," then slid his hands into his pockets to keep from gliding his fingers down her sweat-slickened arm.

"Hey," she said. "Why were you sitting in my driveway?"

How did he explain being here: that the universe had led him to her . . . again, or that he'd asked his aunt to show him what he needed, and she'd led him here, shown him her? They both sounded far fetched, yet both felt true.

Lunden studied a nervous-looking Quade. Something had drawn her attention to the driveway. Imagine her surprise when she'd turned to see him idling there. She'd be lying if she said his presence hadn't had an effect on her. An uncontrollable sensation coursed through her from his closeness.

"Why was I sitting in your driveway?" he said.

The fact he'd repeated her question suggested he was attempting to figure out a plausible response to the question. "The truth," she said. "I deserve that much."

"Honestly . . ." He massaged the side of his neck. "I don't know." He gave a nervous chuckle. "Funny story. I'd actually been headed to

Ms. Jewel's house, but somehow I ended up here. Something led me here."

Something led him here? Lunden wanted to laugh. She studied him again. This time he looked . . . hesitant. "I see."

Quade eyed the house. "Where's Z?"

"Inside playing his game."

He gave a shaky laugh. "That kid loves his games."

A beat of silence played between them.

Lunden waited for Quade to elaborate on the something that had led him here. When it appeared he wouldn't, she decided he'd wasted enough of her time. Pointing over her shoulder, she said, "Well, if there's nothing else, I should really get back to my weeds."

"Just let me say this, and I'll leave. I let my guard down with you, Lunden. Something I haven't done in a long time. When I thought you'd betrayed me, I was hurt."

Did he ever imagine how she'd felt that he would believe such a thing about her?

Quade continued, "I allowed myself to believe you were capable of doing it because I've been deceived so many times before."

The look of sadness in his eyes tugged at her heartstrings. Gosh, it was hard being a sensitive lioness.

"But you're right—I should have known you would have never hurt me like that. That's all I wanted to say." He turned, walked away, stopped as if he wanted to say something else, but a second later continued toward Josie.

"Is that really all you want to say?" she said.

"No."

He backtracked, captured her hand, and scribbled *I love you* into her palm—just as he'd done so many times when they were young—but not the words, the numbers, 1-4-3, just as she had done. One to represent the one letter in *I*. Four to represent the four letters in *love*. Three to represent the three letters in *you*.

A sense of urgency rushed over her as they stood there, silently staring into each other's soul. Swallowing hard, she said, "It's okay to lose your pride over the one you love, but it's not okay to lose the one you love over your pride. I read that somewhere once." Fighting back both tears and fear, she said, "I don't want to lose you again. I know you can't wait to get out of Honey Hill and on to your journey, but once you're settled somewhere that feels like home, maybe we could . . ." Her words dried up before she finished the thought. As much as she loved this man, she refused to settle for a long-distance relationship. As much as she wanted Quade, she had to let him go. "I just hope we can remain friends."

He scrutinized her for a long, paralyzing second before he spoke. "We can't be friends, Lunden."

His words shattered her already fragile heart, but she understood his stance.

"I want to be so much more," he said.

Lunden's brows furrowed; she was unsure if she'd heard him correctly.

"My intentions were to sell the inn and head out on a journey of discovery. But I never realized until this moment that my journey started the second I arrived in Honey Hill. I've been on my journey all of this time. I've been on it with you, Lunden. Dammit, woman. I never saw you coming, and I slammed head on into a type of happiness I've never known. I can't give that up. I can't give this new life up. I can't give *you* up. We fall in love by chance. We stay in love by choice. I choose you to love, Lunden. I choose you," he repeated.

Lunden quivered when he cradled her face. Not from fear, but from the satisfaction of finally feeling his touch again.

"I've felt like there were pieces of myself missing. Standing here with you, I feel complete again. Whole. I think—no, I know—you're the reason. What if I am that man, Lunden? Maybe not the one to operate an inn, but the one who could be content in small-town America?"

Lunden flashed a high-wattage smile, but it dimmed a second later. "Is this what you really want, Quade? I don't want you to wake up one morning and resent me because you feel like I've trapped you here."

Quade chuckled. "You can't trap me in the place where I want to be. And that place is right here with you and Zachary. You're complicated, strong willed, opinionated . . ."

Well, if he was trying to win her over, insults wouldn't do it.

He continued, ". . . warm, loving, kindhearted, passionate, giving, beautiful, soothing, complex. You are so many things. Z is right: you're a superhero."

Lunden swallowed hard to keep tears from falling.

"I'm sorry," he said, "for making you feel like anything less than extraordinary." A tortured expression spread across his face. "The fact that you felt like I was likening you to a whore hurt me to my soul. Please forgive me."

After stalling several seconds for effect, she nodded. "I forgive you," she finally said, because seeing the genuine regret in his eyes made forgiving him easy. "But only if you forgive me for letting my pride get in the way of everything."

"Forgiven."

Quade looked as if he wanted to kiss her, but instead, he allowed his hands to fall to his sides.

"Lunden, I swear to you that I knew nothing about the letters or Danbury's plans. I found out the day of the market just like you, but you were right," he said. "Those parasites wanted to bleed the town dry. Condos and lakes and golf courses. I couldn't let them."

Lunden pressed her brows together. "What are you saying, Quade?"

"I'm not selling the inn."

Both elated and confused, she said, "What? Why?"

One side of Quade's mouth lifted into a sexy smile. "Because it means so much to the town, to me, but mostly because it means so much to you."

He stood to lose millions and was willing to do so for her? Overwhelmed with emotion, she felt a tear trickle down her cheek. She'd never had anyone make such a sacrifice for her.

"The first time I ever wrote those numbers into your palm, I was convinced I would spend my life with you. Then I lost you. I don't want to lose you a second time. I don't know if I can be everything you need, everything you want, but I love you, Lunden Pierce, and if you will have me, I promise to do my damnedest to make you and Zachary the two happiest people on the continent."

"I thought you weren't a family man," she said.

"I didn't think I was until this happy, energetic six-year-old crashed into my life. He showed me I didn't have to be perfect to be someone he could love. I want as many babies with you as you will give me."

Well, how could she argue with that? This time, she cradled his face between her hands. "I love you, Quade Cannon, and yes, I will have you, because you're already everything I need and want."

"For how long will you have me?" he asked.

"Hmm. How does forever sound?"

"I was hoping you would say that. It sounds like music to my ears. God, I've missed you."

He pulled her into his arms and kissed her with urgency. After what felt like a lifetime, he pulled away, leaving her wanting more, as his kisses always did.

"I think I'm going to need protection from some of the townsfolk," he said.

"Why?"

"Because their offers were contingent on the sale of the inn."

"Oh. Wow. Well, it's a good thing I'm a superhero. I'll just have to protect you with my superpowers."

"You know this also means you won't be getting that sizable donation," he said.

"Oh, I have everything I need." Happy the landmark was no longer in jeopardy, she said, "What are you going to do with the inn?"

"Well, I'll be too busy to run it, because I plan to purchase Mr. Conroy's shop. That's if he'll sell it to me after all of this. I was thinking maybe you could run the place, if you want."

"Heck yes, I want. I have so many ideas for it." She rattled them off right then and there, until she noticed how Quade was staring at her. "Too much, too soon?"

Quade eyed her in a tender manner. "No, it's not that. I never imagined I'd find love in Honey Hill, but I'm damn sure glad I have. You are stuck with me, Ms. Pierce."

"And you're stuck with me, Mr. Cannon." She paused a moment. "But are you absolutely sure you can call Honey Hill home?"

"Anywhere you are is home, Lunden."

"You don't know how happy I am to hear that," she said, touched by emotion.

He stared deep into her eyes. "I made a wish once . . . I'm so glad you came true. I love you," he whispered against her lips.

"I love you too." The second their lips touched, Lunden knew she would love this man until her last breath.

A second later, Zachary darted through the door, rushed over, and threw his arms around them.

"I knew you loved each other," he said.

Yep, they sure did. And this time would be for forever.

EPILOGUE

Six months later . . .

Lunden stood at the bay of windows inside the inn, peering out. Quade and Zachary sat under the sycamore tree, chatting and laughing like two old men. God, she loved the way Quade loved her son, loved them both.

Moving away, she scrutinized the disarray around her. While Quade's pet project had become the screen printing shop he'd purchased from Mr. Conroy, hers had become the inn. She'd be glad when the renovations were done. While the inn would still function in its original capacity—to an extent—she'd proposed to Quade they market it as a full-service event venue geared toward weddings. As long as their wedding would be the first to take place here, he'd said.

Lunden eyed the gorgeous square diamond on her finger. Quade had proposed at exactly midnight on Christmas Day. Her heart swelled when she remembered the moment and how he'd cried as he'd told her how she and Zachary had changed his life. Well, he'd changed theirs too. While Quade would have married her later that morning, she'd wanted to do it right this time, full wedding and all. In a couple of months, she'd be Mrs. Quade Cannon. Apparently, the universe did always get the last word.

To think—exactly one year ago today, he'd come barreling into her life, shaking her entire world upside down. Who could have imagined what was to come? *Ms. Shugga.*

Marshall Joyner had delivered Quade one last correspondence for Ms. Shugga's estate: a letter. In it, Ms. Shugga explained how she'd intended to honor her sister's deathbed wish until she'd had a dream about Quade and had been convinced she was supposed to get him to Honey Hill. The letter had also given him the closure he'd needed regarding her and his mother by telling him, in her words, everything that had transpired between them. Lastly, she'd asked for forgiveness for not reaching out to him.

Quade had given it, freeing himself from the burden of the past. Lunden had done some forgiving of her own. She thought about Hilary Jamison. The two would never be friends, but Lunden was okay with that.

Lunden still couldn't believe how her life had changed, and all because of a dream. "Thank you, Ms. Shugga."

Quade crept up behind her, wrapping her in his arms. "Hey, beautiful. Who are you talking to?"

"Myself."

He kissed the back of her head. "Have I told you lately how much I love you?"

"Not since breakfast, so I think I need to hear it again."

"I love you more than breathing," he said, kissing her exposed shoulder. "More than walking." He placed a kiss to her neck. "More than talking." He turned her and kissed her gently on the lips. "You are my air, my legs, my words. I can't function properly without you."

Lunden cradled his face between her hands. "You have no idea, no idea at all, how much I love you, Quade Cannon, but I plan to show you. Every single day for the rest of my life." And she knew he would do the same.

"I want to show you something," he said, taking her hand and leading her into the backyard. They stopped in front of the sycamore tree.

Confused, Lunden said, "I've already seen this tree. Countless times."

Before Quade could respond, Zachary ran up, dragging a shovel behind him; he passed it to Quade, declared he was off to ride his bike, then darted away.

"Be careful," Lunden and Quade said in unison.

Eyeing Quade again, she said, "What are you up to?"

He kissed her gently on the lips. "Patience."

Because of him, she'd gotten better at that.

Quade dug up a plot of earth underneath the tree, stopping when the shovel thudded against something. He knelt and removed what resembled a small wooden treasure chest. Lowering himself to the ground, he motioned for her to join him.

"Shugga and I buried this years ago," he said, staring at the closed lid.

Witnessing the sadness on his face, she rubbed a hand up and down his back. "You okay?"

He eyed her. "I've got you. I'm perfect."

"Open it," she said.

Brushing off the dirt, he pried the moisture-swollen lid open, revealing the time-weathered things inside. They went through Ms. Shugga's contributions first: recipes, a gold-and-pearl brooch, a picture of Ms. Shugga and Quade in a loving embrace, and several other items that had apparently been dear to Ms. Shugga.

"Yours next," she said, anxious to see what he'd added inside.

"Go ahead," he said, directing her to remove the rest.

There was candy, some with pit marks, as if it had been enjoyed by tiny creatures. Baseball cards that might have been worth something had they been sealed properly. A bottle cap. A four-leaf clover. "Oooh, what's this all wrapped up tight?" Lunden removed what remained of the aluminum foil. *A ring box?* A second later, her gaze rose to meet Quade's. "What is this?"

"Open it," he said.

Inside was a gold ring. Instead of a jewel in the center, there were two connecting hearts. She eyed him again, still confused.

"Remember how you were irritated with me for spending so much time mowing lawns and doing yard work that one summer?"

"Yes. You barely had time for me."

He pointed to the ring. "That was why. I have always loved you, Lunden Pierce. Always. And from the very first moment I laid eyes on you, I knew I wanted to spend forever with you. Even way back then, I planned my future with you. I was too young to ask you to marry me then, but I knew one day I would, so I bought that ring in preparation."

Tears rolled down Lunden's face, her heart filling with even more love for him. How was that even possible? Swiping the wetness away, she passed the box to him. While she doubted the ring would go past her knuckle, she at least wanted to feel it on her finger. Removing her engagement ring, she placed it on another finger, then held out her hand.

Quade removed the ring, captured her hand, and slid the ring as far as it would go. Pulling her into his arms, he kissed her long and hard. Breaking their mouths apart, he stared into her eyes. "I would ask you this a thousand times. Lunden Pierce, will you be my wife?"

"And a thousand times . . . I would say yes."

ACKNOWLEDGMENTS

My thanks—first and foremost—to God for blessing me with this gift of storytelling.

Thank you to my husband, Marcus, who has supported me every step of the way on this beautiful journey. To my *amazing* agent, Elaine Spencer, who never let me settle for just good enough. *Thank you* for your guidance. To my editors, Lauren Plude and Lindsey Faber, working with you both has been a truly wonderful experience. You've made this book shine! I appreciate you both. To the members of my Joyrider Street Team and my All-Star Readers' Lounge, thank you for all you do and for your unwavering support. To my readers, thank you for continuously riding with me. To anyone who has ever guided me in any way along this journey, I acknowledge you!

ABOUT THE AUTHOR

By day, Joy Avery works as a customer service assistant. By night, the North Carolina native travels to imaginary worlds—creating characters whose romantic journeys invariably end in happily ever after.

Since she was a young girl growing up in Garner, Joy knew she wanted to write. Stumbling onto romance novels, she discovered her passion for love stories; instantly, she knew these were the kinds of stories she wanted to pen. Real characters, real journeys, and real good love are what you'll find in a Joy Avery romance.

Avery is married with one child. When she's not writing, she enjoys reading, cake decorating, pretending to expertly play the piano, driving her husband insane, and playing with her dog.

Avery is a member of Romance Writers of America. Find her books and sign up for her Wings of Love newsletter at www.joyavery.com. Connect with her on Facebook, Twitter, and Pinterest (@authorjoyavery) or email her at authorjoyavery@gmail.com.